I0823984

A SPIRITED SUPPER AT DUNDOON CASTLE

Books by Darci Hannah

A Beacon Bakeshop Mystery

MURDER AT THE BEACON BAKESHOP
MURDER AT THE CHRISTMAS COOKIE BAKE-OFF
MURDER AT THE BLUEBERRY FESTIVAL
MURDER AT THE PUMPKIN PAGEANT
MURDER AT THE BLARNEY BASH
MURDER AT THE LEMONBERRY TEA

A Food & Spirits Mystery

A FATAL FEAST AT BRAMSFORD MANOR
A SPIRITED SUPPER AT DUNDOON CASTLE

Published by Kensington Publishing Corp.

A SPIRITED SUPPER AT DUNDOON CASTLE

DARCI HANNAH

Kensington Publishing Corp.
kensingtonbooks.com

This book is a work of fiction. Names, characters, businesses, organizations, places, events, and incidents either are the product of the author's imagination or are used fictitiously. Any resemblance to actual persons, living or dead, events, or locales is entirely coincidental.

To the extent that the image or images on the cover of this book depict a person or persons, such person or persons are merely models, and are not intended to portray any character or characters featured in the book.

KENSINGTON BOOKS are published by

Kensington Publishing Corp.
900 Third Avenue
New York, NY 10022

Copyright © 2026 by Darci Hannah

All rights reserved. No part of this book may be reproduced in any form or by any means without the prior written consent of the Publisher, excepting brief quotes used in reviews.

Without limiting the author's and publisher's exclusive rights, any unauthorized use of this publication to train generative artificial intelligence (AI) technologies is expressly prohibited.

All Kensington titles, imprints, and distributed lines are available at special quantity discounts for bulk purchases for sales promotion, premiums, fund-raising, educational, or institutional use. Special book excerpts or customized printings can also be created to fit specific needs. For details, write or phone the office of the Kensington Special Sales Manager: Attn. Special Sales Department, Kensington Publishing Corp., 900 Third Avenue, New York, NY 10022. Phone: 1-800-221-2647.

Library of Congress Control Number: 2025945765

KENSINGTON and the KENSINGTON COZIES teapot logo Reg. U.S. Pat. & TM. Off.

ISBN: 978-1-4967-4747-1
First Kensington Hardcover Edition: February 2026

ISBN: 978-1-4967-4749-5 (ebook)

10 9 8 7 6 5 4 3 2 1

Printed in the United States of America

The authorized representative in the EU for product safety and compliance
is eucomply OU, Parnu mnt 139b-14, Apt 123
Tallinn, Berlin 11317, hello@eucompliancepartner.com

To Jan and Dave Hilgers
Beloved parents, cherished friends, enlightened souls,
and guardian angels
This book would never have been written without you

Acknowledgments

When I started writing this book, I never imagined that I wouldn't finish it on time. I strive to hit all my commitments, especially deadlines. However, there are just some things that you cannot plan for, and for me it was the passing of my dear, sweet mother and life-long best friend, Jan Hilgers. I was in the middle of writing this novel, and all was sailing along just fine. We had just celebrated her eighty-sixth birthday in late July, and both of us were looking forward to the launch of my first Food & Spirits mystery, *A Fatal Feast at Bramsford Manor* in August. We talked about it every day. Over Mom's birthday weekend, I realized that my Facebook account had been hacked and stolen. There was no getting it back. It wouldn't have been such a pressing issue, but I had a book launching in four weeks! Then, suddenly, in the beginning of August—two weeks before my big book launch, Mom called and said that she was leaving us, for good. She knew that her time on earth was coming to an end. Oddly enough, she sounded rather joyful about this. I was a mess. My older brother was too.

As you can imagine, without my mother and social media, I wasn't in the best shape to launch my new series. But I did, and everyone who was there to celebrate with me was incredibly kind, understanding, and downright amazing. Cozy mystery readers are truly the most lovely, generous people in the world. Thank you all!

Soon after the launch, I found myself once again back in my childhood home—a big, English manor-style house where both of my parents had passed away. My younger brother, the inspiration for ghosthunter, Brett Bloom, had also passed away. It was no wonder that whenever I was in the dining room, the lights on the lovely chandelier would flicker at me. Sometimes they'd just turn off. It dawned on me then how life imitates art. Because I had just inherited a possibly haunted, English manor-style home—right after writing about one! Only the ghosts, or more correctly spirits, in this home were my family. It would be another three months before I was ready to write again, and when I did finally get back to it, it was with joy in my heart and a new perspective on everything. Life is a precious gift.

I'd like to thank my wonderful agent, Sandy Harding, for clearing the way for me during this time, and to my incredibly patient editor, John Scognamiglio, for being so understanding. I'd also like to thank the amazing Larissa Ackerman for her gentle touch with my schedule, and everyone else at Kensington for not only being supportive, but for being the best at what they do.

I'd like to thank Randy Hilgers, Diane Tarkowski, Dana Hilgers, Jenna Hilgers, Sandy Cobb, Robin and Chuck Taylor, and Jane and Jerome Boundy for the love, friendship, and all the help with the house on Pine Road.

I'd like to give a huge thanks to my son, Jim Hannah, for working tirelessly to get my Facebook account back. And last but certainly not least, a very heartfelt thanks to my wonderful husband, John, and our children, Jim, Allison, Dan, and Matt. Love you forever and always. I couldn't have done it without you!

A SPIRITED SUPPER AT DUNDOON CASTLE

Chapter 1

"We're going to Scotland. Can ye believe it?" Bunny's voice sounded a wee bit petulant, even to her own ears, as she spoke into the phone.

"Well, isn't that . . . good?" Jane, the woman on the other end, floated. "I mean, you're Scottish. You haven't been home in a long while, and you're always telling Ainsley and me how much you miss it." Ainsley was Jane's ten-year-old daughter, charged with taking care of Bunny's beloved pet Holland lop rabbit, Mr. Wiggles, while she was away on business. Jane and Ainsley lived in Connecticut and were Bunny's next-door neighbors. Jane also happened to be Bunny's dearest friend.

"Aye, I suppose that's true enough. But it's complicated."

Wasn't that the truth, Bunny mused, rolling her green eyes at her reflection in the hotel mirror. She shook her head, smoothed a wayward, bright ginger curl back into place, and thought once again about the absurd string of events that had landed her here, in a budget London hotel room, thankfully not haunted, waiting for the airport shuttle to pick her and the lads up for their next misguided foodie, ghosty adventure. She was, after all, one of the hosts of a new reality television show scheduled to air on the Mealtime Network called *Food & Spirits*.

Just over three weeks ago, Bridget "Bunny" MacBride, had been happily working as a menu developer for *Mary Stobart's Memorable Meals*, with a weekly five-minute segment called "Bunny's Culinary Corner." She was proud of her short but sweet segment. It had been a popular part of the show. In retrospect, perhaps a bit too popular for the aging foodie and lifestyle icon Mary Stobart. However, not long after Bunny refused to embrace the spookier side of the upcoming Halloween episode, purely due to her dislike of scary, spooky things, she found herself sitting in the big corner office with her boss, Mary Stobart, and Jerry Goldstein, a powerful network executive. To her great surprise, they had offered her the opportunity of a lifetime—her own travel cooking show with the engaging title *Food & Spirits*. She was to be the *Food* in the title, responsible for creating a delicious, authentic, locally sourced meal that was connected to the place they would travel to. She was told that the *Spirits* part of the show would be handled by someone else, which was fine by her. Bunny was by no means an expert when it came to mixing up fancy drinks. Deep down, Bunny had an inkling that the opportunity set before her was too good to be true. Yet the moment the pen was placed in her hand, she had signed the contract, filled with visions of traveling to sunny Caribbean Islands, eating exotic foods, cooking with exotic spices, and feasting her eyes on exotic, bare-chested men. Och! She couldn't believe she had signed the contract without question. That was just the stupid type of thing people pleasers and optimists do. Bunny, admittedly, was a lot of both.

It wasn't until a few days later, while attending her first

production meeting, that she realized the *Spirits* part of the show wasn't about mixology after all, but, well . . . spirits. As in ghosts, and specters, and whatnot. The trouble was, Bunny wasn't a fan of ghosts. Not in the least. And she really disliked creepy old places too. Unfortunately, the show's primary focus was all about haunted, creepy old places. Bunny, being an up-and-coming celebrity chef, was, as they say, along for the ride. And what a wild ride their first *Food & Spirits* adventure had been!

Jane was talking again, grabbing her attention while giving her a piece of friendly advice.

"Bunny, my friend, life *is* complicated. That's the point of life. You can tiptoe around all the difficult bits, but you won't be satisfied. You'll be tiptoeing forever. And that's no way to live for an adventurous and talented young woman like you. Whatever fear you have of going home, you must face it, embrace it, and get on with it. Besides, Granny Mac sounds like a gem, coming to your rescue when that body turned up at Bramsford Manor. That must have been utterly disturbing for you! Thank heaven for Granny Mac."

"She's the best," Bunny admitted. Frowning a little, she added, "And sometimes a right rascal. She's the reason we're heading to Scotland today, and to my home, where we're staying the night before heading to the castle. She made it sound innocent, like a spontaneous thought, but I think she planned this little homecoming visit the moment she realized I was back in the UK."

"Castle?" Jane was stuck on the word. "You're going to a Scottish castle? That sounds so romantic and dreamy, Bunny."

"It might, if it wasn't so haunted." Much to her dismay, the word *romantic* sparked the image of hunky Brett Bloom, her cohost on the show. In the blink of an eye, her imagination was alive with his glorious, all-American good looks and knee-weakening smile. She was shocked at how willingly she welcomed these untimely mental intrusions. Sure, Brett could be ridiculous, difficult, and a right dunderhead at times, but, if she was being honest, working with Brett Bloom was one of the few perks the show offered, and quite possibly the reason she had decided to fulfill her contract and not tear it up, as she had every right to do. She thrust the tantalizing image aside.

"Right. Haunted," Jane replied without any conviction. Then, choking down a bubble of mirth, she asked, "So, what ghost are you cooking for this time, Bunny?"

Sure, it sounded funny to the outsider, but it was no joke cooking for a ghost. Which, unfortunately, was her main job on the show. Bunny dearly wished that cooking was her only job, but thanks to Granny Mac and the untimely appearance of a ghostly white rabbit, her entire team began to realize that whipping up an impressive meal wasn't her only valuable asset. Bunny had been, and still was, reluctant to face the truth of her unusual psychic gift, one she undoubtedly had inherited from Granny Mac. Quite simply put, Bunny was clairvoyant too. She had tried to run from it, to hide from it, to ignore it, yet it had always been there, a niggling little secret deeply suppressed in the shadow of her soul. It might have remained suppressed too, if it hadn't been for their visit to Bramsford Manor and her encounter with the tragic, ghostly bride who had haunted it. Clairvoyance and pesky ghost rabbit aside, Bunny was an up-and-coming celebrity chef. It was her culinary skills that had brought her here, and that was the nugget of truth she would cling to. Jane repeated her question again. *What ghost was she cooking for?* Even to her own ears it sounded ridiculous. Bunny cleared her throat, and replied, "Och, some long-dead piper." She brushed off the thought.

"Piper? Are you referring to a plumber?" Jane was confused.

"Not a plumber," Bunny corrected. "A bagpiper, a musician. It's a Scottish thing. Nearly every castle has one."

"How fascinating." Jane was hanging on her every word. "And you say this one's dead?"

"As legend would have it, aye. My gran knows all about it. She's friends with the castle owners. That's how she ensnared the lads and our producer, Trig, back in the home office. He called the castle, talked with the owners, and now we're off, quick as Bob's your uncle. Gran is pleased as punch, and my mum's so excited she's cooking up a homecoming feast. It's going to be awkward."

"Awkward? Bunny, it's going to be wonderful! The prodigal daughter is returning home, and your mother is preparing the proverbial fattened beast."

"Quite literally, I'm afraid." This was the truth. The MacBrides of Inverary, Scotland, not only raised the finest cattle; they also raised sheep, chickens, and a few pigs as well. From February to October, the river that ran through their property was thick with salmon, and the pond in the glen swarmed with trout. There were fruit trees, berry bushes, and honey from the bees that pollinated both. And if that wasn't enough, her mum also had a remarkable kitchen garden and made the best jams in the parish. In short, the family farm was a cornucopia of culinary delights, and just like a musical maestro, Maggie MacBride knew how to select the perfect seasonal ingredients to highlight the fruits of their labor. Bunny's culinary journey had started when she'd been a wee bairn, attached to her mother's hip. She had learned from the best. It was a fact Bunny had always been proud of. However, what Bunny was not so proud of, and what she had failed to mention to Jane, was that her parents had no inkling of the true nature of her show, her burgeoning psychic abilities, or the fact that she had made contact with her dead brother, Braiden, her twin, in the form of a white rabbit. She was still grappling with all of this, so how on earth was she to explain it to those she loved most? The mere thought sparked a raging storm of anxiety within her.

"It sounds delightful! You're going to have a wonderful time."

Was she, now? Doubtful, Bunny thought, but she kept those feelings to herself. However, on a brighter note, Jane's sunny voice and misguided optimism were just the things she needed now that her own natural optimism had taken a downturn at the thought of family. Knowing that optimism, like a heartfelt smile, could be contagious, Bunny leaned into the uplifting words as Jane continued. "Look, you have nothing to worry about. Ainsley is doting on Mr. Wiggles, and from what I can tell, he's enjoying all the attention and extra treats. Let your parents dote on you for a while, Bunny. You deserve as much. Then, after being fortified by the love of your family, go out there and storm that haunted castle. You can do this, Bridget MacBride!"

"I can. I will. I've got this!" Bunny responded with renewed gusto. She then locked eyes with her reflection in the mirror and forced a bright smile. I'm going home, she thought. I'm finally going home. She liked the sound of that. Then, with a painful flinch, her smile faded, chased away by a series of rapid-fire knocks on her door.

"Bunny, darling, are you ready?" The perky voice of Gifford McGrady, the third host on the show, called from the hallway. "We're off in five. Chop-chop. I can't wait to meet the fam!"

"Be right there," she called out, fighting a new wave of prickling nerves. Who was she kidding? Going home was going to be more painful than wonderful, and she really didn't know what terrified her more, confronting her parents, confronting her inner demons, or making otherworldly contact with a ghostly piper? Surprisingly, the scales were tipping in the piper's favor.

"Thanks for the chat, Jane, but I've got to run. We're on our way to the airport. Give Ainsley and Mr. Wiggles a hug from me." Bunny ended the call. With one last fleeting glance at her reflection, she picked up her bags and headed for the door.

Chapter 2

After an hour spent navigating the intricacies of Heathrow Airport, the ninety-minute flight to Glasgow, and yet more time retrieving luggage, organizing video equipment, and renting two vehicles, Bunny found herself once again behind the wheel of a saloon, or sedan, as they say in the States, with Gifford "Giff" McGrady firmly buckled into the seat next to her and cameraman Ed Franco lounging in the back seat. Crivens, how travel tried the patience! Bunny, however, was back on home turf, a fact she celebrated by peeling out of the car-rental parking lot, heading for the M8 motorway going northwest. A quick glance in the rearview mirror told her that Brett, Mike, Cody, and all their bloody ghost-hunting equipment in the van were attempting to keep pace. A fleeting thought occurred to her, one that suggested she should have given them their own set of directions in case they got separated. Too late now, she mused, and focused on the task at hand, driving in heavy traffic.

Interestingly enough, air travel had never bothered Bunny. In fact, she rather enjoyed flying. She found that, once up in the clouds, with the miniature world passing slowly below like an endless patchwork quilt, it was easy to relax. Traveling at such great heights minimized her worries, making them seem as distant as the terra firma below. The fact that Brett had sat next to her on the flight and bought her a glass of in-flight wine further worked in her favor. Brett, adorable, fluffy-headed Brett, had wanted to talk about haunted Scottish castles, bagpipers, and ghosts. While not her favorite subjects, she happily engaged in the conversation because of . . . well, Brett. Tall, blond, and distractingly handsome, she especially loved the way his bright blue eyes sparkled when he talked of ghosts. At first, she had found his enthusiasm disturbing, but now, for her own selfish reasons, she encouraged him. All she had to do was drop a comment or two about *spookies*, sit back, and watch the magic happen. Brett, and a glass of wine, had chased all her cares away. The flight from London to Glasgow had been no problem at all.

Unfortunately, the drive from Glasgow to her family farm in Inverary was proving to be a little more difficult. As Bunny guided the saloon farther north, the traffic thinned, and the familiar and often breathtaking roads of Scotland pecked at her brain until at last the floodgates had been breached. It was what she had feared; it was what she had run from, and now, as she gripped the steering wheel of the Ford, she had no choice but to face them. She felt a burst of unconditional love from her parents, the radiating joys of a beautiful childhood, the haunting darkness and pain of losing her twin, and the very real shame of how she had hardened her heart and left her family behind to forge a new life for herself. As Bunny navigated a roundabout a tad too fast, passing slower vehicles on the inside lane before aggressively merging onto the road once again, she thought, youth is selfish. It must be, she reasoned. Youth is for growth and self-discovery, which, by its very nature, is selfish. How was one supposed to know who they are or what they like if they weren't a little selfish? While justifying the self-centered actions of her youth with some hefty mental gymnastics, Bunny suddenly found herself on the crest of a windswept hill, with the western shore of Loch Lomond unraveling below her like a silky blue ribbon. Crivens! She had nearly forgotten about the loch. The mere sight of it knocked the breath from her.

"Whoa!" Giff breathed in awe. "That's stunning."

"I agree," Ed said, peering out the window. "What lake is that, Bunny?"

"Lomond," she told them. "Loch Lomond." As the great body of water came into view, Bunny was hit with a startlingly strong vision of the last time she had sailed on that loch. It was as if she were back there again, sitting in the little sailboat with her twin, Braiden, working the sails as the boat cut through the chilly water. They had been racing in a regatta, and they were in the lead. She heard the motor of a boat, but never saw it, not until it hit them with such force that both she and Braiden had been tossed far from the boat. She felt the rising panic of being underwater, of not knowing where she was or if she would ever fill her burning lungs with air again. And then she felt the hands gripping her ankles, pushing her to the surface just as she was about to pass out. By some miracle she had survived. Braiden hadn't been so lucky. The great big hole in her heart left by the death of her deceased twin still ached as if it had happened yesterday.

"Loch Lomond?" Giff questioned, staring pointedly at her.

His searching look pulled her back to her senses. Bunny noted that he had a white-knuckle hold on the grab handle above the door. For some reason, her driving unnerved him.

"Oh! Lomond!" he exclaimed, suddenly recalling the loch and Bunny's connection to it. He then inhaled sharply. "That's . . . the site of your boating accident." He cast her a tentative look, curling his body ever so slightly in the seat as he did so. He thought her eyes looked a bit red at the edges.

"I'm perfectly fine," she snapped. "It was a long time ago. I've moved past it."

Giff looked in the back seat at Ed, flashing him a deer-in-headlights look. Ed vigorously shook his head, mouthing, *Drop it!* But Giff wouldn't drop it. Instead, he turned to Bunny and suggested, "Why don't you slow down there a bit, Bun-bun, and let's talk about it? Talking's good. It's cathartic. I'm sure you have fond memories of him. Umm, Brandon, was it? Tell us about Brandon. What did he look like?"

"*Braiden*," she corrected through gritted teeth. "His name was Braiden."

"Ooo, sorry. My bad. I'll file that name away in here," he said, tapping the side of his head. "Won't forget it. Now, what did Braiden look like?"

Bunny let out a little growl. "I didn't come to Scotland to talk about it, Gifford. If you'll recall, we're here to drum up a dead piper." Although her nerves were raging, she cleared her throat and attempted to be civil. "I'm to make a feast to coax a long dead piper back to the table, and I'm scunnered by the thought. I don't even know what pipers like to eat."

"But you're Scottish," Ed reasoned, poking his head into the front seat. "You grew up here. These are your people."

Bunny found his convoluted reasoning infuriating. She was about to say so, when Giff offered another unhelpful suggestion.

"You could just ask him. You know, connect with him psychically and float some menu ideas by him."

Bunny couldn't believe the eejet drivel she was hearing from the lads. Taking her eyes off the road to stare at them, she said, "Are you two mental? I'm not contacting a long-dead piper to ask him what he'd like to eat. In fact, *Mr. Man*, I'm not contacting him at all. That's your job."

"You forget, I just play a medium on the show," Giff defended. "Forgive me for thinking that fortune-telling and channeling the dead are pure chicanery." If Giff was being honest with himself, which he seldom was, he was slightly jealous of Bunny's psychic gifts, but he loved her so much, he barely showed it.

"For the record, we have to drive past the loch. It's on the way to the farm."

"And the fam," Giff inappropriately reminded her. "Can't wait to meet them." He couldn't help himself. He had no filter. As a former ad man, he was cursed with a quick wit, a snappy turn of phrase, and the ability to recall every annoying jingle he'd ever heard.

The mere mention of her family caused Bunny's nerves to spring so tightly, they sparked a red brain flare-up. A growl escaped her again as she gritted her teeth and brought her focus back to the road. The moment she did, she inhaled sharply and slammed on the brakes so hard the car bucked and skidded off the road, narrowly missing a thick hedge and the white rabbit that had shot out right in front of the car.

The lads cried in unison as the car skidded to a halt. Their faces were covered as they braced for impact.

Bunny's heart was still racing at the sight when a loud horn, seemingly coming from inside the saloon, kicked it into triple-time. A split second later, a large truck burst from the dense greenery of the hedge, passing a mere three feet in front of their car. It wasn't a hedge, but a side road, and Bunny never saw it. With a sinking heart, she realized that the lorry had the right-of-way. She had missed the stop sign, almost getting them killed. If her nerves had been raging before, they were now ready to leap out of her skin.

Breathing heavily, she addressed the lads. "Are . . . ye

both alright? Is anyone hurt? I'm so sorry. I'm so sorry," she repeated, tears springing to her eyes. The truth of what happened sprang upon her. If it wasn't for the white rabbit . . . She couldn't even think of it.

"Shaken *and* stirred, I'm afraid, but still alive," Giff remarked. His face had gone white as a ghost's.

"I'm okay," Ed reported from the back seat. "Thank God the car stopped in time."

"Yes, thank God," she agreed. Then, venturing into darker territory, she asked, "Did anyone happen to see the rabbit—the one that jumped from the verge and ran in front of the car?" For the sake of her sanity, she didn't dare state its color.

"Rabbit?" A muscle in Giff's jaw twitched as his eyes grew wide as saucers. "I never saw a rabbit. Is . . . that why you stopped?"

His genuine look of terrified disbelief frightened her even more. Although Giff refrained from saying another word about the rabbit, she knew that he understood what she was asking. As if touched by a hot poker, he unbuckled his seat belt and opened the door.

"Bunny, I hate to do this, but I'm taking the wheel from here."

"But . . . you don't know how to drive on the left-hand side of the road," she protested.

"I'll learn. You can be my copilot and keep me on course." As Bunny stepped out of the car, Brett, driving the cargo van, pulled off the side of the road behind them. Bunny had been driving so aggressively that they had fallen behind. Giff walked Bunny to the passenger side and opened the door for her. "We're in Scotland," he told her gently. "Silly us, we didn't realize that this might be difficult for you. Sit back and relax. Everything is going to be fine. The Giffster won't let anything bad happen to you. None of us will. I promise." Before Bunny could protest, he shut the car door.

Although she knew Giff meant what he said, she doubted that he or any of the dear lads could protect her from the storm she felt brewing in the marrow of her bones. She prayed she was wrong, but she knew, as she had always known, that although they faced this journey together, there were just some forbidden places that only she could go. She prayed that when the time came, she would have the courage to do so. Resigned to her demoted position as copilot, she bucked up and held her breath.

Chapter 3

The moment the grand, two-story fieldstone farmhouse at the end of the long drive came into view, Bunny heaved a sigh of relief. It was as beautiful as she remembered, even more so when enveloped in the enchanting colors of autumn. The well-tended garden of shrubs, plants, flowers, and trees that adorned the front of the old house had already shed the bright blooms of summer in favor of the deep greens, bright reds, muted purples, and luminescent oranges and yellows of autumn. She didn't know what she'd been expecting, certainly not this sudden rush of nostalgia and excitement mingled with pride. The original farmhouse, which had been renovated many times over the years, dated from the early eighteen-hundreds. Long, one-story wings sprouted from each side of the main house. Bunny knew they continued perpendicular to the house, creating a lovely, protected courtyard out back, with the farmhouse standing tall in the center. Just beyond the house were more outbuildings necessary for a working farm, including the original stable constructed to match the house. Surrounding the farm was a myriad of colorful fields ready to be harvested. Some were divided by stone fences. Others were bound by thick hedges. There was even a large swath of forest that covered the hillside, providing shelter for the red deer. There was a large pond in the glen behind the house, and a cool, peaty river that bisected the forest and ran all the way to Loch Fyne. Although she was nervous, her heart soared at the sight of her home.

"This is a farm?" Giff asked, eyeing the large stone house before him. He shook his head. "Looks more like a grand estate. I can't believe you grew up here."

"I did," Bunny told him. " 'Tis been in the family for four generations. My brother Angus will inherit next."

"Whoa," Ed remarked from the back seat. "Four generations. That's a long time. I bet it's haunted."

Bunny turned and glared at him in the back seat. "No, it's not haunted, Ed. Remember, Granny Mac lives here too. She wouldn't abide a lingering spirit."

"Good point," he conceded, adding an appreciative nod.

"Park over there," she told Giff, who was finally getting the hang of driving on the left-hand side of the road. She had a lead foot, Giff had a tendency to veer to the right, and honestly, she didn't know which was more dangerous.

As he guided the car to the gravel parking area at the side of the house, he cried, "Speak of the angel, and there she is!" He pointed to the front door, where Granny Mac had just stepped onto the stone landing, her bright, pixie-cut hair rivaling the red leaves of the two burning bushes that flanked the doorway. She was wearing her signature tunic-style top, this one in a flattering shade of sage green, with embroidered flowers on the front in white and pleasing shades of pink. Beneath the flowing top, she wore a stylish pair of flared jeans, and plenty of dangly necklaces. Bunny was sure that a few of those necklaces contained crystals.

Ella MacBride, known as Granny Mac, waved excitedly. Bunny's mother, Maggie, appeared next, wearing a hunter-green sweater that complemented her light ginger hair, a color that Bunny had inherited, followed closely by her father, Davie. The sight of her family standing together on the landing, waving excitedly at them, compelled Bunny to leap out of the car and run to meet them.

The moment her parents' arms came around her in a fierce, parental hug, all her trepidations vanished. Although she talked to her parents all the time, thanks to the internet and smartphones, being home was different. In their arms, she could feel their unconditional love, their collective joy, and even their relief that she was at long last safely home. Even though she was no longer a child, she understood, in that moment, that to Maggie and Davie MacBride, she would always be their child. It caused a flicker of guilt to well within her, and even a pang of regret as well. Both were swiftly thrust aside by her mother's words.

"My dear lass, we are so proud of ye and all ye have achieved in these past years. 'Tis wonderful to see ye looking so bonny and happy. Welcome home."

"I agree," her father said, wrapping her in one more hug. "'Tis grand to see ye, my wee Bunny. I know you're busy and important, but thank ye, thank ye for comin' home!"

Bunny chanced a look at Granny Mac over her father's shoulder. Big mistake. The look in the older woman's wise eyes issued a telepathic message that rang loud in Bunny's head. It spooked her the way her gran could do that, but now that her own gifts were beginning to emerge, there was no denying her granny's voice. And, quite frankly, she hadn't learned how to block it. *Home is where you need to be*, the mind-thoughts declared. *For it is only when surrounded by the love of your family that you can begin to make sense of your unique gifts and come to terms with the fact that Braiden, your twin, is your spirit guide. Don't be angry.*

"I'm not angry," Bunny said to the older woman, with a hint of anger in her voice.

"What did ye say?" Davie stepped away, looking confused.

Dang it! She hadn't meant to speak out loud. Obviously, she didn't know how it worked yet. Bunny looked at her father and covered her mistake by explaining, "What I meant to say is that I'm . . . not important, Dad. But I have missed you. A lot. Even your grumpiness."

That made him laugh. "I doubt ye've missed that, m'dear. Anyhow, I canna be grumpy now that you're home. And dinna be so modest. Ye are a big telly star. Ye've brought a whole crew with ye. Please introduce us to your friends. I'm chuffed everyone is staying the night. I hope everyone's hungry. Maggie's been cooking for days."

After introductions had gone around, including a hefty amount of small talk, everyone was then shown to their rooms. Brett and Giff were given the upstairs guest rooms, while Mike, Cody, and Ed were given rooms in the east wing. Bunny, of course, was given her old bedroom at the end of the upstairs hallway. As she stood before her door, she glanced at the room directly across the hall from hers, the room that would forever remain empty, and felt an ache in her heart. She schooled her thoughts enough to open her own bedroom door. The pink-and-white-striped wallpaper, the frilly white bed piled high with decorative pillows, and the boy-band posters on the walls had softened the ache in her heart to a nostalgic pang. Although she had taken most of her personal items with her to New York, the room still hummed with a teenage vibe—her teenage vibe—and she was amazed at how easily the past ten years dropped away in exchange for the warmth of childhood memories.

After depositing her suitcase and freshening up a bit, Bunny stepped into the hallway again, only this time her focus was on the door to the empty room. It was a room she had avoided like the plague, and yet she knew that she might find him there. It had been a long time since she'd stepped foot in Braiden's room, and she figured they must have cleaned it out by now.

The moment she opened the door, she was proven wrong. They hadn't changed a thing. Lord help her, it was as still and untouched as a tomb.

Unlike the organized mess it had always been, Braiden's room had been cleaned and preserved as if time had stood still. The blatant lack of dust told her that her mother cleaned it weekly, a thought that caused tears to well in Bunny's eyes. She stood in the center of the room, tears rolling down her cheeks, and took in every painful detail. His meticulously made bed, covered with the blue, white, and beige striped bedspread, and the Scottish flag pinned on the wall above it. The once state-of-the-art gaming computer looked old and outdated as it sat unused on the desk. The shelves above it still displayed a whimsical collection of sailboats, including the old eighteenth-century warship Braiden had meticulously built from a model kit. Her eyes glanced over the battered and scuffed rugby ball on the floor in the corner and a couple of old fishing rods propped against the wall. When her eyes landed on the bookshelf and his beloved collection of Harry Potter books pressed against a collection of Scottish cookbooks, she heaved a sigh. And the pictures, all the pictures were like stepping back in time. Braiden and his high school friends. Braiden sailing on the loch. Braiden kneeling beside his first deer, and one of a favorite old horse named Red. Yet it was the picture of Braiden and her, leaning out the takeout window of their pop-up restaurant, that sparked another wave of tears. They were grinning as if they hadn't a care in the world, and they hadn't back then. "Crivens," she breathed, reaching for the picture. The moment she touched it, she felt his presence in the room.

"I know you're here," she said, gingerly returning the picture to its spot on the shelf. She turned to the bed, half expecting to see Hopper, but it was still empty. "I want to thank you for what you did back at the loch. I wasn't paying attention. The truth is, I didn't want to come here. I'm not ready for this—any of this," she emphasized with a wave of her hand. "But I'm here, in your room. I have questions. Will you please show yourself?"

She swore she saw twinkling lights dancing in the air above the bed, faint yet just perceivable. She felt, more than she saw, his grin, but he had yet to make an appearance. "Please," she whispered again, feeling crazy. Feeling desperate.

"Bunny."

She jumped at the sound of her name, feeling her heart pounding away like a hammer in her chest. Not pleasant. She spun around and faced the door.

"I didn't mean to startle you," Brett apologized, looking afraid to step any farther into the room. He knew whose room it was, just as he had some inkling of why Bunny was standing in the center of it. The look on her face frightened him. Then, spying a white butterfly heading his way, he shifted, allowing it to flutter past him into the hallway.

"A white butterfly," Bunny remarked, awestruck. She had seen one like it before—many of them, the last time Braiden had appeared to her before fading away into the ether. She looked at the bed again, expecting to see him.

Nothing.

"Damn," Brett said, noting that tears were welling in her eyes. He hated the sight of women's tears, especially Bunny's. It made him feel things he wasn't ready to feel. "I'm so sorry. I . . . didn't mean to bother you." Then, because he couldn't help himself, he added, "This was his room." He felt like an intruder, which he obviously was.

"Yes," Bunny said, attempting a smile as she wiped her tears with the sleeve of her sweater. They both stepped into the hallway, where she searched for the butterfly. Did she really expect it to be there?

"This can't be easy for you. Did . . . you see him in there?" Brett briefly glanced into the room. "The white rabbit? Giff told me what happened. How you saw a white rabbit cross the road. It saved you."

The memory of the incident was still too raw and painful. Nonetheless, she said, "I never said it was white."

"Given your recent history, it was assumed." The corners of his mouth lifted upward, forming the fleeting hint of a smile. Serious once again, he added, "I know that your gifts are all very new and difficult for you, but I for one am grateful for them. I want you to know that. And I want to apologize."

"For what?"

"For jumping at the chance to investigate Dundoon Castle."

"Well, ye told me yourself that Dundoon has long been on your bucket list."

"Mine, not yours. I . . . um, know you've been avoiding coming home to Scotland. I know you're not thrilled with the new psychic abilities you have, or how they've been thrust upon you. I know all this and still, selfishly, I rearranged our schedule to make this happen." The guilt he felt was clear on his face. Bunny found it utterly misplaced, yet endearing.

With hands on her hips and curiosity pinching her pretty features, she asked, "You really think this was all you?"

"Yes," he said bravely. "I did all this. And I'm sorry. Coming here is obviously painful for you."

"Well, Mr. Man, I hate to shatter the illusion, but you're wrong. You didn't do this. This is all Granny Mac."

"She might have suggested it," he conceded, "but I jumped at the chance. I didn't have to. I could have stuck to the schedule, but instead I moved heaven and earth to make this happen."

"As she knew ye would. Look, we've both been played by a master. That's what she does, using her clairvoyant gifts and her grandmotherly wiles. She brought me here to face my past and make peace with it, which I am trying to do. It's part of the process, I suppose. Doesn't make it easy. Dundoon and its ghosts were simply the carrot she dangled to make it happen."

"You're saying that I've been manipulated?" Clearly, the thought had never crossed his mind. He looked perplexed.

"Yes," Bunny said, gently touching his arm. If she was about to add anything else, it was lost in her father's booming voice as it wafted up the stairs, announcing that the farm tour was about to begin.

"That's your dad." Relief washed over him as if he'd just been saved from an awkward situation. Having grown up on a cherry orchard in Wisconsin, he suddenly longed to be in the crisp autumn air with the guys, checking out heavy equipment and trouncing over newly harvested fields. He understood that. What he didn't understand were the complexities of women's emotions and how easily they manipulated their fellow man. "He's giving us a tour of the farm. Are you sure you're going to be alright?"

"I'm fine," she assured him. "Enjoy your tour. See you at supper."

She watched him walk down the hallway, then took a deep breath. It was now time to have a private word with her mum, and Granny Mac.

Chapter 4

Sitting at the cozy little table in the breakfast room with her mother and Granny Mac, Bunny suddenly grew nervous about explaining her burgeoning psychic gifts. She'd always been close to her mum, but distance, a five-hour time difference, a busy career, and the death of her twin had forced subtle changes on them both. They talked weekly, shared gossip and recipes, and ended every conversation with a heartfelt "Love you." However, she found that being in her mother's presence once again was both wonderful and daunting.

True to form, Maggie MacBride had set a lovely table for their little natter, complete with a steaming pot of tea and a plate full of perfectly baked scones. As Bunny smiled at her mother, her stomach plunged to the floor in a nervous knot. She knew that a lot of work had gone into this cream tea. It would be a shame to wipe that doting look off her mother's face so quickly. Instead, stalling for time, she mindlessly plucked one of the golden scones from the plate, slathered it with strawberry jam, added a healthy dollop of clotted cream, and took a bite. Her stomach engaged as her taste buds sailed away in delight.

"Oh, Mum, this is *delicious*!" Bunny realized that she had nearly forgotten how magnificent her mother's scones were. She had her mum's recipe and had made them often herself—whenever she longed for a little taste of home. Her scones were good, but somehow, they just didn't match up to Maggie MacBride's. Maybe it was the homemade jam made from the strawberries picked on their farm, or the fresh, thick white cream straight from the cow that her mother slow-baked for hours, clotting it herself. It was the most buttery, delicious clotted cream in the world, and there was nothing to compare to it. The strawberries in the jam were so ripe and flavorful, Bunny could almost taste the sunshine they had bathed in. When both jam and cream were spread on the fluffy, soft scone that was perfectly crisp at the edges, it was pure heaven. "Why do yours taste so good, Mum? I've made these hundreds of times, but they never taste like this."

Maggie looked at her daughter over the rim of her teacup. "Did ye remember the secret ingredient?" Her deep green eyes sparkled with mischief as she asked this.

Bunny stared at her, dumbfounded. "Secret ingredient? You never said anything about a secret ingredient."

Maggie placed her cup back in its saucer and replied, "Love. I add an extra helping of love to everything I make. That's why they taste so good—and probably the cream. 'Tis near to impossible to get such good, unpasteurized, grass-fed cream without knowing a farmer."

Bunny smiled in agreement. "Very true. You can't get clotted cream like this in the States. This is wonderful, Mum. Just us women, chatting over cream tea. It feels like old times." She then cast a questioning glance at Granny Mac and found the older woman's expressionless face annoying. Bringing her attention back to her mother, she asked, "Has Gran told ye anything about our show, *Food and Spirits*, or our visit to Bramsford Manor?"

Bunny knew that Granny Mac had been at the farm nearly

a week before they arrived. She had contacted her friends, the owners of Dundoon Castle, and had made the proper arrangements for their visit. Bunny had stayed back in Hampshire, England, with the lads to work on the list of post-production items Ed had made before sending the footage off to their producer, Trig Gunderson, back in the States. She would have thought her gran would have shared a little gossip with her mum.

To her surprise, her mother leaned across the table, grinned, and uttered in a conspiratorial tone, "We've talked of little else. I could hardly wait for your arrival. That Brett Bloom is positively scrumptious, my dear! I had no idea that your co-hosts would be so handsome. Gran's told me that Giff is likely not your type, being . . ."

"Gay?" Bunny offered.

Maggie nodded before continuing. "However, I've heard that Brett has his eye on ye. Not bad work after only one episode. Gran told me how he couldn't get enough of your prime rib roast and Yorkshire pudding. Your father couldn't resist such a meal either. Keep up the good work, my dear, and we might hear wedding bells yet." She winked.

Bunny's porcelain skin, a curse she'd inherited from her mother, flushed red as a beet. "Mother, please! We've just started working together. Dinna . . . blow this out of proportion or, for heaven's sake, jinks me!" Crivens, why did she add that last bit? Maggie had heard it too, and like a horse with a carrot dangling before its nose, chased after it.

"I wouldn't dare jinks ye!" her mother exclaimed, looking affronted. "I just want to offer a wee piece of advice. Do not close him out, dear. Ye have a tendency to do that ever since the . . ." She trailed off again, unwilling to bring up the accident that hung in the air between them like an impenetrable fog. Bunny noticed that her mother's face was as red as her own must be. The MacBride women certainly couldn't hide their embarrassment.

"Maggie," Granny Mac said, choosing this moment to finally speak up, "let them work it out on their own. Bunny knows what she's doing. She's a sensible adult, and you must learn to trust her. Now, she has something important to tell ye. Go ahead, dear." After giving her an encouraging nod, Granny Mac picked up her scone and took a dainty bite.

Great, Bunny fumed. They had five days together to chitchat and gossip, and all Gran did was puff wind in her mum's sails with talk of romance and hunky Brett Bloom! Well, it was now or never, Bunny thought, and took a leap of faith, hoping her mother would understand. "Mum, 'tis true I'm the chef on the show, and I enjoy it. However, the show is not just about food; it's also about ghosts. Ghosts are the spirits the show refers to."

"Ghosts? Are you sure?" Apparently, Maggie didn't think this was correct.

"Very, Mum. Brett is a ghost hunter. Giff is kind of a . . . psychic medium." She wiggled her hand in the air to wave off the notion, hoping her mum wouldn't ask any questions about Giff or his abilities, which were fraudulent at best.

"Wait. Are ye telling me Brett Bloom isn't a chef?" Maggie's soaring hopes visibly plummeted.

"Not a chef. A ghost hunter, as in he hunts for ghosts and uses all kinds of weird, techy things to detect them. It's actually kind of fascinating. However, why I'm telling ye this is because when I was at Bramsford Manor, something extraordinary happened to me. I started seeing a white rabbit, only the rabbit wasn't real. It was a ghost rabbit." There. It wasn't eloquent, but the truth was finally out in the open. Bunny quickly took a sip of her hot tea while studying her mother's reaction to this news.

Maggie was visibly confused. "I dinna understand, dear. Rabbits are wee beasts. When they die, they just die. Or isn't that correct?" She looked to Granny Mac for support, knowing that her mother-in-law had more experience in spiritual matters such as this.

While Granny Mac struggled to answer Maggie's question, Bunny blurted, "Remember my white rabbit, Hopper?"

"Your wee pet rabbit that got killed by the neighbor's dogs?" Maggie's eyebrows pinched tightly at the memory. "I do. What a tragic ending that poor wee bunny had."

"Well, I've been seeing him . . . or his ghost." While her mother struggled to comprehend this, Bunny decided to confound her even more by stating, "The rabbit I'm seeing isn't really Hopper."

"Thank heavens!"

"It's Braiden. Your son. My brother. Mum, I think I have psychic abilities."

Maggie swayed unsteadily in her chair. Granny Mac poured her another cup of tea before taking hold of her hands. "Drink that up, dear," she urged. "Then we're going to the kitchen to help get supper on the table. The lads will be back shortly from their tour. While we work, we shall explain everything."

Chapter 5

It was going rather well, Bunny mused, working beside her mother and grandmother in the kitchen while preparing the evening meal. As expected, her mother had been dumbfounded by the news of her burgeoning psychic abilities. It wasn't until Bunny explained her vision of the white rabbit and how it was connected to Braiden that her mother understood the beauty and, yes, the curse of such a gift. After all, Bunny was talking about her son.

"Is this true? You're not making this up?"

"She's just beginning to discover her abilities, Maggie, but I assure you they are real. Give her time," Granny Mac advised.

"What . . . does he look like?" Maggie asked as tears spilled from her eyes.

"Handsome," Bunny blurted, wanting nothing more than to ease her mother's worries. "I only saw him for a moment," she explained, recalling her last night in the very haunted Fleur-de-Lys room at Bramsford Manor, the only time Braiden had shown himself. It had only been for a fleeting second, but it was a second that had burned an image on her memory she would never forget. She longed to see him again too. "He looks exactly like you remember him, Mum, only he was surrounded in a shimmering brightness." She left it there, unwilling to explain the white butterflies that had surrounded him. How could she when she didn't understand them herself? Instead, she said, "He wants you and Dad to know that he's okay and that he loves you."

That simple statement released another torrent of tears streaming down her mother's cheeks. Bunny gently removed the paring knife from her mother's hand, set it on the chopping board, and wrapped her arms around her, holding her tightly. Maggie returned the hug.

"I'm sorry I kept all this from you, Mum, but I didn't know how to tell you."

" 'Tis okay, love," Maggie cooed, giving Bunny one last squeeze before releasing her. "Ye know that ye can always talk to me . . . about anything. Even Brett Bloom."

"What?" Bunny saw that her mother was grinning.

"I'm so proud of ye, Bridget. And I cannot wait to hear more about what you discover. I've always thought that such abilities, like the ones Granny Mac possesses, are a blessing. How marvelous that you've inherited the gift."

Bunny wasn't so sure but was happy her mother thought so.

Then, hearing deep voices and the stomping of booted feet in the mudroom, Maggie lowered her voice and said, "However, I think 'tis best if we keep your special abilities from your father. He's not as open-minded when it comes to communicating with the spirits."

Her mother had just picked up her paring knife once again when her father sauntered into the room, infused with high spirits and surrounded by her coworkers. From what Bunny could tell, it looked like everyone had enjoyed a pint or two in the stables before coming to supper.

"Guess what, Maggie?" Davie said, addressing his wife. Bunny didn't think her mum was in any shape to play guessing games, not after the tea, scones, and emotional conversation they'd just had. Thankfully, her father didn't wait for an answer. "These fine fellas here are ghost hunters!" Davie let out a roaring laugh at that. "Did ye hear that? Ghost hunters! That's why they're going to old Dundoon, not for the piping competition, as they should do, but to drum up the ghoulish piper. Lord, I've heard it all!" he exclaimed, grinning broadly at the men. Giff wrapped his arm around the older gentleman and gave him a hug. As he did so, he tossed Bunny a convivial wink.

"We thought your dad knew the nature of our show," Brett explained, having the decency to blush.

"We were told it was a cooking show. My daughter's a famous chef, after all." Davie offered, eyeing Bunny. "Did ye know about this?"

What to say to that? The truth was a little complicated, so she offered, "It's so unusual and exciting that I wanted it to be a surprise, Dad. I'm sure they told you that I handle all the cooking. And speaking of cooking, who's hungry?" Bunny was happy to change the subject.

"We're hungry," said a familiar voice from the hallway. Bunny turned and smiled with delight.

"Angus! Pippa!" she cried, laying eyes on her older brother and his wife. "I'm so happy you're here! Come, meet my friends."

The table was set, and the food was out of the oven. It was time to celebrate a homecoming.

As Bunny sat at the crowded table in the large dining room, two things became apparent. The first was that her family seemed annoyingly entertained by the idea of her cooking on a ghost-hunting show. Even though her father was too practical to believe in ghosts, that didn't stop him from delighting in the stories Brett, Mike, Ed, and Cody were telling them. They, after all, had worked together for five years on their own ghost-hunting show, *The Ghost Guys*, before embarking on *Food & Spirits*. The second thing Bunny noticed was the distant coldness in her brother's greeting. It was as if Angus was annoyed at her for some reason, and she couldn't fathom why. She loved her older brother dearly, but admitted that they had never been particularly close. At least not as close as she and Braiden had been. Whatever issue he had with her would just have to wait. Bunny had a job to do and couldn't be bothered with guessing games. Angus, she knew, was the stoic type who held his feelings close to the vest. If Pippa was aware of the issue, she wasn't about to show it. No, Pippa had been overjoyed to welcome Bunny home.

After a starter of delicious cock-a-leekie soup, two large shepherd's pies were served next, along with freshly baked loaves of crusty bread to sop up the juices. Her mum's recipe called for sautéed chunks of lamb in a rich gravy that was mixed with fresh peas, carrots, and wild mushrooms. The meaty base was spread in a baking dish before being topped with creamy mashed potatoes. Before the pie was popped into the oven to bake, the potatoes were topped with a layer of grated cheddar cheese. Warm, savory, bubbly, and topped with cheesy goodness, the dish was utterly divine. By the time the dinner plates were removed, there was hardly a scrap left of the meal. Maggie then brought out a warm apple cake and a bowl of freshly whipped cream to top it with. It was one of Bunny's absolute favorite desserts.

"Well, now," Davie MacBride said, just after taking a bite of the scrumptious apple cake, "ye are going to the castle in the morning to drum up Dundoon's legendary ghost, the piper of Dundoon." Bunny noticed that he couldn't help smiling at the word *ghost*. "However, did ye know that this is the weekend that Dundoon hosts the National Solo Piping Championship on the old parade grounds beneath the castle?"

Brett nodded. "We have heard a little something about that, sir. I believe Ella mentioned it to us when she made the arrangements."

"I did," Granny Mac was quick to acknowledge. "When I paid a visit to Sir Jordy and Lady Elizabeth, they were especially delighted to have you come during their most auspicious event. The National Solo Piping Championship is held there every October in honor of the noble clan pipers, both past and present."

"Do ye remember the tale?" her dad asked Bunny.

For the love of her, she didn't—not much of it, at any rate—but she nodded all the same. What she did remember was that Granny Mac had delighted in telling them about the ghostly piper when they were kids, mostly to spook them, and probably to relay a little bloody Scottish history as well. Unfortunately, history was lost on her.

Her father, thankfully, glossed right over the ghostly piper as well, focusing instead on the piping competition. "The top ten pipers in Scotland will compete for the national title, and this year one of the judges will be none other than Major Scotty MacDonald!"

"Who is . . . ?" Bunny prompted, noting that both her brother and father seemed excited by this news.

"The personal piper to the late queen, Bunny," he chided, before bringing his hand over his heart, adding, "God rest her soul," Angus, Pippa, and Maggie followed his example.

"The late queen, you say? Impressive," Giff offered, being a fan of pomp, circumstance, and the royal family.

"Major MacDonald won the competition twenty years ago," Davie explained. "His skill on the great Highland bagpipes took him all the way to the royal palace, the highest place of honor for a piper. 'Tis going to be just grand!" He grinned in anticipation of the event.

"Are you going?" Bunny asked.

"Aye, your mother, Angus, and I will be there to watch the competition. We'll be in the stands at the parade grounds tomorrow afternoon, should you like to pop over and say hello."

Bunny noticed her mother's forced smile. She knew her mother wasn't a fan of loud noises or any instrument that sounded like an animal in the throes of a painful death. It was a little flaw her father kindly overlooked.

"I'll be in Oban doing some shopping," Pippa explained, having somehow escaped the family outing.

"Are ye certain ye dinna want to come with us, dear?" Davie asked. "There's nothing like the sound of the pipes played by a gifted piper echoing off the hillsides."

Pippa adjusted her tawny blond hair and offered a kind smile. "I wish I could, but I'm afraid the shopping won't wait."

Bunny secretly applauded her sister-in-law's lie. However, even she had to admit that, while the bagpipes were not her favorite instrument, there was something nostalgic and soul-stirring about their sound. It surprised her, but she found that she was looking forward to visiting the old castle. She wondered what the kitchen would look like.

"Mum," she said, turning to the woman sitting next to her at the foot of the table. "All this talk of pipers has me wondering. What do ye suppose a piper from the sixteen-hundreds would like to eat?"

Angus shot her a disapproving look. "Are ye joking? Are ye seriously worried about cooking for a ghostie? You, Bridget Bunny MacBride, America's *favorite* celebrity chef? Och! Ye should have never left Scotland."

She could tell that the lads were as taken aback by the outburst as she was. The comment infuriated her. In one fell swoop, Angus had stripped the last ten years of hard work from her, reducing her to silly little sister, a role she had always played. Well, she wasn't a child any longer, and she certainly wasn't going to take that from him. Bunny shot out of her chair, ready to yank Angus out of his. He was far taller than she, and as thickly muscled and brawny as their father, but she didn't care. Maggie shot out of her chair as well, but to Bunny's surprise, it wasn't to defend her. Maggie was trying to divert her instead.

"I know just the thing!" she said, in an uncharacteristically loud voice. "Come with me to the storehouse and we shall put together a meal not only fit for a piper, but the laird and lady of the castle as well."

Bunny parried her brother's derisive look with one of defiance. "Thank you, Mother. I believe Angus would like to join us as well, since he seems to have an opinion on the matter."

"Very well," he said and rose from his chair. He dropped his napkin on the table, excused himself, and followed them out of the dining room.

Chapter 6

"Rack of lamb," Maggie said, marching across the courtyard with purpose. She was heading for the storehouse beyond the farm office. "I have a case of beautiful rack of lamb that just came in from the butcher. It'll be perfect for the occasion. We can cut some herbs to go with them tomorrow morning. The tatties have been pulled up as well. You can take a sack of those too. Bunny, are you coming?" Bunny could hardly believe her ears. Her mother was dancing around the thousand-pound elephant that had just crashed their party—namely, Angus and his palpable anger.

"Mother. Stop it. I mean, thank you. That would be lovely, but I'd like to have a private word with my brother."

Maggie stopped and turned around, staring at her grown children under the scant porch light that illuminated the courtyard. One was tall and broad-shouldered, with the same dark hair Davie once had, only now her husband's had gone gray. The other was slim and fair, and far shorter, with a head full of beautiful ginger curls that fell to the middle of her back. They were both so dear to her. It was a chilly, moonless night, and she was afraid to leave them alone in the darkness. "What? Now? Do ye think that's wise? I mean, you've just come home, Bridget."

"Aye, and she'll leave again in the morning," Angus remarked. "She's good at that. Leaving."

So that was it, Bunny thought. She had left, and he resented her for it. "Mother, please go back inside. Angus and I need to talk."

After a moment of hand-wringing and hesitation, Maggie nodded and walked back to the kitchen door. Before she disappeared inside, she turned to them, demanding, "Please be civil."

Bunny faced her older brother and stared up into his face. "I've obviously offended ye, Angus. 'Tis been a long time since I've been home, and now when I am here, with my cohosts and film crew, you pick this moment to air your grievances? You're an eejet!" She was so mad at him, she was gulping air like a racehorse.

"Do ye want to know why I'm angry with you? I'll tell ye why, Bridget. I'm angry because Braiden died, and then ye left. Ye left and never looked back."

"What? Is that what ye think?" She was aghast. "That's not it at all, Angus. I was gutted that day. But I had nothing to do with his death!" She thought about that for a moment, feeling a twinge of remorse for being the one who survived. It had been a familiar feeling, regret. It was that feeling which drove her to make something of herself and not squander the gift she'd been given. She doubted Angus could ever understand that.

"I dinna say ye did, Bridget. We all know it was an accident. What I said was that ye left. Ye left, and he died, and for them, it was like losing ye both. How can ye not understand that?"

"What?" His words stunned her, gripping her heart like a vise and squeezing the life from her. Could that be true?

"We all grieved for Braiden," he reminded her in a shaky

voice. "Mum and Dad were still encumbered by that grief when ye took off on your grand culinary adventure. Ye left the country, and to them it was like a death too."

"They . . . never said a word about it." At the mere mention of her grieving parents, tears sprang to her eyes. She had never meant to cause them pain. "If I had known, I would have stayed. They encouraged me to go, Angus."

"Aye, of course they did. They love ye that much. They knew ye were hurting, and they wanted that for ye. They wanted ye to be happy and follow your dreams, even at the expense of their own happiness. But I was here, Bridget. I remained, and I watched how losing the both of ye nearly destroyed them. They tended the farm like a pair of ghosts, moving about without any joy in living." There was no anger in his voice as he spoke, only sorrow and the remnants of fear, and it thoroughly undid her.

"Angus, I'm so sorry," she sobbed. "Why didn't ye say something to me before this? Why didn't ye call me, or mention this the last time I was home?"

He cocked his head and stared at her through the scant light. "The first time ye came home, I was too angry. Your selfishness made me so. The next time ye were home was the last time, and it was my wedding. I was a wee busy then. Why couldn't ye have stayed in Scotland and gone to a cookery school like everyone else?" he finally asked her. The beseeching look on his face caused a *smirr* of fresh tears. Her fears had been realized. Coming home was worse than she had imagined.

She wiped her wet cheeks with the sleeve of her sweater before admitting, "It was too hard. Everything here reminds me of him . . . of us," she added, gesturing to him and the house at large. "We were a happy family. When Braiden died, the happiness was sucked out of us." She could see that he agreed. Then, feeling she owed him more than her selfish motives, she confided, "You might not have known this, but it was Braiden's dream to go to New York and become a renowned chef, not mine. It's hard to explain, Angus, but when he died, I felt I had to go and chase the dream for him." Survivor's guilt and fear of his ghost had driven her to do it. But she knew Angus wouldn't understand. Instead, she offered, "To make good on a promise. I thought he would have wanted me to go."

Even in the scant light, she could tell he was shocked by this. "He wanted to go to America?" Obviously, the thought had never occurred to him.

"He had so much talent," Bunny reminded him. "Far more than me. Braiden would have had his own restaurant by now, for sure. I've cocked it up. I doubt he would have ended up cooking for ghosts on a reality telly show."

Angus gave a huff of a chuckle at that. However, to Bunny's surprise, that little chuckle grew and grew until it was deep belly laughter. Bunny couldn't help herself. Angus's laughter was contagious. Although her eyes were still dewy with tears, she began laughing too.

"Cooking for ghosties?" he remarked. "Braiden would ha' loved that!"

"Would he?" She lifted an eyebrow at him. "I doubt he would. But if on the off chance he landed in the same spot as me, he'd know far better what to cook for them than I do. For the most part, I'm just making it up as I go."

Her older brother stared at her a beat too long, then doubled over as another wave of laughter took him. "God love ye, Bridget! That's the most ridiculous thing I've ever heard. Ghosties, m'dearie, don't eat. They're dead!" He said this as if she needed reminding.

He had a point. It was a ridiculous notion. However, she had hitched her wagon to both the idea and the ghost-hunting lads and was now on her way to the most haunted castle in

Argyll. She felt inclined to remind her brother of his heritage—of the fact the Scots were the ones who shortened the old Christian term All Hallows Eve to Hallow E'en, which became Halloween, the now ubiquitous name for the holiday. It had been purposely held on the old Celtic celebration of Samhain, the night between October 31 and November 1, when, the old ones believed, the veil between the living and the dead was the thinnest and ghouls and demons roamed the earth in the darkness, looking for victims. In Scotland, bonfires were lit, and neeps (turnips) were hollowed out and carved to look spooky. Once illuminated, they were put on windowsills and outside front doors to ward off evil. Parents would dress their children in disguises to outsmart the spookies, in the hope that they would be overlooked as they went door-to-door, performing tricks for treats such as fruit, nuts, and wee cakes. Families would host a feast and set a table for their departed loved ones, welcoming home the good spirits while warding off the evil ones. It was known as the dumb supper, or silent supper, and she was certain Angus knew about it. Then again, he was a bit thick these days, so maybe he had forgotten.

"Do ye remember the dumb supper that the old ones held on Samhain?" she finally asked him.

"What? You're talking gibberish."

"Our show is based on the dumb-supper tradition, which, in a nutshell, states that if ye want to welcome a departed loved one to the table, ye set a place for them, make their favorite food, and voilà! The ghost of that person is drawn to the table like a fly to honey."

"That's utterly daft, Bridget. Ye know this, right? The dumb supper is a myth like the selkie, the kelpie, and the fairy dog."

How she wished he was correct! However, it had worked on their first try. Maybe it had been luck . . . or the opposite of luck, however one looked at it. She tilted her head and smiled at him. "Ye could be correct. It could be just a myth. At any rate, my job is to cook for a ghost, but here's a little secret, brother: it's the living who eat what I make."

"There's the rub!" he cried. "You're invited in to make a good meal. For your lads, you're their ticket of entry. Verra canny! Speaking of your friends, Granny says that blond fella, Bloom, has his eyes on ye. I'm no judge of character, but personally that McGrady fellow seems more your type. Nice gents."

Bunny smiled inwardly. "I'll tell him ye think so. Thank you, Angus. So, are we okay here?"

"Only if you promise to come home more often. Mum and Dad are getting older. And Granny . . ." he paused to shake his head, "She's marchin' toward the grave. Sometimes I think she's a wee touched in the head as well." He tapped his head, indicating what he thought of Granny Mac. Not to make light of his worries, Bunny gave a solemn nod. However, she knew better. Granny Mac was full of life, vigor, and the second sight, a gift her father and Angus had no use for.

"I promise that I'll come home more often."

"Good," he said and gave her a firm hug. "We're the only family ye have, Bridget, and we love ye."

After the confrontation with Angus, her heart felt a measure lighter. Yet there was still a gnawing guilt for having been so selfish all those years ago. As designed, her visit home was short. She was leaving early tomorrow morning, but there was one place she needed to visit before she left again. After helping her mother with the dishes, and after saying good night to the lads, Bunny left the farmhouse.

Once outside, she wrapped her coat tightly around her to fend off the late-September chill, turned on the torch, and struck out on the familiar path. When the light fell upon the old shed, she stopped in her tracks and held her breath. It hadn't changed at all.

After struggling with the latch, she finally slid open the door and was hit with the familiar scent of barnwood and dust mixed with a hint of dried herbs. In an instant, she was back there once again, cooking in the little pop-up restaurant beside her brother. She flipped on the lights, realizing that nothing had changed. The old electric stove looked the same, as did the sink their father had put in for them. Her eyes scanned the mismatched collection of pots on the rack and frying pans hanging on the wall. Besides her mother's, this was the first kitchen she had worked in. This was where she had found her love of food. What made it extra special was the fact that Braiden had been beside her, encouraging her to think big. Although it was small and rustic, she welled with a longing to be back here, working with the bounty of their own land and creating wonderful little meals for the locals.

"We had good times in here, didn't we?" she said to the room, knowing he was listening. "Thank you. But I need to say goodbye now. I love you, but I really can't have you hanging on." A muffled chuckle hit her ears, and she spun around, expecting to see Braiden. However, it wasn't Braiden who stood in the doorway. It was Granny Mac.

"Unfortunately, it doesn't work that way, my dear," her grandmother said. "We might wish it did, but it doesn't."

"You knew I'd be in here," Bunny said. Her grandmother nodded. "I've been so afraid of coming back here because of what it might unleash in me. I was only thinking of me, and Braiden. I never thought about Mom, Dad, or Angus."

"I know, but now you are thinking of them. Coming home to your family brings about clarity that you otherwise might not get. You have begun to embrace your psychic gifts, and that's good. You have even shared your secret with your mother and have brought her greater comfort than you will ever know. It will strengthen the bond between you."

"And Angus? I had no idea he was so angry with me," Bunny told her, welling with guilt.

"But now you do know. You will be more mindful of your family and their feelings. Hopefully you will visit more often."

"I will. I promise, but what about Dad? How do I make this right with him?"

"He's always been proud of you, Bunny. Both your parents are. That's why they encouraged you to go to America and chase your dream." Granny Mac paused a moment, then added, cryptically, "Now that you're going to Dundoon, I have a feeling you and your father will connect over his favorite instrument, the bagpipes."

"Fat chance of that," Bunny said with a huff. "I'll be in the kitchen cooking for ghosties."

"I'm afraid there's no escaping the sound of the pipes at Dundoon."

"What is that supposed to mean, Gran?"

"It means to be prepared. Now, we have an early start tomorrow, and I cannot wait for you to meet Jordy and Elizabeth Malcom. They're charming, but their castle is frightfully haunted. They could really use your help."

"Frightfully haunted? Why frightfully?" Bunny didn't like the sound of that at all. As Granny Mac guided her out the door, she paused to look at the older woman. "Gran, what have you gotten me into?"

"Us, dear," she reminded Bunny, as they began their trek back to the house. "I'm coming with you and the lads. And I should warn you, the piping can be bloody awful."

Chapter 7

"Get a load of this traffic," Giff remarked, staring out the window. "My understanding is that Dundoon is somewhat isolated. I realize that there's a bagpipe competition going on somewhere in the vicinity, but this is crazy."

"A bagpipe competition in Scotland is a very big deal," Granny Mac informed him as she gingerly guided the rental car along the crowded, winding road that led to the estate. The road was narrow with cars pressed bumper-to-bumper, navigating the curves and bends like colorful scales on a slithering snake. After Bunny had packed the coolers from her mother's kitchen into the car, Granny Mac had volunteered to drive them, knowing the way to Dundoon like the back of her hand.

Giff leaned forward, addressing Granny Mac from the back seat. "That's becoming apparent. Silly me, I thought it was just going to be a couple of guys knocking around in kilts while playing 'Amazing Grace' on the bagpipes."

Bunny gave him a stern look and tried to clout him on the

arm for that ridiculous comment. Giff was full of ridiculous comments.

"What?" he shot back, grinning with amusement. "It's an honest mistake. I mean, we know that Davie MacBride is a self-admitted superfan of the instrument, but how many bagpipe geeks can there be?"

"Apparently, a lot," Ed remarked, looking just as amazed as Giff by the sight of the traffic.

"You lads will enjoy it immensely. It's very Scottish," Granny Mac assured them. "However, I do recommend earplugs. The sound has a remarkable piercing quality to it."

"We're just going to be at the castle, investigating," Bunny said. "We're not involved in any of this."

"While you're here, I suggest that you all make it a point to wander around the fairgrounds and enjoy the competition," Granny Mac told them. "It's quite an experience. Also, dear, your parents and Angus will be here."

"If I have a moment, I will, but that's doubtful. I'll likely be too busy getting ready for tonight's spirit supper."

"Well, I'm certain your efforts will be most appreciated, especially by the Malcoms and their guests."

Giff hadn't heard about the guests. He thrust his head into the front seat again and asked, "Guests? Anyone famous?"

"I'll be there with a dear friend of mine. Also, the three judges of the competition are staying at the castle, as they always do. Did you know that Dundoon is thought to be the oldest continuously occupied castle in Scotland?"

"No, I didn't," Bunny said, knowing that her grandmother was a font of Scottish knowledge. She then thought to ask, "Have you ever heard him, Gran, the ghostly piper of Dundoon?"

Ella MacBride shook her stylish red head. "The truth is, I've never stayed at Dundoon past supper. It is said that the piper only comes out at night after everyone has gone to bed. However, just because I've never heard him play doesn't mean he's not there. I've felt him, and others. As I've mentioned before, the castle is very haunted."

"Great." It was said with a lack of enthusiasm. Giff, Bunny knew, wasn't a fan of spooks either.

Ed flashed Giff a grin before remarking, "You might not find it pleasant, but Brett's going to geek out over this place. As for me, I hope we hear him. That would make for incredible television. Speaking of ghosts, I hope you've got something tasty up your sleeve, Bunny. Something certain to draw this piping specter to the table."

Bunny turned to look at him and smiled. "Rack of lamb."

"I'm listening." Giff cocked his head and leaned forward.

"I planned the menu late last night with my mum. I wanted the meal to be both locally sourced and historic, with a modern Scottish twist. For instance, for starters I'm making Cullen skink—"

". . . and you lost me." He flopped back into his seat.

"Cullen skink is delicious," Granny Mac informed him, looking at him in the rearview mirror. "It's a smoked fish chowder, much like your New England clam chowder, only much better."

"Better than clam chowder? Doubtful," Giff remarked. Ed, sitting next to him, looked doubtful as well.

Granny Mac continued. "Cullen is the small fishing village in the north that first made the soup famous. *Skink* is an Old Scottish word for shin. Soups and stews back in the old days were usually made from tough cuts of meat, like a shin or a knuckle. Therefore, Cullen skink simply means soup from Cullen."

"I'll take your word for it, Ella," Giff said, still looking doubtful.

"As I said," Bunny continued, "Cullen skink for starters, followed by herb-crusted rack of lamb served with creamy gratin potatoes and honey-roasted baby carrots. Dessert will be a hearty Dundee cake, my dad's favorite. As for drinks, we're in Scotland, gentlemen. It's whisky neat, whisky on the rocks, or a whisky sour—you chose."

"I chose whisky. All of it. Oh, would you look at that!" Giff stared out the window in awe.

They had turned onto the long, pine-flanked drive that bisected the hilly castle grounds. It was breathtaking. The moment the tall pines thinned, the land before them opened, revealing a scene that displayed all the colors, crowds, and pageantry of a county fair. In the distance, on a dramatic rise, sat the brooding castle of Dundoon. Thanks to Granny Mac, Bunny knew that Dundoon sat on a vast 5,000-acre estate, nestled in the wild, rolling hills of Argyll, and with nearly six miles of rugged coastline below the high cliffs. She found the lush, green parade grounds beneath the castle a sight to behold. Large, canopied vendors' tents lined the perimeter of the grassy field, selling food, drink, clothing, art, and just about anything else one could wish for. The competition arena in the center was flanked by high bleachers already crowded with fans. Beyond the competition grounds and down in a lower field near the forest, Bunny spied two dozen or so tents. She thought the colorful domes looked more like an infestation of vibrant mushrooms than a campground. Across from the tent campers was a long row of large caravans, or RVs as they were known in the States, parked one beside the other, all with their awnings propped out, protecting the inviting groupings of chairs beneath them. To Bunny, the thought of staying in a caravan was just a wee bit more pleasing than the thought of bunking for the night in a haunted guest room, which wasn't saying much.

Tent camping in the crowded field was out of the question. She pondered her haunted accommodations when the sound of bagpipes struck even louder, pulling her attention to the parade grounds once again.

As they drove past the parade grounds, Bunny could see at least ten bagpipers marching onto the field, each accompanied by a drummer. To her amazement, they were all playing the same loud tune, which echoed off the castle walls and the distant hills. It was hard to hear anything else.

"Great Scott!" Giff cried in a mimicking boom. "The racket! The pageantry! Is it wrong that I can't take my eyes off them?"

Bunny had to admit that there was something very attractive about a Scottish man in full Highland dress. A piper always stuck with tradition, which was part of the charm. Each gentleman marching into the arena wore a plaid kilt in his clan tartan, cut just above the knees to show off a nice amount of lower leg. The kilt was secured with a black leather belt, while a sporran pouch danged front and center at the waist. Some pouches were fur, some were leather; really, it was up to the piper. Covering the torso was a smartly cut wool jacket worn over a white-collared shirt. At the neck, each piper wore a black silk tie. Below the kilt, wool socks covered the lower leg up to the knees and were secured with garters. The shoes were always black and leather. For the head, a piper could choose between the stiffer, sleek-fitting Glengarry bonnet, shaped like an upside-down ship with a rosette cockade on the side and a ribbon down the back, or the rounder, softer Balmoral bonnet, with a pom-pom on the top of the flat crown, also with a ribbon down the back. However, neither should be confused with the rakishly floppy, flat-topped tam-o'-shanter, which was Bunny's personal favorite. She turned to look at Giff.

"Welcome to Scotland. Impressive, isn't it? I'm going to be busy in the kitchen, but you lads will have a great time out here, filming your B-roll."

As they chatted, Granny Mac guided the car through the private castle gates, but not before pointing out the stately gateposts. "Notice the stags gracing the top of each gatepost."

"Whoa!" Giff remarked, swiveling his head to get a better look at them. "Those must have cost a pretty penny."

"Jordy's father commissioned them when he inherited the castle. Those stags are now an iconic symbol of Dundoon. Nearly everyone who comes to visit snaps a picture of them."

"Now that's savvy branding," Giff said, appreciatively. However, the former ad man in him just couldn't keep from offering a bit of advice. "Although . . . the new owner might be better served by replacing the deer with a bagpiper. You know, go all in with the legend. That sort of thing. A piper is more on-brand for this place than a deer. Anyone can have a deer. But a piper?"

"Giff," Bunny chided from the front seat, "they're already holding the National Solo Piping Championship. I think they're doing fine. Leave the stags alone. They're gorgeous."

He narrowed his eyes at her. "Stay in your lane, Bunnykins. I'll have a word with the laird. Do they call him a laird? Look, here's the old fellow now . . . followed by his loyal hound and three members of his adoring staff. *Nice*. Can anyone be a laird?" he asked. Everyone ignored him.

As Granny Mac parked the car, she explained, "That's Jordy Malcom, my dear friend, and his black Lab, Winston. Jordy also happens to be the Malcom clan chieftain and laird of Dundoon. Laird, Gifford, is a title one is usually born into," she explained, unbuckling her seat belt. Yet before she alighted from the car, she pointed to the lovely older woman standing next to Jordy. "And that dear lady with the honey-colored hair and wearing the plaid skirt with the lavender cashmere sweater is his wife, Elizabeth. Her friends call her Lizzy. The middle-aged couple beside them are part of the Malcom's small staff, Mary and Westley Collins. They've worked at the castle ever since I've known the Malcoms."

While Granny Mac was warmly embraced by the older couple, Bunny was greeted quite excitedly by Winston, their big black Lab. Although she loved bunnies and rabbits, Bunny had a real soft spot for dogs, and Winston was a sweetheart. Before she knew it, all the lads were standing beside her, petting Winston and being introduced to the Malcoms and Mary and Westley Collins.

"This place is amazing. Better than I imagined," Brett whispered to her. "Ancient and stately. I'm sure it's filled with fascinating history. Also, that piping competition is going to make for some amazing B-roll." (Didn't she know it!) "I can't wait to see the inside."

"Ella, we are so overjoyed you've come!" Elizabeth said in her lovely, lilting voice. Turning to Bunny and the lads, she added, "We are honored to have you visiting as well, especially during the competition." She didn't need to say more. The din from the parade ground swirled around them like an urgent call to arms. Remarkably, she ignored it. "We've heard so much about you, Bridget, from your grandmother. Please, introduce us to your friends."

"Thank you for having us here on such short notice," Bunny told the Malcoms. "We understand this is a busy time for you, but I believe this will be a remarkable opportunity to showcase your beautiful home—"

"And investigate your legendary ghost," Brett finished for

her. "Your castle is well known in the paranormal community. I honestly can't believe we're here. Has Granny Mac—Ella," he corrected, "explained our show to you and how we work?"

Jordy Malcom, a thickly built man in his mid-sixties with a head of gray hair, a round, jowly face, and sharp blue eyes, flashed a cunning grin at Brett. "Aye, we've heard a bit about it. I'm particularly enchanted with the part where this bonnie lass," he pointed a stout finger at Bunny, "makes a fine meal for the hosts. The famous Bridget Bunny MacBride will be cooking for us! Lordy, that's going to be something. I'm always saying how we could use a decent meal around here. What's on the menu?"

Bunny gave Winston one last ear rub and offered, "It's a surprise."

"Don't worry, Mr. Malcom," Brett said. "Everything Bunny makes is delicious. You're in good hands there. As for Giff, Cody, Mike, Ed, and myself, we can't wait to make contact with your legendary ghost, the piper of Dundoon Castle."

"Aye, he's here, sure enough. He's been making a racket lately. I surmise it's from that lot out there." He jabbed his thumb over his shoulder to indicate the piping competition on the parade grounds below the castle. "They're all acting up, the ghosts."

"There's more than one of them?" Giff asked, making a face that indicated he wasn't pleased about that little bit of news.

"Quite a few of them, actually. Dundoon's an old castle with a romantic and bloody past, my dear sir. Most don't bother us, but it seems a new one has wandered in of late that has the staff on edge. It's a bally-strange thing."

"A new spirit?" Brett questioned, fascinated by the prospect. "What is it? What's it doing that has everyone so nervous?"

"Howling. Capering. That sort of thing." Jordy gave a nonchalant wave of his hand. "But we'll talk about that later. First things first. Welcome to Dundoon Castle. Come along. We cannot wait to show you around. I think you'll find that we have a very interesting history here, and the perfect setting for your most unusual show. Sorry about the pipes," he apologized, ushering them up the walkway to the massive front door. "Try as we might, it seems there's no escaping them here."

Chapter 8

"Dundoon was originally built in the thirteen-hundreds on this rocky point, which strategically overlooks Loch Crinan. That is important to our story," Jordy explained as he led them into the generous entry hall. "I'm afraid all that remains from that era is the curtain wall, which has been rebuilt and fortified by all my warring ancestors. This part of the castle, including the tower house, is relatively new, having been built in the seventeenth century."

Elizabeth graced her husband with a patient smile. "Of course, it has been improved upon and renovated many times over the years to keep up with modern tastes, such as electricity and indoor plumbing."

"Thanks to you and Jordy, you've achieved far more than basic comforts, Lizzy," Granny Mac said. "This castle is lovely."

"I have to agree," Giff remarked, pausing in the doorway of the great hall. "Look at this room," he said, waving Brett and the crew over to see it. "It's stunning. Swathed in manly oak paneling, with a large fireplace surrounded in white marble, and all this lavish furniture. I could live out my days in this room."

Although Bunny rolled her eyes at him, she understood what he meant. She had always known about Dundoon Castle and the legend of its piper, but had never ventured inside. She found the luxury of the great hall surprising. She had pictured Dundoon like so many other rundown old strongholds that had been kept in the family purely out of pride and not common sense. They were expensive to live in and expensive to run, and heaven only knew how much renovations would cost on something so old and historic. The windows of the great hall overlooked the loch, providing a dramatic view. Not only was the room beautifully decorated in an old baronial style, but there was also a stunning crystal chandelier dangling from the ceiling that added a touch of class to the manly decor. She was also happy to note that the walls in this room were adorned with ancestral portraits of kilted chieftains, favorite hounds, and stunning Highland landscapes instead of the many stag heads and old swords that seemed to be the favored motif of the large entry and main hallway. She really couldn't fathom why men thought that animal heads and old weaponry made good decorations, but obviously they did.

As Bunny stepped back from the threshold of the great hall, she made the mistake of looking up, straight into the dead eyes of yet another taxidermized, twelve-point buck head on the opposite wall. She gave a slight shiver, uttered, "Excuse me," and averted her eyes, settling them on a doorway a little farther down and opposite the grand room. She walked past her host and hostess, gave Winston a pat on the head, and stepped into the equally opulent dining room.

As her eyes took in her sumptuous surroundings, her breath caught in her throat. The beautiful dining table and chairs, the focal point of the room, could easily seat sixteen guests. The dark walnut of the elegant table and chairs matched the wainscoting on the walls, which were also covered in a rich, velvety textured wallpaper in pleasing shades of green. Another gorgeous crystal chandelier hung over the table, catching and reflecting sunlight from the wall of arched, mullioned windows that overlooked the parade grounds below. As Bunny stood in the splendor of the sumptuous room, facing the sunshine as it streamed through the wall of windows, all her worries about ghosts and family began to fade. She was in her element, and it was going to be a real pleasure setting out a feast in this room. Thoughts of her scrumptious supper swirled in her mind. She could almost smell the savory scent of the roasted meat and the sweet tang of the buttery honey glaze on the carrots. The word *whisky* floated to the surface of her mind. She could practically smell it on the walls of this old place. Thankfully, she had come prepared, bringing two bottles of good Scotch whisky for the occasion. She thought she smelled whisky again and looked in the direction it seemed to be emanating from. Her eyes unexpectedly locked on the picture in the middle of the far wall. She smelled the drink again, causing the back of her neck to prickle uncomfortably.

"Crivens," she uttered, steeling herself. She was staring at a painting of a piper, *the piper*, she surmised, due to the old manner of his dress, the antiquated instrument in his hands, and the haunting scent of spirits. The painter, whoever he was, had captured the piper's profile as he stood on the battlement of a castle, facing the choppy waters of a loch. "It's you, isn't it?" she whispered to the painting, sensing a strong male presence in the room with her. It was unsettling, especially in broad daylight. However, she fought her rising fear and attempted to clear her mind enough to connect with the spirit. She closed her eyes, focusing all her energy inward.

The second she did, the blaring sound of bagpipes erupted around her, causing her to jump a good two feet in the air.

"*Aaah*!" she screamed. Winston was beside her, wagging his tail excitedly. He looked beyond her and barked, causing Bunny to spin around and face the racket. To her surprise, it wasn't coming from a ghost, but a tall, gangly young man barely out of his teens. The fringe of hair surrounding his bonnet was a deep, rusty red. It complemented his ruddy cheeks, giving him the look of one who spent a good deal of time outdoors. The gangly piper continued into the room from another doorway, blowing and squeezing on the great Highland bagpipes under his arm for all he was worth. Enchanted by his own music, he took two more steps into the dining room, saw Bunny, stopped abruptly, and spit out the mouthpiece, letting the instrument groan to an ignominious death. The woman coming up behind him, carrying a fully loaded tea tray, nearly crashed into him.

Winston barked again before running to greet the woman carrying the food.

"You eejit, Jasper!" the woman chided. "Dinna stop in the doorway like that when I'm carrying tea. Well, hello, Winston. I've got a treat for ye too."

"Sorry," the piper said, dejected. "But I dinna expect her to be here."

It was then the woman noticed Bunny. She smiled broadly, and cried, "Bunny MacBride!" Gracefully stepping around the piper, she added, "You've made it. We are so excited to have ye here at Dundoon. I'm Jenny Duncan, the Malcoms' cook. And this dunderhead is Jasper Savage. Pleased to meet ye. I thought you and your team would like some tea and wee cakes while Jordy blithers away about our ghosties."

Bunny smiled at the woman, who was near her own age. Bunny found her very pretty, with crystal-blue eyes and shoulder-length hair the color of dark chocolate. "I'd love a cup of tea," she told Jenny, happy to see the large silver teapot and a plate bursting with scones, tea cakes, and finger sandwiches. Her nerves were still dancing on end, thanks to the portrait on the wall and the bagpipes. "It's a pleasure to meet you, Jenny. We'll be cooking together this afternoon. I can't wait to see the kitchen."

" 'Tis not much to look at. All the money was spent on these rooms, meant to impress. But we make do. Please excuse Jasper. He works on the estate as well. As for the noise, he's just learning how to play."

"I've been practicing," Jasper announced, adding a wistful glance at the windows. "We have the most prestigious pipers in the land staying right here at Dundoon. I've been listening to them all morning. Also, 'tis tradition to pipe the laird of the castle to his supper."

Jenny set her tray down on the table and made a face at the younger man. "Aye, supper, not tea. We shall let the professionals handle that."

"Great idea," Bunny concurred, and she helped Jenny pour the tea.

"As I've explained, this is an old castle," Jordy Malcom began as he stirred a lump of sugar into his tea. "However, the story of the ghostly piper who haunts Dundoon begins in the mid-sixteen-hundreds, when civil war broke out in England. I won't bore you with the details of that strife, but eventually the Highland clans became embroiled in it too, which led to an armed conflict in this country between the MacDonalds and Clan Campbell. During that time, the Campbells held Dundoon Castle. However, the MacDonalds were led by a legendary warrior known as Colkitto. He had a piper with him, a man renowned for his great skill on the bagpipes. His name is lost to history, but in some tales, he's known only as *an tè dearg*, or the red one."

"Why is that?" Granny Mac asked.

"Hard to say," Elizabeth remarked. "However, I like to think he had red hair, the beautiful red color of Bunny's."

"Right," Jordy said, then cleared his throat, eager to continue his story. "Well, to cut to the chase, the story goes that Colkitto and his MacDonalds took Dundoon Castle in a bloody fight, forcing the Campbells into the heather. Colkitto pushed on, heading across the Sound of Jura, but before he did, he left a small garrison behind to hold the castle. One of these men was his loyal piper. With the mighty warrior gone, the Campbells launched a bloody counterattack. They made short work of it, killing every MacDonald in the process. The one exception was Colkitto's piper."

"It is woefully bad luck to kill a piper," Elizabeth added. "Here in the Highlands, pipers hold a place of high honor."

"Right you are, my dear," Jordy said, picking up his story. "Pipers are educated, important men who can read, write, and play every tune a laird might wish of him. Every clan chieftain worth his salt has a loyal piper. You see, a good piper inspires warriors, leading the troops into and beyond the jaws of death. Now, back at Dundoon, having slain all the warriors, the Campbells settled in, waiting for Colkitto's return. While they waited, the piper was ordered to play for them."

As Bunny plucked a tea cake from the plate, sliced it open, and slathered it with butter, she chanced another look at the painting of the piper on the wall. Had she really felt him, or had it been her imagination? She hoped it was the latter, but it still didn't explain the strong scent of whisky she had smelled in the room. She then mused that, with so many Scots around, there was sure to be a lot of whisky in the castle. It wasn't out of the question that a good deal of it had been spilled, soaking into the carpet and the wood of the floor. That was it. That was likely what she'd been smelling. Also, if she was being honest, the incessant racket coming from the field below the castle was beginning to set her nerves on end. It was a bloody mystery to her how her father, the sensible Davie MacBride, could enjoy this type of music so much. She took a big bite of her tea cake and looked at Jordy. He's relishing this background elevator bagpipe music, she thought, watching his animated face as he told his ghostly tale. She supposed that the same instinct that prompted men to hang the stuffed heads of animals on a wall also made them love the discordant blaring of the bagpipes. As she pondered this strangeness, fighting the urge to flee the noise and the painting, she happened to shift her gaze to Giff. Clearly, he was touched by the same strangeness as the rest of them. He gestured with his nicely styled head to the painting on the wall, winked at her, and offered a thumbs-up. Really, men could be so insufferable.

"Now, the Campbells," Sir Jordy continued in his deep baritone voice, pulling Bunny's attention back to him, "were planning an ambush for Colkitto and his men. When Colkitto's boat was spotted one foggy morning out on the sound, the Campbells ordered the piper to the battlement, where he was to play his master's homecoming song, luring Colkitto into their trap. The piper had no choice but to play. However, he was determined to outsmart the murdering scoundrels. He picked up his bagpipe and began to play, but the song he chose wasn't his master's homecoming tune. It was instead a mournful, soul-stirring lament. When Colkitto heard it wafting across the waves, he was confused at first. Why such a sad lament? However, he soon caught on and understood the message his piper was sending him. The castle had been taken. An ambush had been set. Colkitto turned his boat around and sailed away, saving his men, but leaving his piper behind forever."

"Great story," Brett said. "Colkitto's piper was left behind, and he's still here to this day."

Jordy looked at him. "Well, yes, but there's a bit more to

it than that. You see, when the Campbells realized what the piper had done, depriving them of their ambush, they were furious. Determined to teach the piper a lesson, they lopped off both his hands, making sure he would never again play the pipes. They say the piper bled to death from his wounds, right here in the castle. It wasn't long after his death that the haunting began, heralded by the sound of bagpipes. They are still heard to this day, as you well know. Some can even spot his ghostly image as he plays."

Bunny raised her hand. She wasn't sure why, but the moment Jordy looked at her she asked, "What about that painting on the wall. Is that supposed to be the piper from the tale?"

"It's supposed to be him, but that picture was painted in the eighteenth century, a good hundred years or so after the event. However, the artist, Alistar Blair, who was staying at Dundoon at the time, claimed he'd been visited in the night by the piper. It was such a haunting experience, it prompted him to paint that picture."

"I imagine so." Bunny then cleared her throat and asked, "Was this piper known to have a favorite drink . . . such as whisky?" She noted the way Granny Mac looked at her as she asked this, giving Bunny the feeling that her gran had smelled the whisky too.

"Why, my dear, he wouldn't be a good Scotsman if he didn't like a wee nip o' whisky."

"Where has he been spotted?" Brett asked, unable to conceal his excitement.

"Mostly on the battlement," Jordy explained. "However, before you get all excited, I should warn you that if you hear the tune this ghostly piper plays, it'll strike to the marrow of your bones. It is not of this world. The mere sound sends the hair on the back of your neck on end, and many are driven to tears. It's a sound one never expects to hear, but it is never to be forgotten. An interesting note is that when construction was done on the castle in the late eighteen-hundreds, a skeleton was discovered under some flagstones. When the workers exhumed this skeleton, they realized that the hands were missing, confirming the story of the bagpiper of Dundoon. Elizabeth and I hope you have the pleasure of hearing him play during your investigation tonight."

"We do too," Brett said, clearly moved by all he had heard. "You also mentioned there was a new spirit here?"

Jordy and Elizabeth exchanged a troubled look. "It's a rather troubling matter," Elizabeth explained. "We don't know quite what to make of it. However, I cannot emphasize this enough: be careful at night."

"Careful?" Giff poo-pooed, wrinkling his nose. "We're talking about a ghost—a shimmering vapor with memory issues. How dangerous can it be?"

Jordy narrowed his eyes, looking pensive. "I didn't say it was a ghost. The piper's a ghost."

"Not a ghost?" Bunny could see that Brett was trying to wrap his head around this. "If it isn't a ghost, then what is it?"

"A beast," Jordy said. "It's been spotted outside the castle, roaming the hills and the heather. However, there are occasions when it comes near the castle. We know this because when it does, Winston can sense it. The hackles on his back go up, and he starts growling at the wall. Winterton, our ghillie, or groundskeeper," he clarified for the Americans, "caught a glimpse of it on a wall in the old tower. He's a brave man, Winterton, but it scared the devil out of him. Said it was large and shaped like a wolf, with red, glowing eyes."

Jordy's description made Bunny shiver. She looked at her

gran, noting that the older woman had a tight grip on her crystal necklace. Bunny turned to Elizabeth, and asked, "What . . . do you suppose it is?"

The older woman shook her head and looked to her husband for an answer.

"We believe it's a *cù-sith*, a fairy dog," Jordy said. "For the life of us, we don't know how to get rid of it."

Chapter 9

Fairy dog? Bunny was too sensible to believe in such nonsense. Thanks to Granny Mac, who loved to tell tales of the fairy folk, she was familiar with the beast. A fairy dog was said to be a spectral hound that roamed the Highlands. Like the grim reaper, the fairy dog was a portent of death. If an unsuspecting person happened to stumble upon one while hiking, the prevailing advice was to run, because hearing the howl of a fairy dog three times meant certain death. Anyhow, Bunny knew that it was all a load of rubbish. She didn't doubt that the Malcoms had seen something that spooked them, but it wasn't a fairy dog. It was probably just the wind howling through a crack under an old doorway or a trick of the light. Likely both. Whatever the case, Brett, Giff, and the lads were mightily intrigued by the notion. Bunny dearly hoped it would be an uneventful investigation. However, she knew Brett couldn't resist drumming up a little more drama for the cameras by suggesting that, along with a ghostly piper, Dundoon boasted a fairy dog as well. It was all part of the charm of their show. However, just to be safe, she thought it best to pose the question to Jenny, who lived on the castle grounds.

"What's this nonsense about a fairy dog on the property?" Bunny asked as Jenny led her down a short hallway to the kitchen. While the rest of her party had continued with the grand castle tour, Bunny had ended hers in the dining room. She was anxious to get cooking. Jenny stopped before a door at the bottom of a short flight of steps and looked at her.

"It's not nonsense, Bunny. I saw it with my own eyes, dashing through the fog near the castle one morning. It gave me the fright of my life. It was enormous, with glowing red eyes. It is not of this world." After her ominous warning, she crossed herself and put her hand on the doorknob. "But enough about fairy dogs." Jenny waved her other hand in the air, as if to dispel the odious fairy creature. "Time to get cooking." She thrust open the door, announcing, "Welcome to the grand scullery, which, as you can see, isn't so grand. But we make do. I like to say the Malcoms have simple tastes to match their simple budget."

"I find that unsettling," Bunny said, responding to Jenny's encounter with the fairy dog. Once her eyes settled on the Dundoon kitchen, she smiled.

Unlike the beautifully renovated kitchen at Bramsford Manor, Dundoon's kitchen hadn't seen an upgrade in the last fifty years, possibly longer. It was old and outdated, with stout red tile that looked medieval and thick wooden shelving crowded with old pots, pans, measuring cups, mixing bowls, and jars of spices. When Bunny's eyes settled on the four-oven Aga cooker on the adjacent wall, the word *vintage* sprang to mind, yet there was something very nostalgic and lovely about it. She reminded herself that this was a private kitchen, one that prepared meals for the family, the small staff, and whatever guests happened through the doors. On the far wall was a stunning, arched window that overlooked the loch. Pots of fresh herbs lined the windowsill, soaking up the natural light and perfuming the air with their mingled fragrance. More herbs hung from the stout beams of the ceiling, drying alongside strings of braided garlic bulbs. However, it was the twelve-foot butcher-block island counter in the center of the room that held Bunny's attention. What a workspace! Her coolers were already there, waiting for her, along with her all-important knife roll.

"It's good ye'll be cooking then, due to the modest budget," Jenny informed her. Clearly, the young woman was under the impression that Bunny's last remark was about the modest budget and not Jenny's encounter with the fairy dog. "I'm happy to see ye've brought a whole kitchen with ye. Our larders are emptying faster than we can fill them these days."

"Sorry. I was referring to the fact that you've seen this fairy dog. That's unsettling. Regarding the budget, don't worry. The show supplies all the food needed, including alcoholic beverages. Also, although I'm cooking for the spirit supper and all the guests who will be attending, I also make plenty for everyone else around here who doesn't make it on camera—namely, Ed, Mike, and Cody, who will be filming during tonight's supper. By the way, who brought in my coolers?"

"Jasper. He's very helpful when he's not set on murdering the bagpipes."

They both shared a laugh over that.

"Well, I for one am happy to be in the kitchen. It might not be fancy, but I like it. I can't wait to get cooking." Bunny walked over to her coolers and began unpacking her ingredients. Jenny helped her.

"Ooo, rack of lamb!" Jenny cried, looking impressed as she held up one of the large packages of meat. "Verra fancy." After putting all the lamb in the refrigerator she then began unloading the other cooler. "I understand that you and your team are here to contact the piper, but there is more than one ghost that haunts this place."

Bunny set a sack of potatoes on the counter and looked at Jenny. "I don't really have much to do with the ghost hunt," she lied. She wished she didn't have much to do with it, but now that she had some emerging gifts, she was obliged to join in. "As silly as it sounds, my job is to prepare a meal meant to entice the ghost to the table. The lads take it from there."

"They'll be coming out of the woodwork for the lamb, as will Sir Jordy and his guests. Did he mention that the three esteemed judges are staying at the castle?"

"I did hear about that," Bunny said. "I hope they have a sense of humor."

"I wouldn't count on it. They're stuffy judges. They've been listening to the pipers all day and have the hard task of selecting the very best. Major Scotty MacDonald is one of the judges. Not only is he a dish, but he was the personal piper to the late queen, God rest her soul."

"God rest her soul," Bunny agreed. Then, as a hint of mischief twinkled in her eyes, she added, "As I said, I've brought plenty of whisky. I plan on making orange marmalade sours, lots of them. That should help lighten the mood a measure."

"I'll say." Jenny's round blue eyes sparkled with mischief. "Orange marmalade sours? Never had one. Sounds delish."

Bunny pulled a jar of Dundee marmalade from one of the coolers and grinned. "Fresh from my mum's kitchen. I'll whip up some simple syrup, and we can sample one while I get acquainted with your kitchen. One of the lads will be coming around shortly to film my cooking segment, and I like to be prepared."

"Well then, Bunny MacBride, let's get cooking."

Chapter 10

Jenny deemed Bunny's orange marmalade sour dangerously delicious. It was only noon. Far too early to drink, and yet the scant two ounces of whisky shaken with lemon juice, simple syrup, orange marmalade, and an egg white split between them had created a convivial atmosphere that Bunny found invigorating. Jenny was friendly, vivacious, and highly entertaining. Bunny helped her set out a quick lunch for the Malcoms and their guests, consisting of a variety of sandwiches, a fruit platter, packages of crisps, and shortbread cookies. After making plates for themselves, Bunny and Jenny returned to the kitchen, where Jenny continued to regale Bunny with stories about the castle, its ghosts, and how she came to be the Malcoms' cook.

"My gran was the cook here for forty years. I practically grew up in this kitchen and started working here alongside my gran when I was sixteen. When she decided to retire, I took over. It was a natural fit, since I already knew how to cook what the Malcoms like to eat. My gran's now in a retirement home in Lochgilphead. I visit as often as I can. Did I mention she's a bit of a witch?"

"A witch?" Bunny questioned. "As in she's crabby or a pagan?"

"Neither, really," Jenny said, pausing to pop a juicy, red strawberry into her mouth. Once she swallowed, she added, "Although, with her arthritis, she can be verra crabby at times. No, she's Christian, but she believes in fairies, ghosts, old wives' tales, and folk medicine, and likes to mix up potions, especially love potions."

"Love potions? And here I thought my gran was eccentric." Bunny smiled at that, wondering to herself just how well these love potions worked. Not that she would ever use such a thing herself.

"She sounds a little like my gran, Ella MacBride. She's into crystals and mysticism, and she's clairvoyant."

"I know your gran," Jenny informed her with a grin. "Ella's the best. Your gran's a seer. She can tell fortunes without tea leaves, unlike my gran. However, I don't need either to tell me my love life's in shambles. I know it! What I do want to know is if there's somebody tall, dark, and handsome on the horizon for me, or if I should go straight to the nunnery."

Bunny looked at the beautiful young woman working beside her and laughed. "You? I can't imagine you're having issues finding a man."

Jenny shrugged. "It's more along the lines that there aren't many eligible men around these parts. They're either too old, too young, or undatable."

They shared a chuckle at that and finished their lunches. Bunny had just cleaned the counter and pulled out the ingredients needed to prep for the evening meal when Cody strolled into the kitchen, carrying his camera and a light kit. Jenny took one look at him and grinned like the Cheshire cat.

"Well, hello, tall, dark, and handsome. Cody, is it?" Jenny purred, offering a flirtatious smile. "Come in. It's not every day a big, strong, American man walks into my kitchen. Don't mind us. We've been nursing marmalade sours. Would you care for a sip?" She held up her glass. Cody was under her spell, no love potion needed.

"Umm, yeah. Sure," he uttered, staring at Jenny, totally forgetting why he was there in the first place. He took the glass she offered him, wasting no time taking a few long sips.

As Bunny stared at him, she had to admit that Cody did fit the tall, dark, and handsome bill. He was no Brett Bloom, mind you, but he was good-looking and did have a pleasing shade of dark brown hair that complemented his lighter brown eyes.

"Hello, Cody," she said, forcing him to acknowledge her. "Looks like you drew the short straw again." It was a private joke between them.

"Might be the short straw, but it sure is the best straw," he acknowledged, grinning from ear to ear. He then gave the glass back to Jenny. "That's really good. Did you make this?"

"I made it," Bunny informed him. "Since it's on the menu tonight, I thought we'd try one out and see how it tastes."

"Good choice," he remarked, unable to take his eyes off Jenny. She blushed while emitting a pleasing giggle.

Bunny was going to have to take the bull by the horns on this one. "We've got everything set up here for the shoot, Cody. I think you should start with some footage of this historic kitchen. It's remarkable. Then I'll talk the audience through tonight's menu and how it was designed to entice the ghostly piper to the table. We'll do some cooking shots, and then I'd like to pop into my room for a spell to rest up and change before tonight's dinner. By the way, where are we staying?"

"We're at the White Cottage," Cody informed her. "Winterton drove us there after the tour. However, since it's a good half mile down the road, Ella thought it would be best if you took your nap in her room here at the castle instead."

"Good thinking," Bunny agreed, sending her gran a mental hug.

"Your bags are already in Ella's room," Cody informed her. "Winterton said he'd shift them before dinner, so you don't have to worry. We've got it covered."

"You lads are the best. And where are Brett and Giff?" she asked.

"They went to check out the bagpiping competition. Ed and Mike are filming them. They're getting some great B-roll while sampling food from all the food trucks. I forgot to tell you. We ran into your parents. Your dad bought us all fried Mars bars from one of the vendors. They were tasty."

"I'll bet," Bunny replied, inwardly cringing. Her dad had a real sweet tooth and a soft spot for fried Mars bars. Coming here was likely an excuse to have one.

"I hope they're saving room for dinner," Jenny told him. Looking at Bunny, she added, "The White Cottage is lovely. You should be happy there, if ye don't mind the sound of bagpipes."

"What do you mean?"

"There are five cottages on the estate that are rented out for extra income," Jenny explained. "The pipers in the competition have been booked into the other cottages. 'Tis custom that they stay there, away from the judges, vendors, campers, and their adoring fans. It gives them a little privacy. They'll be your next-door neighbors."

"So what you're saying is that I won't be getting any sleep at all tonight. Good thing I'm taking a nap here."

"Don't worry, Bunny," Cody said. "Winterton told us that there's absolutely no piping after eight p.m. That should work out just fine for us and the investigation tonight." Cody paused, then added, "Although he did tell us not to wander beyond the illuminated walkways at night or beyond the immediate castle grounds because of the fairy dog. He said he's seen it. Claims it's a silent hunter of souls. Do you believe it?"

Bunny rolled her eyes. "I don't believe in fairy dogs, Cody. They're not real, but there might be some animal out there that's dangerous."

"Like a wolf?" he asked.

"There are no wolves left in Scotland," Jenny informed them. "The last one was said to have been killed in the seventeen-hundreds. It's a fairy dog, sure enough."

Cody's eyes grew wide with intrigue, and possibly something else. "You've seen this fairy dog?" he asked. "Would you mind telling us about it while I film you, Jenny? You would look great on camera."

Men, Bunny thought; they were shameless. However, Cody did have a point. Jenny was very photogenic.

"I dinna mind one bit," she told him, pinning him with her big blue eyes. "However, since this fairy dog is elusive, and I've only seen its shadow, how about I tell you about another ghost who lives here. Drunk Gordie."

"I like the sound of that." Cody grinned and hoisted his camera on his shoulder. He gave her a nod, and Jenny began telling her tale.

"Many have heard of our ghostly piper, but there is another in Dundoon as well, Drunk Gordie. It was said Gordie was a fierce warrior and a legendary drinker who lived on the castle grounds in the mid-seventeen-hundreds. The story goes that he caught a wee man by the name of Ian MacDonald trysting with his wife while he was away fighting. Of course, Gordie challenged this man to a duel, but the canny wee man proposed a drinking contest instead. Now, big, strappin' Gordie was a man who didn't lose at anything, be it battle, love, or drinking a man under the table. Since the man before him was much smaller, he didn't think it would be much of a challenge. Gordie would win, kill his foe, and go home to his wife. However, Gordie woefully underestimated Ian's ability to drink. At least that's what he thought. In the company of their men, Gordie and Ian drank all night and well into the next day. By the second nightfall, Gordie was determined to win. He could barely see, he was so drunk, but he could see enough to know that Ian was still sitting across from him, matching him cup for cup. With one last mighty effort, Gordy asked for his mug to be filled again. His mug was filled, and he began to drink. Before the last drop was emptied, however, Gordie fell off his chair, crashing to the floor, never to wake up again. Ian was in poor shape too, but since it was discovered that he was drinking mostly water with his whisky, he survived. It was later found that Drunk Gordie's wife was the one doctoring Ian's drink, ensuring that her lover would survive the ordeal. We can only imagine that this clever woman was likely escaping a difficult marriage. As for Drunk Gordie, he's still here, and he's still angry as a hornet about the deception played on him. It's not unusual to see an ale mug fly off a table and smash into the wall, shattering into pieces. Sometimes it's a wineglass or a plate. Once, when I was going to fetch a bottle of whisky for the laird, I went to the drink cellar, only to learn that Drunk Gordie had gotten there before me. I watched as four bottles of whisky fell off the shelf, one after the other, crashing to the floor. What a waste! However, those are just a few of Drunk Gordie's tricks. Don't be shocked tonight if you see objects move across a table or crash into a wall. That's just Drunk Gordie, working out his eternal frustrations." Jenny's face held an ominous expression as she finished her tale.

"That was awesome!" Cody exclaimed, lowering his camera.

"Agreed," Bunny said. "Thanks for that spooky tale, Jenny."

Unfortunately, she was even more creeped out now than she had been when staring at the portrait of the piper in the dining room. However, she was a professional, she reminded herself, taking a deep breath. "Alright, Cody," Bunny said, pulling her coworker's attention back to her once again. "Let's continue. I have a spirit supper to prepare."

Chapter 11

Once Cody had filmed enough footage of Bunny preparing her specially selected meal designed to entice the ghostly piper to the table, the ladies said goodbye to him. Cody, due to Jenny and her big bright smile, had been hesitant to go. "Shoo," Bunny said, urging him out of the kitchen. She was dead tired and needed a nap.

After putting everything they had made for the spirit supper in the chiller, both ladies took off their aprons. Bunny had explained that she'd return to the kitchen two hours before the spirit supper was to begin, to roast the prepared, herb-crusted racks of lamb, bake the creamy gratin potatoes, gently heat up the smoked fish chowder, sauté the vegetables, slice and plate the Dundee cake, and mix up plenty of the night's special drink, orange marmalade sours.

"I'm going to have a wee rest as well, now that I've been invited to join the hunt," Jenny said with a grin as they left the kitchen. Cody, impulsively, had invited her. Bunny, truth be told, was not only thankful for his crush on the cook, but also his impulsivity. She wasn't overly excited to be trouncing around the haunted halls of Dundoon after dark, but with Jenny along, it was bound to be more fun. Besides, Jenny knew every nook and cranny of the castle, not to mention all the ghost stories. It was a little ray of hope to cling to.

"Have a good rest. I'll see you back here at six," Bunny said, parting company with Jenny. It wasn't until Bunny walked down the main hallway to the grand staircase that she remembered she didn't know where her grandmother's room was located. Thankfully, Mrs. Collins appeared from the library in time to advise her.

"Your grandmother instructed me to take you to her room once you were finished in the kitchen. No need to worry. Mr. Collins has already taken your bags there."

"Thank you. That's very kind of you," Bunny said, and followed the housekeeper up the stairs.

Bunny felt like a mouse in a maze as she followed Mrs. Collins down several hallways on the second floor until finally landing in front of the room in question. Although the entire floor had been remodeled, there was still an oppressive feeling to it that was hard to shake, as if the plaster walls couldn't quite contain the air of unrest that seemed to echo in the stones. Bunny gave a fleeting thought to her room at the White Cottage. Although she hadn't seen it yet, she figured it had to be less oppressively haunted than the castle. However, tired as she was, she realized that if she wanted her much-needed nap, her gran's room would just have to do. With any luck, Granny Mac would be waiting for her, warding off any intruding ghosts. Holding tightly to that thought, Bunny waited while Mrs. Collins opened the door.

At first look, she was taken aback by the stunning opulence of the guest room, from the four-postered, canopied bed wrapped in luxurious bedding, to the beautifully restored antique writing desk and chaise lounge. The room was inviting and meant to impress. However, when Bunny noticed that her gran's bags were there but her gran wasn't, she hesitantly asked, "Have you seen my grandmother?"

Mrs. Collins arched her brows mischievously and said, "Why, she and her gentleman friend went with the Malcoms to watch the competition."

"Her . . . her gentleman friend?" Bunny stammered, thinking she'd misheard Mrs. Collins. Her gran didn't have a gentleman friend.

"Why, the doctor, dear," Mrs. Collins reminded her. Then, realizing she might have put her foot in her mouth, she asked, "You do know about the doctor?" Bunny shook her head. Mrs. Collins grimaced slightly. "Well, he's a fine man, although quite a bit younger, but they seem to get on—"

"*Younger?*" Bunny blurted.

"Marvelously!" Mrs. Collins offered, backing toward the door.

"Marvelously younger? What's that supposed to mean?"

The older woman pressed her lips together, as if willing herself not to say more. But the combination of Bunny's probing look and the juicy piece of gossip was too much for her. "A decade at least, maybe more. But Ella's so feisty and energetic. As for the doc, he's an old soul, a real thinker. Perfect match. There ye have it. Ring if ye need anything. Ta-ta."

Mrs. Collins exited the room so fast it made Bunny's head spin. Great, she thought, one more thing to worry about, as if ghosts, noisy pipers, and folks believing in fairy dogs weren't enough. Thankfully, her bout in the kitchen with Jenny and Cody had exhausted her to the point where she didn't care. The canopied bed was calling to her. Bunny kicked off her shoes, washed off her makeup, threw on a large T-shirt, and set a timer on her phone. Then she climbed under the sheets and expertly turned her mind from everything but the spectacular feast she was about to lay out for the laird, his guests, and the ghostly piper of Dundoon. Pity that all her talent and effort was wasted on a ghost. As she closed her eyes, her brother Angus's words echoed in her head. *Ghosties, m'dearie, don't eat. They're dead!* And that was the truth of it.

Waking abruptly from a nap after a nightmare wasn't a great way to begin the second half of one's day. Neither was spotting the white rabbit of doom sitting at the foot of her bed. Frazzled, Bunny sat bolt upright and addressed the rabbit.

"Dammit, Braiden, I know it's you," she hissed, wiping the sleep out of her eyes. "Can you please just appear to me in the normal way and not be Hopper?"

Even to her own ears, it was a silly request. However, the rabbit ignored her. Typical rabbit. Instead, it wiggled its nose at her before hopping off the bed. Was it a message, or was he just taunting her? Bunny really couldn't tell but was slightly relieved when he disappeared through the solid wood door. As she stared after him, her alarm went off, reminding her that she had work to do.

Showered, dressed, camera ready, and wrapped in a cloak of dread, Bunny left her room and descended the stairs. However, the prevailing dread lifted the moment she spotted Jenny.

"Don't you look beautiful!" Jenny exclaimed, taking in Bunny's white blouse and flowing, wine-colored skirt. "I was just about to come up and get you. They're coming!" she announced, glowing with excitement.

"Who's coming?" Bunny was a tad confused.

"The esteemed judges and the grand procession," Jenny teasingly admonished before grabbing Bunny by the hand.

Bunny soon found herself standing in the empty dining room beside Jenny, looking out the large expanse of window at the scene below. The narrow, snaking walkway that ran from the head of the parade grounds to the private parking lot was flanked on both sides by spectators. The three judges, who now looked exhausted after a trying day, marched along the pathway to the castle, led by a piper and drummer.

"That one with the beefy face and short, dark hair is Fergus Cameron," Jenny told her with a healthy amount of respect in her eyes. "He's the oldest, at fifty-five, and has won the title four times in his day. That big man behind him with the bushy red beard is Rory Fraser. According to Sir Jordy, he's one of the finest musicians this country has ever produced. He's also quite the historian."

"The man at the end," Bunny said, pointing, "he must be Major Scotty MacDonald."

"Aye, he's the youngest and arguably the most well-known, having been the queen's piper."

"That's quite a position of honor," Bunny agreed, watching the men make their way to the castle.

"Aye, but here's the thing. See how the crowd is yelling at them? See how the judges all look pensive? That's because they have a tough decision to make by tomorrow, and the crowd is trying to sway them. Every fan has a favorite," she reminded Bunny.

"I'll bet. I can only imagine what a tough decision it is." This Bunny said partially because all bagpipe music sounded the same to her, and partially because judging music was often swayed by personal taste.

"Well, and here's another thing." Jenny lowered her voice,

as if to impart a secret. "Sir Jordy just told me that, before he returned to the castle to change for supper, he had a word with the judges. According to him, they're at odds with each other, and maybe not just over who should win. It was Jordy's opinion that both Fergus and Rory seem wary of Major MacDonald. And there may be something to it. Jasper told me yesterday that he found Major MacDonald snooping around the castle while the other judges were otherwise engaged."

"Snooping? Why would he do that?"

"Who knows? But there's growing tension between them. I just thought I should give ye the heads up before tonight's dinner. We should seat them between the other guests."

"Good thinking," Bunny agreed. Then, pondering table arrangements, she was just about to turn from the window and get to work when she spied a woman in the crowd grab Major MacDonald by the arm as he walked past her. It was a brazen move, especially since the woman yanked him off the path and began yelling at him. "What in the world . . . ?"

"The crazy witch!" Jenny cried, looking as shocked as Bunny. "Och, she's either a psychotic fan or a jilted lover, maybe a wee bitty of both." She flashed a smile at that. "What a man he is, though," she said wistfully, watching as Major MacDonald remained stone-faced through the entire tirade. "So braw. So brave. Handsome too. No wonder the queen chose him."

Bunny stared at the cook a moment before stating, "That woman is accosting him. Others are shouting at him too. Why aren't the other judges coming to his aid?" As she said this, she watched the major shake himself free of the woman's grasp and continue on his way, as if the confrontation had never happened. It struck her as odd, and incredibly stoic on the major's part.

" 'Tis as I told ye: tensions are running high." Jenny shrugged and headed toward the kitchen.

Bunny took one more look out the window at the three judges marching up the path. She realized that, the closer they came to the castle, the tighter the cold fingers of dread seemed to wrap around her. What was their connection to Dundoon, or to the piper whose ghost remained inside the castle walls? She didn't know, but she felt a storm brewing.

Chapter 12

It was ten minutes to showtime when Brett Bloom sauntered into the kitchen, looking far too handsome for his own good, Bunny thought. He wore tan pants and a trim-fitting sweater in a shade of blue that matched his eyes. His bright blond hair was longer on top, swooped back, and parted on the side, giving him the appearance that he'd just stepped off a sailboat. Her throat went dry at the sight of him, so she smiled instead.

"Smells amazing in here," he announced, strolling over to the island counter, where she and Jenny were putting the finishing touches on the spirit supper. After greeting Jenny, he turned to Bunny, admitting, "I've been eating all day, but somehow I'm starving again. I don't think I've ever had rack of lamb."

Bunny cleared her throat. Fighting hard not to blush under his forthright gaze, she said, "Well, Mr. Man, you're in for a treat, and soon. Everything's ready to go. How was the piping competition?"

"Loud, colorful, dramatic, and surprisingly fun. Fun because we ran into your parents and brother, who told us lots of stories about you." Why did he have to add a cheeky grin after that statement?

"Crivens, I nearly forgot they're here. Don't believe any of them," she advised, feeling her cheeks burn with embarrassment. Why did they have to tell Brett stories about her? Not for the first time did she regret coming to Scotland.

"No, it really was great," he assured her. "They're very proud of you. Said you've been cooking since you were three. What a prodigy you are, Bunny MacBride." He looked serious enough as he plucked a raw carrot from the counter and took a bite. Normally, Bunny didn't tolerate anyone touching her ingredients while she was in the kitchen cooking for an event, but she let it slide. While gnawing on his carrot, Brett added, "We got some fantastic B-roll of the competition as well. Also, Davie insisted we eat a fried Mars bar, or, as I now call it, a fried slice of gooey chocolate heaven. What a crazy idea, deep frying a batter-coated Mars bar, but it works. Then we ate sausages and sampled lots of whisky, and one sly woman even tried handing us a sample of haggis. Can you believe it?"

"Did ye eat it, luv?" Jenny asked, looking up from the pot of Cullen skink, which she was ladling into china soup bowls.

"Ah, no," he told her kindly. "Only because we didn't want to fill up before the spirit supper."

Bunny cast him a skeptical look. "More like you're not brave enough to try it, Bloom."

"Pretty much," Brett agreed. "I've heard stories. However, despite your national dish, I like your country, MacBride. It has style." He tossed her a wink.

"It does have a certain charm," she admitted. She then thought to ask, "Aside from our ghostly guest, is everyone seated at the table?" Although there was always an empty seat reserved for the guest of honor, the ghost, during their first investigation, one of the guests had failed to show up as planned. It had been a disaster. Bunny was hoping that this spirit supper would go as smoothly as a ghost-baiting spirit supper could go. Thankfully, Brett understood what she meant.

"Nearly all the guests are seated, and we've added one more seat for Ella's friend, Doc Beaton. That won't be a problem, will it?"

"He's joining us?" she asked, dropping the piece of orange-rind garnish she'd been fiddling with into a glass. She didn't bother to fish it out again.

"Yes," he said. "Did you know about him?"

"My gran never said a thing. What's he like, this doctor?"

"He's a good guy," Brett assured her. "Doctor Artemus Beaton. He's the doctor in these parts and lives in the village. Seems friendly enough."

"I'm sure he is. I wish my gran would have mentioned him to me before this."

To Bunny's surprise, Jenny answered the confused look on Brett's face. "The Doc and Ella are a couple. Very sweet, isn't it? Finding love at their age." Jenny ran her bold blue eyes over the handsome American standing in her kitchen, prompting her to add, "Finding love at any age is quite wonderful, I imagine."

To Bunny's amazement, Brett blushed and turned away.

"Um, as I was saying, we're almost ready to begin. We're just waiting on Giff, who, to use his own words, is in his room getting 'spiritually connected.' He'll be down shortly."

"Oh my, spiritually connected," Jenny repeated, looking both amused and impressed. "Giff is the medium, correct? The tall, fit man who's a snappy dresser?"

"He is," Brett replied with a remarkably straight face. "So snappy. And he's single. Imagine that?"

"Sounds like a catch." Jenny tossed him a cheeky wink.

"My herb-crusted lamb is approaching peak flavor, Bloom," Bunny warned, pulling them both to the matter at hand. "As I've told you before, it's the mark of a great chef to have all dishes ready to serve at the same time. My supper is ready to be served. If you want to entice your ghostly piper to the table, there's not a moment to lose."

"Got it. We're ready on our end. All the cameras have been set up in the dining room and other hot spots throughout the castle," Brett proudly informed her. "Mike and Cody will be filming during the spirit supper. Ed will be monitoring everything from his control room in the snug."

"The snug?" Bunny questioned.

"Aye. A cozy little room in the left tower," Jenny assured her. "Not only does it connect to the master bedroom, but there's also a set of steps that lead from the snug directly into the great room via a hidden door in the paneling. 'Tis a gem of a room." Bunny took her word for it.

"As Scottish protocol dictates, Bunny, the Malcoms will be piped into the dining room by their man, Winterton," Brett explained. "It'll make a great opening shot. There's no escaping the bagpipes here. You'll follow the Malcoms with the rack of lamb, and Jenny and Jasper will bring up the rear."

"Jasper." Bunny looked at Jenny with near panic in her eyes. "Where is he?"

"On his way. That lad's not good for much, but he'll be fine refilling drinks."

Bunny glanced at the juices pooling beneath her perfectly baked lamb and nodded.

"As I was saying," Brett continued, "we'll get a shot of you entering the dining room with the meal. You'll briefly explain the food you've prepared to the Malcoms and their guests. Once you take your seat, we'll begin. I understand we're starting with soup?" Bunny nodded. "Perfect. Any questions?"

Although her skin prickled with rising anxiety at the thought of the paranormal door that was about to be thrust open during supper, she forced a brave smile. "No questions. We've got this."

She did have it, too; she was totally prepared for the spirit supper, until Winterton's obnoxiously loud piping nearly caused her to lose her grip on the platter bearing her prized rack of lamb. The piercing, penetrating drone echoed off the walls and crashed down around her, causing her to tighten her grip. She wished she had thought to wear earplugs. Unfortunately, it had never crossed her mind. And why would it? It was bad enough that she was cooking on a ghost-hunting show, but she had never, in her wildest dreams, imagined she'd be tormented every step of the way by the horrendous sound of bagpipes. Her nerves were on end as she white-knuckled the silver platter. As Bunny marched into the dining room with Jenny and Jasper behind her, she not only silently cursed the ghostly piper they had come to confront, but every bloody, blasted piper in Dundoon.

The cameras were rolling, and Bunny, if she was anything, was professional. As the pipe music skirled away, she smiled at the camera before setting the platter on the table in front of Jordy Malcom. The delight in his eyes as he looked at the feast made her feel much better. Thankfully, the piping stopped, and she was able to explain her specially prepared feast and why she believed it would entice the resident spirit to the table. Although she explained all of this eloquently, it basically boiled down to the fact that it was a meat-and-potatoes meal, served with plenty of doctored whisky. What Scotsman wouldn't love that? Once she was done, she made the mistake of looking at Gifford McGrady.

An old adage sprang to her mind, the one that stated, *Once you see something it's impossible to unsee it.* And the sight that confronted her was one she wasn't soon to forget. She nearly laughed out loud but valiantly stifled it, due to the guests. Giff was sitting directly across from their host, dressed in his own twisted version of what a Highland gentleman might wear to a ghost hunt. On his head was a rakishly angled tam-o'-shanter bonnet with a bright red pom-pom on top. His white, puffy-sleeved shirt, popular in the eighteenth century, was untied at the neck to better expose his chest and the plethora of dangly, crystal necklaces he wore. Because she was staring at him, Giff briefly stood, proving his commitment to the look. Sure enough, he was wearing a tartan kilt in shades of hunter greens and heather purples. His sporran, of course, was the furry kind.

Cody was standing next to her, filming her reaction. She didn't care. That's what editing was for. Bunny engaged her jaw and said to Giff, "You've barely been in Scotland two days, and look at you."

"What? This old thing?" Giff pretended to be shocked, then tossed her a wink for good measure. "I know, darling. When in Rome." That made everyone seated around the table chuckle.

"The fashion icon of the medium world has just spoken," Brett added, making a face at the camera.

"You mock all you want, Bloom. I had to dress like this. Rocking this look is helping me connect to our ghost. It's my process. Don't question my process."

The three esteemed judges looked more annoyed by this than intrigued. Granny Mac jumped to the rescue.

"Having a touch of the second sight, myself, I can tell you that every medium has their own way of connecting to the spirit world. I applaud Gifford's unique, fashion-focused method. I can't wait to see how it works."

Feeling a one-man show coming on, Bunny couldn't either.

"I'm just going to have to wait and see how the spirit moves me." Giff was about to say something else when Jordy cut him off.

"Excuse me. I don't mean to interrupt, but does the ghostie get a plate of food too?"

Bunny directed her focus to Jasper, who was standing at the foot of the table behind the dreaded, cloth-covered spirit chair. His head was tilted in question as he held a steaming bowl of Cullen skink in his hands.

"Um, yes, technically," Bunny replied, and watched the young man gingerly and very skeptically place the bowl in front of the empty chair.

"Seems a waste," he added.

Jordy heartily agreed. In a loud whisper he confided, "It won't go to waste. I can assure you that." He added a knowing wink.

Jasper grinned and placed a marmalade sour next to the soup bowl. "This ghostie, he'll be wanting a drink too, I expect?"

"Good man. Bring him two," Jordy advised, ignoring his wife's embarrassed expression. "He's about to be called from the dead."

Ignoring the rising panic taking hold of her—for many reasons, including the disturbing picture of the piper overlooking the table—Bunny summoned her professionalism once again. Her job was done. It was time to pass the torch, so to speak. She looked directly into Cody's camera and said, "The table is set, and the feast is about to begin. Be careful who you invite to dinner!"

Chapter 13

Bunny took small pleasure in the fact that her food had been devoured the moment it was served. Had they even tasted it, she wondered? Why had she gone to the trouble? The three judges, after extolling the virtues of the bagpipe and chatting with Brett and Giff, had asked for seconds. While they were talking, Jordy managed to sneak a third plate by trading his second empty one for the full one before the spirit chair. Brett wasn't happy about that, but he was too professional to complain. Regarding the orange marmalade sours, Bunny had lost count, but knew that Jenny had made at least three pitchers of them. For the record, she was on her second one, and they were strong.

The plates were removed, the Dundee cake was served, and the lights were turned low. It was time for Brett and Giff to cajole the shy piper to the table.

Bunny watched as Brett placed the spirit box on the table by the empty chair. The spirit box, she had learned, was a piece of tech designed to catch disembodied voices. Normally, the thought unhinged her, but the alcohol had done wonders for her nerves. There was also a gadget that lit up when a ghost was nearby. Bunny didn't pretend to know how it worked. Instead, she sat back in her chair, took a bite of her delicious cake, and prepared to enjoy dessert and the show . . . until she felt the nagging pressure of her grandmother's eyes on her. Bunny looked across the table at Granny Mac and was startled as her message came clear as day in her head. *Brace yourself, my dear. I feel the presence of an uninvited guest.*

Bunny flashed her a look that relayed her message. *That's the point!*

Granny Mac shook her head and offered another thought nugget. *It's not the piper. This one seems . . .*

Drunk? Bunny mentally offered. Unfortunately, she was feeling way too drunk herself. Thankfully, Brett's voice pulled her from her strange, silent conversation with her grandmother.

"Brave piper of Dundoon, we invite you to come to this table tonight and join us as we feast in your honor and celebrate your skill on the bagpipes. Tell us your name," he said, addressing the staticky spirit box on the table. "What happened to you?"

With all eyes on the spirit chair and all ears straining to hear what might come through the static, everyone was unprepared for the loud screech that came from the other side of the room. Bunny turned her head so fast the room spun. For the second time that night, her jaw dangled. Giff, in his Highland getup, was marching dramatically under the portrait of the piper. Bunny couldn't imagine where he'd gotten the bagpipe under his arm, but one thing was certain, he had no trouble blowing on the mouthpiece. Clearly, it was his first time handling the instrument. To his credit, he knew how to optimize its natural volume.

"Christ! Yer murdering the thing!" Fergus Cameron cried,

shooting up from his chair. He looked like he was at the end of his rope, having listened to bagpipe music all day.

"I've heard worse," the major quipped, looking at him.

"What's that supposed to mean, MacDonald?"

"Gentlemen," Granny Mac chided, shooting them both a stern look. "Please sit down. We're in the middle of a paranormal investigation."

The men did as they were told.

Bunny then noted the look on Brett's face and deduced that he was just as confused by Giff as she was. She had no idea where the "medium" was going with his ridiculous marching and piping under the portrait bit, yet what she did know was that Giff was in the middle of a one-man performance.

With all eyes on him, he spit out the mouthpiece and stopped marching. "Quiet!" he ordered. He then turned to the portrait on the wall and said, "I can't hear you. What was that?" He pretended to hear something and adjusted his hold on the instrument. "Like this?" he asked. To Bunny's amazement, Giff then played three more notes, and this time they all sounded much better. How had he managed that? Then, to her amazement, he froze, convulsed a little, and dropped his instrument on the floor, where it groaned to an ignominious death. Once the bagpipe was silent, Giff turned to the table and began channeling the ghostly piper of Dundoon. Here we go, Bunny thought, doing all she could not to giggle.

With his voice lowered an octave and his chest thrust out, Giff declared, "What a curse it is to be so gifted! I canna help it. I'm a prodigy. People love the sweet sounds emanating from my pipes. No one more so than my chief, my laird." Giff raised his dark eyes to the heavens as his hand came over his heart. "However, I never thought the bagpipes would take me down, but they have. I'm a piper, not a fighter," he told his captive audience. "And for that reason, I'm now stranded here in this moldy old castle."

"Moldy?" Jordy cried, his florid jowls quivering. "I'll have you know that there is no mold within these walls!"

"Quiet down, dear," Elizabeth politely advised. "He's channeling."

"My arse he is," Rory Fraser remarked with a smirk and emptied his marmalade sour. He looked at Jenny and pointed to his empty glass. She ran to fill it.

Giff raised a brow at Rory, then walked to the table. There he picked up his fourth or fifth marmalade sour—Bunny had lost count—before he stared at their host. "This drafty old castle. My point is, they've gone and left me with these . . . these deplorables," he said, gesturing to the table. "They want me to play my pipes for them. As if! But I do. I have no choice. 'Tis a hard-knock life, I tell ye." He walked over to the window and wistfully looked out at the black sky. "He's coming. My chief is coming home. I can see the sails of his ship. But he can't, not with this nest of vipers waiting for him. They're going to spring a trap. They want me to play my pipes. And I will," he said, addressing the table with a cunning look. "I know just what to do."

For the next five embarrassing minutes, Giff channeled the piper, enacting the whole story they'd heard, until he got to the part where they cut off his hands. At some point, Bunny realized that Jenny was standing beside her chair. She had refilled Bunny's drink, but was now drinking it herself, mesmerized by Giff's over-the-top performance.

"My hands! They've cut off my hands! There's so much blood! Oh, God, I'm going to pass out." The moment Giff dropped to his knees, a highball glass flew past his head and crashed on the wall behind him, shattering to pieces.

"Hey!" he said, staring at the table. "Uncalled for! Don't blame me, I'm just the messenger!"

"The REM pod is lighting up!" Brett cried. "We're not alone."

Bunny saw it with her own eyes. Then they homed in on another glass slipping along the table, as if pulled by an unseen force. When it got to the edge, it launched into the air, aiming for Giff. "What in the world . . . ?" She'd seen a lot of crazy things in her life, but this flying glass was next level.

"Ohmygod!" Giff cried, ducking to avoid yet more flying drinkware. "Ohmygod! What's going on? Brett, I've angered the spirits. Stop it!"

Brett, reaching peak excitement, shook his head in wonder, then made a grab for a glass before it launched off the table. "It's warm to the touch. It's moving on its own. I think you have a poltergeist here," he said to Jordy.

"Devil take it!" Jordy cried, looking put out by the thought. He then stood and slapped his napkin on the table. "Come on, Lizzy. You heard what the lad said. We've got a poltergeist." Together, they stalked out of the dining room.

"Giff, duck!" Brett cried.

Giff, amazingly agile, leapt out of the way as another glass sailed past him.

At nearly the same moment, a plate flipped off the table and tumbled into the lap of Rory Fraser. That was the last straw. Everyone got up and ran for shelter. Jenny grabbed Bunny's hand and pulled her out the door and into the hallway. Leaning against the wall, she grinned. "Pity the piper never showed up, but Drunk Gordie sure did."

"Drunk Gordie," Bunny said, frowning at the name. "I should have known."

Chapter 14

After a disruptive—or as Brett termed it, *successful*—spirit supper, the Malcoms retired to their room, as did the three esteemed judges. The spook level in the castle was high, and as the team of *Food & Spirits* knew, that wasn't for everyone. Even Doctor Beaton excused himself, stating that it was a pleasure to meet Bunny and her friends, and hoped they could have a meal together soon, preferably not in a haunted castle.

"He's rather charming," Bunny said to her grandmother as they followed the lads to the third floor of the castle, where the night's investigation was to continue. It had started off with a bang—encountering Drunk Gordie in the dining room—but they really were hoping to contact the legendary piper.

"I think so," Granny Mac said with a gentle smile.

"When were you going to tell me about him?"

"I planned to, dear, but time just slipped away, and you had so much to do in the kitchen. By the way, good work, ladies," Granny Mac said, addressing both Bunny and Jenny. "That was an extraordinary meal."

"Don't change the subject, Gran. How long have you been seeing him?"

"Off and on for five years."

"What?" Bunny pulled her gran to a stop at the top of the steps and glared at her. "Five years! And you're just telling me now?"

"You've been busy. I've been busy. And I thought it would be nice to tell you when you had the chance to meet him. Otherwise, he's just a name without a face."

"So, you knew I'd be coming here." Bunny stewed over this wee tidbit a while.

"Yes," Granny Mac confided. "The moment I met you at Bramsford Manor, I saw the possibility. Don't be mad. Sometimes even fate needs a wee nudge. I find him very handsome."

"He's a yummy dish," Jenny agreed, wiggling her eyebrows for effect. "If I were you, Ella, I'd pin down that man, and soon. Not bad advice for you either," Jenny remarked to Bunny, while watching Brett fiddle with a stationary camera. Jasper was watching him. The young man was also accompanying them on the ghost hunt.

"This conversation isn't finished," Bunny hiss-whispered.

"Ladies. Welcome," Brett said, noting their arrival. He waved them down the hallway, where the men had gathered. Bunny noted that Brett was still in obnoxiously high spirits after their encounter with the petulant ghost.

"We're here, reporting for duty." Bunny gave a mock salute. "Where would you like us?"

"What a night!" Brett exclaimed with eyes ablaze. "The spirit supper went better than I could ever have imagined!" He was so happy that he wrapped Bunny in a big hug and gave her a peck on the cheek before releasing her. "Excellent job, Bunny. And Jenny. This is shaping up to be an investigation like no other."

"Just a note," Giff said, breaking into their little huddle.

"I've already seen enough ghosts for one night. What happened in the dining room has undoubtedly given me PTSD."

"Och, ye poor wee man," Jenny cooed, mockingly. "You've had a couple of bar glasses thrown at you by a ghost. Jasper and I have had worse, and we're still here."

"Jenny's right," Jasper agreed. "Just an ordinary day at Dundoon."

"You all deserve a medal," Giff told them, being serious.

"Okay, everyone, we're about to begin part two of tonight's ghost hunt," Brett said, taking control of his team. He turned to Bunny and Granny Mac. "Cody will escort you two to the tower room. That's where the piper is often spotted. We're hoping you can pick up his energy there."

"I'll be wearing an earpiece, as planned," Giff told Granny Mac, tapping his right ear. "If you happen to contact the piper, or anyone else, just say the word, and I'll jump into action. However, if any other devil in this place starts launching dishware at me, I'm outta here!"

"I don't blame you, dear," Granny Mac told him, placing a calming hand on his shoulder. "That petulant entity was something else. It takes a lot of energy for an earthbound spirit to move an object like that. I could feel his residual anger, which might be expected after learning of Drunk Gordie's death. However, I don't believe all of that anger was coming from him."

"What do you mean?" Brett looked fascinated by this.

"While there's a certain amount of anger and unrest brought by the entity Drunk Gordie, it's my opinion that he was feeding off the anger and unrest already present in the room."

"Whoa!" Giff breathed. "Mind blown. I didn't know that was possible. Whose negative vibes are we talking about?"

"The judges," Bunny replied. She had felt it too, but until now, she hadn't been certain where it all had come from.

"The judges were responsible for that glassware flying off

the table?" Jasper asked before Brett had the chance. Mike and Cody had captured the entire incident on their cameras. Ed had been freaking out in his control room in the snug. It had been one of the wildest paranormal experiences they had ever captured on film.

Granny Mac, unwilling to get into a long conversation about entities and energy, shrugged. "For a person who is energy sensitive, like Bunny and me, the tense energy between the judges was palpable. It is my belief that the entity, having been drawn in by the meal, the spirit box, and Giff's . . ." Here, she paused, not certain what to say about Giff's outlandish channeling debacle. However, unwilling to crush his exuberant spirit, she offered, "unique performance. My point is that the entity came into the room and might have fed off the existing energy in order to move the glassware. Now, ladies and gentlemen, if we want to confront the piper, I say we get on with it. I don't know about you, but I'm getting tired."

Jenny and Jasper accompanied Brett, Giff, and Mike on their investigation inside the castle. While they talked through their strategy for the night's investigation, Cody escorted Bunny and Granny Mac to the tower room. It was an old stone tower perched three stories above the main castle. It also opened onto the battlement, which was where the piper was sometimes seen playing his haunting tune. Ed, comfortably seated in the snug with all his monitors running, gave them the green light to continue the night's investigation.

"I didn't realize it would be so cold up here," Bunny remarked, taking a seat in the folding chair beside her grandmother. "Will you be okay sitting here?"

"I'm fine. Just a wee bit tired is all. It's been a long day."

Bunny took the long scarf from her neck and wrapped it around her grandmother's head, making a loopy hat for her. "This won't do much to wake you up, but it might keep you warmer. Can't have you freezing." She smiled at her grandmother, then added, "I had a nice nap in your room, until the white rabbit woke me. I forgot you spent the day at the piping competition with your boyfriend."

"Please don't be mad at me for not telling you about Artemus. I wanted you to meet him. Now, about the white rabbit. He woke you? What did he say?"

Bunny let out a breath of a chuckle. "Nothing. I think he just wanted me to know he was there. They haven't touched his room at all, have they?" Her gran knew exactly what she was talking about.

"Everyone grieves differently, my dear. No one should be judged on how they grieve."

Bunny let out a deep breath, accepting this with a nod. They sat in silence for a long while, until Bunny asked, "Regarding the piper, are you sensing anything? I honestly thought that, with all the bagpipes at the castle, the competition, and Giff's homage to the piper, he would have come forward by now. Do you think Drunk Gordie is trapping him here or keeping him from appearing, like the black lady at Bramsford Manor?"

"No," Granny Mac replied. "They are two separate entities. I know the piper is here, but he seems unwilling to come forward. I want you to close your eyes and try to reach him."

"Me? Why? I'm perfectly fine sitting in this room with you, keeping you company."

"I know you are. But you have abilities, and now is a good time to stretch them and see just what you are capable of. You smelled the whisky in the dining room when we arrived this morning."

"You knew about that?" Granny Mac nodded. Bunny continued, "So that means he's here; he just won't come out and play?"

"Correct. In my experience, spirits have free will. You can put the call out, so to speak, but they are under no obligation to answer it. Others are quite willing to step forward. Those are the easy ones."

Bunny did as her grandmother asked. She closed her eyes and tried to connect with the piper in the vast spiritual realm. At first, there was nothing. Nothing but silence. Then, however, she sensed an elusive male presence, coupled with the scent of stale woodsmoke, wet earth, salt air, and whisky. Good, she thought. He's here. However, the closer she pushed toward this presence, the farther away he seemed to recede into the ether. She didn't feel that he was shy or purposely trying to avoid her. No, that wasn't it. It was something else, something she couldn't quite put her finger on. However, she got the very distinct feeling that he wasn't going to appear just because she wanted him to. She opened her eyes and shook her head.

"I can't reach him."

"Not to worry, dear. There's enough in this castle to keep the lads busy. I do hope they won't be too disappointed if they don't find the ghost they have come to see. I'm afraid I'm about to fall asleep," Granny Mac told her with a yawn.

Bunny decided to call it a night, and together they left the tower room. Jenny was tired as well and volunteered to escort Granny Mac to her room before heading to her own. As they said goodbye, Bunny desperately wanted to join them but decided to stay with the lads. They were still in high spirits, having heard disembodied voices during their investigation. Giff and Jasper even swore they had heard the warning growl of a fairy dog, although they didn't capture it on the recorder. Before they called it a night, Brett suggested that everyone head to the battlement of the castle. He wasn't about to give up without hearing from the piper of Dundoon.

It was two-thirty in the morning. Bunny was sitting against a stout rock wall while attempting once again to contact the ghostly piper. The lads were with her, aimlessly wandering about with their ghosty gadgets. A dense fog had rolled in, nearly obscuring them from her view as well as cloaking the dark, dramatic landscape in an eerie gray blanket.

"Don't fall asleep," Brett called out to her. That made her smile. She was tired. If she fell asleep, so be it. She assured him she wouldn't and closed her eyes.

Bunny had no idea how long she'd been sleeping when she awoke with a start. The hair on the back of her neck prickled painfully, causing her to open her eyes. The sight of the white rabbit, sitting just beyond her feet in the fog, jolted her awake. She scrambled to sit up as Hopper bounded farther into the fog and disappeared. That's when she heard it. The haunting sound of bagpipes.

Chapter 15

"Bagpipes!" she cried, scrambling to her feet. "I hear the pipes!"

The men had heard them too and had come running to get her. It irked Bunny to see how excited they all looked. "It's the piper of Dundoon!" Brett declared. "Bunny, you've done it!" He was so excited, he wrapped his arms around her and gave her a fierce hug. It was a great hug, warm and protective, and Bunny did everything she could to prolong it. She hugged him back.

"Um, excuse me," Jasper said. Bunny had almost forgotten that they were not alone and that the impetus for Brett's yummy hug was a ghost. She released him and stepped back. Everyone was staring at Jasper. The young man was glowing with excitement. "I thought perhaps we should go find him. Ye know, the ghost."

"Good thinking," Giff said, although it was clear that he'd had enough of ghost hunting for one night, if not a lifetime. After swiveling his head in all directions, he said, "Well, I don't see him up here. Good thing we've got it on tape. Great investigation, everyone. Shall we call it a night?"

"No, we're not calling it a night," Brett huffed. "The piper's not up here; the sound is coming from out there." He pointed beyond the castle's crenellated wall.

"I must say, that makes sense," Jasper told them plainly. "Sometimes, ye can hear him in the castle, marching through the hallways and playing his sad tune. Other times, he's out there on the clifftops, chantin' away on his pipes. He usually sounds better out there. Must be the open air." It was an interesting remark, one Giff picked up on.

"As you know, I'm far from an expert on bagpipe music, but that noise out there sounds earthly to me."

"And here we thought you *were* an expert, especially after playing three perfect notes at the spirit supper. How did you manage that?" This Bunny asked, unable to help herself. It was a question she'd been dying to ask him all evening. Although she cherished Giff's friendship, she knew he didn't have any real mediumistic abilities. Also, she was nearly certain he had never touched a bagpipe before their visit to Dundoon.

With a hand over his heart, Giff said, "I was channeling, Bunny dear. The spirit moved me."

Brett, ignoring them both, wrinkled his brow as he listened to the eerie bagpipe music faintly wafting in their direction through the fog. "On second thought, I have to agree with my esteemed college, Giff. It sounds like a human is out there playing the pipes. Which is odd, because whoever is out there is clearly breaking the 'no piping after eight o'clock' rule that Winterton not only told us about but promised. Clearly, someone didn't get the memo."

"To the untrained ear, it may sound human," Jasper agreed. "But I've been around bagpipe music all my life, and I have heard the ghostly piper. That's him."

Bunny knew they could go on like this for a while, arguing ghost or no ghost, but the fact remained, there was a piper on the moorland. Also, she had a little issue of her own at the moment. Hopper, the ghostly white rabbit, had appeared again, sitting at her feet, and this time she knew what he wanted. "Um, lads," she said, wiggling her fingers in the cold night air to get their attention. She had the sinking feeling she was about to regret the next words out of her mouth, but she said them regardless. "You know that issue I have regarding rabbits? Well, I think we should, um . . . go this way," she told them, watching Hopper hop through the solid oak door.

"Would that rabbit happen to be white?" Giff asked. Bunny nodded. "Fellas, when the white rabbit appears, we listen."

Jasper, clearly befuddled, said, "What white rabbit? I don't see a white rabbit."

"It's our metaphor for 'ghostly trouble,'" Giff lied.

"'Tis what I've been telling ye!" Jasper remarked, losing patience. "The ghostly piper of Dundoon is out there."

Ed's voice crackled over Brett's walkie-talkie then. "I hear it too. Take your gear and chase that down."

"Will do. Switching to silent mode," Brett informed him, not wanting to scare the ghost piper away.

In a flash, they found themselves marching across the foggy moorland, with Bunny in the lead, heading into the unknown to confront the person or ghost playing the haunting tune. Unfortunately, the fog seemed thicker outside, making travel difficult. They could barely see three feet in front of them, and the torches only made it worse. Due to some miracle, call it Hopper's glowing red eyes, Bunny could still see the rabbit leading her to the source of the music. They were gingerly making their way across the rocky, grass-covered hillock and were over halfway there when the piping suddenly stopped. Bunny stopped too, causing everyone else to pull up before bumping into her.

"Why'd he stop playing?" Giff whispered in her ear.

"Probably because he can sense us getting near," Jasper

offered in a clandestine whisper. "He's a ghost, remember. They have abilities."

Bunny really had no idea what was going on, until she noticed that Hopper was gone too. Her heart sank further when she realized she had no idea where they were. She silently cursed Hopper before mentally berating herself for being such an idiot. She gritted her teeth and was about to call after the rabbit (as if he would ever listen to her!), when the back of her neck prickled with such intensity, she grabbed it with her hand to ease the pain. As she began to rub her neck, she heard a noise that knocked the breath from her. It was a low, guttural growl.

"Ohmygod!" Giff hiss-whispered. "Ohmygod, did anyone else hear that? That sounded demonic!"

"Shhh!" Jasper warned, his face pinched with fear.

They were now huddled together, surrounded by fog and whatever sinister thing lurked just beyond their view. Then the beast let out a loud, earth-shattering bark.

"Lord, help us!" Jasper squawked, crossing himself. " 'Tis the fairy dog. Cover your ears! Now! If he barks two more times, your soul is his." Jasper dropped to the ground, curled into a fetal position, and covered his ears with his hands.

Giff looked at Bunny. Frightened far beyond his comfort zone, he bravely quipped, "When in Rome," before crunching into a tight little ball on the ground with his new Highland plaid over his head.

Bunny was so freaked out she didn't know what to do. The blasted rabbit had left her, and now a beast was wandering through the foggy heather with them. Urgh! This was not what she had signed up for! Crouching low, she realized that Brett, Mike, and Cody were not cowering on the ground beside them, but bravely holding their ground while pointing night-vision cameras and digital recorders into the fog in all directions. What on God's green earth were they thinking? She was just about to pull Brett down beside her when they heard a very human grunt, as if someone had had the wind knocked out of them. It was coming from the vicinity of the bagpipe player. More thumps and grunts followed, indicating a scuffle and that there were at least two people on the moor with them.

Brett, not making a sound, turned in the direction of the scuffle with his digital recorder thrust out before him like a torch. Mike and Cody did the same with their equipment as well.

As for Bunny, she had barely made sense of what she was hearing when the beast let out two more unearthly barks. A blood-curdling scream followed, chilling the blood in her veins. When she realized it was fading, as if swiftly moving farther and farther away, she cringed, instinctively knowing what would come next. And it did. They all heard the loud, echoing thump accompanied by one last blast of the bagpipes. The piper was human, and something or someone had just pushed him off the cliff. The fact that a beast had barked three times didn't bode well at all.

"Ohmygod!" Giff cried, emerging from his plaid like a reluctant turtle. "Did everyone hear that? That wasn't the ghost piper. That was someone falling off a cliff!"

"Shhh," Jasper warned.

That's when they heard the unmistakable sound of footfalls swiftly retreating from the spot where the piper had screamed. Bunny found it chaotic and hard to tell whether it was a man or beast running away.

Brett, acting on instinct, dashed into the fog, aiming for the retreating footfalls. Jasper dashed off after him and instantly tackled him to the ground.

"What the . . . ?" Brett uttered, stunned.

"Shhh!" Jasper warned again. This time they all understood why. Something was lurking just beyond their vision, breathing loudly and quite closely. Everyone pressed together, keeping their eyes on the dark fog. Bunny nearly yipped when the giant shadow of a dog appeared, looking like a prickly, snarling whale in the mist. With her heart beating loudly in her ears, she held her breath and prayed.

It was a tense few moments. The beast had sensed them, yet something prevented it from coming any closer. It then flinched, gave a little grunt, and disappeared. A moment later, Bunny saw the glowing eyes of Hopper thinly veiled in the fog. She let out her breath. The white rabbit never appeared, but whatever had occurred between them and the beast, she was almost certain Braiden had intervened. In fact, she felt it. "Thank you," she whispered, directing it to her guardian angel, even though the rest of them could hear her.

"That was close," Brett admitted, as Jasper finally let go of him.

"I didn't expect that," the young man admitted. "But the fact remains that there's a fairy dog out here, and a cliff just over there." He pointed into the fog. "One wrong step and you could meet the one or go over the other. In fact, we nearly did meet the one, and I'm not ready to die."

"Neither are we," Brett assured him." Thank you for your quick actions, Jasper. This fog is very disorienting. I have no idea where I'm going, but I know that a person has just gone over the cliff."

"Aye," the young man agreed. He then motioned for them all to stay on the ground and listen to what he had to say. "The fairy dog has barked three times, and his victim has gone over the cliff; his soul has been whisked away—"

"You can't know that!" Giff chided. "While that hairy fairy dog out there is intimidating, it still doesn't change the fact that the piper who was pushed off the cliff might be alive. We've got to get down there."

"I agree," Brett said. "Jasper, can you help us?"

It was clear that the young man was still shaken by their close encounter with a possibly otherworldly beast, yet Bunny could see that Brett was determined to get to the bottom of the cliff. Jasper knew it too. With a nod of his head, he relented.

"Aye, if ye insist. I know a pathway down," he said. "But 'tis dangerous, especially in a fog as thick as this." This was undoubtedly true. Even Bunny could see that Jasper was troubled by the thought of climbing down a cliff in the dead of night. He obviously knew the gravity of the situation. "Alright, I'll take Brett with me. The rest of ye stay here. Or better yet, go back to the castle and call the police. Maybe the doctor as well. Who knows what we will find down there."

Everyone agreed to the plan. As Brett and Jasper headed into the fog, Bunny thought it best to waste no time calling the authorities. Once she made the call, she thrust her phone back into her coat pocket and prayed that the mysterious piper was still alive. "Ready?" she asked Giff, Cody, and Mike.

Giff turned in the direction they had just come from and stared into the fog. "I don't even know where we are, or if that beast is still out there. Maybe we should stay here and wait for the police to find us."

"We can find our way back," Mike assured him. "Just as we can find out where Brett and Cody will be." He pulled out his iPhone and opened a tracking app. "For security reasons, we all agreed to share each other's locations. This red dot here is Ed, sitting comfortably in the control room waiting for our call. That reminds me. We should call him and let him know what's going on."

They were just about to call Ed and head back to the castle when another sound wafted through the air, penetrating the fog like a butter knife. It was coming from the direction of the castle.

"Oh, dear," Giff said. Beneath the healthy tan of his face, Bunny could see him turning as white as the fog that surrounded them.

"Oh, dear, is right," she agreed.

Mike nearly dropped his phone.

The ghostly piper of Dundoon had finally come out to play, and the tune he played was as haunting as it was chilling. Never in her life had Bunny heard anything like it. It was a beautiful, soul-stirring lament, with a haunting quality to every note that felt spectral and otherworldly. To her utter astonishment, tears welled in her eyes and spilled down her cheeks. The music moved her beyond all comprehension. Although the piper was hidden by fog and separated by time and space, she could still feel the pride he carried for his skill on the instrument and the soul-wrenching sadness in his heart. She now understood why he played.

The piper who had gone over the cliff was dead.

Chapter 16

"This is a terrible turn of events. Just terrible!" Jordy said, wrapped in his dressing gown as he sat in his cushy, wing-back chair in the great hall. Bunny felt that the fluffy mess of gray hair on his head was a testament to the fact that, upon being woken at four in the morning, he had come directly downstairs to join them. He gave his loyal dog, Winston, a pat on the head, then leaned back in his chair. "You say a man was playing the bagpipes out there and now he's gone over the cliff? I didn't hear a thing."

Elizabeth looked just as worried and tired as her husband, although she had had the presence of mind to run a brush through her hair before joining them. With her sleepy, sad eyes trained on Bunny, she explained, "We're very sound sleepers. We put cotton in our ears."

Bunny didn't blame them one bit. When living in a haunted castle, and theirs was very haunted, one must do whatever it took to drown out all the little bumps and thumps in the night, including the soul-rending music from a ghostly piper. Bunny was certain that, had she inherited such a monstrosity as Dundoon, she would have handed it directly over to the National Trust for Scotland and let them deal with it. She didn't have the stomach for drunken ghosts, forlorn dead pipers, and fairy dogs. However, the Malcoms, for better or worse, embraced their heritage.

"Artemis is on his way," Granny Mac informed them, walking into the room. After learning that a person had gone over the cliff, she had immediately called him. Winston, with his tail wagging in welcome, left Sir Jordy's side to greet her. After giving him a loving rub on the head, Granny Mac added, "We hope for the best, yet prepare for the worst. If that poor piper didn't survive the fall, they'll need someone to call the time of death."

"Good thinking," Jordy said. He then turned to Giff. "Did you at least get a look at this piper?"

"Which one?" Giff remarked, still looking a tad pale. "We had the displeasure of hearing two pipers tonight. One living and the other dead."

"Ye gads! Ye heard the piper of Dundoon as well?" Jordy's jowls quaked as he said this.

Giff, Cody, Mike, and Bunny nodded in unison. Ed added, "I heard them both as well, but only over the live feed."

"Well, I'm happy ye heard him. It is, after all, what ye came here for in the first place. What I meant was, did you see the man who went over the cliff?"

"The fog was too thick," Mike informed him. "We could barely make our way out there, let alone see anything."

"You didn't see him? Then how exactly do you know he went over? This fellow could have walked away."

"We heard him playing," Bunny gently explained, "which caused us to walk out there and get a look at him. We thought he might be the piper of Dundoon. Jasper confirmed it, saying he'd heard him playing out there before. So we went to get a look at him. However, as Mike just mentioned, it was too foggy to see much of anything. Then, after hiking over halfway there, we heard growling and the bark of a . . . a dog," Bunny concluded, looking at the sweet black Lab lounging on the floor at Jordy's feet. Dog sounded kinder than beast or fairy dog. "Then we heard a thump and a scuffle coming from the direction of the piper. It was swiftly followed by two more barks, and a loud, frightened scream."

"Good heaven," Elizabeth breathed, clutching her robe tightly at the neck. For a woman who lived in a haunted castle, Bunny felt she looked unnaturally frightened. "What dreadful bad luck. It sounds like the work of a fairy dog to me."

Bunny noted that Giff's handsome, dark head was nodding in vigorous agreement.

Ed, who hadn't experienced the growling beast in the fog himself but had listened to the audio, said, "Look, I'm on the fence regarding this mythical fairy-dog creature. After listening to the audio Mike captured, there is evidence of a large dog or wolf out there, but, as Bunny has just told you, I distinctly heard a thump, then a scuffle, followed by two barks. After that, there was a scream that faded until another, distant thump was heard in conjunction with a burst from a bagpipe. In short, someone got pushed over the cliff. There was also the patter of human feet running away. At least one pair, if not two. Maybe more. Or even a human and a dog. It was hard to tell after just one listen, but I might be able to be more specific once I clean the audio up a bit and isolate the sound."

"They might not be related, the human and the dog," Mike offered. "If there was another person out there on the cliff who pushed the piper over, which is what we think happened, he might have been spooked off by the fairy dog as well."

"That's an interesting take on it," Granny Mac said with a nod.

"Gran, do you believe in fairy dogs?" Bunny asked. It was a silly question. Of course, her grandmother did.

Granny Mac folded her hands and leaned back in her chair, thinking. Bunny had the feeling that the older woman was searching the ether for an answer, and not her personal superstitions. Finally, she offered, "I've never encountered one, but I have heard the stories. I do, however, feel that there is some strange creature out there, lurking in the darkness and wandering the hills. I think it's out of place," she concluded.

Great, Bunny thought. That wasn't the answer she was looking for. A definite yes or no would have been helpful.

Jordy pointed his stout finger at Granny Mac. "Listen to Ella. She knows. She has the second sight. Can you tell us what it is?" he prodded.

"No." Granny Mac shook her head. "That is beyond me. But I do feel that there is something very evil lurking here."

Bunny felt chills race down her spine at that.

"Ella," Giff chided, "please. We know there's something evil out there. It almost ate us and pushed a man over a cliff. What I want to know is if you have any more protective crystals on you, or a magic potion. I'm feeling very vulnerable at the moment." Giff was still in his sexy Highlander getup, wearing a plaid, a kilt, and a puffy-sleeved shirt, with plenty of crystals dangling around his neck.

Granny Mac leaned forward and addressed the man she'd been trying to coach on how a medium actually worked. He wasn't a quick learner. "You're confusing me with a witch, Gifford. I am not a witch!"

"You might be right," he said, rubbing his hands together as he sat in his chair near the large fireplace. "I apologize.

But how about those crystals? Got any for this situation? You know, to ward off evil spirits?"

"Black obsidian, perhaps?" she offered, narrowing her green eyes at him.

"I don't have anything black yet. Like a magpie, I'm attracted to bright, shiny, sparkly things. Not a fan of black, but if that's the color to ward off evil, count me in. How much for a rock about this size?" He cupped his hand, indicating a three-inch circle.

"I'm fresh out," she told him.

Bunny was just about to tell him to zip it, when her phone rang. It was Brett.

"I wish I had better news," he said. "We've just made it down to the shoreline under the cliff. Had to hike over a mile out of our way to get here. We were too late, Bunny. Maybe he never stood a chance. It's rocky and hellish down here on the shore."

"Are you okay?" she asked, her voice thick with concern.

"Not really. The piper is dead. He's one of the three esteemed judges. The poor man. Lord knows what he was doing out here playing his bagpipes at three in the morning."

"One of the judges?" she uttered, eyeing the Malcoms. Jordy cast a glance at the ceiling, thinking what everyone else was. One of the three judges was no longer in his room. But which judge went over the cliff? "I'm going to put you on speaker," Bunny told him. "We're all here, Brett. The constable should be here shortly, and Doc Beaton."

"Good. Thank heavens. Bunny, I don't know how to say this. I'm sorry. Major Scotty MacDonald, piper to the late queen, is dead. God rest his soul."

Chapter 17

The news had shocked everyone seated in the great hall. As for Bunny, her mind was reeling. It was such sad news, and yet all she could think of was that her father was going to be very upset. Major Scotty MacDonald was a hero to Davie MacBride. In retrospect, had she known anything about bagpipes other than the fact that they made a lot of noise, she might have admired the major's last tune. With the exception of the spectral piper, whose music was unearthly, Major MacDonald was likely the most skilled bagpiper at the competition, if not in all of Scotland.

As Bunny meditated over pipers, wishing for the first time that she had some inkling about the instrument instead of a petulant loathing, one thought kept pestering her. What was Major Scotty MacDonald doing out on the fog-covered clifftops at three in the morning, playing his bagpipes? Was he merely practicing? Was it just his way of blowing off a little steam after a trying day? Or was he, perhaps, saying good night to his old friend, the queen, playing what her father had described as a soul-stirring sendoff of "Sleep, Dearie,

Sleep"? The title of the song and the fact that it had been played for the queen's memorial moved her. How she wished she could bear the sound of bagpipes to appreciate the gesture. However, if she was being honest, she couldn't. The sound to her was like nails on a chalkboard being played over a squelchy amplifier. Tolerable for a second or two, but pure torture any longer than that. She supposed that bagpipes, like a good Scotch whisky, were an acquired taste. No, no, that's not quite right. Developing a taste for good Scotch whisky was far easier on the ears and nerves than bagpipes.

Bagpipes. The word echoed in her sad, sleepy head, and for good reason. Whatever personal thoughts she had regarding the instrument, she couldn't deny that it was somehow at the heart of this troubling matter. As she sat in the great hall with the others, watching them mourn the loss of a national treasure while awaiting the arrival of Constable Craig and Doc Beaton, Giff suddenly slid into the chair next to her, grabbing her attention.

"Murdered," he whispered close to her ear. "That prickly piper was murdered. You and I both know that he was."

Bunny's forehead creased in consternation as she studied him. She dearly wished they hadn't gone out on the foggy moors to investigate the ghostly piper. She dearly wished they hadn't heard the scuffle just before a thump that was swiftly followed by a fading cry. Never mind hearing the bark of some type of beast. Major Scotty MacDonald, piper to the late queen, had gone over the cliff, and they could only assume from what they had heard that he'd been murdered. Clearly, the thought intrigued Giff, whereas it frightened her. However, as every great murder mystery on the telly suggested, jumping to conclusions never worked when trying to get to the bottom of a mystery. And this was a mystery. She leaned over to Giff and corrected in a whisper,

"It sure sounded that way, but it was too foggy to see anything. We don't know who was with him when he went over that cliff, or what, for that matter." This she added as visions of a hellish fairy dog sprang to her mind. Then, playing the devil's advocate, she offered, "For all we know, he could have jumped off himself, either from fright after seeing a fairy dog, or . . . or maybe he had just realized that he'd wasted the best years of his life blowing into a bladder and squeezing the daylights out of it to make it sing."

Giff pretended to flinch as he mouthed, "Ouch!" He then whispered, "Don't tell me you hate the sound of bagpipes more than I do?"

"I thought you liked them?"

"I did. For five whole minutes," he confessed. "After that, I wanted to cut off my ears and run for the heather, as they say in these parts. In retrospect, I was simply blinded by the men in kilts who play the horrible thing. You must admit, there's something about a man in a kilt." He stopped talking then, clearly having an epiphany. "Wait. Maybe that's it? Maybe that's why he was pushed over the edge? The major was playing his instrument in the middle of the night, and someone might have snapped from pure annoyance. As Brett pointed out earlier, the piper on the cliff was clearly breaking the 'no piping after eight p.m.' rule. I mean, who could blame them if they did?"

"That's a horrible suggestion," Bunny admonished. "If someone had been highly annoyed by the sound of the major playing his bagpipes after hours, they could have simply asked him to stop."

"Or, more likely, they would have wrestled the pipes from him and tossed them over the cliff, not the major. I understand," Giff nodded. "After all, we are firmly in the heart of bagpiping fandom. Everyone has come to Dundoon Castle to hear the pipers play, even us, but our favorite piper is a ghostly one. I don't believe I'm saying this, but I'm not sorry we heard him."

"Me either," Bunny softly admitted, recalling the haunting tune and the powerful emotions it had invoked in her. She exhaled and offered a wan smile. "Ever since Braiden died, I've been running from ghosts. Now, ironically, I'm chasing them. Even stranger? I feel their emotions. There's something especially compelling about that ghostly piper, Giff. The moment I heard that first haunting note he played, I knew the piper on the cliff was dead."

"Really? And the loud thump at the bottom of the cliff coupled with the dying *WRAHaaaaaaa* . . . of the pipes wasn't enough for you?"

Bunny ignored his sarcastic comment. "True. It was horrible. However, what I'm telling you is that I think somehow that the ghostly piper and Major MacDonald are connected."

"Well, they're both dead now, so you might be correct there."

She flashed Giff a look of mild displeasure. "The thing is, Granny Mac and I might be able to contact the major's ghost. However, I'm not sure it would do any good. As we've learned, the dead . . . or newly dead, can't tell us what happened, often because they don't know it themselves."

"Most importantly," Giff cut in, "ghostly testimony doesn't hold up in a court."

"No, so that means we have to find a way to prove that Major MacDonald was murdered."

"Whoa, MacBride, you're getting way over your skis here. We've only just learned who the victim is. We don't know anything about him, and although we have solved a murder, only because we had to, we're not private investigators. We're ghost hunters."

"Correction. I'm not a ghost hunter. I'm a chef. I have no business doing this." She wiggled her hand in the air, adding, "Whatever this is."

"But you do have a gift, Bunny dear. And we need you. I say we leave this mess to the constable."

"I . . . I agree. But there is one thing that's bothering me. What was the major doing out there in the wee hours?"

Giff exhaled, as if he'd just lost a bet. "If we figure that out, it might lead us to a motive. And if we find the motive, it will lead us to the person or fairy dog responsible for his death. In short, we will solve the murder, Bunny. Do you really want to play this game?"

"I'm going to regret saying this, but I think we should. We owe it to Major Scotty MacDonald. We were there, Giff. We heard him go over the cliff. Also, it might help us discover why the ghostly piper is still haunting this castle."

"Any suggestions where we should start?" he asked.

She did have one, but at that moment, Mrs. Collins ushered Constable Craig and Doctor Beaton into the room, both men clearly shrugging off the last vestiges of sleep and damp fog as they prepared for the long morning ahead of them. Winterton was fast on their heels, looking wild and deeply troubled by the news.

"We just learned that the man who went over the cliff is Scotty MacDonald," Jordy informed them. "He was a guest at the castle. This is terrible news. Just terrible."

"And he's dead," Elizabeth uttered, delivering the last little tidbit of information with a tremor in her voice.

"Dead?" Doc Beaton asked. "It's been confirmed?"

"We were informed a few minutes ago," Granny Mac told him.

Constable Hamish Craig, a tall, sinewy man in his mid-forties, with auburn hair and deep-set, amber eyes, looked at

Bunny. "You must be Ms. MacBride, the young woman who called and reported that a man had gone over a cliff on the Dundoon estate."

"I am," Bunny said. "Pleased to meet you," she added, walking over to him.

"The call came in at three in the morning. What were you doing out there that you witnessed this incident?" he asked.

"Three in the morning?" Winterton blurted, shooting Bunny an extreme look of displeasure. "Did I no' tell ye that 'tis not safe to be wanderin' aboot the grounds after dark?"

"We're ghost hunters, Constable," Bunny answered, ignoring Winterton and his anger. "Well, technically I'm a chef, but we"—she gestured to Giff, Cody, Mike, and Ed—"are filming an episode of our paranormal show, *Food and Spirits*. We are here investigating the ghostly piper of Dundoon."

"One of our resident ghosts," Jordy added with a proud nod.

"Yes," Bunny agreed. "We were inside the castle when we heard bagpipes being played out on the moor. We thought it was the ghost."

"A ghost?" Constable Craig looked suspicious as he eyed the team of *Food & Spirits*. It took a little convincing from Ed, Cody, and Mike before he understood the nature of their show, and why hiking across a fog-covered moor in the wee hours was a totally normal thing for them to do.

"We're getting amazing results," Ed informed him. "I was in the control room while the rest of the team headed outside to investigate the bagpipe music."

Constable Craig, who was frantically scribbling information down in his notebook, suddenly looked at Ed. "You were inside during all of this? At what point did you realize that the piper wasn't a ghost?"

"When we heard a scuffle," Bunny offered. "It all happened so fast. Before we knew it, we could hear the piper go over the cliff."

"You heard the piper, but you didn't see him?" the constable questioned.

"The fog was too thick to see anything," Giff said. He then proceeded to tell the constable and everyone else in the room what transpired after that.

"So, there are two men with the body, correct?" the constable asked. "I'm calling in a recovery team from Glasgow, along with backup." Constable Craig made the calls, then turned to Winterton. "It's still damn foggy, but I'll need to see the body. Can you lead us down there?"

"Aye," Winterton said with a curt nod. "I have the quad out front. We can drive to the trail that'll lead us down to the bottom."

"I'm coming too," Doc Beaton told them, slinging his medical bag over his shoulder. A moment later, they were out the door, heading for the spot below the cliff where Brett and Jasper were waiting with the body.

After the men had gone, Granny Mac turned to Bunny. "Dear, why don't you and Giff make us some tea. It's going to be a long morning, and I for one could use a cuppa while we wait for the emergency vehicles to arrive."

Although Granny Mac was suggesting one thing, her eyes and her mind were willing Bunny to act on another suggestion. It was Bunny's good fortune that she was thinking along the same lines as her grandmother. Because the message she was getting was, *Take your time with the tea. I'll keep everyone here while you check out the major's room.*

"Excellent suggestion, Gran." Bunny sprang to her feet and grabbed Giff by the arm, pulling him into the hallway with her. Giff bristled.

"You seriously want me to help you make tea? Well, here's

my dirty little confession, Bunny. I've never made a pot in my life, mostly because I can't stand the stuff."

"Get over yourself, Mr. Man, because we're not going to make tea just yet. You and I are going to check out the major's room before anyone else thinks to do it."

Giff inhaled sharply. "You're a genius."

"Thank you. But you're not off the hook yet. You're still helping with the tea."

Chapter 18

There was just one problem with their plan. Bunny remembered how to get to her gran's room on the second floor, but once there, she wasn't certain which door led to Major Scotty MacDonald's room.

"According to the Malcoms, there's no more room at the inn, because they've all been taken," Giff offered, staring down the long hallway. After traversing an even longer hallway that held the laird and lady's master suite, they turned the corner, walked down a short hallway, and found another, where the door to Granny Mac's room was visible at the end. "Granny Mac's room is down there, you say? That means one of these three doors must lead to the room in question. Let's start knocking."

"What?" Bunny didn't like the sound of that. "We'll wake the other judges."

"As we should," Giff told her, eyeing the nearest door with suspicion. "A man's been murdered! Also, one of them might be to blame. Look, we could all feel the tension between them during the spirit supper. Clearly, they're at odds, whether over the competition or something else, we don't yet know. But we need to find out. One of them could have easily followed MacDonald as he walked to the cliff with his bagpipes and done the deed. Or maybe one of them led him there, you know, setting up a secret rendezvous where he tricked him and pushed him over the cliff instead? At this point, I'm just speculating, but now's our chance to see if one of them looks too chipper for this time of morning."

Bunny looked at him, nodded, and braced herself as she stared at the first door in question. After taking a deep, fortifying breath, she gave a quick rap on the door and waited for someone to appear. When no one answered, she knocked again, this time louder. "Dare we?" she asked, eyeing the doorknob. Giff shrugged and gave it a turn. He was surprised when it opened.

"What are the odds?" he whispered with a grin and entered the room.

Walking into the still room recently occupied by a near stranger was an odd sensation indeed, Bunny thought, following Giff's lead. Once they were certain there wasn't a body in the slightly rumpled bed, Bunny covered her hand with her sleeve and turned on the lights. "Be careful not to touch anything," she warned him. "We don't want to be murder suspects again."

The first thing that struck her was the relative tidiness of the room. Although smaller than her gran's guest bedchamber, this room was another beautifully renovated space. The walls were covered with wide-striped wallpaper in alternating shades of sky blue and light blue. The bed near the wall was a double, perfect for a single occupant. In the corner by the bed stood an antique chair with a pair of neatly folded men's plaid pajamas on it. The old hearth on the opposite wall, which had once kept the room warm, had been bricked over, the mantle painted white, and a large vase of flowers now occupied the empty space inside. It was a nice touch, she thought, focusing on the smaller of the two black rolling cases that sat on the floor beside it. She pointed to it the same moment Giff saw it. "I think that smaller one is a bagpipe case."

Giff agreed and covered his hand with his blanket-like plaid before opening it. "Interesting," he uttered, noting that a bagpipe was still in the case. Bunny was surprised as well. She crossed the room and stared down at the lovely instrument neatly packed inside along with other bagpipe accoutrements.

A thought came to her then. "We do have the correct room, don't we? I mean, is this Major MacDonald's room, or someone else's?"

It was a good question. The door had been unlocked, and they had naturally assumed it belonged to Major MacDonald, because it was empty. Panicked by the notion, Bunny walked to the wardrobe and opened it with a sleeve-covered hand. Along with the few shirts, sweaters, and pants that hung there, she spotted the ceremonial uniform of a bagpipe judge, including the jacket, kilt, sporran, and bonnet. She wished she remembered what Major MacDonald had been wearing yesterday evening as he walked up the pathway to the castle. None of the judges had been wearing their uniforms at the spirit supper.

"I can't tell if this uniform is his or not," she said to Giff, feeling frustrated.

"It's his," he told her confidently. "I never forget a man in uniform." Bunny raised a questioning eyebrow at this, causing him to confess that Major MacDonald's name was on the official black leather binder sitting on the tiny desk in the corner.

"This is his competition binder," Giff said, gingerly lifting the leather cover of the notebook. He pulled out his phone and snapped a few pictures. "Bunny, take some pictures of the bagpipe and his closet. I don't know what we're looking for, but we might never be in this room again."

"Good thinking," she agreed, and began snapping away. "It looks like he got up, got dressed, and left the room, leaving his bagpipes behind in the case. So, if he wasn't playing his own instrument, whose was he playing out there?" she asked.

"Beats me. My guess is that he had two sets with him, a good one and a junker."

"There's only one case here," she pointed out.

"Yeah, that's the good one," he said without hesitation. "The junker doesn't require a case. It's at the bottom of a cliff."

"It is now," Bunny agreed with a sinking heart. They had seen enough. She turned off the lights just before softly closing the door behind them.

"Now what?" she asked, standing in the hallway.

"Isn't it obvious? We wake the other judges and see how they'll respond to the news." Bunny wasn't fully onboard with this, but it didn't matter. Giff was already rapping on the next door.

"What in God's name are ye doin', bangin' on my door like that, you eejet?" Fergus Cameron barked, stiff and grumpy with sleep.

"We're sorry to wake you, but there's been an accident," Bunny informed him.

"What type of accident?" Fergus studied them with a hefty amount of skepticism, still obviously miffed that he'd been woken from his slumber.

"I don't know how to sugarcoat this, so here it is: Major Scotty MacDonald is dead." Once he'd delivered this news, Giff crossed his arms, cocked his head, and watched the judge's reaction.

"What do ye mean, dead?" Fergus snapped. "He's right next door." He jabbed a petulant finger at the door in question. "That's his room there."

"We know where his room is, and he's not there," Giff told him plainly. "The reason he's not there is because his soulless body is now laying at the bottom of a cliff . . . out there." He pointed a finger in the general direction of the cliff. "Our friend Brett is with the body at this minute, and he knows a thing or two about the dead, having spent a good deal of his life chasing them. By the way, where were you an hour ago?"

"What are you insinuating, sir?"

"Isn't it obvious?" Giff challenged, getting under the man's skin.

"Here!" Fergus shouted, "I was here in my bed! I don't like what you are insinuating. Mr. . . . ghost-hunter person."

"Gifford McGrady," Giff reminded him. "And I am a psychic medium."

"An' my granny's the queen," Fergus snapped, narrowing his eyes at him. He then stepped into the hallway and asked, "How did you get those glasses to fly off the table at you like that? Were you wearing a magnet or something? Pretty good parlor trick."

"He didn't, Mr. Cameron. I can assure you that was real. Bunny MacBride," Bunny said, reminding the judge who she was, should he have forgotten. "We're sorry to wake you, but this really is an emergency."

"Yes," Fergus said, softening his tone. "I know who you are. Very fine meal, Bunny. And I do apologize. You both shocked me. I don't like being pulled from a deep sleep. It ruffles my feathers. And this, if it's true, is terrible news." For the first time since opening his door, Fergus Cameron looked crestfallen. Or maybe it was guilt. Bunny couldn't yet tell.

Just then, Rory Fraser opened his door and stepped into the hallway. It didn't escape Bunny's notice that he was fully dressed, although perhaps hastily so. "I heard the ruckus out here. What's going on?"

Fergus looked at his fellow judge. "They've just told me that MacDonald's dead. That he fell off some cliff."

"What? In the middle of the night? I'm not buying it. MacDonald might be a right uppity bastard, but he's not about to leave his warm bed for a chilly, predawn stroll." Rory shut his door behind him and crossed to the room Bunny and Giff had just investigated. Giff put out a hand to stop him.

"He's not there, Mr. Fraser. He really did go for a predawn stroll. Tell me, is there any reason Major MacDonald would hike out there and play his bagpipes on the top of a cliff in the middle of the night?"

Bunny noted that both men looked troubled by this. Rory Fraser shook his head. "We didn't know him well," he admitted. "However, MacDonald was the type of man whose reputation preceded him, having worked for such an esteemed client as the late queen. Fergus and I travel in the same circles and have competed against one another over the years. More recently, we have worked together judging various piping and band competitions. We know each other's judging style, taste, and what makes an extraordinary bagpiper. MacDonald was his own man," he added with a nod, indicating that the major brought a different set of standards to the competition.

"Would I be correct in assuming that you both were at odds with Major MacDonald regarding the competition?" Bunny asked.

A guarded looked passed between the two judges before Fergus Cameron admitted, "We were at odds. These things happen. We were working it out."

"And we most certainly have nothing to do with his death," Rory Fraser stated. "He was a bit aloof, and maybe not fully present at times . . . distracted like, but we looked up to him. He has an extraordinary gift for the pipes that cannot be overlooked."

"And you have no idea why he would have left his room in the middle of the night to play his bagpipes?"

"Not a clue," Fergus assured them. Bunny wasn't quite so convinced.

"What about bagpipes?" Giff asked. "How many would the major have had with him?"

Both men shrugged. "Likely just one," Fergus answered. "One's all ye need. As judges, we're not called upon to play at the competition, but 'tis good to have one with ye just in case."

"Gentlemen," Bunny said, "it's going to be a long day for you both. Everyone is gathering in the great hall as we speak, awaiting further details from the constable, who has gone to investigate the body. He'll be conducting interviews shortly, I imagine. If there is anything we can do to help with the competition, please let us know. Tea will be served shortly."

"Thank you for alerting us," Rory said.

Bunny watched as the two men returned to their rooms, presumably to finish dressing. She then turned to Giff. "Neither of those men look too broken up by the news of Major MacDonald's death. I find that a little suspicious."

"Agreed," Giff said with a nod.

"Well, are you ready to make tea?"

"Ready as I'll ever be." He wrinkled his nose to let her know what he thought of tea. "Hey, let's put on a pot of coffee too, for us Yanks. No disrespect, Bunny dear, but coffee is our cup of tea."

Chapter 19

Although Giff was no help in the kitchen, which didn't come as a surprise, Bunny still managed to make several pots of tea along with a large pot of coffee. The pots, cups, saucers, mugs, spoons, and a full cream and sugar service were put on a tea trolly. She then ordered Giff to push it into the great hall. Bunny was happy to serve the tea, but once she realized that Brett, Jasper, Doc Beaton, and Constable Craig still weren't back, she decided to head to the kitchen and make herself useful by cooking up a big, hearty breakfast.

"I'll ring Jenny and have her assist you," Elizabeth said.

"Let her sleep," Bunny advised, knowing that the cook had gone above and beyond the call of duty yesterday by helping her in the kitchen, then joining them for the ghost hunt. The poor thing had been tired and left the hunt well after midnight, along with Granny Mac. Bunny knew that the lack of sleep would catch up to her soon, but until it did, she was determined to keep her hands busy.

The moment she stepped into the old kitchen and flipped

on the lights, she let out her breath. She hadn't even realized she'd been holding it. But the tension of the ghosts in the castle and the dead body beneath the cliff, not to mention the two remaining judges and the unfinished bagpiping competition, had gotten to her. The only place to escape the drama, besides passing out into a deep, dreamless sleep, was the kitchen. The kitchen was Bunny's happy place, and having the large, lovely, historic Dundoon kitchen all to herself was just what she needed. Since she was in Scotland, her homeland, her hands were itching to make a full Scottish breakfast. That would keep her busy. Using a clean cloth, she wiped down the butcher-block island counter with warm, soapy water. Once it was thoroughly dried, she took out the bin of flour, found some cold mashed potatoes in the fridge, along with butter, and began making tattie scones, or potato scones, which weren't at all like tea scones. No, tattie scones were flat, round, cut into wedges, then fried in butter. They were perfectly delicious, and no proper full Scottish breakfast would be complete without them.

Once the tattie scones were done and warming in the oven, Bunny began frying pounds and pounds of bacon. To Bunny, the perfect piece of bacon was somewhere between floppy and crispy. A lot depended on the heat of the pan and the amount of drippings allowed to accumulate. She drained the fat often, then placed the cooked bacon on a sheet of kitchen paper to absorb the grease, before putting them into a warm oven. She then cooked sausage links, and Lorne sausage, a beloved Scottish staple, and began frying slices of that to add to the warming oven. She sautéed mushrooms, cooked a pot of beans, and fried juicy, round slices of tomato. She found a loaf of bread and began toasting and buttering that too, because you had to have toast at a Scottish breakfast. Thankfully, she had plenty of orange marmalade to go with it. Cooking like a madwoman, she rummaged through the fridge, looking for haggis, but found black sausage instead. Perfect, she thought, and began frying slices of that as well. As she flipped the black sausage in the pan, she couldn't stop thinking about Major MacDonald. He was an icon in the piping community. If Fergus Cameron and Rory Fraser were to be trusted, they said he acted aloof and often distracted during the competition. A thought popped into her mind, something Jenny had told her. Jasper had found the major snooping around the castle. What was he looking for, if anything? Did that have something to do with why he was out on the clifftop, playing his bagpipes in the fog? Also, was he even playing his own set of bagpipes? Bunny was beginning to doubt that he was. In fact, the more she thought about what they had heard in the fog—the barks, the thumps, the wrestling, the cry, and the final, horrific thud on the rocks below—she realized that nothing was making much sense.

Stick to the facts, she told her sleepy, troubled mind as she gently placed the fried black sausage on a platter and put it in the crowded oven. All that was left were the fried eggs. She wouldn't start those until everyone was seated in the dining room. As everyone knew, eggs were best served hot and freshly made.

Bunny took the eggs from the fridge and placed them on the counter, then began washing the various frying pans she'd recently used. She'd need them for her eggs. Once that was done, she'd head to the great hall and alert everyone to the fact that she was setting out breakfast. She desperately wished that Brett would be back by then.

The moment she thought of him, standing at the kitchen sink with her hands deep in dishwater, the kitchen door opened, and the sound of his voice hit her ears. Her heart leapt.

"I heard you were in here. But, of course, you would be. This is your favorite place in the castle."

With her hands still in the soapy water, she turned and

saw his teasing grin, which faded as fast as it had appeared, revealing a troubled expression. He also looked extremely tired. I must too, she thought.

"I'm so glad you're back," she said, drying her hands on a kitchen towel. "I was worried about you . . . and the others." This she added, not wanting to sound like she'd been pining after him, which she had been a wee bit.

"It smells amazing in here. But it always does when you're in the kitchen. Once again, I find that I'm starving. What am I smelling?"

"A full Scottish breakfast. Under the circumstances, I thought we could all use a good meal."

"You're an angel."

She could see that he meant it, and blushed as he crossed to the island counter. Her mother once told her that the way to a man's heart was through his stomach. At the time, she really hadn't understood what that meant, but staring at hunky Brett Bloom, she was pretty sure she was figuring it out.

"I'm glad to be back in the castle," he admitted, leaning against the island. "It was horrible down there, Bunny. I'll spare you the details, but that poor man." He closed his eyes and shook his head. "I can't fathom who would have done that to him. But somebody did. We all heard it."

"We did," she admitted, recalling the eerie sounds in the fog. She then had a thought. "Tell me, was there a bagpipe with him?" She knew Major MacDonald had been playing one, but she couldn't get the thought of the bagpipe, the one she and Giff had seen in his room, out of her head. The same person who had pushed him over could have recovered the instrument, snuck back to the castle, and placed it back in his room. They would have had enough time to do it. She focused her vibrant green eyes on him, anxious for his reply.

"Yes," he nodded. "It was under him. Why do you ask?"

Bunny lowered her voice. "Giff and I snuck into Major MacDonald's room while the constable and the doctor were on their way to the body. We were the first ones there—"

"Tell me you didn't touch anything."

"Of course not," she said, slightly offended. "As you might recall, this isn't our first rodeo, as you Americans say."

His face darkened, making his vibrant blue eyes seem even brighter. "Don't remind me. This is my third body, Bunny. My third in as many ghost investigations!" He raked a troubled hand through his messy hair, messing it up even more. Bunny was sorry to think that she wanted to run her hand through his hair too. She clasped her hands together, banishing the thought. Brett was overly tired and very upset.

"The first body we found was in Beacon Harbor, Michigan, when we made the mistake of catching it on live feed, airing it to the world on *The Ghost Guys*. That ended our show. Then we narrowly escaped disaster at Bramsford Manor, having the good sense to record and edit the show before airing it. Thankfully, we abandoned the cameras while you wandered off in the middle of the shoot to discover the body."

"I . . . I honestly didn't know that I was about to discover a body," she reminded him.

Brett acknowledged this with a pained look while squeezing his eyes shut. He gave a curt nod. His eyes sprung open again, revealing how troubled he was. "And now this! Another dead body during our second *Food and Spirits* ghost investigation, only he wasn't dead when we heard him playing his bagpipes. Was he? No. This time we witnessed the murder, Bunny!"

"More like heard," she gingerly corrected.

"Is it wrong of me to say that I'm happy it was so foggy? Well, I am. Because the truth is, I don't know what's going on anymore. I really don't. I don't know what a fairy dog is, but everyone else seems to think they're real. I don't know why Major MacDonald was pushed over a cliff while playing the bagpipes. And I really don't want to stare at any more freshly dead bodies. I chase ghosts! I don't want to deal with bodies and murders. Is that too much to ask?" Bunny was about to reply when he cried, "God help me, I'm cursed!"

Bunny could recognize a breakdown when she saw one. Breakdowns happened all the time in kitchens. The pressures of speed and perfection—of perfectly preparing selected ingredients—could be too much for a sous chef or a cook. Even the best chefs had snapped at some point during their careers. Brett Bloom was now in her kitchen—well, technically not her kitchen, but he was there, leaning against the island counter with his head in his hands. She saw his shoulders tremble, as if he was crying, which she knew wasn't at all like him. He was noble, stoic, even when it came to his own feelings. As for the feelings of others, she had learned from personal experience that he ran from the sight of a woman's tears.

She told herself that she was acting on instinct and not longing as she walked over to him and wrapped him in her arms. A thrill rippled inside her as he melted against her, allowing her to hold him. She reveled in the solid feeling of his fit six-foot-four-inch frame. He was far taller than she was, yet he still was able to rest his head on her shoulder. She was just about to run her fingers through his hair when she caught herself and smoothed it instead, cooing, "There now. There now, my wee man, you are not cursed at all."

"I am," he countered, talking into her shoulder, afraid to lift his face. "How else can you explain it?" A minute passed in total silence before he lifted his head and took a step back, breaking the connection. "I'm sorry I got you into this."

His earnest admission made her smile. "Well, I'm not

sorry I'm here. I'm really not, Brett. And I don't think that you are cursed." She had his attention. "My gran likes to say that there are no accidents in life. That everything happens for a reason. Good, bad, weird, cool, fun, or frightening—all our interactions are somehow linked. Granny Mac's old, and I know that old people like to say things like that. She's also pretty woo-woo and spiritually connected. But she might have a point."

"Are you saying that I'm stumbling on dead bodies for a reason?" She could tell he was having a hard time wrapping his head around this.

"Maybe," she ventured, hoping it was true. "Look, being a part of a ghost-hunting reality television show was never on my radar. And yet, somehow, I'm here. I'm still not comfortable being around ghosts and likely never will be, but I needed to be pushed out of my little protective bubble to understand my gifts. Not those of a chef," she clarified. "My other gift. My paranormal gift."

"You would have been happier had you never met me," he said, dejectedly.

"That's not true. Mary Stobart was a bit of a tyrant and would have held me down with her thumb had this opportunity to get rid of me never come along. And you, you chase ghosts. It's your fascination, and you're good at it. When people die, they turn into ghosts. Correct?"

"Technically speaking, the spirit leaves the body upon death. Regarding ghosts, I'm still trying to figure out what they are. Hence this show. Also, I don't mind spooky things. Murder, however, unhinges me."

"I see. Well, have you ever considered that maybe this dead body issue you're having isn't about service to self, as in, how does it help you, but service to others, as in, how you can help them?"

"What do you mean?"

"What I'm suggesting is that on some karmic or spiritual level, the murders happen because you are here."

"You're suggesting that the person about to be murdered is murdered while I'm here because you think I can help them? That's wacked, MacBride, even for you." Although he said this without humor, she could see a smile starting to form on his lips.

"But you *can* help them, Brett. You told me once that you thought a ghost was a soul that was either trapped here due to a traumatic event or that upon death they failed to go into the light. Thanks to you and Granny Mac, I was able to help cross an earthbound soul into the light. Murder is a traumatic death. I'm just learning, but I know we can help these newly departed on their journey. Three bodies during three consecutive investigations, Brett, isn't a coincidence. The universe is speaking to you. To us. We need to help."

Brett leaned against the counter again, frowning as he thought about this. He then looked Bunny in the eyes. "You might be correct, MacBride. We might be able to help figure out who killed Major MacDonald. You mentioned that you and Giff have already searched his room? While Jasper made a call to Winterton, trying to wake him up, I searched his pockets. I found something very puzzling."

Bunny's eyes flew wide in interest. "What did you find?"

"A note wrapped around a weird little object. I'll tell you all about it, but not now. Not here. I say we eat this big Scottish breakfast of yours, then get a few hours of sleep. I don't know about you, but I'm about to pass out."

Chapter 20

Bunny was in the process of laying out the full Scottish breakfast on the sideboard in the dining room when Jenny appeared.

"Why dinna ye wake me?" she asked, staring in awe at the overflowing serving platters on the sideboard. "You've cooked all this! I could have helped." Bunny could see a flash of guilt cross the cook's sleepy face as her eyes softly chided Bunny.

"I couldn't sleep," she told her honestly. "And I didn't want to wake you."

"Aye, I've heard about Major MacDonald. Mrs. Collins woke me and told me the news. Said you were in the kitchen as well. This is just terrible, Bunny, and in the middle of the competition to boot. What's going to happen now?" Bunny shrugged. Jenny, very kindly, took the platter of tattie scones out of Bunny's hands and gently placed it on the sideboard beside the other dishes. She then straightened her rumpled shirt and turned to Bunny again. "I heard you and the lads were out on the moor when he went over the cliff. I never thought ye'd be daft enough to wander beyond the castle walls in the middle of the night, especially knowing there's a fairy dog out there looking for souls to steal." Jenny's large blue eyes grew even larger as she said this. "Glad I missed it. It must have been terrifying for you."

"It was. Utterly terrifying. But the fog was too thick to see anything."

Jenny shook her head. "Ye were all taking a great risk. Why did ye leave the castle in the first place?"

"Because we thought we heard him, the piper of Dundoon."

"Oh, dear," Jenny whispered, looking pensive. "But it wasn't him, was it?"

"We didn't know who it was, because we couldn't see a thing." Bunny thought it best to leave out all details of the fairy dog they possibly encountered in the fog. "Then we heard a scuffle, and the sound of someone falling off the cliff."

"Lord, ha' mercy," Jenny breathed, and crossed herself. "I want to hear everything, but first I'm going to get the Malcoms and their guests to the table. You've been working in the wee hours, and I dinna want this breakfast getting cold."

Bunny agreed, and together they announced that breakfast had been served.

It was a full table, and everyone was grateful for the hot meal. Even Doc Beaton and Constable Craig had joined them, having marched across the moor at sunrise after examining the victim and the crime scene. Although the constable couldn't give out all the details, he was willing to give them the basics. After all, everyone at the castle would be interviewed shortly after breakfast. It didn't escape Bunny that they were quite possibly sitting at the table with a murderer.

Bunny watched as the constable dipped his tatty scone in a golden glob of egg yolk before taking a hearty bite. Beneath the trim auburn hair, his amber-colored eyes scanned the table, as if searching for clues. When they landed on Giff, Giff smiled and read it as an invitation to ask questions. Bunny silently prayed he wouldn't mention anything about searching the victim's room.

"By any chance, do you know if the bagpipes lying at the bottom of the cliff beside the victim were his?" Giff lifted a perfectly trimmed, dark brow in question. "Because we distinctly heard him playing the bagpipes."

Constable Hamish Craig set down his fork and wiped his mouth with his napkin. "That's a good question, Mr. McGrady. The entire area above the cliff and the shoreline below have been cordoned off as the crime scene. Once the fog lifted a measure, we were able to discern on the clifftop above just where the victim had been standing. There are three distinct sets of footprints there, as well as the pawprints of a large canine, possibly a wolf."

"Or fairy dog," Jasper Savage offered, looking pale. "We heard him, sir. We heard him bark three times."

Bunny noted the way Granny Mac was staring at the young man, as if she was reading his innermost thoughts. It wasn't out of the realm of possibility. Granny Mac had certain uncanny gifts. Then, however, she shifted her focus to Bunny, as if knowing that her granddaughter was staring at her. Bunny shrugged. The constable continued.

"While I appreciate a good dose of folklore, Mr. Savage, I'm afraid there was nothing at the crime scene to confirm that the prints came from a fairy dog. A dog, yes. A fairy dog? Likely not, because they don't exist. Now, regarding the bagpipes found at the scene, I believe Doc Beaton can better speak to that."

Doc Beaton was sitting beside Granny Mac, nearly shoulder to shoulder, Bunny noted. What was more, they appeared to be holding hands under the table. Bunny could feel her porcelain skin turning bright red at the thought.

"You see, I play the bagpipes too," the doctor offered proudly. "Been playing since I was a wee lad and have seen my share of instruments." Granny Mac smiled adoringly up at him as he said this. The endearing look caused Bunny to lose her appetite. "Major MacDonald was a professional and the top piper in the land, if not the world. His personal pipes would be heirloom quality, likely from Queen Victoria's time. The wood used on the pipes would be made of ebony. The bag of the pipes would be made of animal hide, commonly sheep or cow. The ferrules would be sterling silver, and likely engraved. The projecting mounts would likely be made of ivory, which is quite illegal to use these days, due to the Trade in Endangered Species Act of 1989. However, the old instruments made before the ban get a pass on the law. That's what makes them so valuable."

Bunny knew that she had pictures of the major's bagpipes on her phone. She'd taken them while in his room and was dying to have a look at them, but didn't dare. That would open a whole Pandora's box of questions she wasn't ready to answer. However, even without looking at the picture, she knew that the fine instrument she and Giff had seen was similar to what the doctor was describing. He continued.

"The pipes lying next to MacDonald were modern, the bag was made of a nylon material, likely Gortex, covered with a cotton plaid for decoration. The pipes were Polypenco, a plastic common in newer instruments, and not the more expensive imported woods, which are still used. The slides were polished nickel, not silver. Granted, the modern great Highland bagpipe made from such materials is cheaper and more durable, especially in inclement weather. When tuned properly, it would be hard to tell the difference in sound. But some can. Not me. No, the pipes found next to MacDonald were not his primary pipes. They could be a second set, but again, a man of MacDonald's profession would have a nicer set than the ones found next to his body." Doc Beaton frowned slightly as he contemplated his next words. He removed his hand from under the table, laced his fingers together, and leaned on his elbows. He looked at Hamish Craig and offered, "Truthfully, I doubt MacDonald was even playing them, but forensics will be able to prove that."

"What?" Bunny blurted. "You think there's a possibility that Major MacDonald wasn't the person playing the bagpipes on the cliff last night?" She had never considered this. "Clearly he was the person who fell to his death . . . with a set of bagpipes in his possession."

"That's all true, Bunny," Brett agreed. "But we never saw who was playing the bagpipes. What we heard was a scuffle followed by a person falling to their death— "

"And the bark of a fairy dog," Jasper ghoulishly reminded them. "A harbinger of death, for sure."

Cody sat up higher then and addressed Doc Beaton. "You say that Major MacDonald might not have been the one playing the bagpipes last night on the cliff? Would you be able to tell by listening to them? We have an audio recording we took last night."

"You have an audio recording from last night?" The constable's interest was piqued. "Why didn't ye say so, lad! We're going to need to confiscate that . . . for the time being. That will be valuable evidence."

"We'd like to listen to that as well," Rory Fraser said, nodding to Fergus, who was sitting next to him. "We're bagpipe judges. We'd be able to tell if it was Scotty MacDonald out there or another."

"Aye, I'd be able to tell as well," Jordy Malcom said with

the confidence of one who'd inherited both title and wealth without ever having to prove himself on the battlefield. "I've got all his albums. Isn't that right, Lizzy?"

Elizabeth choked on a piece of marmalade toast, before smiling at her husband.

It was then agreed that, after breakfast, the lads of *Food & Spirits* would play last night's recording for the constable, Doc Beaton, and the two remaining judges, before handing it over to the authorities for further examination.

As Bunny finished her breakfast and her third cup of tea, she thought about the beautiful bagpipe in the case in Major MacDonald's bedroom and the one at the bottom of the cliff next to his body. It had squealed like a dying animal as it struck the rocks below. What malarky had occurred last night on that clifftop? Was it MacDonald who had played, or another piper, one perhaps startled to find the major there? Had the scuffle been an accident, or had it been planned? And what of the other piper, the ghostly one they had come to find? He had made an appearance last night too. It was something she would never forget. His haunting lament had brought her to tears, and as he played, she believed she understood why. The ghostly piper had played a piper's lament for a kindred spirit. Turning her mind to spirits, she wondered if Major MacDonald was still at Dundoon in spirit form, or perhaps he was a ghost? She really didn't understand the difference; it might be a good idea to probe the ether and see if he was still around. And if he was, perhaps he had unfinished business. She'd need to talk to Granny Mac about it. Just as this thought popped into her head, she felt her grandmother's eyes on her.

Bunny looked up and saw her grandmother nod.

Bunny gave her a thumbs-up, acknowledging the telepathic message loud and clear. However, in her current sleep-deprived state, it hurt her head just to think of ghosts and murder.

"Bunny," Brett said. She hadn't noticed that he'd been standing beside her. "You're about ready to drop off in your chair. Come with me. I'll take you to your room at the White Cottage. We've saved the best one for you."

Chapter 21

Unlike the large, ancient, and frightfully haunted Dundoon Castle, Bunny found the White Cottage utterly enchanting. It was a cozy, white-painted cottage, tucked away down a gravel road half a mile from the castle. She saw that a handful of other holiday cottages were located near it as well and recalled that the ten pipers in the competition were staying in them. Thankfully, it was still early in the morning, too early for the piping to begin. They'd get the shock of their lives upon waking, but she didn't want to think about that now. All she could think of was her bed.

Inside the cottage, Bunny saw that it was light and airy, with hardwood floors, large windows, a charming sitting room, a compact kitchen with an eating area, and three bedrooms on the first floor. A narrow set of steps led to a dormer bedroom on the second floor, where Ed, Cody, and Mike would sleep. Yet, for all its charm, the cottage only had one bathroom, which, Bunny mused, might be difficult given the five men she was sharing the cottage with. However, all thoughts of complicated bathroom schedules faded when she saw the bedroom reserved for her. It was feminine and cozy in all the best ways. The walls were covered in white wallpaper printed with tiny rosebuds. There was a vase of fresh wildflowers on the bedside table and a rose-colored area rug on the floor. Yet it was the bed, covered in a fluffy, white comforter with plump pillows, that called to her.

"Please wake me at noon," she said to Brett, before shutting the door. She kicked off her shoes, threw on a nightgown, and climbed into bed.

"Coffee?" Brett asked, handing Bunny a steaming mug. It smelled like heaven and was just the thing she needed to wipe the sleep from her eyes and the cobwebs from her brain. She had been in such a deep, dreamless sleep, she'd nearly forgotten where she was. The sight of Giff lounging on the couch in the cozy sitting room with his own coffee mug cradled between his hands brought the horrors of last night flooding back to her. She cringed at the memory.

"Morning, princess," he greeted her with a grin. He then scooched over and patted the vacant seat beside him. "Come. Sit. I've been up a whole two minutes before you, so I'll give you the scoop. Brett has something to tell us."

"About the ghost hunt or Major MacDonald's death?" she cautiously asked.

"Both," Brett answered, taking the cushioned chair opposite them. "I mean, they're now connected. Look, I don't like this any more than you do, but we're tangled up in this mess, so it's now in our best interest to untangle it as best we can."

Giff tilted his ruffled head. "That's one way to look at it. Or how about this? We call this one a mulligan and leave. I've been assaulted by the disgruntled ghost of a drunken oaf, a man died, and the piper played. Oh, and there's a fairy dog on the loose. There's a reason the Romans walled off

Scotland. It's too scary. We've got some good footage, Bloom. Let AI do the rest."

For once, Bunny silently agreed with Giff.

Brett, clearly made of stronger stuff, didn't agree at all. "I'm going to pretend you didn't say that, my friend. Dundoon is clearly haunted. That's why we're here. This place is a gold mine of ghosts and bloody history. But more than that, Major Scotty MacDonald, one of the three judges in this highly competitive competition, was pushed off a cliff last night, and I want to know why. Don't you?"

Giff swayed a little on the couch, then shrugged. "I guess."

"Bunny?"

Although her first instinct was to run, she made the mistake of looking into Brett's dreamy eyes. She found herself answering, "Och, aye. I'd like to know. We owe it to him, don't we?"

"Do we?" Giff wasn't quite onboard yet. Not to worry. Bunny knew how to get his cooperation.

"For the late queen," she told him. "The royal family will be ever so grateful."

"You're right, Bun-bun," he sighed and placed a hand over his heart. "This one's for the queen. Okay, Bloom, what did you want to tell us?"

"While Jasper and I were with the body, waiting for the authorities, I checked MacDonald's pockets."

"That's right!" Bunny said, remembering something about that. "You mentioned it to me in the kitchen. You said you found a note wrapped around a weird little object."

"I did. I left it where I found it, but not before taking a picture of it." Brett then pulled out his phone, found the picture in question, and showed it to them. The object in the picture was hard to identify, being small, white, and shaped like a disk. The hand-scribbled note that had been wrapped around it contained only one word, and Bunny was shocked to read it.

"*Brigadoon*," she said, reading it out loud. "Do you think it's a reference to the play about the mythical Scottish village that only appears once every hundred years?"

"Ohmygod!" Giff exclaimed, covering his mouth with his hand. "MacDonald was unhinged! He was playing his pipes, hoping the mythical bridge to the mythical village would appear in the fog. Maybe that white disk is the ticket in? Here's my take. I think he saw the mythical bridge of doon, heard the bark of the fairy dog, grew nervous, and fell to his death trying to cross the bridge."

"Are you listening to yourself?" Bunny chided. "That man was pushed to his death, Giff. We all heard it."

"Fairy dog. Brigadoon," he counted off on his fingers. "Clearly we're in crazy town."

"There's definitely something weird going on, but let's stick to the facts," Brett advised. "We heard a scuffle. Constable Craig thought there were at least two men on the cliff with the major, as well as the prints of some type of dog. Major MacDonald fell to his death, and there was one set of bagpipes that may or may not have belonged to him. Which leads me to my next point. We need to consider a scenario in which the major wasn't the person playing the pipes."

Bunny set down her empty coffee mug and looked at him. "He could have been the person whom we heard walking across the moor. He could have been the one who surprised the bagpiper player, causing the scuffle. Maybe the major meant to push him off the cliff?"

"It's a possibility," Brett said with a nod. "But what is this odd little object in his pocket, and what does Brigadoon have to do with any of this?"

"Could be a reference to the play," Giff remarked. "Maybe he was trying to segue into acting and didn't get the part? Maybe he was bumping off the competition, so to speak. I've known people who'd kill for less. Acting is a cutthroat business."

Bunny and Brett were staring at him, not sure how to respond. Fortunately, they didn't have to. Bunny heard Granny Mac's voice calling from outside the cottage. A moment later, the front door opened, revealing Granny Mac and Jenny.

"Hot toddy, anyone?" Granny Mac grinned as she raised the vintage, plaid thermos in her hand. Jenny was carrying a picnic hamper.

"Glad to see that ye are all awake," Jenny greeted, walking to the kitchen. "After the mornin' ye've had, I thought ye might like some sandwiches and the latest gossip."

"You thought correctly," Brett said, coming to greet the new arrivals. He relieved Granny Mac of her thermos and pulled out five mugs.

Jenny, after casting a wink at Giff, opened the picnic hamper. Giff was beside her in a flash, helping her unpack the roast-beef sandwiches and packets of potato crisps.

"You have some gossip?" he prodded.

"Of course," she cooed. "I live for gossip."

"Me too." Then, extending his hand, Giff invited her to spill the tea.

"The competition's been suspended," she informed them, motioning for everyone to take a plate and a mug of Granny Mac's hot toddy. "Under the circumstances, I don't think they had a choice. There are only two judges left, and they need a third to make it fair. They're trying to work out who it should be. Also, due to the murder, no one connected to the competition is allowed to leave Dundoon yet, including the pipers and the vendors. As for the spectators, they've been asked to make a statement if they believe they've witnessed anything suspicious regarding Major MacDonald's death. Otherwise, they're free to go, if they choose. Most, I hear, have decided to stay because the nation's best bagpiper hasn't been selected."

They were all seated around the kitchen table when Granny

Mac took a meditative sip of her whisky-laced tea. "You all must stay as well, having witnessed this terrible event through the fog. But I don't think it was a coincidence that you were there," she said, focusing her bright green eyes on Brett. "I don't believe in coincidences."

Bunny saw Brett flinch. "Are you suggesting that we were meant to be on that moor when the murder happened?"

"That's exactly what I'm suggesting. Because you were out there in the fog, recording what you heard, Artemus, Constable Craig, and the two remaining judges were able to conclude without a doubt that the man playing the bagpipes on the edge of the cliff last night was not Major Scotty MacDonald. It was another."

Bunny inhaled at the finality of this. "How can they be so sure?"

"Well, aside from other bagpiping intricacies, the glaring fact was that the person playing that particular tune last night had made a mistake. He played it wrong. Everyone agreed that Major MacDonald wouldn't have made such a mistake."

All the blood drained from Bunny's face as she looked at Brett. "If it wasn't the major playing the bagpipes, that means the piper from last night is still alive. We need to find him. How are we going to do that?"

"I say we start with the remaining judges," Brett suggested. "We all know they were at odds, and I want to know why."

"While you and Bunny are doing that, I'm going to look a little closer to home," Giff informed them. "I'd like to ask old Winterton a few questions. After all, he manages the grounds here. He gets around. He might have some insight about who was playing the bagpipes last night. Also, he seems to be the local expert on fairy dogs."

"Good thinking." Brett looked genuinely impressed by Giff's initiative.

"There's just one problem. How do I get to the ghillie hut?" His questioning brown gaze landed on Jenny.

"There is no ghillie hut, pet. The man lives in a cottage." She quirked her lips and flashed a disparaging look. She then took out her phone. "I'll text Jasper to come get ye. Can't have ye getting lost on the grounds. Heaven forbid ye meet a fairy dog out there."

Giff shivered at the thought.

"There is one more avenue I think you must investigate as well," Granny Mac offered, pulling their attention back to her. "The piper of Dundoon. We need to contact him. I think he just might hold the key to what is going on here."

Chapter 22

After wandering the competition grounds, Brett and Bunny finally tracked down the two judges. They were in the judges' tent, which was logical, given that they were judges. However, what they hadn't been expecting was the group of men that surrounded them, including Jordy Malcom.

"Excuse me," Bunny said, entering the inner sanctum of the bagpiping world. The men were standing around a table, talking and arguing about some grave matter. "I don't mean to interrupt, but . . . what's going on in here?"

Jordy Malcom's eyes lit up at the sight of her. "Och, it's the ghost hunters I was telling ye about! Gentlemen, this is Bridget Bunny MacBride, the famous chef, and my friend Ella's granddaughter. Brett Bloom is a renowned ghost hunter, or so they tell me." That got a few chuckles and some guarded glances. "Come on in, you two. I was just telling these fine gentlemen about how ye made that heavenly supper last night, Bunny, right before ye opened the gates of Hell. Ghosts, fairy dogs, and a dead man! What a terrible turn of events. I don't blame ye young ones, of course. How were ye to know? It was a very turbulent night at the castle," he added with a solemn nod.

"Ye were there when it happened?" a short, smartly dressed gentleman in a kilt questioned. Noting the shocked expressions on Brett and Bunny's faces, he extended his hand. "Forgive me. Let me introduce myself. I'm Wes Wexford, president of the Great Highland Bagpiping board. This is just terrible news."

"Brett Bloom," Brett said, introducing himself to the men at the table. "As Jordy has indicated, I'm a paranormal investigator. And I'm afraid that it is true. Our team went out on the moor last night after hearing the sound of bagpipes. We thought it was the ghostly piper of Dundoon—you know, the famous ghost that haunts Dundoon?" Apparently, actual pipers were less impressed with this apparition than he was. "However, it was too foggy to see anything. We heard a scuffle. We heard a man go over the cliff. We are very sorry for your loss."

"Major MacDonald's tragic and untimely death has touched us all," Jordy said. "We have gathered here for two purposes. The first is to elect another judge so that the competition can continue. The second reason is that we are arranging a piper's tribute for Major MacDonald to be held this evening. He was a giant in the piping community."

"That sounds lovely," Bunny said sincerely. She was touched by the thought. "We won't keep you. Brett and I will leave you to it, but first we would like a word with Mr. Cameron and Mr. Fraser in private."

"What's the meaning of this?" Fergus Cameron asked the moment they were behind the tent. "We're in the middle of planning a tribute."

"I appreciate that, sir," Brett said, respectfully. "We would just like to ask you a few questions about your relationship with Major MacDonald."

"What, are ye police now?" Bunny could see that Fergus was ruffled by this. "We don't have to tell ye anything."

"Of course, you don't," Bunny said gently. "We're not the police. But we did host a supper last night, and we couldn't help noticing that there was a lot of unrest in the air between you three judges. We're not suggesting that either of you had anything to do with the major's death. We would simply like to know what you were arguing about."

Fergus shot Rory a guarded look. Apparently, Rory had nothing to hide. He offered, "We disagreed about who should win. I think I suggested that to ye before. You see, the rules of the competition state that all three of us must come to an agreement, but MacDonald insisted that we were favoring the wrong piper. Fergus and I dinna take kindly to that."

"He was a right uppity bastard, that one," Fergus shot out, not bothering to hide his anger. Puffing his full cheeks, he slowly let out his breath and continued in a more civilized tone. "The truth is, I did have a bone to pick with MacDonald. It was years ago, but I too was in line to be the piper to the late queen. As you can imagine, it was stiff competition, but I was favored to win. The job should have been mine."

"What happened?" Brett asked, tilting his head in curiosity.

"What happened?" Fergus repeated. "Och! She chose him instead. Personal preference. Blah-blah-blah!" He waved his hand to indicate what he thought of that.

He was jealous of the major, Bunny thought. Fergus Cameron had never gotten over the fact that Major MacDonald had been chosen by the late queen over him. Clearly, he was a prideful man. But could it have been enough to take revenge on MacDonald after all these years? There was only one way to find out. Plastering a kind smile on her face, she asked, "And how did you two get along here, during the competition? Any bad feelings?"

"Of course, there were bad feelings!" he grumbled. "MacDonald wasn't paying attention to the pipers. He was backing the wrong man."

Rory Fraser stepped in, offering, in a milder manner, "He'd make notes, sure enough, but he appeared distracted. Clearly, his mind was elsewhere."

Bunny made a note of this. Jenny had mentioned to her that Jasper had found the major snooping around the castle. She didn't know where he'd been caught snooping, but when she considered that he'd been distracted during the competition and snooping around the castle, it suggested that Major MacDonald had been looking for something. Then there was that note in his pocket, along with that odd little white disk. Whatever he'd found had been enough to pull him out of his warm bed in the middle of the night and walk across the foggy moorland. Clearly, something was going on, and she believed one of these men, if not both, knew what it was.

"Brigadoon." The random word rolled off her tongue, surprising them all. Brett shot her a questioning look. "Does it mean anything to you? Is it a type of bagpipe, perhaps?"

"As far as I know, it's a mythical village from a play," Rory Fraser said. "Never heard of a Brigadoon bagpipe, but who knows? Maybe Burgess Bagpipe Emporium sell them."

"What is Burgess Bagpipe Emporium?" Brett asked.

"They're a vendor here. One of the largest bagpipe purveyors in the nation," Rory explained.

"Are we done here?" Fergus, having had enough of them, was ready to head back inside the tent.

"Just one more question," Bunny piped up, grabbing his attention once again. "Who was the woman yesterday that pulled Major MacDonald off the pathway as he walked to the castle. She was berating him. Why?"

An uncomfortable look passed between the two judges

before Rory answered them. "Her name is Tabatha Compton. She wasn't berating MacDonald. She was trying to persuade him—ye know, influence his vote."

"Why would she do that?" Brett narrowed his eyes as he looked at them. Bunny recalled that he hadn't witnessed the brazen act by this woman; she had.

"Because, as we've been telling ye, MacDonald was the holdout," Fergus stated, in no uncertain terms. "Rory and I have slated her son, Tommy, to win. The lad deserves it." And with that said, he disappeared inside the tent, pulling Rory Fraser with him.

"Tabatha Compton," Bunny mused aloud, looking at Brett. "We need to speak to her."

Chapter 23

"I don't know why I was picturing Winterton's lair like a hut. You know," Giff prodded, casting the young man beside him a convivial, wide-eyed stare, "like Hagrid's Hut—a circular stone building with a conical roof, sitting like a rocky lump in the vast, rolling wastelands of Dundoon, with a couple of frolicking fairy dogs on the lawn. This," he said, gesturing to the two-story building in front of them with a manicured lawn and garden, "falls firmly in the realm of ordinary. Rather disappointing."

Jasper couldn't help grinning at the thought of a ghillie hut as they walked up the gravel drive to Winterton's cottage. "Aye. It would be something if we had one, but we're fresh out of ghillie huts. Winterton's a very capable man, but a quiet sort. And a bit gruff. If ye like, ye can suggest a ghillie hut to him. Doubtful he'd like it, though. Old Chandler Winterton likes his creature comforts."

"Don't we all," Giff remarked with a lopsided grin. "I'm glad to see his lawn is free of fairy dogs. Nasty things." He stopped just short of the stone landing and looked at Jasper.

"I find it odd that a gamekeeper, or groundskeeper, or whatever he is, believes in them."

"Fairy dogs, ye mean? Why's that?"

"Because, although Winterton is quiet and a bit gruff, he still seems like a sensible man to me. He undoubtedly knows the animals who live in the area. Embracing a mythical creature like a fairy dog not only takes a leap of the imagination; it also suggests that Winterton might not be as sensible as he appears. Either that or he drinks."

"Aye, he drinks." Jasper gave an affirming nod. "As for believing in the fairy dog, that's perfectly normal in these parts. A fairy dog is part of the fairy folk, the old ones. Ye might think it Highland superstition, but to us they're real."

Giff raised a brow at that. He wasn't sure what to believe, having encountered something sinister lurking in the fog last night. It had frightened them all. The fact that it had barked three times just before a man fell to his death only played into his fears. The rational part of his brain knew that there had to be a logical explanation for what had occurred last night. The nonlogical part of his brain, which he was far more comfortable with, tended to believe whatever he was told.

"See all that land over there beyond the fishing pond?" Directly behind Winterton's cottage was a large, meandering pond. Beyond the pond was a seemingly endless landscape of rolling, heather-covered hills, pine forests, valleys, and moorland that reached all the way to the sea.

"All of that belongs to Dundoon?" Giff looked skeptical.

"Aye, it does—"

"Impressive. Truly impressive. Jordy Malcom, the old dog. Living in a rundown old castle when he's land rich!"

"Aye. But my point is, that's forbidden land. No hikers or hunters are allowed on it. 'Tis rife with sinking bogs, deep crevices, caves, and rough terrain. Winterton often remarks how it is the realm of the fairy folk, a race of people similar to you and me, but who live in a universe that's interwoven with ours yet completely separate. They dinna cross into our world much, but when they do, ye have to be on your toes. The fairy dog has crossed into our realm, and now 'tis a real problem." He spoke with such certainty, Giff almost choked.

He stared at the wooden door before them, about to knock, but turned to Jasper instead. "For the sake of this argument, let's say the fairy dog is real. How does one get rid of it?"

"Beats me. I thought ye ghost guys were the experts."

Giff stammered a little, then embraced the role he had created to avoid being unemployed. "Right. We are the experts," he smoothly recovered. "And we're going to get to the bottom of it. Hopefully, Winterton has some useful advice for us." He forced a smile and knocked on the door.

Chandler Winterton was a man who didn't mince words. His unremarkable face was made even more unremarkable due to his stoic lack of expression. He stood six feet tall and was in excellent shape for a man in his late forties, no doubt from all the hours spent working on the estate. His dark hair was sprinkled with gray, and his eyes were a frosty shade of blue that brought to mind glacier ice. He opened the door, looked at the two men standing there, and said with a perceptible lack of interest, "What brings ye here?"

"Tea," Giff replied, poking the man's standoffish nature. "Don't you remember inviting us?" Before the ghillie could answer, Giff was through the door, raking his curious gaze over the cottage. Truth be told, the rustic wood table, the worn leather couch and chair, the old stone fireplace, the faded braided rug on the floor, the dust bunnies, the clutter of tools and gadgets, the messy, outdated kitchen, and all the hunting guidebooks on the bookshelf would have been perfectly suited to a primitive hut. One thing was certain, Winterton was a bachelor.

"I dinna ask ye for tea." His gray eyes flicked to the dish-filled sink, just in case the matter was pressed.

Giff, also looking at the dirty, dish-filled sink, remarked, "On second thought, hold the tea. Can I ask you a question instead?"

Winterton might have been gruff and aloof, but he wasn't a fool. "Och, so that's why you've come. Ye want to ask me a question. Well, out with it."

"As you know, my colleagues and I have come to the castle to investigate the ghostly piper of Dundoon. Last night, on the battlement, we thought we heard him, only the sound of the pipes was coming from outside the castle." Giff made a sweeping gesture with his hand to indicate what he meant.

"Aye, and ye went out there against my warning. Even you," Winterton said, hitting his assistant with his cold-eyed stare. "I take Major MacDonald's death personally. I'm responsible for the grounds here, the safety of them, and now a man is dead because he dinna heed my warning." To his credit, the man looked deadly serious as he talked. It was a side of Winterton Giff hadn't seen. Winterton continued. "There's something dangerous here, lads. I understand that ye have both heard the bark of the fairy dog. I've seen it. Now is not the time to have this competition, but there's nothing for it now. Those grounds out there are full of people. Until I can figure out what's going on, I insist that ye keep to the castle or the White Cottage after dark."

"I'm not going to disagree with you there," Giff was quick to add. "Had I been in charge, we never would have left the castle. But my colleagues felt differently, especially after we heard bagpipes wafting across the moor. Jasper told us that the piper of Dundoon sometimes plays out there. Is that true?"

"Aye, he does," Jasper inferred. "I've heard him many times out there." He looked at Winterton for confirmation.

"Right," Giff interjected. "You also told us the piper

sounds better when he plays out there than inside the castle, which he did. Because the man playing on the moor isn't a ghost. Never has been, I'll bet. So, my question to you, Winterton, is how long has that man been playing the bagpipes out there on the moor in the middle of the night?"

"My understanding, Mr. McGrady, is that the man playing the bagpipes is now dead. As ye well know, 'twas Major Scotty MacDonald playing out there last night, God rest his soul." Winterton crossed himself as he stared at Giff.

"You haven't heard?" Giff tilted his dark head as he stared at the man. "The bagpipe found at the bottom of the cliff with Major MacDonald wasn't his. Also, it's been confirmed by the constable, Doc Beaton, and the two remining judges that Major MacDonald was not the man playing the bagpipes last night."

Obviously, Winterton hadn't heard the news. His face turned as gray as his once-white shirt. "What d'ye mean he wasn't playing? How can they be certain?"

"Because, our excellent team was recording our entire foggy folly on the moor last night," Giff explained. "We were, after all, still investigating the ghostly piper. We caught the piper playing his tune. We also caught a scuffle and the barking of the hellhound. It all sounded Greek to me, but once the authorities took a listen, they were able to determine that it wasn't MacDonald playing the bagpipes."

"What on earth was Major MacDonald doing out there at that time of night?" Winterton's eyes were studying the floor as he thought about this.

"That's what we're trying to figure out. Being the ghillie, you must have some idea of who's been playing out there in the middle of the night."

Winterton looked at Giff and shook his head. "I dinna know who plays out there. Many folks in the area have bagpipes, Jasper and I included. I suppose it could be anybody.

But I've never heard them at that hour. I'm well asleep by then and too far away to be bothered."

"That makes sense," Jasper nodded, before flashing a look at Giff. Giff shrugged. Jasper then asked, "What do ye make of the fairy dog? He was out there last night. We heard him bark three times."

"And a man died," Winterton added gruffly. "'Tis bad business, lads. I'll ask ye again to be careful and to no' wander alone after dark."

"I'm onboard with that," Giff said, then asked one more question. "Does the name Brigadoon mean anything to you?"

Winterton hit him with his icy stare. "Brig o' Doon is a mythical bridge that leads to a Scottish village time forgot. It only appears every so often."

"One day every hundred years," Giff corrected. "Do you believe in it?"

"'Tis fiction," Winterton stated without humor.

"But you do believe in the fairy dog?"

"Until I learn differently, then, aye, I believe in the fairy dog."

Chapter 24

"Fancy meeting you here," Giff teased, appearing beside Brett and Bunny, who were picking up their drink orders at the coffee truck. After his meeting with Winterton, Giff left Jasper to his work and texted Brett. He was told they had another lead, whereas all he had learned from his little excursion was that Winterton had the personality of a tree stump and was a sound sleeper who believed in fairy dogs. It wasn't quite what he'd been hoping for. Bunny picked up two cups, one tall, the other small, and handed the tall one to Giff.

"The pumpkin spice latte you ordered, sir."

"You're an angel," he told Bunny, gracing her with a beatific smile. To Brett, who was staring at him with a questioning look, he quipped, "Don't judge me until you've tried one," before taking a sip.

"How did it go with Winterton?" Brett lifted a blond brow while stirring cream into his black coffee.

"Why do you think I ordered this?" Giff held up the latte, then took another sip. "Nothing like sugar, cream, caffeine, and pumpkin goodness to erase a throbbing trauma like

Winterton." He leaned in and whispered loudly, "He's not what you would call chatty. Frosty and lame's more like it. He goes to bed at a reasonable hour, is a sound sleeper, and believes in fairy dogs. Thanks to Jasper, we know it wasn't the first time someone has played the bagpipes out on that clifftop. But Winterton claims he's never heard them. He's a quiet man by nature. The kind of man who doesn't say more than he needs to. I don't know if I believe him, but there's really no reason why I shouldn't. But enough about me." He waved his hand in the air before asking, "How was your meeting with the two remaining esteemed judges?"

"We didn't get a confession, if that's what you're asking," Brett supplied before taking a sip of his coffee. "However, we did learn that they're planning to honor Major MacDonald tonight in a piper's tribute ceremony. Fergus Cameron and Rory Fraser were spearheading the event. Jordy was there as well, along with the entire pipe-band committee."

"Well, that's good of them," Giff acknowledged. "The competition has ground to a halt, so they might as well keep the pipers busy."

"That's one way to look at it," Bunny replied, offering a wan smile. She had ordered her coffee strong and black, hoping it would carry her through the day. After taking a cautious sip, she added, "I'm still not convinced they're innocent. Although both judges had issues with Major MacDonald—namely, they disagreed on who should win the competition—Fergus Cameron's issues went a little deeper. We learned that he and Major MacDonald were both competing for the same job."

"Don't tell me. The queen's piper?" Giff looked enchanted by the notion. "Bagpipes aside, MacDonald was far easier on the eyes. In other words, who wore it better? He did. The old girl made the right choice . . . God rest her soul," he thought to add, being surrounded as they were by Scotsmen.

"I'd say he's the better piper too," Bunny added, stifling a grin. "But Fergus Cameron is still angry about it."

"We should keep an eye on him. He has motive and means."

"Means?" Brett looked at Giff, waiting for him to explain.

"After Bunny and I searched MacDonald's room, we knocked on Fergus's door. We didn't know it was his door, but we figured it must be one of the other judges. Anyhow, when Fergus answered, he looked like he'd been sleeping, but he could have easily done the deed and hightailed it back to the castle before anyone noticed. Enough time had passed by then. Either one of the judges, or both of them, could have lured MacDonald out there. Both play the bagpipes, and with MacDonald out of the way, they removed the only opposition to their unanimous agreement. By the way, who do they favor?"

"A young man by the name of Tommy Compton," Bunny told him as they began walking down the main thoroughfare, heading away from the parade grounds. "Interestingly enough, I witnessed Tommy's mother, Tabatha Compton, berating Major MacDonald yesterday evening as he was walking back to the castle. She was trying to sway his vote in her son's favor."

"Yikes. Berating the man?" Giff looked shocked. "Major MacDonald didn't look to me like a man who was so easily swayed."

"I agree." Bunny nodded. "And he wasn't, I don't think. The major just stood there like the soldier he was as she pulled him off the walkway by the arm and lit into him like a scorned lover . . . or, more likely, a protective mother. Fergus Cameron and Rory Fraser just continued on their way, as if nothing was happening."

"I wonder if they're in cahoots?" Brett suggested. "Both judges choose this woman's son to win, and then she goes after the one judge standing in her way. Also, would she have been privy to that information?"

"That's a good question," Giff said, pursing his lips as he thought about this. "It was a two-day competition, and MacDonald was bumped off in the wee hours of the second day. Hold up," he said, suddenly reaching into his pocket. He pulled out his phone and found the picture he'd taken in MacDonald's room. "I found his competition binder on the desk. I opened it and took a picture. Looky here." He blew up the picture and pointed to a name at the top of the list. "After adding the day's scores, MacDonald put Jamie Livingston at the top. Tommy Compton is the third on this list."

"That confirms what Fergus and Rory told us. I'm glad you thought to take a picture."

"I wonder why they disagreed with MacDonald?"

"Maybe Tommy's mother can help us understand that," Brett suggested.

"And do we know where this Mommie Dearest lives?"

"We're heading there now," Bunny told him. "According to Rory Fraser, Tabatha Compton is staying in one of the campers in the lower field."

They found Tabatha Compton sitting in a folding lounge chair under the awning of a camper, listening to "Dreams" by Fleetwood Mac on a portable speaker. She was wrapped in a fake-cheetah fur coat to fend off the autumn chill, with a cup of coffee in one hand and a cigarette in the other. Bunny recognized her immediately as the woman who had accosted Major MacDonald yesterday evening.

"Tabatha Compton?" she asked, gingerly stepping under the awning. The woman took a long drag on her cigarette, then blew a stream of smoke in Bunny's direction. "Who's askin'?"

Brett and Giff had kept their distance, standing in the grass beyond the awning, while Bunny greeted the woman. Giff leaned over to Brett and whispered, "Well, doesn't she look fun?"

Brett ignored him.

"I'm Bunny MacBride," Bunny continued. "These are my friends, Brett and Giff." Noting that the men were hesitant to join her, she waved them closer. She waited until their halfhearted greetings were over before continuing. "We're guests at the castle this weekend. As you probably know, Major MacDonald died last night under mysterious circumstances. We're here because I witnessed you having a sharp word with him yesterday as he walked back to the castle. I'd like to know what made you so angry with him."

Tabatha turned off the music and sat up higher in her chair. "Ye want to know why I was angry with him? That's easy, luv. Because he was a pigheaded man." She crushed her cigarette into the ground and stood. "Got any more questions?" she challenged.

Whoa, Bunny thought as Tabatha got in her face. This woman was a bully. However, Bunny wasn't so easily deterred. She had faced her share of bullies before in the kitchen. She steeled her nerves, held her ground, and said, "We know that your son, Tommy, has the backing of the two remaining judges. I find it interesting that you would accost the one judge who felt differently. It didn't look like Major MacDonald was easily swayed, and now he's dead. Where were you last night between the hours of two and three-thirty in the morning?" There, she had said it. However, it wasn't helping that Tabatha was glaring at her as if she wanted to wring her neck. Then, however, the faux cheetah fur–clad woman did something unexpected. She burst into a scathing cackle.

"What business is it of yours where I was? Ye are no cop. I dinna have to tell ye nothin'."

Giff nudged Bunny aside and swooped in. "Darling, of course you don't," he soothed, flashing Tabatha his winning smile. "How silly of us. We're not the police. What we are is paranormal investigators. Our focus is not on the living, but the dead. And that's why we're here. Major Scotty MacDonald, God rest his soul, is very out of sorts in the afterlife. He's not moving on. He's got . . . issues."

Tabatha's brown eyes were wide and unblinking as she stared at him. "You're talking rubbish," she said with a hint of question. Obviously, she was willing herself to believe it.

Giff shrugged. Then he froze in his tracks. In a movement that shocked everybody, he thrust his open hand toward her, as if willing her to stop. "Whoa there. It's coming to me. You, madam, have a deeper connection to Major MacDonald!" He made an imaginary circle in the air in front of her. Tabatha yipped and dropped her coffee mug; it shattered on the ground.

"How . . . did you know?" she stammered.

"Because, silly, he's here with us." Giff was in full acting mode, and Bunny silently applauded him. Tabatha, believing in his abilities, was growing visibly nervous.

"Ye are lying," she said, forcing a smile. Her smile wavered. "Aren't ye?"

"I'm afraid he's not," Brett offered. He then handed her his phone. "You should probably read this."

"World renowned medium and fashion icon . . . ?" She looked up from her phone and stared at Giff. "This is you?"

"In the flesh," he said, and bowed.

Looking troubled, she handed the phone back to Brett. She looked at Giff and said, "Ye are really a medium, as in ye can talk to the dead?"

"Yes. And to answer your next question, yes, it is a curse." Giff placed a hand over his heart and made a face that relayed deep personal pain.

"That wasn't my next question," she told him.

Giff waved a hand. "Next. Third. Fourth. My point is, it was coming."

"I dinna know that it was," she said, with a healthy amount of skepticism.

"Trust me. Now, your son, Tommy." That was all he had. He ended there, hoping she would pick up the sentence, telling them something they didn't know. Unfortunately, she wasn't playing along yet.

"What about Tommy?"

Giff focused on a space above her left shoulder, then nodded. "Major MacDonald is saying that you need to tell us what you told him."

"That . . . Tommy should win?" she questioned. Giff nodded, encouraging her with his welcoming gaze to elaborate. Thankfully, she did. "He knew it too. My boy deserves to win this competition. Tommy's worked hard for this. We dinna have much. I'm a single mom trying to raise a son. What little I do have I spend on Tommy and his lessons. Winning this competition would change his life for the better. Scotty knew it too, and instead he chose—"

"Jamie Livingston," Giff added, surprising her.

"How did ye know that?" Tabatha looked a bit frightened.

"How did *you* know that?" he threw back at her. "No one but the judges were privy to that information, especially on the day before the final event in the competition. That speaks of collusion." Giff flashed a look at Brett and winked. After all, Brett had been the one to suggest that Tabatha and the judges might have been in cahoots.

"There is no collusion," she insisted. "I knew by the way he was looking at Jamie as the lad played. I knew because that bastard, Scotty MacDonald, was trying to punish me."

Giff clapped his hands together and declared, in an *a-ha!* moment, "Because you were lovers!"

"Because I told him that Tommy was his son," she corrected.

No one had been expecting this. Bunny's mind was reeling with possibilities, while Giff was still stuck on, "So, you *were* lovers."

"It was a long time ago." She frowned slightly at the memory.

"And how did Major MacDonald take the news?" Giff ventured.

"You tell me." She crossed her arms, looking fit to be tied.

"Not well?" he shot back a little too quickly. "Yes, I can see that now. Not well. So . . . is Tommy MacDonald's son?

"There's a very strong chance he is. After all, Tommy dinna get his musical gifts from me."

"But . . . you don't have proof?" Giff found this a little unsettling.

"I have Tommy. He's all the proof I need. I'm curious," she added, tilting her head while staring at Giff. "What does he say about it now that he's dead?"

"Ah . . . let me ask him." Giff crossed his arms and stared off into the middle distance. A moment later, he shook his head. "I've got nothing. You probably should have had a paternity test done. Why didn't you?"

Because she was afraid to, Bunny thought, when Tabatha didn't answer. Tabatha had told them enough, and what she had revealed, Bunny found disturbing. Mothers wanted the best for their children, and sometimes those mothers took extreme measures to get it. There was one more question left, and Bunny was determined to ask it.

"Thank you for telling us this, Tabatha. I know how difficult this must be for you. You wanted Major MacDonald to acknowledge Tommy for his musical gift, one he might have inherited from him. But he wouldn't do that, at least not at that time. And now he's dead. You do understand how this looks?" Tears began to form in Tabatha's eyes as she nodded. "Where were you last night between two and three-thirty in the morning?"

Tabatha dried her eyes with the sleeve of her cheetah coat. "I was here in my caravan."

"Can anyone corroborate that for you?"

Tabatha suddenly grew red with embarrassment. "Aye, Seth Burgess can. We had a few drinks together last night and fell asleep. He left this morning." She fumbled in her coat pocket, took out a pack of cigarettes, pulled one out, clamped it between her thin lips, and lit it.

Seth Burgess. The name sounded familiar to Bunny, but she couldn't quite place it. Thankfully, Brett was thinking along those same lines as well.

"Where might we find Mr. Burgess?" he asked.

Tabatha took a long drag on the cigarette and slowly blew it out, looking better for having the nicotine flowing through her veins. "At his tent, Burgess Bagpipe Emporium, I expect. They're the largest bagpipe emporium around. Tommy plays one of their instruments."

With all this new information buzzing around in their heads, Bunny, Brett, and Giff thanked Tabatha and took off once again in the direction of the fairgrounds.

Chapter 25

"It looks to me like we might have a real *Mamma Mia* situation on our hands," Giff informed them as they marched along the gravel road. "You know, one lady, three possible baby daddies. It's a real head-scratcher. I suggest we get a DNA sample and figure this out."

Bunny stopped in her tracks. "Three baby daddies? That's a leap. And we're not getting a DNA sample. We're not the cops. And we're certainly not taking a sample from a dead man."

"Dear Bun-bun, where's your sense of adventure?" he chided, with a mocking twinkle in his eyes.

"My sense of adventure is limited to the kitchen, thank you very much," she snapped. Then, noticing the way Brett was looking at her, she added, ". . . and maybe other places too. But not swabbing the cheeks of the recently dead. No, Gifford. We need to keep our nose to the trail and follow the leads. We need to talk with Seth Burgess to see if Tabatha was lying."

"Why would she lie about a man staying with her in her

camper?" Brett flashed Bunny a questioning glance. "If you ask me, she looked embarrassed by it."

They had just made it to the main thoroughfare, which was lined with booths and food trucks. They continued weaving through the crowds of people, searching for the tent of Burgess Bagpipe Emporium, when Bunny heard her name. She stopped and turned in the direction of the sound. That's when she spied her mother, brother, and father standing at the counter of the fried Mars bar food truck.

"Bunny. Brett. Gifford. Halloo," Maggie MacBride called out again, waving them over to where they stood.

Davie, preoccupied with the short menu, turned around and smiled at the sight of his daughter and her friends. Turning back to the man in the window, he said, "Add three more of those fried bad lads to my order, if ye will."

"Good man," the cashier said with a wink and swiped Davie's credit card once again.

"It's so good to see you, dear." Maggie ran up to her daughter and gave her a big hug. After greeting Brett and Giff, she added, "We heard about Major MacDonald. What a tragedy. Your father is in mourning," she added, gesturing to the food-truck window. "Comfort food."

"Poor Dad," Bunny cooed, exchanging a morbidly comical look with her brother. Regaining her composure, she offered, "It is a tragedy. Unfortunately, we were out on the moor when it happened."

"You were there?" Angus asked, in a voice tinged with skepticism. "Why were you out on the moor at that time of night?"

"Because, dear brother, I not only cook for a ghost, but I help find them too."

"You were looking for a ghost out on the moor?" He was trying to wrap his head around that.

"Aye. I told you back home. We're here to find the

ghostly piper of Dundoon Castle. We heard the bagpipes coming from outside the castle last night and went to investigate. As you now know, it wasn't a ghost playing those bagpipes, but a man."

Davie joined them and began handing out the fried Mars bars.

"Dad," Bunny chided, taking the little basket that contained the battered and deep-fried candy bar. "You know these aren't good for you."

"Of course, they're not. That's the point of it, m'dear. Even the Mars candy company has taken steps to distance themselves from this delicious abomination we Scots have created out of their humble candy bar, stating that batter-coating and deep-frying their candy bar doesn't align with their commitment to a healthy lifestyle." He shook his head. "A candy company said that. What eejets! But to your point, Bridget, I told myself yesterday that one is all I'm getting. However, in light of this terrible news regarding the death of a national treasure, myself is allowing me one more."

"Here-here!" Giff applauded and took a bite of his Mars bar abomination. The moment he did, he let out a little moan of delight. It was surprisingly delicious.

As they sat at a picnic table eating their gooey treats, Bunny, Brett, and Giff told them all they knew about what had occurred last night on the foggy moor. Bunny learned that Granny Mac had called her folks this morning with the news. She could see that her father was taking the death of Major MacDonald very hard.

While the men were talking, Maggie whispered near her daughter's ear, "Do ye have any premonitions about who the murderer is, dear?" Unfortunately, her father heard the question as well.

"Dinna ask her such barmy questions, Maggie. Bridget is wise, no' clairvoyant. Dinna confuse the two. Clairvoyance is a sham." He gave a nod to the gentlemen and leaned in closer. "My mother claims to be quote-unquote clairvoyant to amuse her friends. Makes her popular at parties."

"Dad," Bunny said, hoping to change the subject, "you play the bagpipes. Maybe you can help us with something." That got his attention. "Brett has a picture of an odd wee object that he found in Major MacDonald's coat pocket this morning. I'm wondering if you might know what it is?"

On Bunny's cue, Brett pulled out his phone and showed Davie the object in question. Angus leaned in as well. Both men seemed to recognize it immediately.

"That's a projecting mount," Angus offered. "A right fine one at that."

"Aye, 'tis. They are mostly decorative on a bagpipe, but they also serve to protect the wood of the drone from splitting where it attaches to the tuning slide," Davie informed them. Bunny, not sure what a drone was, nodded anyway. "Why do ye suppose he was carrying that in his pocket?"

Brett then told them about the note found with the object. They were all puzzled by what it might mean. Then Angus spoke up.

"Now that ye mention it, I remember something odd about yesterday. I was at the Glenlivet tent, waiting to purchase a couple shots of whisky for Da' and me, when I saw Major MacDonald talking with another man. But it didn't seem like a normal meeting. Two things struck me as odd. The first is that they were behind the Glenlivet tent. I saw them through a wee flap in the back. The other was that the man MacDonald was talking to was dressed in a black suit. He looked very out of place at an event like this."

"The dude in the black suit?" Giff questioned. "I saw him yesterday, too."

"Where?" Bunny asked.

"I was inside the tent that sells kilts," he explained. "Once

I spent enough money, the nice man working there showed me how to play a few notes on the bagpipes. He had the patience of a saint."

"So, that's how you did it!" Bunny exclaimed, remembering his bizarre act last night during the spirit supper. "The spirit didn't move you. A man taught ye how to play those notes!"

"You found me out," he said, placing a hand over his heart. "I can't keep my secrets of the trade a secret from you, Bunbun. Remember," he added, leaning over to Davie, "I just play a medium on the show. Clairvoyance is a sham." He winked, then continued. "I recall the man in the black suit because he stood out due to his lack of plaid. He looked out of place as he slinked along the alley behind the tents."

"I wonder what they were talking about," Maggie offered. "It could be important to this case." She looked at her daughter and gave another clandestine wink. Bunny wished her mother didn't look so excited by the prospect of her and the lads hunting down a murderer.

"Well, should he turn up again, ye should ask him why he's here," Davie suggested.

"We'll be on the lookout for him," Brett assured them. "By the way, does anyone know where we might find the tent for the Burgess Bagpipe Emporium?"

"Aye." Angus grinned and pointed his finger over their heads. "'Tis the one with the big banner across it proclaiming Burgess Bagpipe Emporium. It also happens to be right next to the entrance of the competition grounds. They always have a big presence at these competitions. They sell bagpipes of all sizes and price ranges. I bought my own set there a couple of years ago. If ye are all done with your wee treats, I'll take ye there now."

"Thank you for the fried Mars bar, Dad." Bunny gave her father a kiss on the cheek. She hugged her mother, promising she'd keep her posted on any new revelations in the case regarding Major MacDonald. She also promised she'd visit them soon. Before she left to follow Angus, she had one more question for her father.

"Dad, did you know Gran is seeing a doctor?"

Davie laughed. "Why, at her ripe old age, I certainly hope she is!"

Chapter 26

Once the Burgess Bagpipe Emporium tent was in sight, Bunny waved the lads ahead and dropped back to have a word with her brother.

"Does Dad know that Gran is seeing someone?"

Angus let out a little chuckle at the question. "The doctor, ye mean? Aye, he knows. He's just having a wee bit of fun with ye, is all."

"Is he okay with Gran seeing him, a younger man?"

The smile faded from Angus's lips as he replied, "Granddad's been gone a long time now, Bunny. At first, I think Da' had a hard time with it, but he wants his mum to be happy. What about you. Are ye happy?" The concerned look in his eyes melted Bunny's heart.

"I am, for the most part. Thank you for asking. And . . . what about you, brother? Are ye happy?"

"Aye, I am. But I worry a great deal. 'Tis my job to worry. That's what men do. Worry. I worry about Mum and Da'. I worry about Pippa. I worry about being a father."

"Wait," Bunny stopped him. "Is Pippa pregnant?" Her

eyes glittered with hopeful expectation. When Angus gave an affirming nod, Bunny cried, "That's wonderful news! I'm going to be an aunt! You're going to be a father! Angus, why didn't you say something to me about this before now?"

"Well, I'm telling ye now, aren't I? But I'm not finished, Bunny. I worry about ye too. What were ye doing out on that moor so late at night? Ye told us you were the chef on the show."

"I am. That's true. But there's a little more to it than that. Can you keep a secret?" She wasn't sure she should tell him about her gifts. She wasn't sure how he'd react. However, Angus was her brother, her only remaining brother, and she felt he deserved to know the truth about why she had gone out on that foggy moor in the wee hours.

"Aye, I'm good at keeping secrets," he said, with a hint of suspicion.

Well, here goes nothing, Bunny thought, and crossed her fingers. "Here's my secret. I have psychic gifts, just like Granny Mac."

"Funny," he said, and nearly chuckled. For some reason, Bunny was annoyed.

"Not funny, Angus. 'Tis not funny at all, because it's the truth. Sometimes the dead talk to me."

"Ye're pulling my leg, now. I suppose I deserve it for the way I went after ye back at the house. Ye got me, Bunny."

"Angus, listen to me. I'm telling the truth. It started shortly after Braiden died. I started seeing him."

"Wait. Ye are serious? I thought in Gran's case it was all an act. Are ye telling me 'tis real?" His face was so contorted with skepticism, Bunny almost laughed.

Apparently, relaying this little secret of hers was going to be harder than she thought. A fleeting part of her wished she'd never bothered. But she had stepped in it with both feet this time, and there was no going back now. She took a deep breath and said very plainly, “Braiden appears to me. That’s why I went to New York. Yes, I was following his dream to become a famous chef, but I was also trying to escape the ghost of him. I was afraid of what was happening to me, Angus. ’Tis not a pleasant thing, seeing or feeling ghosts. I was avoiding it. I didn’t want to face it, and the irony is, it was working.”

“What happened?” he asked, noting that she was very serious now, so serious it frightened him. Great, one more thing to worry about, Bunny seeing ghosts. His list was getting way too long.

“What happened, ye ask?” She gave an ironic shrug of her shoulders before stating, “I foolishly signed a contract that landed me on a food-baiting ghost-hunting show. That’s what happened, brother. It was sold to me as a travel cooking show, for all love. And I believed it. Look,” she waved her hand, “that’s all water under the bridge now. I’m happy doing this. I adore the lads I work with. But here’s the thing, Angus; because of my gifts, I was out on the moor last night trying to connect with the ghostly piper of Dundoon. Instead, we overheard a man being pushed off a cliff. Very disturbing any way you look at it.”

“Ye were trying to connect with the piper of Dundoon?” Angus was still trying to wrap his head around this.

With a surrendering gesture to the sky, she added, “That’s what I do. I cook, and I converse with ghosts.”

“That’s messed up.” She didn’t disagree. Noting she was being entirely serious, Angus asked, “What . . . does he look like, Braiden? Lord, Bunny, I’d give anything to see our brother again. Ye can really see him?”

Noting that Brett and Giff were inside the Burgess Bagpipe Emporium tent talking with a large, burly man, Bunny swiftly told her brother about Braiden appearing as Hopper. She told him how Granny Mac was helping her cope with her gifts. Poor Angus. He had so many questions, most of which she couldn't answer herself.

"Thank you for telling me all this," he said. Bunny noted that his prior skepticism had now morphed into a troubling pensiveness. She was sorry to think that skepticism suited him better. "Listen, please be careful. There's a person out there who pushed a man to his death. 'Tis dangerous. Call me if ye need me. I'm serious, Bunny. Call me. I'm so glad ye've come home."

"Bunny, this is Seth Burgess," Brett greeted her, introducing the large, thickly built, slightly balding, middle-aged man they'd been talking with. Bunny noted the twinkle in Seth's eyes as they rested on her, making her feel slightly uncomfortable. "Seth is the owner of Burgess Bagpipe Emporium," Brett continued, unaware of the look. "He's a bagpipe aficionado. Knows everything there is to know about the instrument. He's been showing us around his impressive pop-up shop. Look over there," he said, pointing to a rack a few feet away. "They have a whole basket of projecting mounts." Brett cast her a knowing look before excusing himself to investigate.

"Pleasure to meet you, Bunny." Seth took her hand and didn't let go. Bunny began to panic in earnest when she realized that the man was intent on bringing her hand to his thick, glistening lips.

Who did that anymore? she thought in disgust. Only lords and lechers, of course. And this man was clearly no lord. "*Boop!*" she said, yanking her hand from his grasp. Answering his affronted look, she glibly lied, "I have a saliva sensitivity. Can't be braking out in a rash right before making supper, now can I?"

"Forgive me. I was merely trying to be courteous. 'Tis not every day such a beautiful lady walks into my shop. Is this your first visit to the piping competition?"

Noting that Brett was preoccupied with the projecting mounts, Giff came to her rescue. "It is," he said, wrapping his arm around Bunny's shoulder in a brotherly hug. "Nice pipes. Impressive collection."

"The best in Scotland," Seth added with the air of a challenge.

"Right. I'll take your word for it."

"Are ye and your friend over there in the market?" The way he lifted one of his unruly eyebrows made Bunny wonder just what market he was referring to.

"Not at all," Giff assured him with an air of indifference. "We're good friends of the laird." He lowered his voice and added, "We're helping Jordy with a troubling matter."

"Troubling matter? Ye wouldn't happen to be talking about the unfortunate death of Major MacDonald, now, would ye? God rest his soul." The portly bagpipe purveyor made the sign of the cross without removing his probing brown gaze from them.

Giff grinned at the man as he tapped the side of his nose. "Nothing slips by you, does it?"

"Very little," he agreed, tossing Bunny a wink.

This was too much. Bunny knew that Giff could make small talk all day. Brett, she noted, had wandered to the back of the tent. He reminded Bunny of a hungry child in a sweetshop, as he stared at the staggering array of bagpipes lining the walls. Quite frankly, Seth Burgess gave her the creeps. It was time to take the bull by the horns, so to speak. "The reason we're here, Mr. Burgess is that we were just talking with a friend of yours, a woman named Tabatha Compton."

The prickly, gray eyebrow rose even higher on his brow at the mention of the name, validating for Bunny that he at least knew the woman. "And what did she say, now?"

"That you spent the night with her," Bunny stated, looking to see how he'd react to that bit of news. She hadn't expected the lecherous grin to appear so willingly.

"Just like Tabby to brag. Well, the old girl makes good company on a chilly autumn night, if you know what I mean."

"I'll bet." Giff offered a conspiratorial grin. "And you were with her the whole night—until *dawn's early light*?" Giff, channeling his proud American voice, sang these last notes.

Unfortunately, Seth bristled at the question. "Why are ye so interested all of a sudden in my nocturnal dealings, young man?"

"I've already told you. We're looking into the troubling matter of Major MacDonald's death."

That's when Brett swooped in. Apparently, he had gleaned everything he was going to from the bagpipe shop. "We're paranormal investigators," he stated proudly. Bunny wasn't so certain that was the best thing to lead with.

"Did ye say paranormal or private investigators?" Seth looked confused.

"Yes," Giff said. "Answer the question, please. What time did you leave?"

"An hour or so before dawn. Why? Do ye suspect her of wrongdoing?" His eyes darted between the three faces staring intently at him. He didn't like that one bit.

"We're not sure," Bunny told him. "However, we know that her son, Tommy, is doing quite well in the competition. Two of the judges favor him. Yesterday evening, I witnessed the one judge who didn't favor him get a berating from her. That judge is now dead. Now we find out that you were with her last night but left sometime before dawn. You understand how this looks?" Bunny noticed that Seth's face had gone white. He waved them farther away from listening ears.

"Look, I'm going to be honest with ye. Tabatha has big plans for her son. That's not a secret. She's an ambitious woman. Tommy's a gifted lad, but they cannot afford the type of instrument the top pipers play. Ye see, a piper at that level is not only judged by his skill on the pipes, but also on the quality of the instrument he plays. Most grand pipers play with historic sets, handed down from one generation to the next. If not, they buy a rare set for a hefty sum. Poor Tommy is not so lucky. However, his mother and I have worked out a wee deal so that Tommy could have a grand set to play during the competition. 'Tis grand to see him doing so well."

"You and Tabatha worked out a deal? What type of deal?" Bunny eyed the man suspiciously.

"The only kind she can afford," Burgess stated with a leering grin. "Like I said, Tabatha is an ambitious woman. I can vouch for her whereabouts last night. Mine too. Any more questions?"

"Yes," Giff said. "Did she happen to mention to you anything about Tommy's father?"

"Tommy's father? Didn't know that there was one."

"Come now," Giff chided. "Everyone has a father."

"Aye," Seth seethed, "I know that. I've known Tabatha for some time now. What I mean is, she's no stranger to bagpiping competitions. A bit of a groupie, I'd say. I don't think she's ever been married, but she does have a type. And that type plays the bagpipes."

"Got it," Brett said. "Thank you for your time. If you think of anything else, please let us know." Brett then handed him his card as he ushered Bunny and Giff out of the tent.

"Paranormal investigator?" Seth Burgess called out after them. "It says on this card that you're a ghost guy!"

Chapter 27

"That man gives me the creeps," Bunny said as they headed into the parade grounds. There were a few people seated in the bleacher seating, watching a handful of pipers, who were paired with drummers, practicing for the evening's tribute. As Bunny and the lads headed toward a group of empty seats, she added, "Taking advantage of a woman like that. I can only imagine what sort of unholy payment he talked her into."

Brett took a seat beside her. "Burgess is clearly an opportunist. But you have to consider that Tabatha was willing to pay his price. I never knew that bagpiping competitions were so cutthroat."

"Well, I don't trust either of them," Bunny said, staring at the pipers and drummers on the field. The discordant noise was giving her a slight headache. "Was I the only one who found it odd that Seth wasn't clear about the time he left Tabatha's caravan? He said it was an hour or two before dawn. That's a large time window. Tabatha could have easily set up a clandestine meeting with Major MacDonald, walked from her caravan to that clifftop, then pushed the unsuspecting man to his death. For all we know, Seth Burgess could have been with her, playing the bagpipes."

"It's plausible," Giff added with a nod. "But here's another scenario to consider. What if it was Tommy on that clifftop playing the pipes and not Seth Burgess? MacDonald receives a note or an invitation of some type to speak with Tommy. After all, Tabby is under the belief that he's her baby daddy. When MacDonald shows up to talk with Tommy, she pushes him off the cliff. I mean, with a she-wolf of a mother like Tabby, anything's possible, right?"

"These are both worth considering," Brett agreed, leaning across Bunny to look at Giff. "But it doesn't explain the note in MacDonald's pocket, or the fact that he was carrying a projecting mount. Also, if you'll remember, no one spoke a word out there. There was a piper, a struggle, and the barking of a possible fairy dog. How does it all fit together?"

"I'm not sure," Bunny admitted. "However, if you consider that Tabatha and her son stand the most to gain from MacDonald's death, it puts her in the running for murderess. With MacDonald out of the way, Tommy has the best chance to win the competition. Good for Tommy. There's likely prize money and accolades to go with winning. Good for Tommy, and Tabatha. Regarding Seth Burgess, I'm not sure there's any benefit to him. If Tommy gets the money needed to pay for his fancy set of bagpipes, then his mother's debt to Seth would be paid off in full. In other words, she'd be free of the creep."

"True," Brett said. "But I still say we keep Seth Burgess on our suspect list. I'm going to play devil's advocate here, but if Tabatha truly believes that MacDonald is Tommy's father, why would she want him dead?"

For a ghost-hunting enthusiast, Brett had a way of cutting through the noise regarding murder suspects. Bunny cast him an appreciative glance before stating, "She wouldn't . . . unless MacDonald was holding something over her head."

"Like not choosing her son to win the competition?" Giff suggested. "That, my friends, brings us right back to the beginning. Two judges favor Tommy Compton. One favored Jamie Livingston, and now that judge is dead." He forced a huff, causing his warm breath to ruffle the perfectly styled swag of dark hair on his forehead. "Is one of these pipers truly better than the other? Or is it a matter of taste? Or, better yet, is one of them paying off the judges? I say we ask them ourselves. Now's our chance. Looks like things are wrapping up on the field, thank heaven."

After inquiring with the steward, who kept track of each piper in the competition, they learned that Tommy Compton wasn't playing on the field, but Jamie Livingston was. They found the piper in question sitting on a sideline bench with his head bent, his bagpipes beside him, and his bonnet clutched between his hands. For a man at the top end of the competition, Bunny thought he looked deeply troubled.

"Excuse me, Jamie?" she ventured. At the sound of her voice, the piper lifted his head. He looked to be in his mid-thirties, Bunny thought, with a strong, handsome face that was partially covered by a closely trimmed, chestnut-colored beard. It was a perfect match to the hair on his head, which was also nicely trimmed and styled. Bagpipe music aside, Bunny was ashamed to think that had she been one of the judges, Jamie's strong, manly appearance would launch him right to the top of her list to win. Thankfully, she wasn't a judge. She silently cursed herself for being so shallow. When she realized he was waiting for her to speak, she offered shyly, "You're . . . really good with those things." To illustrate what she meant by *things*, she pointed to his bagpipes. Crivens! What was she doing? And with Brett and Giff beside her, no less. Noting that Jamie Livingston was now staring at her with an expression that bordered on pity, she rapidly fired, "We'd like to ask you a few questions. That won't be a problem, will it?"

Jamie eyed them skeptically. "Are ye reporters?"

"No, we're ghost hunters," Brett clarified with a hint of misplaced zeal. Before Jamie could excuse himself and head for the exit, Brett placed a hand on his shoulder. "It's about Major MacDonald. We were out on the moor last night when the accident happened."

That got the man's attention. "Ye were there? Ye saw MacDonald go over the cliff? For the love of God, why didn't ye stop him?"

Giff clapped his hands like the fun-loving medium he was. "Let's back up a moment, shall we? To clarify what my esteemed ghost-hunting colleague just said, we were on the moor chasing ghosts. Don't look so surprised. Not everyone has musical talent. What lured us out there in the first place was the sound of bagpipes."

The piper raised a chestnut brow in irony. "Why, I'd think you'd hear the sound of bagpipes everywhere around here. That's the point of being here during the most prestigious piping competition in the country."

"Not at three-thirty in the morning," Brett said, crossing his arms. "We're here to investigate the ghostly piper of Dundoon. We thought we heard him."

"Come again?" Jamie Livingston clearly didn't know what to make of this.

Feeling there was no need to dwell on the folly of chasing a ghostly piper, Bunny jumped in. "It was too foggy to see anything, but we did hear a scuffle, followed by the sound of a man falling to his death. As you can imagine, it was quite terrible. We now know that man was Major Scotty MacDonald. How well did you know Major MacDonald?"

"Not very," Jamie said, looking glum. "Major MacDonald

was well known in the piping community. He was an inspiration to me. I looked up to him. We all did. I can't believe something like this could happen to him."

"Are you aware that Major MacDonald put you in the lead to win this competition?" Giff focused his probing gaze on the piper as he said this.

"No." The piper looked more humbled than elated as he gripped the bonnet between his hands tighter. He then took a deep breath, letting the information sink in. "I'm honored. Truly. However, just because I scored well on day one of the competition doesn't mean I'm going to win the whole thing. 'Tis a bit more complicated than that. Also, how did ye know this? The judges haven't announced anything yet."

"So, this is news to you." Giff found that interesting. They all did.

Bunny cleared her throat. "The only reason we know is because the other two judges admitted as much to us."

"Also, I saw his competition notebook," Giff admitted with a mischievous grin. "Are you telling us that this isn't the usual way piping competitions are judged?"

"This is your first competition." The piper eyed the three ghost hunters wearily. "Look, competitions like these can run in a couple of ways, depending on the particular competition. Larger ones are structured by different skill levels. The top few pipers in each level advance to the final, usually held on the second day of competition. Every piper on every level is graded on three major things, the first being the quality and sound of his bagpipes. The bagpipes ye play have a huge bearing on your score. The second is how well ye play the grace notes, which are those short, ornamental notes played just before the main note. They add a touch of flourish and flair to the melody without affecting the rhythm or timing of the tune. It's personal style," he added with a bob of his head. "The third thing one is graded on is how well the music is played. A piper is judged on accuracy, rhythm, and the tone of the piece. We all play what is known in the piping world as MSR, which stands for March, Strathspey, and Reel. Those are traditional tunes one plays on the bagpipes. Ye might have heard those yesterday."

"We did," Bunny was quick to assure him. "There was no escaping it."

"Aye. Very true. Well, since all ten of us in the competition are level-one pipers, our score sheets are not publicly posted at this final competition, although we all have some idea of who's hovering near the top. But that can change. We all advance to day two, where we play a melody selection, a well-loved tune that we personally arrange and perform. 'Tis a crowd favorite."

"We're truly sorry the competition's been postponed." Bunny was sincere when she said this. After all, the handsome piper seemed like a nice man. "So, what you're telling us is that although Major MacDonald slated you as the leader going into day two, the competition is far from over."

Jamie shrugged. "I wouldn't say far from over. There's always the possibility of mucking up your final tune. However, if there are a few of us with the same score, then we all battle it out on the field on day two. I wonder if we'll get the chance to do it."

"You said that you are judged heavily on your bagpipes?" Giff questioned, staring at the set on the bench beside the man. "Those look very nice."

"Aye, they are. They're a vintage set that belonged to my great-grandfather and have been passed down through our family for generations. I consider myself lucky to have them."

Bunny looked at the bagpipes and ran her fingers over the ornate projecting mounts. "What are these made of?" she asked.

"Ivory," Jamie admitted a little sheepishly. "Can't use ivory these days, for obvious reasons, but 'tis what they used back in the day these were made. It makes them incredibly valuable."

"Are you scored higher because of the ivory decoration?" Brett asked.

Jamie shrugged. "Maybe a wee bit, and the quality of this instrument as well. However, 'tis mostly on how the pipes are tuned and how they sound when played."

"Thank you." Brett then asked where they might find Tommy Compton.

"He's doing quite well, for a youngster," Jamie replied. "I haven't seen him yet today. As ye can imagine, we've all been very upset by the news of the major's passing. Ye might check at the Bothy."

"The Bothy?" Giff asked. "And where might that be?"

"'Tis the wee cottage he's staying at, just down the Castle Road."

They thanked him for the information and struck off once again, this time aiming for the little stone cottage not far from their own, known simply as the Bothy.

Chapter 28

Tommy Compton was sitting alone in the intimate courtyard outside the gray stone cottage, clutching a steaming mug between his hands and looking a tad too big for the decorative, white-painted, cast-iron chair he was sitting on. The moment Bunny spotted the tall, gangly teenager alone at the little café table, she felt a pang in her heart. He looked young, much younger than all the others in the competition. The wild tuft of red hair on his head and his smooth, boyish complexion reminded her in the subtlest of ways of her brother Braiden. His youth said a lot about his talent on the bagpipes. Braiden had been talented for his age too.

"Tommy?" she asked in her high, lilting Scottish voice as she walked into the courtyard. Although her tone was light and friendly, it must have shocked the lad. At the first sound of his name, he let go of his mug and sprang out of his chair with the speed and agility of a cat about to be dumped in a bathtub.

"Aye. That's me," he chirped, facing the newcomers with bright, probing eyes. The moment his gaze landed on Bunny and the lads, he took a deep breath and asked more calmly, "Can I help ye?"

"We're sorry to bother you," Brett said gently. "There's no need for alarm. My name's Brett, this is Giff, and this is our friend, Bunny. We've just come to ask you a few questions."

"You're an American," Tommy said, staring at Brett. "I can tell because of your accent. Cool. Have ye come all this way to hear the bagpipes?"

"As a matter of fact, we have, only the bagpipes we've come to hear are of a very different nature."

"I'm not following ye." Tommy tilted his head as he studied Brett. "What other kind are there?"

"I can't believe I'm saying this," Giff huffed, pausing long enough for a deprecating eye roll, "but the bagpiper we've come to hear is a ghost. The ghostly piper of Dundoon. Perhaps you've heard of him? No? Brett's a ghost hunter, I'm a psychic medium, and Bunny here is a celebrity chef. We're here to film a paranormal investigation for our show, *Food and Spirits*, at the castle."

"Seriously?" The boy's face filled with enchanted skepticism as he stared at them. "You're here because of some pipin' ghost?"

Bunny could tell it wasn't quite what the young piper had been expecting. "I'm afraid we are, Tommy." she said. "But we are really enjoying the competition as well," she lied.

"*Nice.*" He gave them all the once-over, relaxing a measure as he did so. "I've heard dafter things. What is it ye want with me, then?"

Brett took the opening as an invitation and hit him with, "How well did you know Major MacDonald?" At the sound of the name, the boy stiffened again, becoming instantly wary.

"Terrible what happened to him." Tommy shook his head. "I heard he went over a cliff. The police have already been here, talking to us. Jeremy Taylor, another piper in the competition, is staying here too, only he left to practice for tonight's tribute. I was going to join him in a few minutes. I just . . . needed some time, now that the competition's been put on hold."

"We're sorry. It must be hard for you," Brett offered, with a lack of expression. "But you didn't answer my question. How well did you know Major MacDonald?"

Tommy shook his head. "I knew him, but not well."

"The reason we're here at all, Tommy, is because we've talked with your mother." Giff sat in one of the little cast-iron chairs and waved for Tommy to do the same. Once Tommy was seated, Giff added with a forced smile, "Charming woman. Did you know she accosted Major MacDonald last night when he was on his way to the castle?"

"No," he said with a touch of disdain. "I dinna really know what my mother does."

"But you must know that she's gone to great lengths to get you the best set of bagpipes she can afford for this competition." Bunny crossed her arms as she looked down at the young man sitting across from Giff.

With his eyes glued to his folded hands resting on the table, Tommy admitted, "I do. I appreciate what she does. She's well aware that I cannot compete at this level without a bespoke set of bagpipes."

"I bet they're lovely," Bunny said. "Can we see them, Tommy?"

The boy flinched before he shook his head. "No. They're not here."

"Well then, where are they?" Giff politely asked. "We'd like to see them."

"Why?" he snapped, looking at them. "Why do ye need to

see them? You're not part of this competition. You've just said ye are ghost hunters. I dinna have to show them to ye."

"That's true," Bunny agreed. "You don't have to show us anything, but we'd like to see them, Tommy. Major MacDonald was pushed off a cliff last night. We were there. We heard it happen. And now, for better or worse, we're embroiled in this mystery. We want to know who would push that man off a cliff and why. Unfortunately, our enquiries have led us to you. Did you know that the other two judges have you at the top of their list, slated to win this competition?"

With a very sheepish look, Tommy nodded.

"How did you know this?" Brett asked.

"My mother told me. Look," he said, jumping up from the table again, "I had nothing to do with that man going off a cliff. I swear it!"

Tommy was nearly as tall as Brett, Bunny noted, but unlike Brett, the boy clearly had a chip on his shoulder—namely, his mother. He was definitely hiding something, but could it possibly be murder? He was a young man with a great talent, and Bunny didn't want to believe he could be capable of pushing a man off a cliff. However, she could sense a lot of anger bubbling within him. The poor lad, she thought. With a voice full of empathy, she addressed the young piper. "I bet your mother puts a lot of pressure on ye, doesn't she? She's vested in you winning this competition, isn't she? That must be very hard for you, being so young."

Anger, frustration, embarrassment, sadness—whatever emotions were swirling inside the lad—were taking a toll on him. It couldn't be good. Bunny could recognize a meltdown when she saw one, and this poor lad's emotional dam was about to be breached, and fast. His face was red, and his eyes shimmered with the sting of unshed tears. "I love her," he seethed, "I do, my mother, but she's a devil on my back I cannot shake! You've met her. We're not rich. And piping doesn't pay much. But to her, 'tis everything! Had I to do it all over, I would ha' never picked up the blasted instrument, but she insisted I learn to play. It was my damn poor luck that I'm good at it. She'll do anything for me. She'll do anything to help me win, but she's not a murderer. She's not!"

Brett gently asked, "Were you out on that cliff last night, Tommy?"

"No. I was here. Jeremy will tell ye."

Giff stood from his chair as well. He looked at the boy and asked plainly, "By any chance, was Major MacDonald your father?"

"What? No. Jesus Christ," he swore under his breath. "Did she tell ye that?"

"She did," Giff nodded, looking slightly disappointed by this news. His delicious, scandalous, *Mamma Mia* theory was crumbling like a stale cookie before his eyes.

"She's a liar," Tommy said. "She likes to think he is. 'Tis her sick fantasy. She used to date him before I was born. She told me that he was. She even wants me to lie about that too, but I won't. I won't because he's not my father."

"Do you know who your father is?" Brett asked, annoyed with himself for having to ask such a question of a young man.

"Aye. Last year I took one of those genetic tests that match ye with relatives. Fortunately, for me, my biological father did too. I've met him. Told my mother about it even. He checks out. They were engaged to be married, but she decided to break it off. She was pregnant with me at the time. I dinna resent her for it, but I do resent her making up lies about it. I'll tell ye who he's not. He is not Scotty MacDonald."

"I'm very sorry, Tommy," Bunny told him, not having the heart to press him any further. She knew he'd been pressed enough and manipulated by his mother, the poor lad. "Thank you for answering our questions. We shall leave you alone now. However, I have to ask, where are your bagpipes if they're not here?"

"In my mother's trailer, both sets," he offered.

"You have more than one set?" Brett was surprised by this.

"Aye, most of us do. One for competitions, the other for everything else. And they can stay in that damn trailer, for all I care."

Chapter 29

As Bunny, Brett, and Giff left Tommy Compton to his own thoughts once again, they all agreed that the fact the young man didn't have his bagpipes with him was cause for concern.

"The set found at the bottom of the cliff with Major MacDonald could be one of Tommy's," Bunny pointed out. "As far as we know, those bagpipes have yet to be identified. Tommy could have been the person playing out there last night, with his mother lying in wait. Major MacDonald, having been led out there for a clandestine meeting, could have wrestled the bagpipes away from Tommy, allowing Tabatha to shove him off the cliff. Thanks to Tommy, we now know that MacDonald wasn't his father, taking that little obstacle, if it ever was one, off the table."

"Highly disappointing," Giff interjected with a frown. "I was hoping it was true. There's nothing like a good, scandalous, baby-daddy surprise as a reason for murder."

Bunny ignored him. "Which means that both mother and son would benefit with Major MacDonald out of the way. Tommy would likely win the competition . . ."

"And Tabby would win mother of the year," Giff added. "Her dream title, according to Tommy."

"Something like that." Brett shook his head at his friend and continued. "However, Bunny's correct here. Thanks to Seth Burgess, we know that Tabatha's alibi has a large hole in it right around the time of the major's death. We will need to check Tommy's alibi. He claims he was at the Bothy all night and that his fellow piper, Jeremy Taylor, can corroborate this. But they have separate rooms, making it plausible that Tommy could have slipped out at night without anyone knowing."

"I agree," Bunny said, smiling at her cohost. "It appears that both mother and son have holes in their alibis." They were standing in the middle of the gravel road that in one direction connected the cottages to the castle, and in the other led back to the fairgrounds and beyond that the campsite. Bunny pointed to an unseen spot in the distance. "You two are going to have to go back to Tabatha Compton's trailer and see if Tommy's bagpipes are there. We know Tabatha is a liar. I don't want to think it, because I truly feel for poor Tommy, but he could be lying as well."

"Where are you going?" Giff asked, noting that Bunny wasn't about to walk all the way back to the campground.

"Back to the castle. I'm meeting Granny Mac for a wee natter. I also have work to do for tonight's supper. It'll be a small affair, since we're not filming."

"Don't need to film supper," Brett agreed. "Last night's spirit supper was epic. However, will you make sure it's okay with Jordy and Elizabeth that we continue with our investigation tonight?"

She assured them she would and headed for the castle.

"Granny!" Bunny found the older woman sitting on a beautifully upholstered couch in the fancy great room, with

Doc Beaton beside her. She gave her gran a kiss on the cheek, greeted the doctor, and took a seat on the sofa across from them. Bunny was happy to see a silver tea service on the coffee table, with an extra teacup and saucer. There was also a plate of delicious-looking shortbread cookies. She was certain Jenny had made them. She poured herself a cup of tea and said, "I'm only going to stay a minute. I have a lot of prep work yet to do in the kitchen for tonight's supper. Jenny's already in there, working away. It's going to be a very casual affair tonight. Poached salmon with dill sauce, mashed acorn squash with brown butter, and seasoned new potatoes. I'm making a raspberry sponge cake for dessert."

"Doesn't sound very simple to me, dear. But it does sound delicious."

"Thank you. Will you two be joining us?"

"We wouldn't miss it for the world," Granny Mac assured her. Then, looking somewhat apologetic, she added, "However, since dinner will be rather late, due to another ghost hunt, Artemus and I are going to have a bite to eat beforehand."

Doc Beaton frowned. "I do hope you're not planning on stirring up any more mug-tossing ghosts at tonight's supper." Bunny assured him that supper was just going to be supper, without a show. The doctor looked relieved to hear it.

Granny Mac set her teacup on the coffee table and began to refill it as she asked, "How is the investigation going?"

Bunny quickly brought the elderly couple up to speed, telling them everything they had learned so far. "Unfortunately, there are a lot of possible suspects," she said, feeling overwhelmed by the possibilities. "There's Tabatha Compton, who was seen accosting Major MacDonald yesterday evening; her son, Tommy, who is favored by the two remaining judges; and speaking of the judges, Fergus Cameron and Rory Fraser are not off the hook yet. Then we have sleazy Seth Burgess, the owner of Burgess Bagpipe Emporium, who provided Tommy with his bagpipes. I'm not certain he's a suspect, but I don't trust him. There might be more suspects that we haven't thought of. In fact, I'm certain there are more, but no one is really jumping to the forefront on this one. I suppose that's to be expected."

"Well, ye and the lads have certainly been busy," Doc Beaton said. "As fate would have it, I've just come back from the postmortem."

Bunny, having just finished off her second cookie, set down her plate and leaned forward, anxious to hear what the doctor had to say.

"As expected, Major MacDonald died from his injuries suffered during his fall. I've checked with Constable Craig. The forensic team has gone over the area on the top of the cliff with a fine-tooth comb, so to speak. As the constable indicated earlier, there are three distinct sets of footprints on the clifftop and those of a large canine. They've been able to identify the set belonging to MacDonald. The other two are a mystery."

Bunny, thinking of Tabatha Compton, asked, "Do we know what shoe sizes these footprints happen to be? I'm only asking because Tabatha has a pretty strong motive to want the major out of the way."

"I'm not certain. I suppose we could check, but I've been led to believe that the footprints found at the site were all larger in size, with deep imprints, indicating that they had some weight behind them. Is Tabatha a big lass?"

Bunny shook her head. "Not particularly. She's slender and just slightly taller than I am."

"I'll check with Constable Craig to make sure. However, given the current evidence, it's doubtful that she was there last night. Her son, maybe."

"Thank you for checking," Bunny said. Doc Beaton continued.

"Also, there is no doubt that Major MacDonald was pushed to his death. Due to the skid pattern left at the cliff's edge, combined with the audio your cameraman captured, we've been able to confirm, without doubt, that this was no accident. It was done with intent."

Just hearing it made Bunny shiver slightly. "What about the bagpipes found next to the body? Is there any more news regarding those?"

"They were badly broken in the fall," the doctor offered, tilting his distinguished, slightly graying head as he looked at her. "They were a fine, modern set. If the pipes were a second set of the major's, that would make sense. However, as we've indicated earlier, there is serious doubt that he was the man playing them last night on the top of the cliff. How they ended under him during the fall is still a mystery."

"Do they know who they belong to yet?"

"Not yet. As you can imagine, no one has come forward to claim them. Forensics is running a DNA test on the saliva, so it's only a matter of time. I did learn an interesting fact. Constable Craig told me that the bagpipes found in MacDonald's room, although vintage and quite valuable, did not contain ivory projection mounts, as first thought. Craig looked into this and learned that the late queen, being a notable animal lover, insisted that all ivory mounts in her service be retired to discourage the use of ivory on such instruments. Ivory is now replaced with high-end plastics, made to resemble ivory. To add more flourish, projecting mounts and tuning slides are still embellished with decorative sterling silver, making them appear like the real thing. Och!" he exclaimed, suddenly remembering something important. He raised his brows at Bunny and told her, "I almost forgot to tell you the most interesting part. Major MacDonald was found to be carrying a real ivory projecting mount in his pocket. Imagine that? It was wrapped around a note with the word *Brigadoon* written on it." The doctor shrugged, clearly not knowing what to make of that.

Bunny looked at her gran, marveling at the way the older woman pretended to be amazed by this news. Of course, they had told Granny Mac about the note back at the White Cottage and had shown her a picture of the projecting mount; only then, they hadn't known what it was. However, no one imagined that the projecting mount had been made of real ivory. What did that mean? Bunny wasn't certain, but she was determined to find out. Somehow, all the moving parts they had discovered—and those yet to be discovered—would eventually fall into place and make sense. Some were important. Others were spare pieces. Yet together they would tell the story of Major MacDonald's murder. There was one piece Bunny had yet to examine—namely, the ghostly piper. Like spooky magic, Granny Mac picked up on her thoughts.

"You really do need to contact him tonight, dear," Granny Mac said, adding a soft, grandmotherly smile. "As I've said before, I think he holds the key to unlocking this mystery." Doc Beaton, sitting beside her, stared at her.

"Contact who?" he asked.

"The piper of Dundoon, dear," she told him gently. "Bunny needs to connect with him, the sooner the better."

"She can do that?" His brows were pinched together in puzzlement as he addressed Granny Mac. "I know that ye have certain, remarkable gifts, Ella, but your granddaughter has them too?" He looked doubtful, or perhaps disturbed. Bunny wasn't certain which.

For her part, she just smiled at him and shrugged. She wasn't certain that she could contact the piper. She had tried, but he seemed so aloof, removed, shadowed. The sound of his pipes, however, was another story. It was perfectly haunting and soul-rending. The thought of pursuing the ghost wasn't pleasant. In fact, if she really thought about it, it was quite terrifying. However, she knew she had to try.

"As I've told you, I've already talked with Jordy and Elizabeth. They're pleased that you're going to try to get some answers here. Also, and I hardly need to tell you this, dear, but Jordy can't get enough of your cooking." Granny Mac tossed her a cheeky wink. "If he wasn't so strapped for money, I'm sure he'd try to lure you away from your show to work here."

For some reason, the thought of her replacing Jenny annoyed her. "Crivens, Gran! Jenny's a fine cook. And I like what I'm doing."

"She's fine enough, alright, for his budget," Granny Mac offered with a grin. "Jordy's always had champagne taste. Unfortunately, his budget is more suited to beer."

"And whisky, obviously," she added. "There's so much of the stuff here that I'm convinced the floors of this old castle have bathed in it. The smell can be overwhelming at times."

"It can be, and there is a hint of whisky throughout this place," Granny Mac conceded. "However, I believe that smell is attached to one of the spirits here."

"Drunk Gordie!" Bunny said, realizing why the smell was so strong in certain places. Doc Beaton appeared to be stuck on Bunny's burgeoning psychic abilities.

"Are you certain that's a good idea, Ella? Having Bunny contact a ghost? After last night's debacle, I'd say it was downright dangerous. What's he going to do, anyhow? He can't tell her who murdered MacDonald, can he? Also, may I remind ye that there's still a murderer on the loose." Bunny found the doctor's concern endearing.

"Not to worry, Artemis." Granny Mac gave his leg a gentle pat. "I'll be with her. As for the murderer, I'm confident we'll be able to sniff out the guilty party in due course. But it's not going to be easy. I still feel a storm brewing in the marrow of my bones."

Great, Bunny thought. Why did she have to say that?

"Well, that's me away," she said, excusing herself. Bunny then picked up the tea tray and headed for the relative safety of the Dundoon kitchen, attempting to block all thoughts of ghosts, murderers, and brewing storms from her mind.

Chapter 30

Bunny had been in the kitchen just above an hour when she received a call from Brett. She answered without thinking, but the moment she heard the heavy breathing and the urgency in his voice, she knew something was wrong.

"Giff and I found him," he said, breathing sporadically, as if he was running.

Without waiting for him to finish, she asked, "Who, Brett? Who did ye find?"

"The man in the black suit . . . the one your brother and Giff saw yesterday talking with MacDonald. He's just come out of the Burgess Bagpipe Emporium tent and is heading for the car park. He's moving fast. I need you to get the van and meet us in the car park."

Bunny, knowing Jenny was staring at her, scrunched her nose and gave a helpless shrug. "But . . . I don't have keys for the van," she reminded him. She also didn't have keys for the saloon. Granny Mac had those, and she and the doctor had left the castle, taking that car.

"They're in the glove compartment," Brett fired off. "It's unlocked."

"It's unlocked?" Bunny found that very irresponsible. "The van is unlocked, and you left the keys in there? Who does that sort of thing?"

"I grew up in rural Wisconsin!" he snapped, as if that was all that needed to be said on the matter before ending the call.

"Well, well, what was that all about?" Jenny asked with a suggestive grin. "Ye are not gone above an hour and lover boy cannot bear to be without ye. He's smitten. Guess the love potion Ella and I mixed in the hot toddy this morning worked."

Bunny, rushing to get the last plump, hothouse raspberry on the top of the gorgeous cake, nearly buried it in the decorative dollop of whipped cream. "Love potion?" she cried, feeling the heat rise to her cheeks. "Tell me you did not use a love potion on Brett Bloom!"

Jenny laughed and took the cake from her hands. "Of course, we dinna. We dinna need to, not with that one. Now shoo. Dinna keep your lover boy waiting," Jenny teased, heading for the refrigerator.

"Are ye sure? I hate to leave you without finishing the prep."

"Ye are not the only cook in the kitchen, MacBride, now are ye?" Jenny chided and shooed her out the door.

The van was indeed unlocked. Remarkably, and quite negligently, the key was right where Brett said it would be, in the glove box. In a matter of moments, Bunny, channeling Brett's urgency, found herself racing down the Castle Road at an exhilarating speed. It wasn't a well-groomed road on a good day, she mused, and the current flood of traffic did nothing to help it. Also, the rental van needed better shock absorbers. As Bunny bounced and jostled down the lane, aiming for the car park, two men jumped in front of her, causing her to slam on the brakes.

"Crivens!" she cried, skidding to a halt. The moment she did, Brett swung open the passenger-side door and slid into the seat. Giff, for reasons of his own, buckled up in the back seat. In a scolding tone, she cried, "I almost hit you two!"

"But you didn't, princess," Giff called out from the back. "Now step on it, Bun-bun. He's already out the main gate!"

The man in the black suit was driving a black saloon, which, to Bunny's way of thinking, wasn't very original. Remarkably, even with a good five-minute head start, he was only three cars ahead of them, which spoke volumes about the desolate land Dundoon castle lorded over. The black saloon was heading for the small village of Crinan, located on the south side of the loch of that same name. It was the closest village, yet incredibly small. Bunny doubted Crinan was the man's destination. Nope, he was likely racing off to Glasgow, where he'd give them the slip in a heartbeat. Bunny, who was known for her lead foot, wasn't about to let that happen. She had left the kitchen in the middle of preparing the evening's supper to chase this possible baddie. If she was going to be called from the kitchen so abruptly, she was bound and determined to make it count. Therefore, filling with purpose, she floored the pedal and passed a pokey car, going a speed she doubted the van had ever reached before. Her target was just two cars away. The black saloon, which she just realized was a BMW, picked up speed and disappeared around a bend in the heavily wooded landscape.

"I think he's onto us," Brett cautioned. "Don't drive so fast, Bunny. Hang back a little. We need to blend in."

"*Blend in?*" She cast him a look that suggested he was mental. "Are ye kidding me right now? I'm driving a white Ford Transit van. Last time I checked, only kidnappers and misguided ghost hunters drive such things."

Giff leaned forward as far as his seat belt would allow. "She has a point, Bloom."

"If this person is connected to Major MacDonald's murder, we need to talk with him," she reminded them. "For heaven's sake, Brett, ye pulled me away from the kitchen. It is not going to be for nothing!"

Unfortunately, sporty BMWs go much faster than clunky rental transit vans. The man in the black suit had smoked them, and Bunny found herself more than a little miffed as she turned down the high street of Crinan.

"What do we do now?" she asked. "Do we keep driving or do we turn around? Clearly, I'm not a mind reader. I have no idea who he is or where he's headed."

"You're psychic," Giff reminded her. "Can't you just tap into his brain and find out?"

She desperately wanted to glare at him in the back seat for that ignorant remark, but she refrained, hesitant to take her eyes off the road. Instead, she offered, "Ye might be confusing clairvoyance with remote viewing, Gifford, a skill that some psychics have where they can tap into a location they've never seen or a person they've never met. The Ministry of Defence attempted a program in 2002. I think the Yanks know more about it. I'm doubtful it works. And anyhow, I don't do that. In fact, I barely even know what it is that I do regarding psychic abilities."

"Got him!" Brett cried, pointing at the black Beemer in a parking lot off the high street they had just driven past. "He's right there. That's his car. He's at the hotel! What are the odds?" he asked with a wide grin. His high spirits faded as they continued down the road. "What are you doing? We have to turn around."

"I'm on it!" she barked. "But I can hardly do a three-point-turn in the middle of the road in this clunky van, now, can I?" Noting that this was true, Brett held his tongue as Bunny drove to the nearest turnaround, which was a little shop down the road, and did the deed. Once turned around and heading in the right direction, they motored straight back to the seaside hotel, thankful that the black saloon was still there. Bunny parked the van in a wider spot at the end of the lot and turned off the engine.

"What's the plan?" she asked, looking at Brett for direction.

"Yes, what is the plan, Bloom?" Giff had unbuckled his seat belt and was now squatting behind their seats.

"There's no plan. We find the man and politely ask him what he and Major MacDonald were talking about yesterday behind the Burgess Bagpipe Emporium tent."

"What if he has a gun?"

"Gun?" Bunny quipped, looking at Giff. "We're not in the US. People don't carry guns in the UK."

"007 does," Giff replied with a raised brow. "For all we know, he could be MI6."

Brett shook his head in frustration and opened the door. "Are you two coming?"

The moment they walked into the hotel, they spotted a little gastro pub just off to the right. Warm, inviting, with a rack of fine spirits on display and large windows overlooking the loch, it seemed like the most logical place to begin their search. Unfortunately, the moment they entered, they saw no sign of the man in the black suit, just a smattering of random patrons enjoying a pint with nibbles. On second look, a couple in the booth in the back corner looked familiar.

"That's my gran! . . . And she's with the doctor! So this is where they disappeared to," Bunny huffed and headed for the secluded booth. Brett and Giff followed.

"Bunny, what a pleasant surprise," her grandmother said, pulling her eyes from the handsome doctor sitting across from her. Bunny got the distinct impression that she was interrupting something. Crivens! Were these two canoodling in the back of a gastro pub? Trying to banish the thought,

Granny Mac forced a wee smile at her granddaughter. "I thought ye were in the kitchen, dear. What brings you three to the hotel?"

Brett, with eyes restlessly scanning the room, said, "We're looking for a man in a black suit." He shifted his gaze to the elderly couple as he explained, "Angus saw him yesterday talking with Major MacDonald behind the Burgess Bagpipe Emporium tent. Giff saw him as well. We think he might be somehow involved in the major's murder."

"The fit, dark-haired man in the black suit?" Doc Beaton questioned. "Aye, he was here," he assured them, pointing to the bartender. "He was talking with the gent behind the bar. I have no idea where he got off to after that."

They thanked the doctor and went straight to the bar, where Brett addressed the bartender directly. "Good afternoon. I hope you can help us. We're looking for a man who was just here, dressed in a black suit. Did you, by chance, catch his name or know where we might find him?"

The bartender raked them with a scrutinizing gaze before nodding. "Och, aye, I saw him. And I can do ye one better," he said. He turned to the back counter and, to their surprise, selected a pint glass. Without asking after their order, as though assuming they were in for a pint, he placed the glass under a tap and drew a beautiful, bubbly, amber beer with a thick, foamy head. He slid it over to Brett before slapping a note on the counter.

"I . . . I didn't order this. I don't understand?" Brett said, looking at the mug of beer and the note. "What's this?"

"The man ye just asked after said to give ye this when ye came looking for him. Paid for three pints before he left." He cast them a wink, then grabbed another glass from the back counter and began filling another pint. Bunny wasn't normally a beer drinker, but she had to admit, it smelled divine.

Noting that Brett and Giff were ogling the beer, she picked up the note and read it before handing it to the lads.

This is a warning. Do not stick your nose where it doesn't belong. Have a pint instead.

"Ohmygod!" Giff exclaimed. "He's warning us to back off, which means we're getting close. Also, he bought us beers. I don't know whether to be frightened or flattered. Truthfully, I'm a little of both. What a mysterious man."

"Damn it!" Brett seethed and ran out the door. Bunny and Giff followed him. Just as they expected, the black BMW was gone. There was no sign of it at all, not up or down the road. The man had slipped out right under their noses. He was good. Mysterious, but good.

"Well, no use wasting a good beer," Giff said and headed back inside.

"That man's involved in this." Brett waved the note as he looked at Bunny. "This warning confirms it. I don't know how or to what extent, but he's involved."

"All we can do is keep looking for him," Bunny softly suggested, reading the frustration so clear in his eyes. "But first, let's have that beer. I'd say we've earned it."

Chapter 31

"Have some chips," Granny Mac said, sliding the plate of thickly cut, perfectly crisped potato wedges across the table to Brett, Bunny, and Giff. The three were pressed together on one side of the booth, clutching their pints for fear of spilling, while Granny Mac had joined Doc Beaton on the bench across from them. The couple had been sharing a plate of fish and chips, with extra chips.

Bunny knew that her gran was a tad woo-woo, being a seer and all, and a bit of a health nut to boot, but the woman had a real soft spot for chips, or, as the Americans called them, French fries. Well, good for her, Bunny thought, warming a little to the idea of her gran and the doctor as a couple. Everyone needed a guilty pleasure. Was that what the doctor was? Or was he something more? She had to admit that they seemed to enjoy one another's company. That was something. He was a tad pedantic, but no one could deny that he was smart. He also seemed very caring and empathetic, which were both good qualities for a doctor to have. Bunny had spent the last ten years of her life living alone. Well, not totally alone. She had Mr. Wiggles, her pet Holland lop. Although he was adorable, with his long, floppy ears, his puffball tail, and his curious, wiggling nose, he wasn't all that skilled with conversation, being a rabbit. No, a person needed human conversation. A person needed someone to share their triumphs and tribulations with, and to laugh with over a good meal. Loneliness could wear on the soul.

With that thought gripping her heart, Bunny cast a covert glance at the tall, blond-headed man squished beside her. She wondered, not for the first time, how lovely it would be to spend her days with him. *Stop it!* she mentally berated herself. Now was not the time to entertain fantasies about hunky Brett Bloom. He was consumed with this murder case, and, of course, the upcoming ghost hunt. Also, they might, just possibly, have narrowly missed confronting MacDonald's murderer.

"These fries aren't half bad," Giff announced, shoving another one into his mouth. As he chewed, he offered, "Not as good as a hot sleeve of Mickey D's, but passable."

"Are you referring to McDonald's?" Doc Beaton questioned, staring at Giff as if he was a patient with a puzzling ailment.

"Yes, but he's dead, so I didn't want to bandy his name about in reference to French fries. Ella would agree, that's bad juju." Giff cartoonishly executed a cursed look as he clutched the clear white crystal dangling over his sleek black turtleneck. "Am I right?" he asked, holding Granny Mac in his slightly mocking, yet utterly curious gaze.

"A MacDonald, with a different spelling, and without any connections to French fries, good or bad, has indeed died, Gifford." There was a slightly exasperated look on Granny Mac's face as she offered this. She was a patient woman, and Giff was a very dear young man, but he was not even at the baby-steps level in understanding spiritualism, mediumship, clairvoyance, meditation, and what it means to open one's third eye. He loved crystals, that much was clear. He believed in their magical powers, which was a wee disconcerting. But there was no harm in it. She took a deep breath, forced a serene smile, and said, "You will not anger the spirits or those dangling just beyond our reach in the fourth dimension with idle chatter. Now, about this mysterious man in the black suit. What do ye suppose he was doing with Major MacDonald?"

"Ye told us that he was seen talking with MacDonald behind a tent at the competition," Doc Beaton stated. "Was it a friendly chat, do you recall?"

"We have no idea," Brett admitted. "What we do know is that it's highly suspicious."

"Aye, clandestine meetings are often suspicious. However, how can we be certain that the man in the black suit wanted MacDonald dead?" the doctor pointed out. The co-hosts of *Food & Spirits*, gingerly sipping their beers, nodded in unison. "Then let us consider another possibility. He was a friend. Or perhaps they were working together? The mere presence of the man in the black suit lurking around in the shadows might suggest that there's something bigger going on here. I propose we use the method of decomposition to break this seemingly complex problem of murder into smaller parts. We can then address them individually in the hopes that they will eventually lead to a solution for the larger problem, which is finding the culprit who pushed the major off the cliff last night. I often use it regarding a collection of puzzling symptoms a patient might be struggling with to diagnose the proper disease."

"Whoa, slow your roll there, Doc!" Giff aimed a wink and a gun-finger at the older man. "I mean, this isn't rocket science or brain surgery. There's no need to overcomplicate the matter. The problem is murder. The question is who?

We're looking at suspects, motives, and the facts to find the guilty party. Am I right?" In an effort to get him to behave, Bunny reached next to her and squeezed his knee. "Ouch! I was just stating the obvious."

"I agree with the doctor on this one, buddy," Brett said, offering his friend a gentle smile. "Let's break it down to its basic parts. Is MacDonald's death due to the competition, or is it about bagpipes? Maybe it's a little of both? Here are the facts as we know them. We have two remaining judges who, for all intents and purposes, are aligned regarding their pick to win the competition. In order for their man to win, they needed to sway MacDonald's vote, which they didn't do. Also, judge Fergus Cameron admitted to being resentful of Major MacDonald's relationship with the queen, making him stand out a little more than Rory Fraser."

"Mr. Cameron claimed he never left his room," Giff said. "When Bunny and I went to wake them at four this morning, Fergus Cameron appeared sleepy, was rather cranky as well, and called us eejets for waking him up. It could have been an act."

Bunny nodded in agreement. "Rory Fraser, on the other hand, was dressed, but hastily so. He likely heard the racket, got dressed, and popped into the hallway to see what was going on. I agree that he's far less suspicious than his friend, Fergus Cameron. There's also Tabatha Compton to consider, Tommy's mother. Tommy is the favorite to win. There's an air of desperation about her that gives one the impression that she's capable of murder. However, Doc Beaton told me earlier that the footprints found at the crime scene didn't appear to belong to a woman. So, we can possibly rule her out on the grounds that the evidence doesn't suggest she was there last night."

"That's good to know," Brett said, looking relieved by narrowing down the suspects. "Tommy, on the other hand, could have been the one playing the bagpipes. We didn't have time to tell you, Bunny, but we went to Tabatha's trailer, and she wasn't there. We never did locate either of Tommy's set of bagpipes."

Granny Mac, gazing into the middle distance with that unfocused look in her pale green eyes, offered cryptically, "This is all about the bagpipes. Bagpipes. Pipers playing, old and new. Songs wafting across the water." She snapped back inside herself, her wise, clear eyes focused once again on Bunny and the lads. "No one has yet come forward to claim them. Why would that be?"

"Because if they had," Bunny began, her large green eyes focusing on her gran's, "it would place them on the top of that cliff. It would implicate them in the murder of Major MacDonald."

"Yes. But this person wasn't alone," Granny Mac pointed out. "There were at least two people there, and a . . . a"—she looked at Doc Beaton sitting next to her and landed on "dog. Has anyone seen a large canine running about the grounds?"

"Just Winston," Bunny offered. "He's the sweetest thing. Wouldn't harm a soul. No. Gran, you are correct. There's another dog or fairy dog here somewhere. And let's not forget the ivory projecting mount found in the major's pocket. What is that all about, do you suppose?"

"It's part of a bagpipe," Brett offered plainly, having examined a bunch of them that afternoon in the Burgess Bagpipe Emporium tent.

Giff, with a spark of an idea blazing behind his eyes, said, "It could be a marker. You know, a way to identify certain bagpipes from others. You must admit that there are a lot of bagpipes at this event. Every bagpipe here has a set of projecting mounts, ivory, plastic, or otherwise. What if the one MacDonald was carrying is a match to other sets,

sets of bagpipes carrying something they're not supposed to be carrying—"

"Like drugs!" Doc Beaton blurted for him, both men having the same epiphany. Remembering where they were, the doctor lowered his voice. "The man in the black suit! That explains it. He looks like a Scotland Yard man to me. I hate to say it, but this forlorn, sparsely populated coast has long been plagued with drug smuggling. I think we've hit the mark on this one, lads . . . and ladies."

"Brigadoon could be the name of their covert operation," Bunny added, having seen enough high-octane shows on the telly to know how these drug smugglers worked—code names, surreptitious meetings in dark places, foggy nights, men in dark suits, a marquee event in the background to add distraction and misdirection, and, of course, murder. All the moving parts were beginning to align, she thought. There was just one glaring problem. The bagpipes at the bottom of the cliff. Who did they belong to?

"It's getting dark out," Brett said, indicating to the window, where the fading autumn sun was dipping below the watery horizon. "We best get back. The pipers are holding their tribute soon."

"Don't want to miss that," Giff offered, sarcastically. "Bagpipes! Just can't get enough of them. Am I right?"

"I'm not going. I've got supper to get on the table," Bunny reminded them. "I'd dearly love a nap too, but I'm afraid there's no time."

"I could use a nap as well, but as they say, Bunny, there's no rest for the wicked," Brett teased, holding her in a gentle smile. "Our investigation tonight won't be as late as last night, I promise. We're not filming during supper, and the only ghost we're trying to contact will be the piper of Dundoon. We'll give it our best shot, but if it can't be done, Bunny, it can't be done."

"I'll be there to help," Granny Mac assured them. It was obvious to Bunny that Doc Beaton, from the spooked look on his face, was perfectly happy to sit this one out. She envied him. Her gran continued, "There are ways to pull the illusive piper from the shadows. It can be done. I get the feeling he's ready to play. However, gentlemen, it is best that ye gird your loins," she warned, focusing her sea-glass eyes on Giff and Brett. "I've a feeling that these ghosts won't go gently into that good night."

Chapter 32

Full of determination, Brett coaxed the large white van along the castle road through the swelling crowd. The line stretched from the car park to the parade grounds, making it appear that every bagpipe enthusiast in the nation had come to witness what was sure to be a moving tribute to the late Major Scotty MacDonald. In fact, the moment they had driven through the main castle gates, Bunny had been astonished by the change in atmosphere. The light, fair-day mood of the competition had shifted with the setting sun. Torches now lined the road all the way to the castle, the wavering flames fighting against the cold, damp, onshore wind from the sound. The castle on the hill had also changed, looking like the impenetrable medieval fortress it was. As Bunny stared at the towering walls underlit by the glow of fire, a shiver washed over her. At the same moment, an echo of the unearthly bagpipe tune rang loud in her head. She had not imagined it, yet she was certain the lads had not heard it. He was calling to her. The piper. Dear God, it was happening.

Just then, Brett's phone rang, forcing the unearthly tune out of her head. He answered it on the van's hands-free system. It was Ed Franco. "Hey, Bloom, we're at the castle. Where are you guys?"

"Nearly there. We're caught in the tribute traffic. We haven't seen you since this morning. How is everyone? Well rested, I hope."

"We got back from the police station late in the morning and slept all afternoon. I trust you'll bring us up to speed regarding Major MacDonald when you get here. We're ready to go, but we're starving. Bunny, darling, are you there?"

"I'm here, Ed," she assured them, forcing a smile, even though he couldn't see her. Her arms were tightly crossed over her torso in an attempt to stop the shivering that was no fault of the cold wind. "Supper will be ready once I get there. If you're starving, find Jenny. She'll set you up with some lovely cheeses and an assortment of breads and crackers."

"Sounds perfect. Will do. Looks very promising down there at the parade grounds. I'm just wondering if you want us to take a camera to the tribute. Jordy told us that they're playing a piper's lament. Sounds so moody and somber; it would make great B-roll. We might even catch something relevant on camera again. Should we head down there?"

Although Brett hadn't planned on going to the tribute, something in the crowd caught his attention. He stepped on the brakes, let a handful of people cross in front of him, then made a quick turn onto what looked like grass. "No," he said to Ed. "Keep the cameras there. We're not here to cover a murder or a tribute to the victim. We are here to cover a paranormal investigation. We are here to find answers regarding the ghostly piper of Dundoon."

"Gotcha!" Ed replied.

"One more thing. We're going to be delayed a bit. Best get some cheese and crackers."

The moment Brett ended the call, Bunny asked, "What are you doing? Why are you driving on grass?"

Brett flashed her one of his *I'm on the hunt* grins. "This lane goes behind the vendor tents. I just saw the shadow of a man farther down crossing the lane. He disappeared behind one of the tents. It was our man in the black suit."

"No," Giff offered in a scandalized breath. "Brett, we were told, via a hastily written note, not to stick our noses where they don't belong. Correct me if I'm wrong, but I don't think our noses belong down this Highland back alley."

"You can stay in the van if you'd like," Brett told him. "Why didn't I think of this in the first place?" As Brett berated himself, looking at Bunny as he did, he parked the van behind one of the vendor tents. "Of course, he'd be here. The pipers are paying tribute to the man he either murdered or was trying to help. He gave us the slip at the pub, then doubled back here. Are you coming?"

Bunny nodded and got out of the van. Giff, reluctantly, did the same.

"What's your plan?" she asked.

"He went this way," Brett pointed to the dark, narrow space between two tents. "Let's split up. I'm going to follow him this way. If you spot him, or anyone suspicious, call me. Otherwise, we'll meet at the gate to the parade ground in ten minutes."

"Gotcha, boss," Giff sent Brett off with a salute before watching him disappear between the tents. He looked at Bunny. "You have to admire his tenacity. I'm merely humoring him. I'm not about to split up with a murderer on the loose. Let's head this way."

Leaving the safety of the van, they walked down the grassy lane that ran behind the vendor tents until they spied one tent glowing in the near distance.

"Isn't that the Burgess Bagpipe Emporium tent?" Even in the darkness, Bunny could see that Giff was intrigued.

"I think so. Which is odd. Everyone here seems to be heading to the tribute. So, who's at the bagpipe emporium?" she questioned.

"Once again, I'm clueless. I'm not getting any psychic visions. Are you?" he teased.

Bunny responded with a rebuking grin. "I'm fresh out of visions, which means we're going to have to check it out in person."

Bunny, with Giff following, slipped between two dark tents, which opened on the main, torchlit thoroughfare where Brett had disappeared into the crowd of people heading for the entrance to the tribute. Not far from the entrance stood the Burgess Bagpipe Emporium tent, with its flaps wide open and bright lights illuminating the people milling inside. Bunny could see Seth and another employee behind the counter, serving a line of customers.

"Why is Burgess Bagpipe Emporium open for business, you ask?" Giff cast Bunny a sly grin as he posed the rhetorical question. "Because, silly, Seth Burgess is capitalizing on this tragedy and pushing the dated, event tchotchke as a memento of the day the music died, aka, the bagpipe maestro, Major MacDonald."

"Well, that's just rank opportunistic, and a wee bit slimy," Bunny seethed.

Giff, lightening the macabre mood, offered, "Hey, when a man dies and the pipers come out to play, people need trinkets. Which reminds me. I don't have enough souvenirs of this little ghost hunt, do you?" He pulled Bunny with him and entered the tent.

As Bunny scanned the crowd of shoppers, looking for a nondescript man in a dark suit, which was the only description the lads had given her, Giff, remarkably, was shopping.

"Look, Bunny," he called to her over the heads of intent shoppers. The moment she looked at him, he hoisted up a stout white mug with a bagpiper on it. "It's the piper of Dundoon! What a handsome devil. Brett clearly needs this. Want one? Or would you prefer the CD of classic bagpipe hits? Your choice. I'm buying." He made the slightest gesture with his head, pointing to the back of the tent.

Bunny looked and saw the tent flap flutter back in place, as if someone had just gone through it. Giff, you brilliant man, she thought. You're not shopping, you're creating a diversion. Yet just as she was about to investigate, the deep baritone of Seth Burgess filled the tent.

"Och, ye ghost-hunter kids. What are ye doing here?"

"Same as everyone else," Giff replied loudly. "Mourning the death of a national treasure. Do you have any T-shirts?"

While Giff put the press on Seth, Bunny, bobbing through the crowded aisles of merchandise, dashed to the back of the tent and went through the flap. To her surprise, she found herself in yet another tent, a smaller one illuminated by a bright, battery-powered lantern. It was filled with boxes and crates. She realized it was a makeshift stock room, and there was a good amount of stock, from the look of it. As Bunny eyed the boxes, the flap in the back of this smaller tent burst open, revealing a youngish man wearing jeans and a flannel, Carhart jacket. He grabbed one of the crates, then stopped in his tracks when he noticed her.

"Who the hell are ye?" He scrunched his eyes at her in a hostile manner.

Bunny didn't care for it at all. She also didn't like it when people came at her oozing aggressive attitude. She held her ground and offered a defiant lift of her chin. "I might ask ye the same question, Mr. Man. What are *you* doing here?" She eyed him suspiciously as she stepped around him and looked out of the flap he'd just walked through. Her heart gave a painful lurch at the sight. She was staring at the back of a cargo van, one similar to theirs, but unlike theirs, this one was filled with crates. She dropped the tent flap and turned to the man again.

"You're stealing bagpipes during a tribute? That's low."

"Stealing?" That clearly confused him. "It would be, if these weren't already mine."

"But they're not yours, are they? They belong to Seth Burgess. If you take one more, I'm going to run back there and get Mr. Burgess."

"Ye do that, sweetheart," he said, hoisting the box onto his shoulder. He flashed a wicked grin before disappearing outside. Bunny, without thinking, followed him.

"Where are you taking these?" she asked, watching him load the crate into the van.

He turned and walked past her. He was about to disappear back inside when he replied, "Back to the shop, the one in Paisley. That's our main store."

"Wait, you work for Seth?"

"Work for him?" A derisive chuckle escaped as he offered, "I'm the man's son. Peter's my name. I dinna catch yours."

"Bunny," she said meekly, as her cheeks burned with embarrassment. "Oh, dear. I'm so sorry. I just thought . . ."

"I know what ye thought. Ye made it clear. But ye were wrong. 'Tis Sunday. Technically speaking, this is the last day of the competition, and we're closing the pop-up shop. My da's selling what he can, but the rest needs to be packed up and taken to Paisley. If ye are planning on going to the tribute, ye better leave now, darlin', or you'll miss it." He brushed her off with a twist of his lips and went to get another crate. Bunny followed him.

"Please forgive me for thinking the worst of you," she hastily apologized. "I don't normally do that. I'm just on edge due to the"—she was about to say murder, caught herself, and offered—"unusual death of Major MacDonald."

"Unfortunate, that." He raised a brow while delivering a grimace in apology. Then he plucked another crate off the pile.

Bunny, certain this man was brushing her off, and still feeling guilty, decided that helping him load a box or two would make up for the ejeet, knee-jerk accusation she had made. She watched Peter slip out through the flap again before picking up the next hefty crate from the stack. The moment she did, she regretted it. The crate was much heavier than she had bargained for. She had assumed that, since it was marked with a capital B, the crate contained bagpipes. Not knowing much about the instrument except for the basics, she had naturally assumed that a crate of them would be manageable. With the crate gripped tightly between her hands, she took a few steps toward the flap, then a few backward to gain her balance again, but her arms were burning, threatening to let go. She could feel her fingers slipping when Peter burst through the flap, aiming for another crate until he saw her. Clearly, the last thing he expected was to see her still there, ready to drop the crate in her hands.

"What are ye doing?" he snapped, taking the crate from her.

Peter was of average height and build for a man, yet clearly, he was stronger than he looked. With another wave of embarrassment washing over her porcelain skin, she uttered, "I . . . I'm trying to help."

"Help? I dinna want your help. I dinna even know who ye are, lady," he growled, clearly angry that she was still there. "Just leave. Get out of here."

"But . . . but," she stammered.

"Go!" He pointed to the flap that led back to the shop.

Knowing that her confrontation with Peter had gone way off the rails, she gave a curt nod and ducked back inside the main tent, relieved to be out of there. Although there was still a crowd of people shopping, she immediately spotted Giff. He was carrying a large bag that she was certain was full of bagpipe memorabilia.

"Who was back there?" he asked, as they hustled out of the tent.

"Seth's son, Peter. Unlike his father, he's not the friendly type. He was packing up stock. They're leaving tomorrow. Come on. Let's find Brett and get back to the castle. It may be haunted, but I'll take haunted over rude any day."

Chapter 33

Bunny's nerves were still tingling painfully under her skin as she headed for the castle kitchen. It had been a frustrating day, spent talking with possible suspects, chasing a mysterious man in a black suit, and finally being barked at by the petulant son of Seth Burgess, who was by no means a peach himself. She was tired and dreaded the thought of another ghost investigation. Although Brett, Giff, and the lads would be with her, she knew it was up to her and Granny Mac to contact the ghostly piper of Dundoon and hopefully gain some insight into what the heck was going on here. It was always an unsettling, draining experience for her, especially since she felt ghostly emotions. Her own were bad enough to deal with at times. Really, she didn't need anyone else's!

Already feeling drained, Bunny thought of the warm, cozy bed waiting for her in the White Cottage, tantalizing her with a peaceful night's sleep. "Go away!" she said aloud, in an attempt to shoo the image out of her thoughts. She didn't have time to sleep. She had supper to get on the table.

"Och, you look as if ye could use a good night's sleep,"

Jenny remarked upon seeing her. *Why did she have to bring up sleep?* Bunny thought. "Aye, I'll not disagree with you there. I'm a wee bit tired, but I'll be fine. I'll push through. 'Tis all part of the job. By the way, that salmon looks lovely." And it really did. The dear lass, bless her, was already hard at work on supper, plating the poached salmon and garnishing it with slices of fresh lemon and a dollop of the fragrant dill sauce Bunny had made earlier. The dish looked so lovely that Bunny felt a pang of guilt for not being there to help with the supper she had planned.

"Why, thank ye." Although a touch of rose graced the tops of her cheeks at the compliment, Jenny grinned and made a little bow. "I hope ye dinna mind that I started without ye. It'll be a cozy group tonight without the judges. They're dining in the village with the pipers from the tribute. Good riddance to them all," she declared with an eye roll. "It'll be just the family, us employees, your gran, her man," she flashed an impish grin at this, "and ye and your lads."

Bunny nodded before crossing to the butcher-block island to help Jenny plate up the meal. She gave the bowl of roasted and mashed acorn squash a stir, inhaling the delicious, savory aroma as she did. She had made the brown butter sauce earlier, which Jenny was reheating on the stove. It had a touch of brown sugar in it, with a pinch of cinnamon and nutmeg to boost the natural flavor of the vegetable. It was one of Bunny's favorite ways to eat acorn squash. As she began adding the squash to the plates Jenny was working on, she offered, "I'm glad the judges won't be here. Aside from all that tension between them last night, I don't trust them."

Jenny looked up from the plate she was working on. "Do ye think they're guilty of murder?"

Bunny shrugged. "Hard to say. One of them possibly. Fergus Cameron was jealous of Major MacDonald's employment by the late queen. He told us today that they had both auditioned for the job and that both were in the running to get it. However, the queen made the final decision and chose Major MacDonald instead."

"Aye, as she should have done. Major MacDonald was far easier on the eyes." Although Jenny punctuated this statement with a teasing grin, Bunny knew there was some truth in it. "I suppose it'll all shake out once Constable Craig gets the forensic report back from the lab," Jenny added. "As of yet, no one is claiming ownership of the bagpipe found at the bottom of the cliff."

Bunny agreed. They were just about to add the seasoned, boiled potatoes to each plate when the kitchen door burst open, revealing a very disgruntled Winterton.

"They're gone!" he cried, marching into the kitchen. "They're bloody gone!"

"Good evening, Winterton," Jenny said with a wry grin. Clearly, she had no idea what he was talking about. "A pleasure to see ye too. What are ye missing this time? If you're looking for your glasses, they're on your head." She pointed to his head, stifling a giggle.

Chandler Winterton's fingers fumbled around a moment before latching onto the pair of eyeglasses hiding on his fluffy, silver head. He then frowned and shoved them into the pocket of his Highland coat. "Thanks, but they're not what I was looking for. 'Tis my pipes. They're not in the closet where I keep them. Have ye seen anyone with them?"

Jenny shook her head.

"You keep them here, at the castle, and not at your home?" Bunny asked, thinking it odd.

"Aye, I keep them here. I use them to pipe the Malcoms to their supper and little else. I'm getting ready to do that now, but I canna. Not without my pipes."

"Does Jasper know where they are?" Jenny asked.

"Why would the lad know? He's not the keeper of my pipes. He's got his own set."

Bunny could see that the stoic ghillie was beginning to panic. Although she felt sorry for him, it got her wondering. Missing bagpipes? Could they be the unidentified set found at the bottom of the cliff with Major MacDonald? She turned to the ghillie, and asked, "When was the last time you saw them?"

"Last night. After I piped Jordy and Elizabeth to the table, with your cameramen filming. Once I was done, I went back to the closet, as I always do, and stored them away."

"Where is this closet?"

"Behind the kitchen storehouse. 'Tis in the hallway just off the back entrance."

Bunny's curiosity got the best of her. She asked to see the closet in question. Jenny set down her knife, wiped her hands on her apron, and followed Bunny.

It was exactly as Winterton had described it. The old closet in question was just off the kitchen, across from the back stairway, and near a doorway that led to the back courtyard. Jenny told her that it was the entrance the staff commonly used. Along with a couple of rugged barn coats and a few well-worn hats, Bunny saw a set of bagpipes hanging on a hook.

"Here they are," she said helpfully, pointing to the bagpipes.

"Those are Jasper's," Winterton told them.

"Mr. Winterton," Bunny began as the inkling of a possibility began to burn bright in her mind, "have you, by chance, seen the set of bagpipes that were found with Major MacDonald?"

He shook his head, indicating that he hadn't. "When Jasper called me with the news, I was sound asleep. I got dressed as fast as I could, started up the quad, and came right here. I then picked up Doc Beaton and the constable and drove them to the spot Jasper had indicated. It was not only dark, but, as you know, mightily foggy out there as well. Jasper was waiting for us. He then led the doc and the constable down the cliffside trail, while I stayed back to wait for the service vehicles to arrive. What are ye getting at, lass?"

"It's just a hunch," she told them, before making a call to Constable Craig.

Bunny and Jenny got dinner on the table while they waited for the constable to arrive. Everyone was seated, including Granny Mac, Doc Beaton, Jordy, Elizabeth, Winterton, Jasper, and the lads. Even Mrs. and Mr. Collins had joined them for supper. The moment Constable Craig arrived with the picture of the unclaimed bagpipes found at the bottom of the cliff with Major MacDonald, it became instantly clear who they belonged to.

"Dear God in heaven," Winterton breathed, looking at the photo of the ripped bag and broken drones of his beloved pipes, "what were they doing down there?"

"That is the question," Constable Craig said, taking back the picture. "We know they weren't Major MacDonald's, nor did they belong to either of the two remaining judges. Jasper, who was at the crime scene, didn't recognize them either."

"In my defense, sir," Jasper piped up, with a slightly wild look on his face, "there was a dead man lying on top of 'em! The drones were sticking out from under him like the tentacles of a squished octopus, all broken and askew. I dinna give them a second thought, under the circumstances."

"Here-here, lad," Jordy rallied his employee. "I likely wouldn't have recognized them either in that condition. I don't play myself, but I will declare until my dying breath that nothing stirs my soul like the sound of bagpipes at dusk."

"Mr. Winterton," Bunny said, grabbing the ghillie's attention once again. "We know these bagpipes didn't belong to either Cameron or Fraser, but could either one of those men have seen you put them away in that closet?"

He thought a moment before answering, "Aye. They might have. But as long as we're talking about judges, MacDonald might have too. Jasper told me that he found the man poking around the castle, looking in cupboards and closets and other folks' rooms. Those pipes dinna belong to Major MacDonald, but that doesn't mean he wasn't playing them the night he was murdered. If, in fact, he was murdered?" Winterton's dark eyebrows rose high on his forehead as he posed this question.

"Aye, regarding all the evidence, it appears that he was pushed to his death," Constable Craig confirmed. "Whether it was premeditated or a crime committed in the heat of the moment is yet to be determined, as we do not have any suspects in custody. What we do have are the facts, which are that three people and a dog of unusual size were out on that clifftop in the wee hours of the morning, one of them playing the bagpipes. Was it mere tomfoolery, or was something nefarious going on out there? Again, we cannot say. However, I can assure you that we are still searching for the other two people who were out on the clifftop last night with Major MacDonald."

"Dog of unusual size?" Giff, stuck on this one phrase, finished the last of his wine before returning his glass to the table. "Is that what we're calling it now, this fairy-dog creature? A dog? Because, last night, I distinctly remember seeing a pair of glowing red eyes through the fog. Call me crazy, but there's no dog breed I know of that claims glowing red eyes. It's unholy! Ladies, gentlemen, we can all agree that there is something very strange going on here."

"Aye, there is," Jordy said, with a frown that made his

jowls quake. "The ghosties are one thing. Lizzy, Winston, and I have made our peace with them long ago. This murder, however, is confounding."

"About those ghosts," Brett began, his blue eyes holding onto Jordy's, "I want to thank you for allowing us another chance to continue our investigation tonight. I don't know if Ella told you, but Bunny heard the ghostly piper last night, just after MacDonald went over the cliff."

"Ye heard him?" Jordy tilted his head as he looked at Bunny. "But you're the chef."

"My granddaughter has inherited some of my clairvoyant abilities," Granny Mac proudly informed the table. "Then there's the fact that she has some all her own that she's learning to cope with."

"Och, ye poor dear." Elizabeth's hand came over her heart as she held Bunny with her gentle, understanding gaze. Then, quick as the snap of the fingers, those same eyes began sparkling with curiosity. "What was it like, reading the mind of a ghost?"

Umm, how to explain it, Bunny thought. She could barely make sense of it herself. Sure, she could communicate telepathically with ghosts, but it was the fact that she could feel their living emotions that she found daunting. It was getting late, and she had no wish to belabor the thought of ghostly, ghastly emotions. She could feel more than sense that she was about to be visited by more ghostly emotions, and relatively soon. She landed on the word: "Unsettling. I'm not very good at it yet. But surely, you've heard the piper play?"

"Aye," Elizabeth said. "It is a sad, unearthly tune he plays. You've all heard the story. The piper played a warning for his master, Colkitto MacDonald, and his hands were lopped off by the Campbells because of it. I saw him once up on the battlements. He had no hands. He's a handless piper. I often wonder if the tune he's playing isn't a little off because he has no hands."

"Yikes!" Giff said aloud. He raised his empty wineglass to their host. "Jordy, my good man. As you know, we're about to tap into the fourth dimension and rile up your handless ghost. Would you mind passing around some more of that fine wine? It's going to be a long, hair-raising night for the team of *Food and Spirits*, and I, for one, could use all the Dutch courage I can get. Cheers!"

Chapter 34

"Ella and I are in the snug, ready to roll," Ed informed them over their walkie-talkies. "The camera feed is up, and we're recording. Keep it rolling, boys."

"Will do," Cody said, and winked at Bunny.

"I don't know why you're so happy about this." Bunny might have snarled at him as she said this, and she was a little sorry about that. However, in her defense, she was in the beginnings of a paranormal nerve storm, and she highly doubted Cody understood what that was like. "You're not going to be able to film what I experience. You're just not."

"Maybe not, but I'll be right there with you, tucked into a corner with my camera pointed at you, conveniently out of the way. I won't let anything happen to you, Bunny. Also, Ella will be right here," he said, holding up his walkie-talkie, "in case we need her."

It wasn't the most comforting thought, but since the ghostly piper seemed to have a connection with Bunny, it was agreed that Granny Mac would sit in the cozy snug with Ed, staying warm and connected, while monitoring the proceedings from there. As for Bunny, it was decided that she would go back to the battlement and try connecting with the piper there. It was the place her spirit guide, Braiden, had brought her to last night in the form of the white rabbit. She knew in the marrow of her bones that that was where she needed to be. It would be cold, but she was prepared. She was bundled in a heavy winter jacket, with a warm hat on her head and thick gloves encasing her fingers. Cody was also dressed for the weather.

"We're ready to begin the hunt over here," Brett's voice came loud and clear over the walkie-talkie. Brett and Giff arguably had the most difficult assignment of the evening. They were bound and determined to get to the bottom of the fairy-dog sightings in the old east wing. Mike would be with them, filming their adventures.

"Woe to the fairy dog that barks at me," Giff added, jokingly.

"Stay safe," Bunny told them. "We're climbing up to the battlement now, lads. Wish us luck."

As Bunny and Cody arrived at the top landing, Cody opened the door. A cold gust of wind coming off the choppy water below hit them square in the face, ruffling the hair beneath their warm hats. It was going to be a chilly night. Bunny walked across the flat, rooftop structure surrounded by a stout, crenellated wall and peered out at the night-dark landscape that engulfed them. The hair on the back of her neck stood on end at the sight that greeted her. During the day, the battlement overlooked the Sound of Jura and the hills of the Western Isles across the water. It was breathtaking. At night, however, with the full autumn moon overhead reflecting off the black waves like a watery beacon, it felt ancient and eerie. It was a dramatic setting for a ghostly encounter. Bunny knew the place hadn't changed much since the piper's day. She walked to a spot along the wall and stood there a moment, feeling a slight hum as her blood pumped through her veins. She knew that this was where the piper had once stood, looking out over the sound, waiting for the sight of his master's ship to return. It was as if the stones in this very spot held the memory of that tragedy long ago. Bunny took one last full breath of the cold, night air and turned from the wall. As she walked to her spot, the same one she had occupied last night, sitting with her back against the castle wall, she saw Cody. He was sitting in the corner of the battlement with his camera aimed at her. She gave him a silent nod as she sat back against the wall. She then closed her eyes and regulated her breathing, turning her thoughts inward, turning them to the ghost of the piper who haunted the castle.

Bunny wasn't aware of just how long she'd been sitting like that until she felt the bump against her leg. Her eyes flew open, and she immediately saw Hopper. His fluffy butt was resting on the floor, while his white front paws dangled over her legs.

"I figured you'd show up eventually," she told him, adding, "when you were good and ready." He wiggled his nose at her in understanding. "I'd like to contact the piper, Hopper. Can you bring him to me?"

With another wiggle of his pink nose, Hopper pushed off her leg and bounded along the battlement, leading her away from where she'd been sitting.

Bunny scrambled to her feet and followed him. The moment she rounded the corner, she stopped and let out a little gasp. The ghostly piper was standing right where she had been a few minutes ago. His back was to her as he stood facing the water, and Hopper was sitting at his feet. She stared at the rabbit, wondering how to begin. The rabbit was no help.

"Um, hello," she said, merely because she didn't know what else to say.

The moment she spoke, the piper turned around, facing

her. That was a mistake. Not only was he missing his hands, but the moment he saw her, she felt everything he did. Her heart began pounding in her chest with the pain of fear and excitement. It was pounding so hard that Bunny feared she might have a heart attack. Her senses filled with the smell of him, the tang of whisky, the sweet scent of oiled leather, and the pungent reek of wet wool. Yet more than any of these, she could feel the urgency in his purpose. Life-and-death urgency. This wasn't a game.

"I have heard you play," she offered. The piper, with the old instrument under his arm, gave a curt nod of his bonneted head. "Did you know that the song you played saved your master?" A welling of pride filled her as she asked this. Again, he nodded. "Are you aware that you are a ghost?"

He was still a moment, unmoving, causing Bunny to question this. Then, however, he nodded again. "Aye," she heard him say in a gruff, spectral voice.

"Why . . . are you still here?"

"I am trapped," he told her with simplicity. "I am a prisoner. I am waiting."

Bunny's heart clenched painfully at this. The ghostly piper was still at the castle because he was trapped. She swallowed the lump in her throat and asked, "You say that you are a prisoner and that you are waiting. What are you waiting for?"

"For my master Colkitto's return. I used my pipes to warn him of the treachery here. He understood and guided his ship away, saving them all from certain death. The men are all gone now, and I am still here. Alone. I will never see them again in life, but I still play. I play because one day my master will hear the song I play and welcome me home."

Bunny's heart ached for the man this ghost once was, ached for the bravery he had displayed by defying his captors and playing a song that had saved the people he belonged to. A selfless act. An act of incredible bravery and loyalty. Bunny thought that she had never encountered such fierce loyalty before, until she thought of her brother, Braiden. Her twin.

Bravery. Loyalty. Love. The emotions of this ghost had rendered her speechless and clouded her eyes with tears, because those qualities defined her brother as well. Even in death, he was still with her, albeit in the form of her beloved white rabbit.

She took a deep breath, fighting for control again.

Thinking of this ghostly piper's haunting tune and the piper who had recently died, she asked, "You have another fallen comrade, I believe. Another MacDonald piper who served the queen. I heard you play for him."

"Aye," he told her. "He battled a foe on the cliffs and lost. I did my duty and played a lament that has carried his soul home. My kinsmen are all safe on the other side."

"Your kinsmen are safe," she acknowledged, feeling out of her league with this noble spirit. She found the fact that he acknowledged Major MacDonald as a kinsman a good sign. "He was a piper too," she stated. "Was he the man playing on the clifftops before he . . . died?" She wasn't sure that talking to a ghost about death was acceptable. Thankfully, the piper didn't seem to mind.

"No. It was not him. It was an amateur who misplayed the tune."

"I was told that you misplayed a tune as well," Bunny reminded him. The ghost agreed.

"Aye. I sent a message of warning by misplaying a tune. My master understood, because I had never misplayed it before. I saved him."

Taking a chance, Bunny asked, "Do you know who was playing the bagpipes out on that clifftop?" The ghostly piper shook his head. Bunny then asked, "Would you like to go home?"

She felt his answer in her chest, hitting her with the force of a football kicked at close range. It was a feeling of heart-aching longing, of sadness, of despair, with just a glimmering of hope. Granny Mac would know how to move this spirit from his current earthbound purgatory to the glories waiting on the other side. She was certain of that. But how?

"I am waiting for my master's return," he stated again with confidence, which Bunny felt was misplaced.

Before she could tell him that she would try to help him, he turned away from her. And just as he was fading into the ether, shimmering like a stray moonbeam in the darkness, he began to play his haunting lament. Bunny now understood why the ghostly tune was so sad, so powerful. He was trying to reach his master on the other side. The piper was trying to find his way home. The helpless feeling that overwhelmed her was crushing her soul. Hopper was fading too.

"Oh my God!" Cody cried, pulling her out of her meditative state and bringing her into reality. She felt exhausted, both emotionally and physically. "He's here! The piper is here! I got him on camera. I saw the ghostly piper of Dundoon! Can you hear that?"

She could, and the sound was not only haunting, but heartbreaking as well. "I can," she told him softly, as tears streamed down her face. "I've connected with him, Cody. It was . . ." She searched for the right word to describe her paranormal connection, but words fell short. She landed on "incredible," leaving it at that. As thoughts and emotions of her recent encounter swirled in her head like fallen leaves swept up in an eddy of wind, she offered, "The man on the clifftop playing the bagpipes last night was not Major MacDonald. It was another."

"Are you sure?" Cody looked at her as if she was not quite in her right mind. Truthfully, she wasn't.

Bunny looked at the fading, shimmering mist in the shape

of the ghostly piper. Hopper was gone. As she stared at it, awestruck, she saw a white butterfly form in the belly of the mist, flittering and fluttering about. With a lump in her throat, she watched as the butterfly climbed higher, reaching the spot in the mist shaped like the piper's head. The moment the butterfly broke through the mist, hitting the cold night air, both mist and butterfly vanished. That was the moment Bunny received an image of Braiden smiling at her in her mind's eye that was so vivid and real, it momentarily knocked the breath from her. Somehow, she understood that the connection with the ghostly piper was a gift from him. Receiving the message, every nerve in her body erupted in a wave of light tingling, from her toes to the crown of her head, waking her fully to the time and place she was standing in. She realized that Cody was staring at her, awaiting an answer.

"Am . . . I sure Major MacDonald wasn't playing the bagpipes last night on the cliff? Aye, I'm sure. A ghost so pure of heart as the piper of Dundoon would not lie. More than that, however, is that Major MacDonald was a professional, like the ghostly piper. The person who was playing last night wasn't a professional, at least that's what the piper thought. This was because the piper last night misplayed the tune he was attempting to play. In other words, he made a mistake, one the ghost picked up on."

Cody, staring at her in wide-eyed wonder, uttered, "Amazing. The ghost recognized the tune? That's incredible. Great work, Bunny! Hey," he said, suddenly thinking of something else. "Doesn't the legend of the ghostly piper of Dundoon state that he also misplayed a tune . . . in order to warn his master of an ambush?"

"As a matter of fact, he did."

With the hand not holding the camera, Cody scratched his chin. "Bunny, do you think . . . ?"

"That it was intentional?" she added for him, deep in thought herself. "That the piper misplayed the tune on purpose as a warning?"

"Exactly. The question is, who was he warning, and why?"

That was the question, but neither Bunny nor Cody had time to ponder it because Brett's strained voice crackled over Cody's walkie-talkie.

"Cody, Bunny, are you available?"

"As a matter of fact, we are," Cody offered. He was about to share the fact that they had just encountered the ghostly piper of Dundoon, when Brett cut him off.

"Good, because I need you two to get down here. Quickly!"

Chapter 35

Bunny and Cody immediately left the battlements and raced down the three flights of tower stairs. They weren't certain where Brett was, but the moment they landed on the second floor, Granny Mac was there to greet them. The fine lines and wrinkles of her face were animated with excitement, making her look younger and more youthful than her seventy-five years. Without saying a word, the older woman wrapped Bunny in her arms.

"Ye reached him, my dear," she whispered proudly in her granddaughter's ear. "I felt your connection. Although I was sitting in the snug with Ed, watching you on the monitor, it was as if I was right there with you as you crossed into the fourth dimension to woo the elusive piper out of the shadows."

"Braiden helped," Bunny whispered back, reveling in her grandmother's warm, comforting embrace. Although she hadn't realized it, her gran's hug was just what she needed.

"Loyalty," Ella MacBride stated as she released her hold on Bunny. The word took Bunny by surprise. Cody too, judging from the look on his face. "I felt such an intense welling of loyalty the moment you connected to the spirit, Bunny, that I believe this is why he remains. Unrequited love was the shackle that bound the ghost of the poor, dear Mistletoe Bride to Bramsford Manor. Loyalty to a kinsman is what keeps the piper here, hiding in the shadows. I'm certain of it."

"I think so too, Gran," Bunny admitted. "I also believe that you can help move him on. But first there's the troubling matter of the fairy dog."

"Ah, yes, the fairy dog." Granny Mac's upper lip stiffened as she said this. "I've been watching the monitors. Very troubling indeed. Follow me." She waved them on as she led them down the hallway.

As Bunny and Cody followed Ella down a series of hallways and stairways, and through a room or two, Bunny's nerves were still quite raw from her ghostly encounter with the piper. She wasn't at all certain she was ready to battle a fairy dog just yet. However, Brett's strained and excited voice had struck something deeply primal and protective inside her. Was it mere loyalty, she wondered, or something more complicated and delicate, something closer to the heart? Her heart was certainly beating fast. Was it normal that her breathing was also fast? She wasn't certain, but what she did know was that Brett needed her.

They landed in a dark, eerie hallway on the second floor of the east wing. Bunny assumed that Brett and Giff would be there to greet them. The fact that they weren't only made her more nervous than before. Her heart was beating nearly as fast as the wings of a hummingbird.

"Where are they?" she asked Cody. That was a mistake. Cody knew as much as she did. He pointed his night-vision camera down the dark hallway and shrugged.

"I don't have a clue. Ella, are you certain this is the right hallway?"

"Not really," she replied, with pinched brows. She was trying to examine the hallway, but it was too dark to see much of anything. "I've never been to this part of the castle before. Although, if I'm not mistaken, this is the hallway that directly connects the renovated bed chambers in the west wing to the stairway that descends just beyond the kitchen. Jordy used to travel this hallway in the middle of the night to get a snack, but that stopped once the fairy dog was sighted."

"The fairy dog was sighted in this hallway?" Cody pointed his camera at her as he asked this.

"This is one of the hallways. Drunk Gordie also can be heard traipsing along the hallway to the kitchen stairs. This part of the castle is very haunted. Does anyone else find it odd that the lads aren't here?"

Bunny was just about to agree with her gran that it was odd, when the sound of a low growl hit her ears. She spun around at the same time Cody did, both facing the end of the long hallway. "Crivens! What was that?"

The question had no sooner left her mouth when she saw a pair of glowing red eyes appear at the end of the hallway. They were slowly moving toward them, accompanied by the sound of more guttural growling. The hair on Bunny's neck stood on end. She wanted to run but held her ground. She needed to find Brett, Giff, and Mike. What if . . . ? What if . . . ? Och, she couldn't even think of it. As she stared at the red orbs, a dark, shadowy body began to take shape. The closer it got, the larger it became. Bunny didn't want to believe in fairy dogs, but she could not deny that the largest, scraggly canine creature she'd ever seen, with red eyes, was prowling down the hallway toward her. There was no doubt in her mind that this hellish fairy creature had taken Brett. The thought enraged her. It made her crazy and irrational. With nothing but clenched fists at her sides, Bunny knew what she had to do. She had to attack the fairy dog before it could bark three times.

"What are you doing?" Cody hissed at her as she crouched into position.

"I'm going to scare it off, or die trying," she told him with gritted determination. Tears at the thought of Brett filled her eyes. She was also quite sorry that Giff was gone too, but even she had to admit that it was the thought of Brett—hunky, handsome, brave Brett Bloom—that spurred her to unreasonable action. "That creature has taken our friends from us, and possibly Major MacDonald as well. I'm putting an end to it. I'm going to send that hellhound back to hell!"

"But . . ." Cody said, trying to reason with her. However, it was too late. Bunny had shot up from her crouch and was now running hell-for-leather down the old stone hallway toward the glowing red eyes.

A loud, earth-shattering howl echoed through the hallway, sparking a new wave of terror coursing through Bunny's veins. That was the first howl, she thought. I cannot let it howl again! Silently wishing she had her chef's knife with her, Bunny tightened her fists instead. Pummeling the air, she closed her eyes and ran even faster toward the beast. She didn't want to see it or hear it. All she wanted to do was pummel its scraggly body into the afterlife. However, as hard as her fists punched air, they weren't connecting with anything at all but, well, air.

"Bunny!" she heard Brett cry.

Bunny's eyes sprang open at the sound. That was when she realized that the end of the hallway was swiftly approaching. She pulled up, trying to stop, but she'd been running too fast. She hit the wall, shielding the blow with her shoulder. The moment Bunny hit the solid stone wall, she spun around and stared down the hallway the way she had come, wondering where the fairy dog had gone. How had she missed it? She was happy to see that her gran and Cody remained. Then she saw Brett standing behind them, lovely, hunky Brett. He looked unscathed. The sight of him lifted her heart. Then Giff appeared, followed by Mike. All three ghost hunters were there, looking absolutely fine. Brett was running toward her. What in the world was going on?

Before she knew it, Brett's arms wrapped around her. She didn't hate that. In fact, she melted into him, feeling safe, secure, and happily still very much alive. Unfortunately, the hug didn't last as long as she might have wished. Then again, they were in the middle of a haunted hallway. The moment Brett released her, she stepped back.

"Where did it go?" she asked him, wildly raking her eyes over the walls. "It was right here. The fairy dog was coming toward us. I heard it howl."

"What were you doing, running like that at the wall?" His light-colored brows were pinched with concern.

"I was going after the fairy dog. I"—she sniffed, rubbed her sticky eyes, then continued—"I thought you were dead. I thought it got you."

"Dead?" That shocked him. "You thought the fairy dog got me?" Bunny could see that he was trying hard not to smile. In fact, his burgeoning humor irked her. She had just risked a run-in with the hellhound of the fairy world to avenge his death, and he found it humorous? "The fairy dog didn't get me. It couldn't get me. It's not real, Bunny. But I do appreciate your bravery. You were trying to chase it off, I believe?"

"Something like that. Crivens!" she suddenly exclaimed, thinking about his words regarding the fairy dog. She looked right at him and asked, "Don't tell me the fairy dog is a ghost!" Why did that thought depress her?

Brett shook his head. "Not a ghost. It's even better than

that. While Giff, Mike, and I set about hunting for this mythical fairy dog, we encountered it here, same as you. Only, unlike you, we weren't as brave. We ran from it, not toward it. Then, however, we encountered it again on that back hallway, the one adjacent to this hallway. That time, we didn't run, we observed it. That's when we realized there was something not quite right with the fairy dog."

"What do you mean by not quite right? That unholy beast is terrifying." Bunny tilted her head as she studied him.

"It is, but it's designed that way. After observing it, we noticed that every five minutes it repeated the same series of growls and howls. Sure, it's scary, and it looks terrifying with those glowing red eyes, but we knew then that the fairy dog wasn't real. It was a projection of some kind."

"It's a projection?" She was having a hard time wrapping her head around that. The fairy dog she had encountered sure appeared real, until it vanished.

Brett held her in a grin of pure excitement. "Come on, we have something incredible to show you."

While they waited for Ed to join them, Brett explained how it had taken them a good long while to figure out just how it was done. Once everyone had gathered in the old hallway, Brett, Giff, and Mike led them to a long-forgotten storeroom in the cold, damp cellar of the castle. Brett walked to the back and stood before a moldy, old lace curtain that looked to be from the nineteen thirties. He then pulled it back with a flourish, revealing a very modern computer, set up on a desk, that was running its own Wi-Fi network. Giff pressed a key on the keyboard, bringing the monitor to life. The moment he did, Bunny couldn't believe what she was seeing.

"This is highly troubling," she uttered, staring at the monitor. It showed four different video feeds from different parts of the castle, including the two hallways where the fairy dog was commonly encountered.

Granny Mac crossed her arms as she shook her red head at the screen. "This computer is the smoking gun we've been looking for. Someone is trying to scare Jordy and Elizabeth, making them believe that a fairy dog has started haunting the castle when, clearly, it's . . ." Her forehead wrinkled as she pondered what exactly it was that she was looking at. The only thing playing on the monitor was the still views from four different hallways. "Could this be a security camera?"

"That's a good question, Ella," Ed said, taking a seat at the computer desk. He typed some commands on the keyboard before informing them, "It's actually set up to be a security system." A moment later, the screen went black, and a line of small green text appeared, scrolling across the monitor. Bunny was no computer expert, but she recognized the gibberish as code.

"It's not a security system," Giff told them. "The Malcoms already have one. Instead, this system monitors these hallways. When someone steps into hallway number two or three," he indicated to the two screens in question, "it trips a sensor." As Giff explained this, Ed continued typing. As another screen popped up, he exclaimed, "Gotcha!"

The screen he was looking at revealed a video labeled FAIRY DOG HOLOGRAM. Ed opened the video and hit the play button. The monitor came to life with a familiar 3-D image, coupled with the soundtrack that had so recently terrified Bunny in the long hallway. The giant, three-dimensional fairy dog was moving on a white background, growling, howling, and walking toward the screen. Ed dragged the mouse around, showing the remarkable image from all sides.

"This is exceptionally complicated," Bunny said, staring

with dripping incredulity at the monitor. "So how does it appear in those hallways?"

"After successfully debunking the fairy-dog haunting," Brett stated, pointing to the video playing on the monitor, "we then went back to the hallways in question and discovered that there is a hidden camera in one of the wall sconces in each of the four hallways. We then figured out that the system is only activated between the hours of midnight and five in the morning. If someone enters one of these hallways during that time, it sets off a sensor, triggering the appropriate holographic projectors and sound systems in one of these two hallways. We discovered that the holographic projectors have been mounted in the ceiling, hidden by fake smoke detectors."

"Absolutely diabolical, isn't it?" Giff arched one of his manscaped brows like a master villain. "Someone has gone to great lengths to pull off his fairy-dog hoax. The question is who and why?"

"I don't know who would do such a thing," Granny Mac said, frowning at this new discovery. "But I might know why. These two hallways open onto the second floor of the renovated wing. I think someone here wants to scare the Malcoms at night, keeping them and their guests in their rooms."

"Major MacDonald had left his room in the middle of the night," Bunny offered. "Maybe he stumbled on this too. Maybe that's why he was out on that clifftop last night. Maybe the person playing the bagpipes is somehow connected to this."

"That is a very decent guess," Brett told her, raking a hand through his hair as he thought about it. "However, remember last night in the fog?" he asked his team. "We saw two glowing red eyes, and we heard a dog growl and bark three times. I don't know about the glowing eyes, but there was clearly a dog out there last night. Constable Criag has even proven there was; he found the large canine pawprints at the scene."

"That's right," Giff nodded, remembering those haunting red eyes. "We know there's a sweet puppy already living at the castle, Winston, the Malcoms' black Lab. He's far from a scary fairy dog, the big sweetie. The constable said that the prints found at the crime scene were too large to be from Winston. So that means there's another dog here that we don't know about."

"It could mean that," Bunny agreed. "But Winston is the only dog I've seen. I know that there haven't been wolves in Scotland since the seventeen-hundreds, but I did hear that there have been efforts to reintroduce wolves. It's not out of the question that what we encountered out there last night was a wild wolf."

Brett nodded at the possibility. "Once again, it looks like we have more questions than answers. But I think we're getting closer to unraveling this puzzling thread." He glanced at his watch. "It's one in the morning. Since this isn't a life-threatening matter, I say we take pictures of everything here, then call the constable first thing in the morning to report this."

One in the morning! Bunny wished that Brett hadn't mentioned the time. All the creepy, spooky excitement had kept her awake, but now she could feel herself fading fast. Thoughts of the warm, soft bed waiting for her in the White Cottage swirled in her mind. She mindlessly snapped a few pictures of the fairy-dog video on the computer while dreaming of sleep. It wasn't until her gran gave her an elbow nudge that she realized Brett had asked her a question.

"We've been so busy here that I forgot to ask. How did it go on the battlement?"

At that pointed question, all thoughts of sleep were thrust aside by the image of the ghostly piper. Bunny was also dismayed to know that, with his image, came a flood of the overwhelming ghostly emotions that bound him to Dundoon. “I had a wee chat with the piper. While he couldn’t reveal much, he did tell me that the man playing the bagpipes last night on the clifftop was not Major MacDonald. We can put that theory to rest, along with the fairy dog you’ve just debunked. Also, you’ll be happy to know that the spirit of Major MacDonald is no longer here. The piper made sure that his soul has crossed over. Heavens, it’s been a long night.”

Chapter 36

Bunny dreamed that she was frying bacon in an old cast-iron skillet in a vaguely familiar kitchen. The bacon was sizzling and popping to perfection. It looked delicious and smelled heavenly, so heavenly that her tummy rumbled, reminding her that she was hungry. That's when she opened her eyes and realized that she was not, in fact, frying bacon in a kitchen, but snuggled under the warm comforter in the soft cottage bed. Despite the recent ghost hunt, her connection to the ghostly piper of Dundoon, and the debunked fairy-dog hoax, she felt remarkably well rested. She stretched her arms over her head and took a deep breath of the cool, bacon-scented air. Someone was definitely frying bacon in the cottage kitchen. Bunny then plucked her phone off the nightstand and looked at the time. Eleven-thirty. No wonder she felt rested. It was nearly noon.

After hastily dressing in a pair of comfy, faded jeans and a thick, white cable-knit sweater and slipping on her fluffy slippers, Bunny left her room, pulled by the scent of bacon. She was delighted to see Jenny standing at the stove. Jasper was beside her, buttering toast and scooping scrambled eggs onto the awaiting plates. As for the bacon, that was all Jenny's doing. Beyond the kitchen, she saw Granny Mac sitting at the head of the table, clutching a mug of tea while chatting with the lads. They were all there, dressed and ready for breakfast. Giff, she noted with an inward smile, was wearing his kilt with the lovely plaid wrapped around his shoulders like a warm blanket. After all, that's exactly what it was.

"Good morning, everyone," she said cheerfully and went to join Jenny in the kitchen. "Sorry I overslept. What's going on?"

"Breakfast, with a side of apology," Jenny replied, casting Bunny a troubled look over her shoulder. "I feel so daft."

"Why do you feel daft? I don't understand?" As Bunny spoke, she took a mug down from the cabinet and poured herself a much-needed cup of coffee. She leaned her hip against the counter and took a sip of the hot, bold black brew.

Jenny pursed her troubled lips. "I feel daft because we've been tricked, and I told ye the tale, the tale of the fairy dog. When I came to the castle kitchen this morning to make breakfast, Jordy and Elizabeth walked in with Constable Craig. The constable told us about your ghost hunt last night, and about the fairy-dog hoax played on us at the castle. It made me so sad, and so angry."

"Aye, it was bloody awful!" Jasper added, his face animated with indignation. "Breakfast was canceled, and we were all sent to the dining room to give statements to the police, and by all, I mean the entire castle staff. They think one of us was clever enough to make that hologram and spook the hallways! As if. I was terrified of that creature! Jenny and I've had several run-ins with it—in those very hallways! It chilled me to the bone, and I've lost more than a good night's sleep over it. I've been scared to venture into that part of the castle for months, all because of some hologram—some bloody hoax! I'm scunnered by it!" He made a face to illustrate just how he felt and plopped a scoop of scrambled eggs on the plate in front of him.

"Well, if it's any consolation, I for one am glad it's a hoax," Bunny told them. "While a hoax is irritating and quite diabolical, I'll take that any day over the possibility of a real fairy dog roaming these hills."

"But that's just it," Jasper said. "If it's all just a hoax, then what did we encounter two nights ago on that foggy moor? I saw a pair of glowing red eyes. I heard that menacing growl. There were paw prints on the clifftop! The beast barked three times, and a man died! How do ye explain that?"

"We're not sure," Brett said. He rose from the table and stood beside Bunny. He cast her a private smile as he reached across her for the coffeepot. "A wolf, maybe? A very large dog? It could be anything. The point is that someone here is using the frightful tale of the fairy dog to keep people out of that part of the castle. Why? What's in that part of the castle?"

"Drunk Gordie?" Jenny offered. "One of those hallways leads to the stairway that's next to the kitchen. I've heard heavy footsteps plenty of times, only to find no one there."

"What?" Jasper attacked Jenny with his wild, wide-eyed look. "Are ye suggesting that Drunk Gordie is a hoax too? Och! I canna take this!"

"No, dear," Granny Mac piped up from the kitchen table. "He's the real deal, a drunk and disorderly spirit. He's belligerent, is that one."

"Phew!" Jasper looked relieved. "I thought for a minute that I've been taking crazy pills. I'm no fan of ghosties, but I'm happy to know that Drunk Gordie is a real haunting, and not a hoax."

Bunny placed a gentle hand on the young man's arm. "If it's any consolation, the ghostly piper of Dundoon is real as well. I connected with him last night. 'Tis an experience I shall never forget."

"Ye did it?" Jenny looked both surprised and pleased. "Oh, Bunny, that's grand! What did he say?"

"Not a whole lot, being a reclusive ghost. But he was very confident that Major MacDonald was not the man on the cliff playing Winterton's stolen bagpipes."

"Did he say who it was out there?" Jenny looked up from her pan of frying bacon. She put the last crisp pieces on the platter, turned off the stove, and tilted her head at Bunny.

"Unfortunately, he didn't. However, he did indicate that the person playing the bagpipes had misplayed the tune. Said the piper was not a professional because of that mistake."

Bunny and Brett helped put the breakfast plates on the table before taking a seat. The table was perfect for six, but felt rather cozy with all eight of them pressed together, drinking hot beverages, and eating eggs, bacon, and buttered toast.

"You said that all the castle employees were gathered this morning to give statements to the police," Giff began. "Is there anyone who works here who is capable of rigging up that complicated system?"

Jenny shrugged. "Well, that's just it. Mr. and Mrs. Collins know how to use a computer, like the rest of us, but rigging such a thing as that hologram is beyond them. Truthfully, it's beyond all of us. I can use my smartphone like an influencer when I'm so inclined, but when I'm at a computer, 'tis a different story."

"Aye, I agree," Jasper added. "I'm more what ye'd call mechanically inclined. If I'm stumped by something more complicated than a bum tractor carburetor, I watch a YouTube video. They're helpful. I also like to game a wee bit.

But when it comes to understanding technology, like holograms or complicated software programs, I'm lost."

Giff leaned on his elbows and hit Jasper with his pointed, brown-eyed gaze. "What about grumpy old Winterton? Could he be capable of rigging that hologram to play in the hallways?"

Jasper shook his head. "Not likely. I'm not sure the man's ever turned on a computer in his life. Don't know if he even owns one. Winterton's not what ye'd call an inside chappy. He's out and about all over those hills. He manages the grounds, keeps an eye on the wild beasts, and leads hunting parties. He also embraces folklore. I know for a fact that he believes in the fairy-dog legend. He truly does. He was just as angry about that hoax as we all were, likely more. Makes him look like a great muckle fool for embracing the myth so wholeheartedly."

"If no one who lives or works at the castle is capable of perpetrating such a hoax," Ed began, shaking his last piece of bacon at Jasper like a pointer, "then who do you think would benefit from such a hoax?"

"There have been workmen at the castle for a while now," Jenny informed them. "The constable was going to contact the general contractor and get a list of the names of every person who's worked here in the past few months. That's when the sightings began, three months ago."

"Very good," Cody said. "So, what's the connection between the fairy-dog hoax and the piper on the cliff? Jasper, you said two nights ago that you have heard the piper play out there before. You also stated that he sounds better out there than inside the castle."

"Aye, I did." Jasper's eyes came alive then, understanding what Cody was getting at. "The person playing the pipes two nights ago has done so before. Many times, in fact. I've heard him."

"How late at night?" Brett asked. "Do you remember?"

"Aye, late. Around two or three in the morning." His cheeks flushed red, as he admitted, "Sometimes I stay up gaming with my lads."

"Do you remember when you started hearing those bagpipes out there?"

Bunny could see the wheels of the lad's mind start clicking into place as he thought on this. "Lordy," he uttered, "that's the thing. Ye see, I started hearing the pipes out there around the same time the fairy dog started stalking the castle grounds. Do ye think there's a connection?"

"Most definitely," Granny Mac said. She placed her elbows on the table and rested her chin on her folded hands. "If this piper has been playing on that clifftop for a few months now, it means that he is either local or is familiar with these grounds."

Jenny and Jasper exchanged a troubled look. Jenny said, "That's troubling. That means there's a murderer among us."

"Or it could be one of the construction workers," Jasper offered hopefully. "Or someone from the town, like maybe the doctor?" He raised a questioning brow at Granny Mac. She shot him down with a hard stare and a wave of her hand.

"Don't be ridiculous," she told him.

"But he's got computers at his office, Mrs. MacBride," Jasper stated. "And he plays the bagpipes. Also, he knows the castle like the back of his hand, being a friend of the Malcoms."

Jasper had a point. Bunny could tell that her gran wasn't keen on the thought of her lover being a murderer, but they just couldn't leave it at that, and Granny Mac knew it too.

"Although it is highly unlikely that Artemis is involved in the murder of Major MacDonald, I agree that no one connected to this castle is above suspicion, even you, Jasper. You also play the bagpipes."

Jasper grew even redder than before. "Aye, but not well! I'm just learning. Also, when we heard the piper out there, I was with them!"

"He was," Cody said, quick to defend the young man. "He was with us the whole night."

"Very well. You have a sound alibi, Jasper," Granny Mac conceded. "Let us focus on what we know, then, shall we? We know that the hologram of the fairy dog only plays at night, triggered by anyone who enters one of those four hallways between the hours of midnight and six in the morning." Mike and Ed nodded in agreement, Ed having been the one who had figured out that little detail. "That, I presume, was designed to frighten anyone from thinking about going to the kitchen for a midnight snack or sneaking out of the castle through the back door at night. In other words, that menacing fairy dog was designed to keep the people in this castle from wandering around."

"I'll bet Major MacDonald had figured it out," Brett said in an *a-ha!* moment. "He was snooping around the castle, which means that he might have been looking for something. Clearly, he wasn't afraid of the fairy dog—possibly because he'd discovered it to be a hoax—because he left the castle in the middle of the night, presumably through the back door, and headed to the clifftop to confront the piper."

"He could have been following one of the judges," Bunny offered, "Judge Fergus Cameron, in particular. Mr. Cameron could be behind the fairy-dog hoax, just as he could have taken Mr. Winterton's bagpipes from the back closet. If he was up to no good, he'd hardly use his own set of bagpipes. Also, the ghostly piper indicated that the piper on the cliff wasn't a professional, because he misplayed a tune, but, like the ghostly piper himself, Mr. Cameron could have purposely misplayed that tune as a warning."

"Very good!" Giff clapped his hands and nodded in agreement. "But you forget, there were three sets of footprints on that clifftop, and, to use the constable's own words, the paw-prints from 'a dog of unusual size.' Which simply means that if Judge Cameron was involved, he had another person and a large dog with him."

"Agreed," Brett chimed in. "Which means we now need to find this other person who owns the large dog."

"What about the man in the black suit?" Granny Mac offered. "You were hot on his trail yesterday afternoon, and he knew it. I don't know if he owns a large dog, but I do have the very strong feeling that he's somehow involved in this."

"I do too, Ella," Brett told her. "In fact, last night, when we were on our way back to the castle, I spotted him walking between the vendor booths. I parked the van and tried to follow him. He was heading to the parade grounds for the tribute, possibly to meet up with Judge Cameron. I really don't know."

"Did you find him?" Mike asked, setting down his empty coffee mug. Brett shook his head.

"I lost him in the crowd. The man has an uncanny way of dodging us."

"Ladies, gents, I think we're onto something here," Bunny said, standing up from the table. She picked up her empty plate and took Jenny's as well. "I say we split up into groups and help the constable tackle this difficult task. We need to find the person or persons responsible for the fairy-dog hoax. We need to find the piper who took Winterton's bagpipes from the castle and misplayed a tune on the clifftop. And we need to find the owner of a dog of unusual size."

Jasper raised his hand, as if he was in school. "I'll go with Ella to interrogate the doc," he offered, casting Granny Mac a sideways glance. "Just to make sure Ella's safe from harm, should things go awry."

Granny Mac shot him a disparaging look for that.

"Excellent," Brett said, standing from the table as well. "Giff, why don't you take Cody, Mike, and Ed and talk to the judges again, and the pipers who are still here. See what you can find out. I don't fully trust Tommy Compton or his mother. She could be hiding a large dog in her camper."

"I'd be delighted to pay Mommie Dearest another visit. She's fun in a slow-motion train-wreck kinda way," Giff flashed a fake smile. "Her unfortunate son isn't far from here either. We'll have another chat with him as well. And where are you going?"

"With Bunny," Brett stated plainly, helping her clear the plates. "While you all are going to search for the who, as in the two people out on that clifftop, Bunny and I are going to attempt to figure out the why, as in why were they there in the first place? Why push Major MacDonald over the edge? Doc Beaton mentioned to us at the pub that this coast, due to its rugged, secluded nature, is known for drug smuggling. Most of the land surrounding the castle has been marked as forbidden to hikers due to that fake hellhound roaming out there. But now I think it's forbidden to hikers for another, very different reason. I'm beginning to think that this isn't about bagpipes and fairy dogs at all, but illegal drugs." At the mention of all that forbidden territory, Bunny stared at Brett, practically reading his mind. She smiled at him and gave a little nod in agreement.

"In light of recent events, it is highly suspicious, but I warn you: be careful," Granny Mac said in a no-nonsense tone. "Whatever is going on here is not only dangerous but deadly. You can ask questions. You can search for answers. You can venture close, but not too close. If you find anything suspicious at all, return to the castle immediately and call Constable Craig. Keep in mind that your specialty is not the law and bringing baddies to justice; it's cooking delicious meals and hunting ghosts for entertainment. In other words, do not be heroes."

"Ella," Giff said in a dramatic tone, "your common sense has overridden my better judgment. And here I was, prepared to throw myself on my proverbial sword for the sake of a dead piper. I guess I'll take off this lovely plaid cape. Capes are for heroes," he said, shrugging the plaid blanket off his shoulders. "However, for the sake of the ladies present, and my dignity, the kilt is staying put."

Chapter 37

"Hello, Angus," Bunny cheerily greeted her brother on the other end of her phone. She'd been in the kitchen, making a quick batch of scones as a snack for her upcoming hike and decided to call Angus while she waited for them to finish baking in the oven. Brett had insisted on taking a shower, which she thought was counterproductive. However, due to the one-bathroom dilemma, it was his time slot, and he was determined to take it. Who was she to argue with that? Therefore, Bunny had the better part of a half hour on her hands. It was just enough time to do a little baking and thinking. With her earbuds in, Bunny stood at the sink filling two metal bottles with water. "Are ye back on the farm today?" she asked Angus.

"I was this morning, but I'm on my way to the pub in Crinan to have lunch with Granny."

"What? Gran never mentioned a thing about that to me." Bunny was slightly jealous that her brother was having lunch in Crinan with their grandmother. Angus, who obviously noted the slight tinge of petulance in her voice, chuckled. The sound did nothing to ease her rising jealousy.

"We have lunch from time to time, Bunny," he explained. "She's my gran too. And I'm her favorite, being the oldest."

She ignored his teasing remark. "Granny has no favorites. You're just closer, living on the farm."

"Aye, well. That may be. However, she told me this morning that you and your lads had another ghost hunt last night with some interesting findings. I wanted to know more about this show you're working on, and your . . . um, abilities."

"Why don't ye just ask me about them?"

"I have, but I want to hear what Granny Mac has to say on the matter. Get a whisky sour in Gran and she'll spill the tea like a bride-to-be at a hen party."

"I'm certain she will," Bunny agreed, knowing that her gran played both sides of the aisle when it came to family dynamics. "What did she tell ye that made ye want to take her to lunch?"

"She's taking me," he corrected. " 'Tis all part of the granny code, taking your favorite grandchild to lunch." Bunny turned off the faucet and rolled her eyes. "She said that you talked to the ghost of the handless piper." Bunny could hear a car horn in the distance, indicating that Angus was on the road. "Since I don't fully believe in paranormal abilities, or handless pipers, Gran said she'd explain things to me. Believe it or not, I do want to understand. Also, and more importantly, I heard about the fairy-dog hoax."

"You did? What do you think of it?"

"I thought what any normal person would think. Of course, it's a hoax! Fairy dogs don't exist, Bunny. 'Tis pure myth and Highland folklore. The fact that you lot believed in them is a topic for another day. What is unsettling about the whole thing, however, is that someone went to great lengths to perpetuate the myth."

"It is unsettling. We're going to find out who did it," she told him in no uncertain terms. "In fact, that's the reason I'm calling. When we were younger, didn't you hike the hills around Dundoon?"

"I did, long ago. Why?"

"The fairy-dog hoax got me thinking. Brett too. Due to the fairy-dog sightings around the castle, most of the moorlands and hills have been marked off as forbidden territory. We know that the fairy-dog sightings were a hoax, so why is all that land off-limits to hikers?"

"It could be due to dangerous terrain, like sinkholes, landslides, or unstable stretches of shoreline. Then there's the obvious reason. Someone is hiding something out there."

"There's a lot of terrain to cover. I was hoping you could give me a little advice on where to start."

"I'd be happy to, sis." Angus then relayed all he knew about the vast hiking trails surrounding the castle, while Bunny took mental notes. "Call me if you need any help," he told her, just as he had before. Bunny said she would and ended the call. Brett was dressed and ready to go.

"Ready for this?" Brett asked, buttoning up his coat.

Bunny gave him a thumbs-up and slung her little backpack over her shoulder. She didn't know how long they'd be hiking across the moors, but she thought it would be a good idea to at least have some food and water with them. "Angus suggested we take the main hiking trail at the trailhead. It's not currently off-limits, but he said it should lead us right to the moorland in question without raising suspicion."

"Excellent," Brett remarked, and together they struck out for the trail in question.

No one could deny that they were hiking through breathtaking country. They had picked up the trail right where Angus said it would be and continued down a well-marked footpath through a dense patch of forest. Bunny marveled at the cathedral of towering pines surrounding them, and she couldn't get enough of the fresh, resinous scent. It brought her back to her childhood on the farm and her many adventures traipsing through the woods with her brothers. She felt a pang of nostalgia for those carefree days.

As the sun streamed through the needly branches overhead, spreading soft, dappled light on the forest floor, she couldn't imagine anything as sinister as a fairy dog lurking in such a beautiful place. A red squirrel, red fox, or red deer, maybe, but not the mythical fairy dog. Why had she been so quick to entertain the idea? Och, she knew why. It was because her burgeoning psychic gifts had clouded her better judgment. The thought depressed her, nearly as much as the fact that, for her, the veil between reality and the paranormal was lifting, causing her to entertain all manner of wild possibilities.

"Look," Brett said, pulling Bunny from her troubling thoughts. She looked to where he pointed and noted that the forest was thinning up ahead. Just beyond the dense tree line, she caught a glimpse of sun-dazzled purple heather. It was the stretch of moorland currently off-limits to hikers. "The trail takes a sharp left up there and heads into the wooded hillside. That's our exit." He flashed a cheeky grin just before he stepped off the trail and began bushwacking through the tangle of woods. Bunny shrugged and followed him.

"Wow," she exclaimed, looking out over a vast expanse of moorland. "That's a lot of ground to cover."

"We're not covering all of it," he told her, running his gaze across the seemingly endless stretch of wilderness to the left and right of them. He then pointed to the waters of the Sound of Jura. "We're just going to head for the coast and hopefully find a way down to the shore. If there is a hidden smuggling ring operating out here, there should be signs."

"What kind of signs?" she asked, following him as he

stalked through the tufts of heather and tall grass. Brett had long legs and the type of stride that made easy work of the rough terrain. Bunny didn't, but she made a good effort as she tried to keep up with him. As Brett headed off to the right, Bunny veered to the left, hoping to cover more ground while looking for the mysterious signs.

"Trampled grass," Brett called back to her. "Litter. Anomalies. Unusual objects not commonly found on a moor." He was calling them out as he walked. Bunny didn't find them particularly helpful.

She headed for the loch, skirting large patches of shrubbery, small hills, jumping over tiny creeks, all the while searching the ground for signs of human activity. There weren't any, as far as she was concerned. Then, however, just as the shoreline was coming into view, she heard something that made her blood curdle. It was the sickening sound of snapping branches, as if something large and foreboding was closing in on her. The sound wasn't close, but not nearly far enough away either. Bunny stopped dead in her tracks and looked wildly around, trying to assess the source of the noise. The land was strangely barren. There wasn't a soul upon it, not even Brett. Brett! Dear heavens, where was he?

"Brett!" she cried, feeling the back of her neck prickle with foreboding. "Brett!" she cried again, this time growing truly frightened. Brett was nowhere in sight. Like a whisp of fog in the heather, he had vanished into thin air.

Chapter 38

Bunny had two choices. She could run back to the castle or run toward the sickening, cracking noise she had heard a moment ago, the noise that sounded like a large creature stalking her. "Brett," she called out again, knowing that the logical thing to do would be to investigate the source of the snapping wood and not run away. Brett was still out here. She was certain of it.

As she walked closer to the spot where she believed the noise had come from, she saw something unusual. An anomaly. Something that didn't quite belong on the moors. It was a large, gaping hole in the ground surrounded by innocent-looking shrubbery. Upon closer inspection, that shrubbery wasn't so innocent after all. It had been used to disguise a large pit that someone had purposely dug. A poacher, perhaps, Bunny mused, as she made her way toward the pit. Wary of the ground beneath her, she got on her hands and knees and gingerly made her way to the edge. She then looked down into the hole. The moment she did, her heart stopped for a beat or two. Her worst fears had been realized.

Lying at the bottom of the pit in a crumpled heap was Brett, and he wasn't moving.

"Brett! Brett Bloom! Answer me, Brett! Brett, are you okay?" The moment she asked this stupid question, she instantly chided herself. Of course, he wasn't okay. He was at the bottom of a pit, either unconscious or dead. No. Not dead. At least not yet, she surmised, knowing in a way only the spiritually sensitive could, that Brett Bloom was still alive, but he needed help. At that moment, she knew she would give anything to hear his voice again.

In full panic mode, Bunny yanked the sling backpack to her front and dug into the pocket, searching for her phone. The moment she had it in her hand and tried to unlock the screen with her face, it gave her fits. It wasn't working! Of course, it wasn't, because she needed it. She cursed technology. After fiddling with it a moment longer, the phone unlocked, and she called her grandmother. "Come on!" she cried, realizing that she didn't have cell service. She danced in a full circle with her phone hoisted high in the air, praying for those pesky little bars to light up. But none did. "Not now! Not now. Urgh!" she cried helplessly, wanting to chuck the stupid phone into the pit with Brett. Thankfully, she refrained. Just as Bunny was cursing her phone, a pain-stricken moaning hit her ears. Brett! She crawled back to the edge and looked at the man lying at the bottom. "Brett? Brett, please say something!"

"Bunny," he croaked, batting his eyes against the lone shaft of sunlight that ran across his face. "I found an anomaly." Although he tried to smile, his face wouldn't fully cooperate. "Never expected this. Never saw it until it was too late. I took a step, then *bam*! This pit definitely shouldn't be here."

"No, it definitely shouldn't," she agreed, trying to hide the panic in her voice. How on earth was she going to get him out of there? "I bet a poacher did this. It's very diabolical. Can you move? Can you stand?"

To his credit, he did stand, but not without great cost to his dignity. Brett was in pain. Even Bunny could see that his ankle had been injured. "Got the wind knocked out of me," he said, trying to control the agony he felt. "I think I sprained my ankle."

With her body flat on the ground, Bunny reached her hand into the pit. She knew it was too deep, but she had to try. "Can you grab my hand? Maybe I can pull you up?"

Brett knew she couldn't but reached his hand up to hers regardless, illustrating the five-foot gap between them. "It's too deep. We need a rope or a ladder."

"I tried to make a call, but there's no cell service out here."

Brett pushed the pain from his voice and said lightly, "I'm not going anywhere, Bunny. Do you think you can make it to Winterton's cottage? It's the closest building and loaded with everything we need. He'll know what to do."

"I can," she promised him. "I'll keep checking my phone as well. The moment I have service, I'm calling the police."

"Excellent. I'll just . . . I'll just sit right here." She watched as Brett eased himself back down, resting his back against the dirt wall of the pit. She was about to run for help when he warned, "Be careful. There might be more pits like this out there."

More camouflaged pits? Dear heavens, now she was really on edge! She had intended to run the entire way to Winterton's cottage, wherever it was. Now she had to keep her eyes peeled.

"I'll be cautious," she promised, then reached into her pack and pulled out a water bottle and a half-dozen scones. She couldn't, in good conscience, just leave him there without food and water.

"Thanks," he said, securing the coveted scones and water

on his lap. "I know I've told you this before, but you really are an angel." She blushed at the compliment. Brett groaned again as he shifted slightly.

"I should go. You're in pain."

"Do me a favor and put a marker—like a large stick or something—to mark this spot in case it gets dark before you make it back. Without cell service you won't be able to track my location."

Bunny nodded. It was the first time the thought of not finding him struck her, causing another painful wave of both panic and urgency. She found a broken stick, stuck it in the ground, and took a picture so she wouldn't forget the spot. "I'll be back soon," she promised one last time and set off for Winterton's cottage.

She had barely gone a hundred yards from the pit when another spine-tingling snapping of twigs stopped her in her tracks. She looked at the ground to make sure she wasn't standing on top of another pit. Then, realizing that she wasn't, her head snapped up, and her heart dropped into her stomach. Standing at the top of a little rise stood a giant, black, shaggy beast of a hound. Its narrowed, yellow eyes were locked onto hers as it bared its sharp teeth. She recognized the beast instantly as the fairy dog from the holographic video they had debunked last night at the castle. However, she knew with certainty that the beast before her was no hologram, but a real, living and breathing canine.

"Crivens," she uttered as every nerve in her body exploded. Not sure of what to do, she uttered, "There's a good doggie," and started backing away toward the pit again. With her mind reeling, she gave a thought to jumping into the pit with Brett. There was safety in the pit . . . unless the beast jumped in with them. Then it would be carnage.

The dog barked.

Bunny screamed.

"Bunny! What's going on?" Brett cried from the bottom of his prison.

"The fairy dog!" she cried, running hell-for-leather back the way she had come, toward the pit. "It's real, and it's after me!"

"What?" The thought spurred Brett to action. He struggled to his feet again and was just able to see the top of Bunny's head as she came barreling to the rim. Dear God, was she really going to jump in with him? That was lunacy. They'd be trapped. Then again, if she couldn't outrun the beast, she'd be mauled. Caught between a pit and a hellhound, he cried, "Run to the loch. Make your way to the shore. Work your way back to the castle from there!"

He heard her yelp as he watched her feet hit the rim of the pit, sprinkling him in a shower of dirt and bits of heather. Then she was gone. He never saw the hound but cringed every time he heard its thunderous bark. Soon the barking faded into the distance, heading, he knew, toward the coast.

Battered and defeated, Brett Bloom sank back to the hard ground once again and prayed for a miracle.

Chapter 39

Brett Bloom, ghost hunter extraordinaire, had plenty of time to contemplate the follies of his life as he sat at the bottom of the cold, darkening pit in the wilds of Scotland. Instead of working on the family cherry orchard in one of the most beautiful places in all of Wisconsin, he had chosen to forge his own path by entering haunted old buildings in search of ghosts. From the time he was a young boy, Brett had always been intrigued by the unknown—by the greatest mysteries in life, which for him were, quite simply: *Are UFOs real? Does Sasquatch exist? Is the Loch Ness monster just a plesiosaur, and could there be one in Lake Michigan?* And the ever-pressing *What happens after we die?* This question had never occurred to him until his beloved grandfather suddenly keeled over from a heart attack. Twelve-year-old Brett couldn't wrap his head around the fact that his grandfather was gone, just gone, after living a truly incredible life. Brett dearly loved his grandfather. Of course, going to church every Sunday, he was told that his gramps had died and was now in heaven. The only problem was that no one could tell him with absolute certainty what heaven looked like. All people ever said was that it was a far better place than earth. In his experience, earth was pretty wonderful. He couldn't imagine anything better than sitting on the lakeshore at sunset eating his Grandma Jenn's delicious, fresh-from-the-oven cherry pie with a large scoop of vanilla ice cream. His gramps had always said it was heaven, that cherry pie.

After college, where he majored in film studies, Brett had informed his parents that he and a few of his friends were going to hunt ghosts and film their adventures for a television pilot. His dad's jaw dangled for a good three minutes after that announcement. His mother had cried. Both thought he was utterly crazy. After spending a couple of hours trapped in a pit with a swollen ankle, he was beginning to see their point.

As he sat with his back against the dirt wall, sipping water and eating Bunny's delicious scones, the possibility that he might never be found crossed his mind more than a few times. Out of pure boredom, he had tried climbing out, but every effort was met with failure and more pain to his injured ankle, which had puffed up like a balloon. And what of Bunny? Did she make it to the shores of the loch? Or had the vicious dog attacked her, leaving her in the heather to die as well?

He cursed at the thought. "Damn it," he cried to the blue sky overhead. "I should have told her to jump in here with me. If we're going to die, then at least we would die together." The thought of Bunny's arms around him made him smile.

Thinking of Bunny, Brett was just about to nod off on yet another nap when something hit him. He startled awake and saw that a rope ladder had landed in his lap. He scrambled to his feet and cried, "Bunny! Hello! Are you there?"

"Not Bunny," came a gruff Scottish voice. "Just me."

Brett looked up and saw Winterton's unsmiling face peering down at him. "Thank heaven. Is she safe?"

Winterton shrugged. "Looks like ye hurt your ankle, lad. Can ye climb out or should I pull ye out with the quad?"

"I can manage," Brett assured him, and he began the painful assent out of the pit.

The moment Brett was sitting on the blessed moorland once again, in the fresh Scottish air, he noted Winterton's look of extreme displeasure. "What were ye thinking? I told ye this wilderness is off-limits. 'Tis dangerous out here."

"I don't disagree." Brett shook his head and began rubbing the bits of grass and dirt off his hands before getting to his feet. "There are pits out here. Did you know?"

"Aye."

That surprised him. "Well, if you knew, why didn't you warn anyone or put a sign out? I nearly killed myself falling into that pit."

"Aye."

"What?"

"I said aye, as in I know. That's the point. To keep meddling folk like ye and your wee friends out of my business. But ye couldnae stay out, could ye?" Winterton then pulled a gun from the pocket of his coat and pointed it at Brett.

The moment Brett saw the gun in the ghillie's hand, everything started to fall into place. "Oh my God! It all makes sense. Your bagpipes were found at the bottom of the cliff because you were the person playing the bagpipes the other night. You knew they were missing, as they were found at the bottom of the cliff, and yet you pretended they had been stolen!"

"Rotten luck, having MacDonald yank my pipes from me as he was about to fall off a cliff. What else was I to do but say they were stolen? I was playing the game, Mr. Bloom. Needed to keep the constable off my trail."

"So, what you're telling me is that you're a liar and a murderer. After all, you pushed Major MacDonald to his death!"

"Nay, that was not me. Now hold yer whist!" he warned and tied Brett's hands behind his back.

"Where is Bunny? What did you do to her? I swear if you hurt a hair on her head, Winterton, I'll kill you!"

Winterton tied Brett's hands behind his back, then gagged him, and thrust him into the passenger seat of the quad. As he drove toward the coast, he asked, "Was the wee little chef out here with you?" Brett nodded. "Aye, then, she's likely dead. Not to worry, you will be too, soon enough."

Yet instead of driving the rugged, all-terrain vehicle to the coast, as Brett thought he would, Winterton stopped it in front of a group of large boulders. Before he knew what hit him, Brett was out of the vehicle, being pushed toward the crevice between the large stones. He watched in amazement as Winterton pushed back a tangled bush, revealing a metal hatch. He then lifted the lid and thrust Brett down a set of long metal stairs.

The going was rough, due to his sprained ankle, yet Brett was buoyed by sheer adrenaline and the burning need to find Bunny. With every step he took, he prayed that she was still alive.

Once at the bottom of the stairs, Brett saw that they were in a dimly lit underground tunnel. As he was thrust farther along the narrow passage by Winterton's gruff and assertive hands, he realized that his drug-smuggling theory was on the mark. Lord, how he wished he'd been wrong. He wished, in an odd sort of way, that the senseless murder of Major MacDonald had been about bagpipes, and not drugs. Drugs were the bane of society. And they were big business. He imagined that this rugged, forlorn coast must be lousy with smuggler's caves. Another observation that made him even more certain was that every step he took brought him closer to the sound of lapping waves. The Malcoms had trusted their ghillie, and in turn, Winterton smuggled illegal drugs right under their noses. The thought enraged him, but there was little he could do about it with a gun pointed at his back.

There was a light at the end of the tunnel. As they continued toward the light, the tunnel began to open, revealing a cave lined with stacks of crates on the cavern floor. A deep river of water ran through the center, flanked by a sizable dock. It was a smuggling operation, alright, Brett fumed, thinking that the place looked like something straight out of a James Bond movie. No, not James Bond. This cavern was natural. The only man-made things, as far as he could tell, were the dock, the tunnel, and what looked to be a storage room right next to where he was standing. To his surprise, Winterton pulled out a key and unlocked the door.

"I'm gonna have to lock you up, lad," Winterton said, opening the heavy metal door.

"No," Brett cried through the gag in his mouth. "Nooo!"

"Ye've seen too much. This is where it ends. Be a good lad and hop in."

Brett didn't hop in. He fought tooth and nail, but it was no use. With his sprained ankle and bound hands, he was no match for Winterton. Before he knew it, the door was shut and locked. Helpless, Brett peered out the barred window at the top and watched Winterton walk away. As he struggled with the rope around his wrists, he didn't know what was worse, being trapped in the bottom of a pit or locked in a storage room hidden in the belly of a smuggler's cave. It was turning out to be a very bad day.

Chapter 40

Brett had just managed to free his hands from the ropes that bound him and yank the gag out of his mouth when he heard the disturbing sound of footsteps approaching. Someone was coming for him, and it couldn't be good. He had seen too much. He knew about the smuggling operation. Devil take it! He wasn't going to die here. He wound the length of rope around both his hands and pulled it taut. He then stood behind the door and waited with bated breath.

The footsteps got closer.

Brett gripped the rope tighter. The footsteps stopped before the door, accompanied by the sound of a dog whining.

"What's in here, lad?" a familiar voice said, just before a face appeared in the barred window. "Brett? Is that you?"

"Bunny! Dear God! You found me!" he cried, staring into her lovely face from his new prison. It seemed that being trapped was a theme for the day. Then he heard the low growling coming from directly beside her. He stood on his tiptoes and was about to look down when the giant face of a dog filled the barred window. "Whoa!" Brett cried, hobbling backward. The dog started barking. “What in God’s name is that?”

“Wallace!” Bunny chided and pulled the giant dog away from the door. “This is Wallace; at least that’s what the name on his collar says. He’s our fairy dog, Brett. What are you doing in there? I thought you were still in the pit.”

“Winterton found me and locked me in here.”

“Winterton locked you in there?” The name set the wheels of her mind spinning. Everything was falling into place. “The villain! That really makes me angry!” Noting that the dog was still growling, Bunny snapped, “Hush now, ye big brute.” Surprisingly, the dog stopped growling. It looked at Bunny, sat on its haunches, and hung its head in shame.

“Wait. Let’s back up a minute,” Brett said. “That creature is our fairy dog? The same one that was chasing you on the moor? It didn’t maul you?”

“Heavens no. I really thought he was going to,” she explained as she picked up an axe near one of the crates and held it between her hands. She walked back to the locked door and peered at Brett once again through the barred window. “I was running away from him so quickly, and without paying much attention to where I was going, that I tripped on a rabbit hole. I thought I was dog food, I really did. Yet instead of eating me or barking three times and sending me to the next world, this big guy just stood over me and started whining. I realized then that he smelled the scones I had left in my pack. I pulled them out and fed him every last one of them. Now we’re best friends. Isn’t that right, Wallace?”

The dog looked up at her with beseeching yellow eyes, as if he understood.

“Now stand back while I whack this thing open.”

Brett did as he was told. After a handful of well-meaning strikes of the axe, Bunny managed to break the lock. She then opened the door. The moment she saw Brett, she wrapped him in her arms. "I'm so grateful you're here. I'm so glad we found you. I thought I'd never find you," she told him, with one last, life-affirming hug.

"But you did find me. By the way, how did you know that I was down here?"

"That was all Wallace, I'm afraid," she explained as they made their way toward the crates. "He had chased me over halfway to the shore. Once I fed him, he led me to a pathway that traveled down the clifftop to the beach. I was set on making my way to the castle when I realized that the beach ended at a rocky point that jutted way out into the water. The thought of climbing back up was daunting. However, Wallace wasn't deterred by it. He found a little pathway hidden in the rocks that led right into the mouth of this cave. Then, just before we got to the mouth, something spooked him. Wallace turned around and scampered into the rocks, where he hid behind a boulder. I did the same. A few moments later, I saw Mr. Winterton exiting the cave. I was about to go get him and tell him about you in the pit, when I saw the gun in his hand. He was talking on a walkie-talkie, waving the gun in the air like a madman. It hit me then that Winterton isn't quite the man he seems. Once we were certain he was gone, Wallace and I entered the cave. It was Wallace who led me to this door. I think this might be where he lives."

Brett looked back inside the storage room. "Well, that would explain the empty dish and the water bowl back there. I was too preoccupied trying to free my hands from the ropes to give it much thought."

Bunny frowned. "Wallace is never coming back here again, my poor wee puppy." She rubbed the tufted fur on the top of Wallace's head. "He's coming with me. I'm officially rescuing him. I'm also going to report Winterton to the police and to the RSPCA, the Royal Society for the Prevention of Cruelty to Animals," she added for Brett's benefit.

Brett tilted his head as he soaked up the sight of Bunny and the giant dog beside her. They made an odd couple, the beautiful, lively chef with the flowing red hair, and the giant, wild-looking beast of a dog. The dog had been wooed by scones. Brett couldn't blame the dog. Bunny's scones were delicious. It was the expression of pure determination on her face that made him glow with admiration, pride, and something a little closer to his heart. "I'll back you one hundred percent on that one, MacBride." He told her with a grin. "Not sure where you're going to keep that dog, but I do know that he's one lucky pooch. Regarding Winterton, he's our man. He's a drug smuggler."

As they walked toward the evidence in question, Brett brought Bunny up to speed on all that had transpired since she'd left him.

"Winterton was the man playing the bagpipes on the cliff!" she exclaimed. "That makes sense, since they were his bagpipes all along. Yet he was very convincing when he claimed that someone had stolen them."

"He's a liar," Brett added. He was now holding the axe that Bunny had used to free him. He was going to pry open one of the dozen or so crates.

"Och, the ghostly piper!" she blurted, suddenly recalling what the ghost had told her. "He said that the man playing on the clifftop wasn't a professional. He had misplayed the tune."

Brett relaxed his grip on the axe to look at her as another thought dawned on him. "I bet Winterton purposely misplayed the tune. Think of it, Bunny. I bet there was a ship out there waiting in the fog for the signal. Just like in the piper's day, a misplayed tune sent a warning. What if *Brigadoon* is the name of the ship that's been running the drugs?"

"I bet that's it!" Bunny exclaimed as her mind raced to put the pieces of the vast, troubling mystery into place. "I'll bet anything that *Brigadoon* is the name of a ship! Brett, you're a genius!"

He flashed her a self-satisfied grin right before shoving the wedge of the axe under the lid of a crate. He was about to pry it open when Bunny stopped him.

"What?" he asked, a tad annoyed.

"There's the letter B on that crate."

"So there is," he said, running a hand over the letter. "Why is that important?"

"Because I saw a load of crates just like these at the back of the Burgess Bagpipe Emporium tent. Peter Burgess, Seth's son, was loading them into the back of his truck. I went to help him, and he nearly bit off my head when I picked one of them up. They were very heavy. Too heavy for bagpipes."

"The Burgesses must be involved in this too. Remember that there were two people out on that clifftop the other night with Major MacDonald, two people and a large dog. You found the dog, and we now know that Winterton was the person playing the bagpipes. When I realized that he was going to kill me, I asked if he pushed MacDonald off the cliff as well. But he denied it. He didn't have any reason to lie to me back there. Peter or Seth Burgess must have been out there with him. One of them killed Major MacDonald. Great work, Bunny! Now let's get this crate open and take some pictures. Then we're getting out of here."

The moment Brett pried open the lid, he took one look at the illicit cargo and swore under his breath. He'd been wrong. Very wrong. It wasn't drugs they were smuggling. It was possibly even worse.

"Am I looking at what I think I'm looking at?" Bunny breathed, feeling sick to her stomach. She was so angry her entire body started shaking. She had never been so outraged in her life. "Are . . . are those elephant tusks? Oh, Brett. This is truly diabolical! They're not smuggling drugs. They're smuggling illegal ivory from poachers!" She was about to ask why they would do such a thing, when the answer hit her. "Oh my God! This is because of the bagpipes! The ivory projecting mount found in Major MacDonald's pocket was no accident. I'll bet anything he was trying to stop this!"

"And got killed in the process," he added, barely able to take his eyes off the illegal ivory. "If I had to guess at what's going on here, I'd say that Winterton is smuggling the illegal ivory and selling it to the Burgesses. They're using it to forge antique bagpipes, because, as we've learned, a piper is judged not only on his musical skill, but also on the quality of his bagpipes. Antique bagpipes with decorative ivory tuning slides are highly sought after."

As Brett and Bunny hastily took pictures of the ivory, Bunny offered, "I bet Tommy Compton has a set of bagpipes with ivory tuning slides. We never did find out where his bagpipes were, and with good reason. If they had ivory on them, and he'd bought them from Burgess Bagpipe Emporium, they're likely a convincing antique forgery. That would disqualify him from the competition."

Brett agreed and closed the lid.

The sound of Wallace growling pulled them back to the problem at hand. It was getting late, and they needed to get back to the castle. No easy task with Brett's sprained ankle.

"I think someone's coming down the tunnel," Brett whispered, pointing to the tunnel behind them.

Bunny nodded, filled with the urge to leave this viper's nest. "Wallace," she addressed the growling dog, "take us to the castle!"

Wallace had no idea what she was saying, but even he knew it was time to run for the hills.

Chapter 41

Wallace, possessing a thorough knowledge of the cave, trotted toward the light, taking a narrow pathway between the side of the cave and the water, which was opposite the way he and Bunny had entered. After climbing over a tumble of boulders at the mouth of the cave, which was no small task for Brett and his ankle, they found themselves once again on the rocky bank of the loch, only this time the turrets of Dundoon could be seen in the distance, sitting like a sentinel on top of the cliffs. It was truly a sight to behold and one that buoyed their spirits, especially Brett's, as he'd been fighting through the pain of his injury. Yet even with a swollen ankle, he limped along at a remarkable speed, trying to keep up with Wallace.

After ten minutes of watching Brett struggle toward the castle, wincing with every step, Bunny jogged beside him and took his hand.

"Let me help you," she said, before wrapping his arm around her shoulders, taking some of the weight off his injured ankle. "The moment we get cell service, I'm calling the police, and then Doc Beaton. If he's as good as Gran says he is, he'll know what to do for your ankle."

"I'd kill for a painkiller right now." He tried flashing her a grin, but it came out lopsided.

"I'd kill for a helicopter," she said, upping the stakes. "We'd be there by now, if we had one."

"What about cell service now?" He turned his head to look at her, then stubbed his lame foot on a rock. That elicited a loud grunt. Bunny cringed. Once Brett was limping at speed again, she pulled out her phone.

"Not yet," she told him, shaking her head.

"We need to get off this beach, Bunny. Winterton isn't far behind, and once he realizes—"

Brett didn't get a chance to finish his sentence. The sound of gunshots ripping through the air above them made the point for him. Bunny gasped and spun around. That's when she saw Winterton running after them with his hunting rifle aimed in their direction.

"Brett! We're being hunted!" Bunny cried, urging him to pick up the pace.

Wallace, who was trotting down the beach just ahead of them, got spooked by the gunshots. The dog took off, racing for a spot below the cliffs.

Not knowing what else to do as Winterton followed them in hot pursuit, Brett and Bunny limp-raced to where the dog was leading them, praying that it wasn't a dead end. Thankfully, the dog knew the landscape far better than they did. He wasn't leading them to a dead end, but to another partially hidden pathway that led up the rugged cliffside to the moors that surrounded Dundoon.

"Damnit!" Brett swore under his breath. "Why do there have to be so many cliffs around here? This is going to hurt." He looked up at the steep cliffside they were about to climb and gritted his teeth. The large, black dog made it look easy. His ankle was killing him.

Winterton's gun rang out again, splintering the rock ten feet to their right. Bunny flinched.

"Idiot!" Brett cried, ducking behind a boulder. He knew that they didn't have a choice. Staying on the beach meant certain death. By climbing the steep pathway to the moors, although it was tough going, they would at least stand a slightly better chance. Also, the closer they got to the castle, the greater were their chances of having cell service. And they needed cell service!

Bunny was crouched beside Brett. "Keep leaning on me, Bloom, and stay low. We've just got to make it to the top." Brett nodded. They were waiting for Winterton to stop firing and reload his rifle. Bunny then added, "And here I thought that hitching my wagon to your ghost-hunting show was going to be lame." The firing had stopped. Bunny flashed a smile before pulling him along with her.

"Lame?" he said, highly offended. "Ghost hunting's not lame, MacBride. It's adventurous."

But Bunny wasn't listening. All her efforts and focus were spent assisting Brett to the top of the cliff. Winterton had reloaded and began shooting at them again. With each agonizing step, she prayed for a miracle. Then that miracle appeared in the form of a white rabbit.

"Hopper," she uttered under her breath.

The white rabbit sprang out of a clump of weeds at the base of a rock to her right. Then, just as she had witnessed before, his white fur began shimmering and fluttering in the wind. Right before her eyes, Hopper morphed into thousands of white butterflies. The butterflies took to the air, fluttering down the cliffside like a snowy white waterfall. She watched in awe as they headed straight for the man with the gun.

"What the . . . ?" Brett uttered in disbelief.

"You can see that?" Bunny cast him a questioning look.

"The swarm of white butterflies that just appeared by that rock over there? Yes, I can see them." He looked utterly dumbfounded by what he was witnessing. "They're heading straight for Winterton."

Winterton had stopped shooting, due to the tornado of white butterflies that surrounded him, blocking his vision. They could hear him swearing on the beach below as he frantically batted at the butterflies. But the butterflies were not deterred.

"What are they doing?" he questioned, awestruck.

"Buying us time. Come on. Let's go."

With Winterton occupied by the kaleidoscope of white butterflies that seemed to have appeared out of thin air to harass him, Bunny and Brett were able to climb to the top of the cliff without being shot at. Wallace was there waiting for them. However, the moment they reached solid ground, the dog dashed away again, heading in the direction of the castle.

"I have cell service!" Bunny exclaimed, staring at her phone.

Brett was bent over, catching his breath, while keeping an eye on Winterton. The ghillie was climbing up the trail after them, although the flurry of butterflies was hindering his progress. The man looked fit to be tied, and rightly so. They had just uncovered his nefarious dealings.

"You'll not make it back alive on my watch!" Winterton warned just before he took aim.

Brett ducked as the bullet sailed high in the air. "Call Constable Craig," he advised Bunny. "If you don't have his number, call Ed. He'll make the call."

Bunny was about to call the constable when a loud bark in the distance caused her to look up from her phone. The moment she did, her heart soared. "Look, Brett," she uttered.

pointing to the top of a gentle rise. Brett straightened and came beside her to witness yet another miracle.

"It's Angus," she said, watching as her brother appeared on the top of the hill, marching across the moorland toward them. Beside him was Wallace, the giant fairy dog, barking and racing ahead of him, spurring him on. "How did he know?" she asked, looking dumbfounded as she waved at her brother.

"Look, Jordy Malcom's just a step or two behind him, with Winston. And he's got a hunting rifle! Way to go, Jordy." Brett hobbled away from the cliff's edge and pulled Bunny with him as he began limp-running toward their saviors. Winterton was going to get the surprise of his life when he arrived at the top.

The two big black dogs, one substantially larger and hairier than the other, looked as if they were fast friends already as they loped and barked ahead of the men. But that wasn't all. Giff appeared next, wearing his kilt and plaid, and looking more like a Highland laird than a . . . well, Highland laird. He waved excitedly at his friends. Behind Giff the entire crew of *Food & Spirits* appeared on the rise, swiftly followed by the entire castle staff. It was a little army, ready for battle. Bunny was so relieved at the sight that tears sprang to her eyes.

"What a miracle," Brett said as they closed the distance between the little army. "Our rescue party has arrived, and not a moment too soon. I honestly don't know if I could have made it to the castle with this damned ankle!"

Chapter 42

It had been quite an adventurous day, too adventurous for Bunny's taste.

Chandler Winterton, after climbing to the top of the cliff, had been shocked to find not only his employer waiting there, but an entire little army of civilians and two dogs. He'd been instantly disarmed and apprehended. Constable Craig had arrived mere minutes later to take him into custody. Once again, emergency vehicles descended on Dundoon like a swarm of bees. Bunny and Brett gave their statements to the police, and the crime scene was secured. Then, finally, Brett was taken to the hospital to have his ankle x-rayed. Doc Beaton, assuming the role of personal physician, insisted on accompanying him. Soon after that, Bunny found herself surrounded in the luxury of the great room, sitting between her brother and Granny Mac, while being fawned over by Jenny Duncan.

"Have some more tea," Jenny insisted, filling her teacup. "I cannot believe it," the young woman exclaimed for the tenth time. "A smuggling ring was goin' on right under our noses, and we never smoked it. Ye are a hero, Bunny."

"I'm really not," Bunny refuted, her cheeks turning bright red at the compliment.

"As I was telling ye, dear, I had a hunch." Granny Mac continued. "Once I had thoroughly convinced Jasper that Artemus was not a murderer, I called Angus and invited him to join us for lunch, as he often does. As you know, he had some questions regarding your abilities."

"I told ye," Angus said with a wry grin. "Also, lunch was very tasty."

"I'm sure it was. So, back to your hunch, Gran. What was it?"

"I felt that you were in grave danger, dear. I saw the image of a large fairy dog baring its teeth." Here she offered a soft smile at Wallace, who was lying beside Bunny's chair. "Then my ankle began to burn. It was very uncomfortable. After voicing my concerns to the table, I tried calling you. But I couldn't reach you. Your phone went straight to voicemail. That's when Angus told us that you and Brett had gone for a hike on the forbidden castle lands."

"What made you believe Gran's hunch?" she asked her brother. Angus shrugged.

"She was explaining some things to me about what 'tis like to be psychic. I dinna really believe most of it. I thought it was just an act, until she stopped talking in the middle of a sentence and her face changed, just like that." He snapped his fingers. "She said ye were in grave danger. I canna even explain it, but I think I felt it too. Then when we couldn't reach ye, I got nervous. Ye and your friends have been poking around here, Bunny, trying to find the person responsible for Major MacDonald's death. Murderers aren't forgiving people, especially when someone is closing in on them. I had the feeling that ye had closed in on them, Bunny, and were in trouble. That's when we drove straight to the castle."

"Jordy called Winterton immediately," Granny Mac explained. "Winterton wasn't happy when Jordy explained that you and Brett went hiking in what Winterton had claimed was fairy-dog territory. Even though we all knew that the fairy-dog sightings at the castle had been a hoax, Winterton was still insistent that it was dangerous territory for a hike. He took off immediately."

"Of course, he did," Bunny said, frowning at the memory. "He was a desperate man about to be found out for his evil doings."

"Well, after an hour passed without hearing from Winterton, Angus decided to take the matter into his own hands."

"I did," he admitted, smiling gently at his sister. "Call it a hunch, but I knew something was wrong."

"Don't tell me! You have it too, a touch of the clairvoyance." Bunny grinned teasingly at her brother.

"No. I dinna. It was just a hunch," he clarified, sounding a lot like Bunny when she had first learned of her abilities. "Jordy and old Winston volunteered to go with me. Giff did too, and the rest of your lads. Before we knew it, every able-bodied person in Dundoon joined us for the search. You know the rest."

Yes, she certainly did, and she had never been more grateful to have her family around her. They continued to chat for a while longer until Brett came hobbling in on crutches, followed by Doc Beaton.

"Did you break your ankle?" Bunny was on her feet, assisting her brave friend, who just happened to be uber hunky and even more adorable on crutches.

"Just a sprain," he informed her. "Doc Beaton says I'm lucky."

"Lucky indeed," the doctor concurred. "Lucky you're young, healthy, and can take a nasty fall like that without breaking your ankle. You'll be right as rain in a few weeks."

"Hear that?" he said, casting Bunny a private grin. "I'll be right as rain. Until then, I'm told I have to take it easy."

"No more ghost hunting for you," Bunny teased.

"No, no, the show must go on," he insisted, looking mildly affronted by the thought of not being able to wander the halls of a haunted castle at night with all his ghost tech in tow. Doc Beaton hit him with a cautioning look, prompting him to add, "However, I might trade places with Ed in the control room for the time being."

They were soon joined by Giff, Cody, Mike, and Ed. It felt wonderful to be beside a warm fire with friends, Bunny mused. The Malcoms soon joined them, as did Jenny, Jasper, and Mr. and Mrs. Collins. Then Constable Craig walked in with another, familiar man, finally ready to explain the extent of the ivory-smuggling ring.

"The man in the black suit!" Giff exclaimed, staring at the man in question. "What are you doing here? You've done a great job throwing us off your trail, and now here you are, in the great room of Dundoon. Well, what is your involvement in all of this? We saw you talking with Major MacDonald. Very suspicious. By the way, thanks for the beer."

The man in the black suit bowed his head in acknowledgment.

"Allow me to introduce Major Oliver Hume," the constable said. "He's with the British Intelligence Service."

"I knew it," Brett mumbled under his breath.

"He's here on official business. I think ye all will be very interested to hear what he has to say."

Constable Craig was correct. The entire hall fell silent as the mysterious man began to speak. "Sorry for giving ye three the slip, but as ye will see, it was necessary," the major said, addressing Brett, Bunny, and Giff.

"Before the late queen passed away, it was brought to her attention by her loyal piper, Major Scotty MacDonald, that during some of the top piping competitions, newer bagpipes were turning up with ivory projecting mounts. This was particularly troubling, since the use, sale, and trade of elephant ivory had been banned in the Ivory Act of 2018. The late queen, God rest her soul, had a passion for protecting endangered animals, including a strong disdain for poachers. When the queen asked why such a thing would be happening, Scotty explained that pipers were also graded on the quality of their instruments. Older instruments with ivory embellishments were scored higher, giving a piper lucky enough to have inherited such an heirloom set a slight advantage. He felt that this practice encouraged the illegal trade in ivory and counterfeit bagpipes. The queen, of course, had other pressing matters to attend to at the time. However, months later, upon her deathbed, she summoned her distinguished and loyal friend to her bedside. There she asked him to get to the bottom of the ivory-smuggling ring and put a stop to it. He swore to her that he would. That's when he contacted me."

"He knew about the ivory-smuggling ring!" Jordy Malcom exclaimed. "That's why he was here, snooping around, I'll bet."

"Correct, sir," Major Hume acknowledged. "Major MacDonald's dedication to the cause brought him here, to Dundoon Castle and the National Solo Piping Championship, where he used his role as a judge to narrow in on the culprits. Major MacDonald was putting two and two together on the ground. My intel suggested that another ship carrying the illegal cargo was scheduled to make a stop during the competition. The reasoning was that everyone would be so preoccupied with the competition that no one would notice. The ship's name was—"

"*Brigadoon!*" Bunny called out. "It was *Brigadoon*, wasn't it?"

"Very good, Ms. MacBride. The smugglers named their ship *Brigadoon*. MacDonald had the name of the ship and the general location, but he still hadn't figured out how it was done, not until he heard a piper piping at two in the morning out on the clifftops. He surmised, and rightly so, that whoever was out in the wee hours of the morning was sending a signal. Thanks to your team of ghost hunters, we now know that the piper on the cliff was Chandler Winterton."

"They were the men wrestling out there! We heard them," Jasper offered.

"Correct. Winterton's been involved in the smuggling ring for some time now. His position as ghillie made him the perfect accomplice to a much larger criminal undertaking. It was also very lucrative. We now know that MacDonald tried to apprehend Winterton when he heard him playing his pipes on the clifftop. However, what MacDonald failed to realize was that Winterton wasn't alone. Peter Burgess was with him. Peter and his father, Seth, were the masterminds behind the smuggling scheme. Seth, being the ringleader, conveniently had an alibi for the night MacDonald died. He was with Tabatha Compton in her trailer. Peter, being Seth's right-hand man, had accompanied Winterton to the clifftop. Peter admitted that they were aware someone was onto their scheme. You see, the Burgesses paid for the ivory, and Winterton arranged for the shipments. The Burgesses then used the ivory to forge the age of a new set of bagpipes, making top dollar on the instruments."

"That's not only scandalous, 'tis diabolical!" Elizabeth Malcom proclaimed, looking outraged.

"I don't disagree," the major told her. He then continued. "Peter has stated that he never meant for anyone to die, but once he realized that they were in danger of being found out, he snapped. He wasn't about to go to jail, so he pushed MacDonald off the cliff, hoping it would look like he slipped. Unfortunately, Major MacDonald had a hold on Winterton's bagpipes as he fell."

"What about the fairy dog?" Giff asked, looking at Wallace, who had turned out to be just a big, lovable pooch.

"He's right there, Mr. McGrady," Major Hume pointed out.

"I know, but what about the glowing red eyes? We met Wallace on the foggy moor that night. We could hear him growling. We could see glowing red eyes."

Major Hume gave another nod of his head. "We know that Peter Burgess and Chandler Winterton were behind the holographic hoax. Peter has even confessed to installing the equipment in the castle when those two hallways in question were closed for remodeling. It was ingenious, really. We know that Wallace was the model for the hoax. We also know that Wallace was often let loose to roam the hills, giving credence to the fairy-dog myth. Winterton confessed to bringing the dog with him when he signaled the ship. The illusion of the glowing red eyes was simply done by strapping a hat above the dog's eyes that contained two red lights. I hear it was very effective."

"Very," Bunny and Giff replied in unison.

Major Oliver Hume was about to take his leave, when he suddenly stopped. He turned to Brett, Bunny, and Giff. "I tried my hardest to deter you three. I didn't want you getting involved in this messy criminal undertaking, but you are the most tenacious group of people I have ever met. The truth is, I'm glad you are. We couldn't have solved this case without you. Thank you. I wish you great success on your . . . show," he said, adding another dip of his head.

They were about to head into the dining room for supper, when the two remaining judges, Fergus Cameron and Rory Fraser, appeared. The men had been questioned by the authorities and were released. They had also made a very important decision.

"We had no idea that all this was afoot during the competition," Rory explained. "Terrible, just terrible. Burgess Bagpipe Emporium has long been a name synonymous with quality bagpipes. Now that name has been sullied by their illegal dealings. We are also here to apologize. We both chose young Tommy Compton as the winner of the competition, never realizing that his bagpipes were counterfeit. 'Tis not the lad's fault, but we've both agreed that he wasn't the best player in the competition. We are also ashamed to admit that his mother might have had some sway over our decision, she being a particularly persuasive lady." Rory blushed as he admitted this.

"Mommie Dearest persuasive? That woman eats pipers for lunch," Giff whispered in Bunny's ear, causing her to stifle a bubble of mistimed mirth.

"Playing the bagpipes is a pure and noble pursuit," Fergus added. "Instruments should not be tampered with, and men should not die defending the sanctity of our competitions. Thanks to Constable Craig, we were able to look at the major's competition folder found in his room. Taking Major MacDonald's scoring into consideration, we have come to a decision on who should win this year's competition. We are proud to announce that Jamie Livingston is this year's winner."

The entire hall erupted in cheers and applause. Bunny could almost feel the bright smile of Major Scotty MacDonald beaming down on her. Admittedly, she hadn't known the man very well, but she did know that he had given his life upholding a promise to his queen. And he had nearly succeeded. Jamie Livingston might have won, but Major Scotty MacDonald was the true champion in her eyes.

Chapter 43

"Are you really going to keep that giant dog?" Brett leaned against the island counter, mindful of his crutches, and flashed Bunny a questioning look.

"I would. He's a great dog," Jasper averred, kneeling on the kitchen floor to better hug the giant fairy dog. "I can't believe this big sweetie was terrorizing the castle."

"The poor, wee baby," Jenny said, placing a giant bowl filled with supper leftovers on the floor for Wallace. The dog gobbled them up with wolfish hunger.

Jasper stood back and leaned against the counter next to Brett, watching his new best friend eat. "I can't believe Winterton kept him in a cave and used him to scare us. What kind of breed do ye suppose he is?"

"I'm no expert," Giff began, pouring himself another shot of whisky, "but he looks like an Irish wolfhound crossed with something black and furry."

"So, are you going to keep him?" Brett pressed again.

Bunny offered a thoughtful smile. "I'd love to, but I'm far too busy to take care of a dog. It wouldn't be fair to Wallace.

As it is, Mr. Wiggles, my bunny, is living at my neighbor's house. No, Wallace needs a lot of space to play. He needs an active owner, someone who likes to roam the hills. He'd be the perfect dog for a young ghillie." She looked at Jasper, hoping he'd gotten the hint. He did.

"Are ye serious? You'd really give Wallace to me?" His face lit up at the thought.

"I don't actually own Wallace. I rescued him," Bunny corrected. "I really want him to have the best home possible, which is right here at Dundoon with you, Jasper. Will you take him? I assure you, he already knows this place like the back of his paw."

"Yes! I do! Do ye hear that, Wallace? Ye get to live with me in the ghillie's cottage. I'm sure Jenny won't mind feeding ye as well. After all, she already feeds the rest of us, including Winston."

"Of course, I'll feed him, ye eejet. Welcome home, Wallace." Jenny picked the empty bowl off the floor and patted the dog's head. "You're going to be very happy here. I just have one question. Do ye suppose he's potty trained?"

Giff crossed his arms and stared at the dog. "I have a feeling you're about to find that out shortly."

After a very busy weekend of ghost hunting, cooking, listening to bagpipes, and murder-solving, there was just one thing left to do before the team of *Food & Spirits* wrapped up their investigation at Dundoon Castle. Bunny had made a promise to the legendary ghostly piper, and she was determined to make good on it. After all, the ghost had been at the center of this mystery all along. As Bunny reflected on the nature of the ghost and the strange, hauntingly mournful music he played, she was reminded again that loyalty to his leader had gotten him killed. Loyalty: it was a powerful emotion, if not a noble one. After all, Major Scotty MacDonald had died for much the same reason. His loyalty to his queen had brought him to this same castle, where he too had died. Yes, they were kindred spirits. The fact that they shared the same surname of MacDonald hadn't escaped her either. Had the legend, in fact, come full circle? In her heart she believed that it had. In fact, it had given her an idea.

Bunny turned to her hosts and asked, "Jordy, Elizabeth, are you okay with what my grandmother and I are about to do?"

Elizabeth nodded right away. Jordy was still on the fence. "The piper's been here for a long time," he mused aloud. "His legend is intertwined with this castle. His story sparks the imagination. His noble deed inspires pipers throughout the land. I hate to see him go. What about Drunk Gordie? Could ye give him a nudge into the light instead?"

Bunny, being very new to her abilities, and feeling very out of her league, didn't know what to say. Thankfully Granny Mac did.

"Jordy, you have nothing to worry about. If we are able to move the piper into the light, then he can come here and visit anytime he chooses, in spirit form. Spirits are different from ghosts. A person's spirit is unique to them, like a fingerprint. In most cases, spiritual energy carries a high vibration. When a person dies, it is their spiritual energy—their life force—that enables them to cross into the light upon leaving their earthly body. Take it from me, spirits are all around us. Ghosts, however, are a different matter. There are many reasons spirits can get trapped in the places where they died. However, by not moving into the light after death, one's spiritual vibration becomes very low. Ghosts, in essence, are low-vibrational energies. They are unable to move on by themselves. They are trapped on the earthly plane. They are often referred to as earthbound spirits. In other words, they need some help to raise their spiritual energy enough to cross over into the realm of spirit, or what we often refer to as heaven. They then become high-vibrational spirits again."

"Cool," Giff uttered, utterly enthralled by what Granny Mac was telling them. Unfortunately, Jordy Malcom was confused.

"Ghosts? Spirits? Crossing into the light? I'm afraid I'm not following ye, Ella."

"No worries. It's quite complicated. Just take my word for it that your lovely castle will still be shrouded in the piper's legend."

"What about Drunk Gordie?" he pressed, looking hopeful. "Can ye lift his energy enough to shove him out as well?"

"He's a drunk ghost," Granny Mac explained with a shake of her head. "That's doubly low-vibrational stuff. He's also angry. I'm afraid we don't have the time or the energy to move him on tonight. Maybe on another visit. Is everyone ready?"

Chapter 44

"Why am I always the one stuck in the room with the uncool ghost?" Giff complained over his walkie-talkie. He was standing in the dimly lit dining room, staring at the table that was now piled with old plates and stained coffee mugs to entice the ghost.

Jasper was with him, ready with the bagpipes. Now that he was the ghillie of the castle, he'd need to work on his piping skills.

Mike, bracing himself for another encounter with the vengeful, drunken ghost, kept his camera rolling as he aimed it at both men.

"First it was that black-hearted joy-sucker from Bramsford Manor," Giff reminded them. "Now it's the ghostly version of a raging alcoholic with relationship issues. Why? Why, I ask you, do we need all these dishes?"

"To keep him busy, buddy," Brett explained over the walkie-talkie. Due to his sprained ankle, he was sitting in the snug with Ed, watching the monitors. It wasn't where he wanted to be, which, if he was being honest, was right beside Bunny on the cold battlement, holding her hand. However, he couldn't complain about the view. There was great feed coming from every camera in the castle.

"Keep him busy?" Giff sounded appalled. "He's a g-dam ghost, Bloom! And he's got good aim. I'm not qualified for this!"

"And yet you look so hot on night-vision," Ed added with a grin. "You're really rocking the whole Scottish laird vibe, m' dude. Viewers are going to love you."

In the control room, Brett grinned and flashed Ed a thumbs-up for the comment.

Back in the dining room, Jasper giggled. Giff grew even more annoyed, which, Granny Mac had told them in secret, was the point. Drunk Gordie needed a burst of energy, nervous or otherwise, to get him going.

"Thank you for saying so. Dressing for every occasion is the one thing I am qualified for. However, your flattery, Edward, has fallen on deaf ears."

Ed smiled at that. "I doubt it has, Giffster. Now, when I say go, Jasper, start playing the pipes."

"Aye-aye, sir." Jasper saluted the camera and put the chanter into his mouth.

Brett spoke into the walkie-talkie, this time addressing Bunny. "Is everything ready on the battlement?"

"Ready as I'll ever be," she told him as butterflies swirled in her stomach. "It's another cold, foggy night up here, but we're all prepared, sitting in a circle and about to hold hands."

"Everyone, hold hands," Granny Mac instructed.

"I'm right here if you need me."

Bunny looked at the group of family and friends, bundled in heavy coats, who had joined their circle to help cross the piper over. Granny Mac sat on her left; her brother Angus was to her right. She had to admit how good it felt to have her gran and her brother there with her. Doc Beaton had also joined them, along with Jenny, Elizabeth, and Jordy.

Bunny squeezed her brother's hand. She could tell that Angus was as excited as he was nervous. She smiled inwardly at the thought that he was about to get the shock of his life.

"We're all set, Brett," Bunny said into the walkie-talkie. "Tell Jasper to start playing."

Down in the dining room, Jasper began playing his bagpipe with more gusto than ability. A discordant racket ensued, summoning the ghost of Drunk Gordie. When the first mug flew off the table, narrowly missing Giff, he cried, "He's here, and his aim seems to be improving!"

Up on the battlement, as they all held hands, Granny Mac suggested, "Love, joy, gratitude, fill your hearts with one of these emotions to raise our collective spiritual vibrations. Let us create a beacon for the piper."

As Bunny looked at her brother and grandma, her heart filled with all of those powerful emotions—love, joy, and gratitude. For ten years, she had run from her family, when, in truth, they were her greatest refuge. She knew that now, with clarity.

It was up on the castle battlement where Bunny had first contacted the ghostly piper. It was the spot where he had once stood, watching for his master's return. It was the spot where he had played his last, earthy tune.

Her eyes were only closed for a minute or two before the haunting sound of bagpipes hit her ears, heralding the piper's arrival. She opened her eyes and saw Hopper sitting in the middle of the circle. With a wiggle of his nose, he hopped toward Angus first, landing on his lap, as if acknowledging his presence, then hopping into the dense fog that surrounded them.

Bunny looked at her older brother, noting that his eyes were focused on the fog. It suddenly dawned on her that he couldn't see Hopper, their brother. But he could hear the piper.

The piper. How was she supposed to summon his master

so that he could return home? She didn't know, so she went with her alternate plan and thought about his other kinsman, Major Scotty MacDonald. As the piper appeared in the fog, playing his spectral tune, something truly remarkable happened. The spirit of Major Scotty MacDonald appeared, shrouded in golden light. Bunny acknowledged his presence with a smile. The major bowed before turning to the piper. That was when another spirit appeared, another kinsman. The name Colkitto filled Bunny's mind, answering her question.

"They are both here," Granny Mac said, awestruck.

Bunny was aware that everyone in their circle was just as awestruck, witnessing the unfolding event. She continued to fill her heart with joy and gratitude for the ghostly piper. Then she told him, "You are no longer a prisoner here, my friend. You are free to go."

The piper looked conflicted for a moment, unsure if he should leave his eternal post. That's when the spirit of Colkitto reached out his hand.

"You have served your kinsmen well, old soul. Your duty is done. It is time to come home."

The spirit of Major MacDonald reached his hand out as well.

The piper stopped playing his bone-chilling tune. He then looked at Jordy Malcom, whom Bunny noticed had tears streaming down his beefy face. He wasn't alone. They all had been moved to tears.

Jordy nodded, giving his consent as the laird of the castle to the ghostly piper. The piper saluted him, then reached for the spirits that had come to escort him home.

Although, in life, his hands had been lopped off by his captors, Bunny saw that the piper was whole again. The moment his ghost touched the spirits of his kinsmen, his foggy image transformed into light.

The fog lifted as if blown away by a powerful force. In thinning gossamer layers, the vast black sky overhead was soon revealed, bejeweled with a million twinkling stars.

The piper of Dundoon had gone home.

Bunny wiped the tears from her eyes and looked to where the ghost had been. The piper was gone, but Hopper was still there. "Thank you, Braiden," she said, then watched as he too faded into the darkness, her brother, her spirit guide, her link to the other side.

Bunny's heart nearly burst with joy, gratitude, and love, realizing what she had done. With the help of Hopper, Granny Mac, Angus, and their friends, she had freed another spirit, this one bound to the castle by loyalty. The entire mood of the castle seemed to brighten the moment he had transitioned.

Bunny looked at her older brother, reluctant to release his hand. "Well, what did you think of that?"

His face said everything. He was amazed. "I've never been so humbled in my life. I was wrong. Forgive me. I thought I knew everything, but . . . Och, Bunny, I'm so proud of ye. By the way, where are you off to next?"

"Home," she told him, still filled with the powerful need to be with the people she loved most, her family.

"Back to Connecticut?" He looked disappointed.

"No, silly, back to the family farm. The lads and I have ten days to kill before our next investigation. I hear we're going back to England, to a little island off the Devon coast where Agatha Christie wrote a couple of her novels."

"Wait," Angus looked skeptical. "Are you going to . . . ye know, ah . . . connect with the ghost of Agatha Christie?"

She could tell that the notion both intrigued and frightened him. Bunny shrugged, and admitted, "I'm going to stay at a nice hotel there, cook a delicious meal for the guests, and see what happens. I'm not making any promises."

"Fair enough. What about your friends? Will they come to the farm as well?"

"Giff has plans. Cody, Mike, and Ed want to do a little sightseeing. I thought the farm might be a good place for Brett to rest while his ankle heals. I know it's short notice, but . . . I hope you don't mind."

"Not at all. Mum and Da will be thrilled. It might nearly make up for the ten long years ye were away."

Bunny smiled. "Dear brother, after ten days with me hanging around the farm again, you and Dad will be escorting me to the train station, making sure I make it to my next engagement. Remember, I've got baggage."

"Dinna we all, sis. Dinna we all." Angus then pulled her up off the cold stones of the battlement and wrapped her in a warm, brotherly hug. "Welcome home, Bunny. Scotland just hasn't been the same without ye, wee ghosties and all."

Author's Note

The Legend of the Ghostly Piper of Duntrune Castle

Years ago, back when I was writing Scottish historical fiction, I found myself doing a lot of research on, naturally, the history of Scotland. One day, when reading a tome of heavy Scottish history, I came across a paragraph—just a little paragraph—that noted a particular Scottish castle haunted by a ghostly bagpiper. I don't know why that particular fact struck me, but it did, and it has stayed with me well over eighteen years.

As I might have stated in a previous author's note, I don't have much experience with ghosts at all, thank goodness. But I do like a good ghost story, and the thought of a Scottish castle being haunted by a ghost that was so thoroughly Scottish intrigued me more than I would have liked to admit. Let's face it, who can think of a bagpipe without thinking of Scotland? Not this author! It was a romantic notion. A picturesque tale of Scottish history. At the time, I didn't even know the name of the castle associated with the ghost. I didn't have any details on the ghost's tragic story, but I was nearly certain it was tragic. I was merely satisfied just knowing that there was a castle in Scotland haunted by a piper.

It's an odd feeling when something from your past pops into your mind as if it happened yesterday. That's what happened to me the moment I began writing my pitch for *Food & Spirits*. Knowing that each book in this series would center around a ghost story, real or otherwise, the ghostly bagpiper immediately popped into my mind. I knew then that I was going to dedicate an entire novel to the ghostly piper, just as I knew that my mystery was going to be about bagpipes. Even though I didn't know anything at the time about the piper's story, I was certain it was going to be compelling, and, boy, was I correct!

The castle associated with the ghostly piper is Duntrune Castle. Of course, I changed the name of the castle because it's privately owned. It really is the oldest, continuously occupied castle in Scotland. After doing a lot of research on the castle and its fascinating history, I then tried to piece together the piper's tale as best I could. As with every good ghost story, the piper's tale is shrouded in myth and legend, with a healthy dose of Scottish history as well. I'm not certain how much of it is true, but it made for fascinating reading. Jordy Malcom, my fictitious laird of Dundoon Castle, entertains the cast of *Food & Spirits* with the piper's noble tale. My story, *A Spirited Supper at Dundoon Castle*, is entirely a work of fiction spun around the legend of the ghostly piper of Duntrune Castle. As you can imagine, I took a great deal of creative license in order to weave both a murder mystery and this ghost story together. I loved every minute of it!

I sincerely hope that you have enjoyed reading this mystery as much as I have enjoyed writing it.

Sláinte!

—Darci Hannah

Bunny's Culinary Corner

Recipes and tips to entertain your family and friends.
(And ghosts, if that's what you're into.)

Orange Marmalade Whisky Sour

Prep time: 2 minutes. Special equipment: cocktail shaker. Makes 1 drink.

Ingredients:
2 ounces whisky
1 ounce freshly squeezed lemon juice
$^3/_4$ ounce simple syrup
1 heaping tablespoon orange marmalade
$^1/_2$ ounce egg white
Ice (for shaking)
Orange peel for garnish

Directions:

Add all the first five ingredients (no ice yet) to the cocktail shaker. Shake vigorously for 20 seconds. Next, add ice and shake for another 20 seconds. Strain into a small cocktail glass. Add a sliver of orange peel for garnish and serve.

Bunny's Classic Scottish Scones

Prep time: 15 minutes. Bake time: 15 minutes
Makes 8 scones.

Ingredients:
$2^1/_2$ cups all-purpose flour
1 tablespoon baking powder
$^1/_2$ teaspoon salt
$^1/_4$ cup sugar
$^1/_2$ cup of chilled butter (1 stick), cubed
1 cup half and half (plus extra for brushing on top of scones)
Sugar for sprinkling on top (optional)
Fruit jam and clotted cream or stiffly whipped heavy cream for serving

Directions:

Preheat the oven to 425°F (218°C).

In a large mixing bowl, sift together flour, baking powder, salt, and sugar. Next, add the chilled butter and rub it into the flour mixture, using your fingertips, until it resembles fine breadcrumbs. You can also use a pastry cutter for this.

Stir the half and half into the mixture, and mix until a soft dough forms.

Turn the dough onto a lightly floured surface and knead lightly to form a ball. Roll the dough out on the floured surface until it is 1 inch thick. Using a $2^1/_2$-inch biscuit cutter, cut the dough into 8 scones.

Place the scones on a parchment-lined baking sheet. Brush the top of each scone with the half and half. If you would like a sweeter scone, sprinkle a little sugar on top of each.

Place prepared scones into the oven and bake for 15 minutes, or until the scones have risen and are a nice, golden brown. Remove from the oven and place on a cooling rack, covering them with a tea towel to keep them warm. Serve with your favorite jam and a dollop or two of clotted cream.

Shepherd's Pie

Prep time: 20 minutes. Cook time: 30 minutes.
Serves 8.

Ingredients:
2 tablespoons of butter for sautéing (may use oil)
1 onion, chopped
2 cloves of garlic, chopped
6 ounces button mushrooms, sliced
2 pounds of ground lamb, or beef (when using beef, it becomes a cottage pie)
1 package of frozen peas and carrots (you may use fresh carrots and peas, but this is a time-saver)
3 tablespoons tomato paste
1 cup lamb or beef stock
3 tablespoons Worcestershire sauce
3 pounds of russet potatoes, peeled and cubed
1/2 cup of milk
1/2 cup butter
Salt and pepper to taste
1 cup shredded cheddar cheese

Directions:

Heat 1 tablespoon of butter in a large frying pan on medium heat. Next, add the chopped onion and garlic, and sauté until the onions are soft. Remove from the pan and set aside. Add the other tablespoon of butter to the pan, and sauté the mushrooms until cooked. Remove from the pan.

Add the ground lamb (or beef) and cook, stirring occasionally, until all the meat has been cooked. Drain the fat, keeping the meat in the pan.

Returning the pan to medium heat, add the onions, garlic, and mushrooms to the meat mixture. Next, add the package of frozen peas and carrots. Stir well. Next, add the tomato paste, lamb (or beef) stock, and Worcestershire sauce. Simmer for 20 minutes until the gravy thickens.

Heat the oven to 350°F (177°C).

While the meat is simmering on the stove, add the peeled and diced potatoes to a stockpot. Cover the potatoes with water and bring to a boil. Cook the potatoes for 10 minutes or until tender.

Drain the potatoes and return them to the pot. Keep the pot on low. Next, using a potato masher, mash the potatoes, adding the milk and butter as you mash. Then turn off the stove, and add salt and pepper to taste.

Pour the meat mixture into a buttered 9-inch x 13-inch baking dish. Make sure to spread the meat mixture evenly. Next, top the meat mixture with the mashed potatoes, spreading the potatoes carefully over the meat mixture. Top the potatoes with the shredded cheese.

Place the baking dish on a rimmed baking sheet to prevent the juices from bubbling over. Then place the pan into the preheated oven and bake for 30 minutes, or until the cheese has melted and the meat is bubbly. Remove from the oven, and cool for 5 minutes before serving.

Cullen Skink

Prep time: 40 minutes. Makes 4 servings.

Ingredients:
7 ounces of smoked haddock
3 cups of whole milk
1 bay leaf
2 tablespoons of butter
1 medium onion, finely chopped
1 pound of peeled potatoes cut into $^{1}/_{2}$-inch cubes
Salt and pepper

Directions:

The first job in making Cullen skink is to flavor the milk. To do so, use the trimmings from the smoked haddock. Simply remove the fillet from the skin and place the fillet aside. Pour the milk into a medium saucepan. Next, add the fish skin and the bay leaf. Put on low heat and bring to a simmer. Simmer for 5 minutes. Remove from heat.

Dice the fish.

In a large saucepan, melt the butter on medium heat. Add the chopped onions, and cook until they are soft.

Next, add the diced potatoes to the large saucepan with the onions. Then, using a mesh strainer, strain the flavored milk while pouring it into the large saucepan. Add the bay leaf back to the saucepan, and bring the milk and potatoes to a simmer. Cook for 15–20 minutes, until the potatoes are soft and tender. You will also see the milk begin to thicken from the potato starch.

Add the diced haddock to the pot, and cook for 5 more minutes.

Salt and pepper to taste, and serve hot.

Herb-crusted Rack of Lamb

Prep time: 15 minutes. Cook time: 20 minutes. Rest time:10 minutes.
Makes 4 servings.

Ingredients:
$^1/_2$ cup fresh breadcrumbs
2 tablespoons minced garlic
2 tablespoons chopped fresh rosemary
2 teaspoons salt
1$^1/_4$ teaspoons black pepper
2 tablespoons olive oil
1 (7-bone) rack of lamb, French-trimmed (removing the fat cap and the bit of meat between the ribs—optional)
2 tablespoons butter
1 tablespoon Dijon mustard
Tinfoil

Directions:

Preheat the oven to 450°F (232°C). Make sure the oven rack is in the center.

Combine breadcrumbs, garlic, rosemary, 1 teaspoon salt, and $^1/_4$ teaspoon pepper in a small bowl; stir in 2 tablespoons of olive oil to moisten the mixture. Set aside.

Next, brown the lamb. Season the lamb with 1 teaspoon of salt and 1 teaspoon of pepper. Using an oven-proof fry-pan, large enough for the rack of lamb, melt 2 tablespoons of butter on high heat. Add the lamb, and sear on all sides for about 1 to 2 minutes per side. Set the lamb aside for a few minutes to cool.

Brush the lamb with mustard, then roll the lamb in the breadcrumb mixture until evenly coated on both sides. Cover the ends of the bones with foil to prevent charring.

Arrange the breaded rack of lamb bone-side down in the same skillet. Next, place the lamb in the preheated oven for 12–18 minutes to reach a nice, juicy medium doneness. Use an instant-read thermometer inserted into the center; the temperature should read at least 130°F (54°C). Continue to cook the lamb until it reaches the desired doneness.

Remove the lamb from the skillet and loosely cover with tinfoil. Allow the meat to rest for 5–7 minutes before carving. To serve, carve between the ribs.

Creamy Au Gratin Potatoes

Prep time: 15 minutes. Cook time: 1 hour 30 minutes. Serves 6.

Ingredients:

2 pounds of thinly sliced, moderately starchy potatoes. Yukon gold work well here, but feel free to use russet as well.
3 tablespoons butter
3 tablespoons all-purpose flour
$^1/_2$ cup finely chopped yellow onion
2 cloves garlic minced
2 cups whole milk
$^1/_2$ cup heavy cream
1$^1/_2$ teaspoons salt
$^1/_4$ teaspoon freshly ground black or white pepper (optional)
2 cups shredded cheddar cheese, reserving $^1/_2$ cup to sprinkle on top of potatoes
$^1/_3$ cup grated Parmesan cheese

Directions:

Preheat the oven to 350°F (177°C).

Heat the butter in a large saucepan over medium-high heat and add the onions. Cook until soft and translucent, about 5–6 minutes. Next, add the garlic and cook for another minute. Next, add the flour and stir to combine. Cook for a minute or two until thickened. Next, slowly add the milk and cream, stirring continually to prevent clumping. Slowly bring the mixture to a boil, then reduce the heat and simmer until slightly thickened, about 5 minutes.

Next, add 1$^1/_2$ cups of the cheddar cheese to the mixture (reserving the other $^1/_2$ cup for the top). Add the parmesan cheese and the salt. Stir until the cheese is melted. Then add the potatoes, and stir until thoroughly combined.

Grease the bottom of a 2-quart casserole dish. Pour the cheesy potato mixture into the dish, and sprinkle with the remaining cheddar cheese. Cover the casserole dish with foil, and bake for 1 hour or until the potatoes are tender (time can vary depending on how thickly the potatoes are sliced).

Uncover and bake for an additional 20 minutes or until the top is lightly browned.

Let sit for about 5 minutes before serving.

Honey-roasted Carrots

Prep time: 10 minutes. Cook time: 15 minutes.
Serves 4–6.

Ingredients:
2 tablespoons of oil for roasting
2 garlic cloves
3 sprigs of thyme
1 pound baby carrots, washed
1/4 cup butter
1/4 cup honey
1 whole lemon, juiced

Directions:

Keeping the garlic cloves in their skin, slightly crush them.

Using a large frying pan over medium heat, heat the oil. Next add the crushed garlic cloves and the thyme. Cook for 1 minute, tossing to coat the pan. Increase the heat to medium-high and add the carrots. Continue cooking until the carrots begin to roast. They should get soft and have slightly caramelized skin.

Reduce heat back to medium and remove the garlic cloves and thyme. Then add the butter, honey, and lemon juice. Cook a few more minutes until the carrots are coated in the honey-butter sauce. Serve immediately.

Raspberry Sponge Cake

Prep time: 15 minutes. Cook time: 35 minutes.
Serves 10.

Ingredients:

6 large eggs, weighed on a food scale (You will see why this is important)
Half the weight of the eggs in sugar
3 tablespoons of hot water
Half the weight of the eggs in all-purpose flour

For the filling:

2 cups of heavy whipping cream
1 teaspoon vanilla extract
1/4 cup powdered sugar, plus more for dusting
1 cup of raspberry jam
1 pound or more fresh raspberries
Parchment paper

Directions:

Preheat the oven to 350°F (177°C).

Crack the eggs into a bowl and weigh them. Write the weight down for reference.

Add half the weight of the eggs in sugar to the bowl. Then add the 3 tablespoons of hot water.

Using an electric mixer with the whisk attachment, beat the egg mixture until it is thick and creamy. This will take around 5 or more minutes. The mixture should be thick enough to hold its shape.

Measure out half the weight of the eggs in flour. Sift the flour into the egg mixture, and gently fold it in. The lightness of this batter will depend on the amount of air that has been incorporated into the whisked eggs.

Grease and flour three 9-inch cake tins. Line the bottoms with parchment paper for easier removal. Then divide the mixture evenly between the three pans.

Place pans into the preheated oven for 30–35 minutes or until the cake has risen and is a nice, golden-brown color. Remove and cool in the pan for 10 minutes.

Gently remove the cooled cake from the pans, leaving the parchment paper on the bottom of each layer. This cake is very delicate, and keeping the parchment paper on will help prevent it from cracking. At this point, the cake can be wrapped in plastic wrap and placed into the freezer for up to one month.

Make the filling:

Pour whipping cream into the bowl of an electric mixer. Add the vanilla and the 1/4 cup of powdered sugar, and beat on high until fluffy peaks form.

Begin filling the layers of the sponge cake. Place the first layer on a cake plate, then remove the parchment from the bottom. Spread half the cup of raspberry jam over the cake. Next, spread 1/2 of the whipping cream over the jam. Next, arrange the fresh raspberries in the whipped cream, covering the layer. To complete the layer, spread another 1/4 cup of the whipped cream over the fresh raspberries. Next, place the second layer of cake and complete the process again.

Place the third layer of cake on top of the second layer of raspberries. Dust the top of the cake with powdered sugar. You can decorate the top with dollops of whipping cream and raspberries if you have extra. Refrigerate for 30 minutes before serving.